Mercy Goodhue

A Puritan Woman's Story
of Betrayal, Witchcraft and Madness

A NOVEL

Elizabeth Kern

HillHouse Books
PETALUMA, CALIFORNIA

HillHouse Books

ISBN: 978-0-9835815-2-9

Library of Congress Control Number: 2014905324

This is a work of historical fiction. Apart from the well-known people, events, and locales that factor into the narrative, all other names, characters, and incidents are used fictitiously.

Book design by Sandra Sanoski www.sanoski.com
Geneva Bible Title Page courtesy of Andover-Harvard Theological Library.
Base photo of Mercy Goodhue © Can Stock Photo Inc. /olga_sweet.
Photo of eye courtesy of Morguefile by imelenchon.

Library of Congress Cataloging-in-Publication Data
  1. Women—New England—History. 2. Women—New England—
  Social Conditions. 3. Witchcraft—Massachusetts—History—17th century.
  4. Puritans—Massachusetts—Colonial period, ca. 1600-1775—Fiction.
  5. Puritans—Massachusetts—History—17th century. 6. Puritans—
  Massachusetts—Fiction. 7. Puritans—Massachusetts—Biography.
  8. Winthrop, John, 1588-1649. 9. Hutchinson, Anne Marbury, 1591-1643.
  10. Hutchinson, Anne Marbury, 1591-1643—Political and social views.
  11. Freedom of Religion—Massachusetts—History—17th century.
  12. Antinomianism—Massachusetts—History of doctrines.

For

Beau

Andie

Katie

Sophie

Emily

Daniel

Matthew

Kelly

Mark

Jake

Luke

Camille

Maya

and

Cameron

May you always live in enlightened times.

Chapter One

~⚬~

Boston, Lincolnshire, England
1629

The messenger was an eager horseman—handsome in his scarlet plumed hat and tan cape, cinched with a brass clasp at his collar. I watched him through the window of our barn where I was milking Parsimony. He slid off his steed and strode assured steps toward our door. In the time it took him to pass the frame of the narrow window, he flung his cape over his shoulder and pulled a letter from his doublet pocket. I heard a rap on the door and his deep voice.

"Is this the home of Gabriel Goodhue?"

"It is," Papa replied.

The messenger's voice was velvet and I strained to hear more, but Parsimony bleated in my ear. "Hush, you silly goat!" I complained, giving her slack udders a squeeze. If I hurried, I could be inside when Papa read the letter, and perhaps I could catch another glimpse of the handsome horseman on my way.

A shiver of anticipation raced through me. It was not often Papa received letters. At one time they came frequently, but that was when there was work in the harbor and his days were filled with more activity than his hours could hold. During the past two years Papa's trade of building ships had slowed to naught, due to silting in our harbor. I had been praying he find work elsewhere.

I flung open the barnyard gate and smacked Parsimony's rump to send her out to graze. The messenger saw me and waved a gloved hand in salute and I waved back, offering him the sweetest smile I could muster. I had not braided my hair that morning, nor had I worn my coif as was proper, but it was just as well. It felt daring to give a stranger a look at my unbound hair. He leapt onto his steed and galloped off beneath a canopy of flickering red pin oak. I scurried backwards towards the door, watching the bouncing form of him fade in a mighty cloud of dust.

Inside, I slammed the door behind me.

"Mercy, slow yourself," Mama scolded. She was seated on the bench at the table plucking feathers from a goose that lay slack in a shallow bowl in front of her. Beneath the flutter of her hands I could see the swell of her stomach. Mark what is most important, I told myself. The child Mama carries matters more than any job could mean for Papa.

Papa was standing behind his tall-backed chair holding the letter in one hand and rubbing the stubble on his cleft chin with the other. Behind him a fire crackled in the hearth.

I set the pail of milk on the far windowsill where it was coolest and hung my cape on a peg behind the door. "A letter arrived, Papa?" I said, trying to appear calm.

He gave me a quick glance.

"It may be about work!" I blurted.

"The letter is Papa's business, not yours, Mercy."

"The girl means no harm, Hannah," Papa said kindly.

As I watched my father, I thought of how melancholy he had become. In better times he was a jester, now he walked about in gloom. His laughter had dried up with his livelihood and he was worried about providing for us. Yesterday evening, like so many evenings before, he sat at our table tallying numbers in his ledger, and when the sums gave him no satisfaction, he slammed the book shut and brooded. Then in a huff, he pushed his chair aside and left the house. We knew he had gone to the Falcon Inn to drink. When enough time had passed for him to lift one tankard and then two, and still he had not returned, Mama sent me to bed. I lay praying he would return home unmolested, for I knew the dangers that could befall a man in the black of night, even one of heft like Papa. It was only after I heard the shuffle of his footsteps on the lane that my heart could rest.

Papa removed a small blade from his pocket and slipped it beneath the ruby seal on the letter's wrapper. He unfolded the letter, held it at arm's length and began to read silently to himself. I wished for him to hurry, but he was taking his time. He raised a curious eyebrow, and then shifted his weight from one foot to the other with a heaviness that made him look older than his thirty-five years. My eyes drifted from his broad shoulders to the loose folds in his white shirt, and to the two untied cords that hung from his neckline and dangled halfway down his chest. He rubbed his hand across the cleft in his chin and cleared his throat.

My twin brothers, Noah and Michael, sat on either side of Mama, playfully picking dappled feathers from her bowl and stacking them in separate mounds. They were but ten-years-old—too young to feel the worries I felt at fourteen. I took a deep breath and placed my hand upon Noah's shoulder, as much to settle myself as to give him sweetness. He tilted his head back and grinned, and I bent and kissed his forehead. His straight blond hair flopped backwards and tickled my chin. It carried the hearty scents of autumn and burning firewood.

"The letter comes from a John Winthrop," Papa said. "William has spoken of him. He is a lawyer and manor lord from Suffolk."

Mama smiled approval.

"Does he wish you to build him a pinnace, Papa?" Michael asked.

"Like the ships you've built before?" Noah added.

Papa furrowed his eyebrows. "Before you see images of pounds and shillings in your heads, let me read you what Mister Winthrop has to say." Through the thin paper angled into a patch of sunlight I could see his tightly-knotted words slanting downward like beads sliding off a string.

"The letter is dated the twenty-third of October. Winthrop wrote it a sennight ago. The young messenger was swift in his delivery." Papa smiled at me from above the page.

I felt my face redden and looked away. Papa knew that if a handsome boy were within sight, surely I would take notice of him and would be gossiping about him with Jane before sunset.

"*My Dear Sir,*" Papa read, "*Although we have not met, I take the liberty of contacting you, because of the religious bond we share and because you come highly recommended by our mutual friend, William Coddington.*"

"He knows William!" Mama interrupted, her eyes dancing with expectation. "William may have recommended you for work." She stopped her plucking and rested her slim arms on the table. Her face was flushed and her cheeks were luminous against her chestnut hair. Mama was blessed with bounteous hair that she usually kept contained within her coif, but in the privacy of our home she allowed it to hang loosely about her shoulders.

Papa began to read more quickly.

"*I have recently been named the governor of the Massachusetts Bay Company, a group of investors that has been granted a charter by His Majesty King Charles to establish a plantation in America. Our company shall depart from Southampton for New England next April, and in my role as governor I have leased a fleet of eleven ships to carry about 700 souls of zeal, ability, and godliness to America, plus provisions and cattle. William Coddington, whom you know has joined our settlement company, tells me that you are highly qualified to maintain our flagship at sea. He says there is no finer a shipwright in all of England. Then, by the grace of God should we arrive safely in America, our company will need a man of your skills to build ships for commerce.*"

Papa straightened his shoulders and stood taller at the flattery of John Winthrop's words. Mama frowned and began plucking the feathers again, this time more vigorously. Like Mama, I knew what this invitation meant. My heart sank at the thought of leaving England and all I knew, especially my dearest friend, Jane, who was like a sister to me. There was hardly a day in our lives that we had not been together.

Although my mind raced in a multitude of directions, I forced myself to listen to Papa read the rest of the letter.

"*We shall settle well before winter on fertile land between the Merrimack River on the north and the Massachusetts Bay and the Charles River on the south, and three miles on either side of the bay. Unlike the other settlements, we shall be free to govern ourselves, and although we shall remain part of the Church of England, we may worship as we please in America. Each investor in good standing shall have freeman status. The Lord has truly blessed us beyond all expectations with such a fine opportunity. It is my sincere hope that you will consider my offer.*"

Papa's face came alive. I noticed a glint in his deep brown

eyes, and behind them a spark of energy that had not been there for a long time.

Our eyes were on him, but it was Mama who spoke. "America is a wilderness, Gabriel. Our child will be born in January and will be but three months old when the fleet sails. We cannot travel so soon." It was unlike Mama to speak of her own needs, but she blurted out her words in a voice surprisingly strong, which made me feel proud of her.

"It is work, honest work, Hannah. Be of good faith."

Mama sighed and bowed her head over her plucking.

"The Lord will guide our path," Papa said firmly.

I saw what transpired then between my parents. At that moment, Papa told Mama that regardless of the perils, we would go to America.

Later, after the others had gone to bed, I unfolded John Winthrop's letter and held it to my nose. I wanted to get some scent of his lawyer from Suffolk, this manor lord, this friend of William Coddington's who had caused such a disruption within our household. A whiff of cologne perhaps, for he was a gentleman, or the aroma of sweet tobacco or spice? But to my disappointment, the thin ivory paper held no scent of the man.

Chapter Two

―――――― ✥ ――――――

1630

Our cart, bound for Southampton, was loaded to the brim with crates, bundles, and Mama's precious cupboard, the only piece of furniture Papa allowed her to take. Jane and I stood facing each other, unusually silent, our fingers entwined like links on a chain. Only minutes remained of our time together.

I looked deeply into her face trying to memorize her every feature so that I could recall her countenance later. *Remember her*, I told myself. *Remember every detail.* Her soft blue eyes tinged with yellow at the centers. The playful curve of her smile. The tousle of flaxen hair that billows out of her coif like rays of brilliant sunshine. That morning Jane wore her pale blue gown, the one with the great silk buttons I so admired.

The past four months had been a prolonged farewell for us. Inseparable, we marked our final adventures together: our last run through Market Square with its crowded booths and colorful streamers and scents of cinnamon buns and spices; our last visits to Butcher Row, Fysshe Row, and Wormgate; our last climb up the blocky bell tower of St. Boltoph's, where from the top we could see the red tiled rooftops of Boston, the cobblestone lanes, lush patches of hawthorn blossoms, and the curve of the Witham River flowing into the North Sea.

I knew I would never see England again.

Remember everything. Remember it all.

By the day of our departure, Jane and I had said everything we needed to say, and said it dozens of times.

"What shall I do without you?"

"And I without you?"

"Who will I tell my secrets to?"

"Who will help me pick a husband?"

When I'd blame William Coddington, John Winthrop, and Papa for turning my dreams to ashes, Jane would reassure me. "Mercy, those brave enough to sail to America are God's chosen people, His saints. You are amongst them."

And I'd retort: "I do not want to live amongst saints. Their sobriety does not suit me. Your companionship is what suits me."

"So, Mercy Goodhue, you wish to live in the company of sinners like me?" she'd laugh.

Then when our days together grew fewer and I became more distraught, she'd resort to the only notion she knew would cheer me. "Imagine all the lads from every shire of England you'll meet. One of them will surely become your husband."

Papa climbed into the wagon. "It's time to leave now, Mercy."

"Farewell to you, Jane," I said one last time.

Jane's delicate fingers slipped away from mine. She opened her arms and I fell into them, nestling my head into the crook of her neck, inhaling the scent of smoke and flowers that would forever remind me of her. Tears streamed down our cheeks.

"You go, Mercy, and one day I will join you in America. I promise you I will."

Chapter Three

------ ❧ ------

America

I thought I smelled the scent of pine—cool pine dampened by the fog of early morning. I stood alone on the upper deck of the *Arbella*, inhaling the sweet fragrance.

"Could it be? Please Lord, make today the day," I prayed into the mist. With all my might, I willed the fog to clear, but it remained a ghostly wall between me and the land I so longed to see.

We had been at sea for fifty-nine days. I had kept private count of them by pressing half circles with my fingernail into the soft wood of the ship's hull, near the floor of the cabin where I slept. Each half moon reminded me that the Lord had spared us from the clutches of the sea still another day. But each mark also told me that while we were closer to America, we were sadly that much farther away from home.

As Governor Winthrop had promised, our family—Papa, Mama, Noah, Michael, my new sister, Grace, and I travelled on the *Arbella* with some of the prime families of Lincolnshire—the governor, two ministers, and the troublesome midwife from our village, Goodwife Hammer, the only one amongst us whom I wished had remained in England.

The *Arbella* was a tri-masted bark that had an oaken hull, polished to a gleam and decorated from bow to stern with stripes of amber and green. Because our ship was once named the *Eagle*, (she was renamed in honor of our most prominent passenger, Lady Arbella Johnson, the daughter of the Earl of Lincoln) she had an eagle's head at her prow that seemed to have grown full blown out of the ship, so much a part of the wood it was. The eagle's bulging eyes were black and its feathers, slicked against its head and neck to look like the wind had flattened them, were black and white. Its golden aquiline beak pointed out to the sea. But now I saw none of those colorful adornments. We were enshrouded in a fog so dense that I felt as if everything around me—the ocean, the sky, the ship and its passengers—had dropped away and I was alone in the world, left to fare for myself.

It had been a wretched voyage. Some days there was naught but boredom and all we did was stare the sea. But other days when it stormed, it was as if the sky had fallen and the sea had risen up in its fury to snatch us. I shall, until the day I die, have nightmares of waves as tall as mountains lifting us up and dropping us into the abyss; of crashing, screaming, the stench of puke, of pitch black nights when we knew not what was up or down; of how, sickened by the heaving waves, we huddled together expecting to die, but praying to the Lord to live. Were it not for Papa, I surely would have gone mad during those storms. But time after time, he calmed me. "Be of good faith, my daughter. The *Arbella* is built to withstand such force," he would say. And through it all, I believed him because I knew he would protect me. He knew ships and he knew the sea, and he was a wise man who understood more than I did the mind of God.

"Good morning t'ye!"

I jumped and turned around.

"I startled you, my daughter."

"Oh, no, Papa. Good morning t'ye."

Papa's breath smelled like oatmeal and cider, and droplets of mist quivered on the dark stubble upon his cheeks, settling within the cleft of his chin. He tugged on the floppy brim of his Monmouth cap, the close-fitting, narrow-brimmed cap sailors wore. Governor Winthrop had given him that cap for the courage he had shown during a storm that damaged one of our masts and nearly took our lives. When even some seamen cowered in fear, it was Papa who climbed the riggings and repaired the mast.

"It has been fifty-nine days, Papa. Shall today be the day?"

His dark eyes were fixed on the ocean.

"What do you see out there, Papa?"

He took a deep breath. "Nothing yet, but there is land behind that fog. I can smell it."

"As do I," I said proudly, remembering the pine.

"Then, my daughter, you have the nose of a seaman," he laughed. "Keep watching yonder," he said, pointing his calloused finger northwest.

A shiver of excitement raced through me and I gripped the railing tighter.

He squeezed my shoulder. The quickness of it told me he was ready to move on. Papa was happiest when he had work to do.

I watched the hazy image of him wend toward the hatch. He was taller than most of the other men, so when I could no longer see the dome of his brown cap bobbing up and down, I knew he had descended the ladder.

By midday, the fog had cleared and the *Arbella* was sailing speedily. Mist sprayed onto my cheeks. People in their sad colors of browns, blues, and blacks began milling about. The sun peered out from behind the clouds giving sparkle to our clothing. High above us, at the top of the main mast, the Union Jack with its combined crosses of Saint George and Saint Andrew whipped and snapped in the breeze. The sight of our flag made me proud of my homeland.

It was a ship's boy perched in the crow's nest who espied land first. At his shout of "Land ahoy!" word spread from tongue to tongue as quick as fire. Passengers below scurried to the upper deck and everyone on the upper deck crowded starboard. I clung to the portion of the railing I had claimed earlier. Elbows jabbed into my back. Bodies pressed into me. Shouts pierced my ears. And then I saw it too: A graceful curve of land stretching out before us like a cat's paw. As far as I could see, there were golden beaches, outcroppings of glistening boulders, and majestic forests. The pine trees that had teased me with their fragrance finally made their appearance. Tall and green, they swayed gently against the cloudless blue sky.

"Land!" I cried. "I see it!"

"Praise the Lord!" voices cried out.

"We are safe! Thank you, God!" I was trembling, shaking, and waving.

"Huzza!" people cheered. Some fell to their knees and prayed. Others wept. Mama, who had squeezed in beside me, held baby Grace in the air to catch her first glimpse of America. Throughout the voyage our two ministers, Reverend Phillips and Reverend Wilson, had taken turns preaching. Now they were both preaching at once:

"Give thanks to the Lord, for he is good."

"Even the sparrow has found a home, and the swallow a

nest."

Then, above the din, came the sweet sound of music. Behind us a tall and lanky ship's boy we called Shrimp, was bouncing from foot to foot, dancing barefoot on the hatch playing a jaunty tune on his harmonica.

His melody was like heaven to me. I started tapping my foot to his tune and swaying my hips. My prayers had been answered. Around me, faces were streaked with tears. Mouths were wide open, and there was laughter and joviality, sobs and whispered prayers.

Then there came another commotion from behind.

"Make way," a woman's voice cried out. "Allow her to come forward." To my annoyance, the crowd was parting for Goodwife Hammer. I had been standing at the railing since sunrise and she had just arrived, and there she was striding forward with a look of privilege on her face, as if she were Queen Elizabeth resurrected from the dead.

Uttering nary a thanks, the crone claimed a portion of railing two women away from me. Goody Hammer wore the wide-brimmed black hat she wore everywhere, and in its shadow I caught a glimpse of her stark white face staring at me, and of her frightfully withered eye.

"G'day to you, Goodwife Hammer," I stammered and forced a smile.

"And to ya, girl," she grumbled.

Gladly, I shifted my gaze to Mama. Tears of happiness were sliding down her cheeks. I wrapped my arm around her trembling body, and wee Grace, whom she held within the folds of her cape.

"'Tis the New Jerusalem!" Mama whimpered, pointing to land with a gesture of her chin. Wisps of her chestnut hair danced in the breeze. A teardrop fell upon her woolen shawl and glistened like glass. Self-consciously, she wiped her eyes in her sleeve and tucked an errant curl into her white linen coif, tied loosely beneath her chin.

When I realized I was crying too, I started to laugh.

"Papa and the boys, where are they?" Quickly, Mama spun around to search the crowd. She was constantly mindful of Noah and Michael's whereabouts for my brothers were lads bent on adventure and ships were dangerous places. Her tension eased upon seeing them with Papa. "Ah, there they are," she said, pointing to the deck atop the forecastle.

A group of men were gathered around Captain Milburne, and a group of boys were gathered around the men. Noah and Michael were leaning over the railing at such a precarious angle that I feared they might fall in. Their shirttails flapped in the breeze like small white sails, and they were waving and yelling their huzzas to land as if we were approaching the majestic gates of heaven. To my pleasure, Joshua Hoyt, a young man I had set my sights upon the day we boarded the *Arbella*, was amongst them. Joshua was from Folkingham, a town I knew nothing about but intended to learn of. He and his father, the cooper Ezekiel, were responsible for maintaining our casks at sea, for making sure that neither leak nor rat spoiled our precious supply of dried meats, peas, grain, and ale. He was eighteen, tall and handsome with high cheekbones, hair the color of split pine, good teeth, and a smile that could make the sun blush. Suntanned and fit in his leather jerkin and breeches that in the wind hugged his muscular legs, he was most appealing to me. He saw me and waved, and I waved back so vigorously I thought my wrist might snap off. Already, I was full of dreams of him.

Papa held a map for our captain to read. After what seemed like a sennight, Captain Milburne stepped to the railing of the deck overlooking us. He lifted his brass trumpet to his lips. "Cape Sable, it is!" he shouted through the mouthpiece. "Prepare to fire ordnance!"

Five gunners sprinted to the gunroom anticipating his order. Their blasts would alert the *Ambrose*, the *Jewel*, and the *Talbot*—the ships we were traveling in consort with—that we had espied land.

"Let me cover Grace's ears," Mama said as the first shot fired, followed by a second and a third. The ship trembled as if shaken by the hand of God. I gripped my mother's elbow just as Grace let out a sharp cry. "Welcome to Cape Sable," I whispered into Grace's wrinkled face.

"Look up!" Mama cried, gesturing toward the mizzenmast.

A pigeon was etching a graceful path between masts and sails and riggings, banking its iridescent gray body as if to survey the sunburnt, tearful mass of us below. Then on a wingtip, it turned toward land, squawking and flapping its wings in salute.

We watched the pigeon glide through the air. I had never taken much delight in those pesky creatures given to nipping our ankles in Market Square. But today was different. After weeks of barren skies, this pigeon was surely a good omen.

It was the beginning of our new life in America and we were all bursting with hope: Papa for prosperity, Mama to do the will of God, Noah and Michael for adventure, and me for all of those things, but also to meet the man I would one day marry.

I COULD HAVE STAYED ON DECK until nightfall, but now there was work for me to do below. I leapt off the bottom rung of the steep wooden ladder leading to our cabin and collided with the one I least wished to see: Goody Hammer. To others she was a midwife gifted with the ability to heal. To me she was a sharp-eyed crone, who since the day of my birth has made it her business to watch my every move. I had no good memories of her. Once she took a willow branch to my ankles when she came upon me swaying to the music of a fiddle in Market Square. Another time she scolded Jane and me in front of the entire congregation for eating fennel seeds in St. Boltoph's that we'd stuffed in our pockets. Those were not the most serious grievances she had committed. Those I could forgive. What I could never forgive was what she did to me the day Grace was born.

"Pardon me, Goody Hammer. I did not see you in the darkness."

The crone pressed her hand onto my shoulder. "Slow yourself, girl." Her voice was a low bray and her breath was sour.

"Yes, ma'am," I apologized. "I'm just happy."

"Mercy, while I have you here, I have news. Governor Winthrop will address the lot of us, tonight at dusk in the Great Cabin. He has sent me to tell everyone. Tell your parents, will you?"

"Aye, ma'am." Then I blurted, "Will he tell us when we will set foot on land ... when we will settle ... when the ships will return to England with our letters?" I took a deep breath and waited for an answer, but she just stared at me.

In my excitement I bounced from foot to foot, not knowing where to stand. Goody Hammer was a woman of girth I did not wish to interfere with. I ducked into the small space behind the ladder to allow her room to pass. She looked at me with a tilted face. She gripped the sides of the ladder and hoisted herself onto the first rung, which put her a head above me.

My smile faded. I waited for her to ascend the ladder, but

she did not budge.

I studied her face through the frame of wood. Her white skin was drawn upon her bones so tightly I thought the Lord had run out of skin in the making of her. But what frightened me most was her left eye. It was withered and sightless. No matter how hard I tried to avoid looking into that ghastly eye, it drew me in. It was an eye I had known my entire life. It was probably the first sight of this world I had seen, for Goody Hammer had assisted Mama in my birth. Once, I told Jane that her eye looked like a spider floating in a cup of coddled milk, and we both chucked over the humor of it. But later, when I repeated it to Mama, she did not laugh. "Goodwife Hammer was born with a withered eye, Mercy. 'Twas surely a punishment from God for a sin her parents had committed before she was born."

"Mercy, I am in a rush and I have no time for folly, but Providence put us here for a reason, so let me speak my mind and speak it to you plain." She stretched her tall body to its full height. "Day after day I have been watching you starin' at the ocean," she said disapprovingly. "All that time, did you not have work to do carin' for Grace, and lookin' after your brothers who dart about like monkeys aboard this ship?"

"But Papa allowed me to rise at first light and keep watch. He wanted me to be the first in our family to see America," I tried to explain, thinking that mentioning Papa's name would soften her. But my words were to no avail. I also wanted to remind her that Noah and Michael were as spirited as any boys their age, but hardly as rowdy as many of the other lads aboard.

"But, ma'am . . ."

"Hush, girl." She wagged her finger beneath my nose and puffed hot breath on my face. "Let there be no buts but contrition. Satan shall find work for you if you're not at work for God."

"Aye, ma'am."

"And the land we saw. It was there all along, was it not? We only had to wait for the Lord to reveal it. All your watchin' didn't make it show any faster now, did it?"

"No ma'am."

"How old are you now, girl?"

"Fifteen now, just last month, ma'am."

"The age when temptations come. You are a beauty like your mama with those brown eyes and that beguilin' smile. From watchin' you I can see you take pleasure in the vanities of this world, I can tell you that."

"Ma'am, I do not . . ."

She looked at me harder. "I saw you encitin' that ship's boy, dancin' to his tune. You don't know it yet, but I can see more with my one eye than you can with two. Yesterday I also saw you struttin' past Joshua Hoyt on the main deck temptin' him with your smile. He had that look in his eyes that boys get. Watch yourself with him, Mercy. I have seen too many lightskirts give themselves up to men with misguided appetites. Be you not one of 'em."

I felt myself blush. Aye, I had been stealing away from the others during prayer to wander about the ship looking for Joshua. Off on my own, I'd hitch up my skirt and climb a tall ladder to the forecastle, and from there, high about the other decks, I'd watch for him. I had come to know his schedule. Every afternoon, shortly before supper, he would emerge from the hold carrying a cask of ale above his head to deliver to the galley for our evening meal. At the sight of him, I would dash down the ladder to a spot where we were sure to meet, stopping when he stopped, walking again when he did, marking my every step and hoping he would say to me more than G'day."

But that was all he ever said, "G'day."

"The eye of God sees all you do, girl."

Her hand moved through the wooden frame of the ladder to my face, and with a cold finger she touched the cleft in my chin. Then she pulled her finger away as quickly as if she had just touched an ember. "You know what they say about these, don't you?"

"No, ma'am."

"A dimple in chin, a devil within," she cackled. "You do not wish Satan to take a pluck at you now, do you?"

"Certainly not." I said, flustered.

She stepped back into the grainy shadows, and in a blink she was gone.

By then I was trembling from her accusations and too angry to think. Aye, I relished the attention of boys, especially Joshua's. And aye, I knew the Lord was watching. But I'd done nothing to warrant such harshness. Alone in the dark space, I gripped the sides of the ladder. Tears were streaming down my cheeks. I did not want to cry, not on such a glorious day. But the hag's rebuke made me feel like a sinful child. Did she not know the burn of her words?

I scurried to our cabin, my arms locked across my chest. "She is a witch," I said.

I did not care who heard.

Chapter Four

After supper I helped the women tidy the Great Cabin in preparation for Governor Winthrop. Feeling the sting of Goody Hammer's scolding, I did more than my share of the work. I rinsed our wooden cups in a tub of rainwater and stored them in a cabinet beneath the table. I gathered up bedrolls that had cluttered the floor since morning and stowed them away. All the while, I kept a watchful eye on Goody Hammer who sat hunched over the table drying our thin wooden trenchers with a coarse dishrag. I wanted her to see me work.

When she lifted the last trencher, I forced myself to approach her.

"May I stow these for you, ma'am?"

Painstakingly, she dried the final bead of water from the corner of the plate, placed it on top of her stack as carefully as if it were the Queen's china. She glared at me. "Do not topple 'em, girl."

"Aye, I mean, no ma'am." I grabbed the trenchers and hurried off.

WHEN THE WORK WAS DONE, I sat on the edge of our berth surveying the Great Cabin. For the past two months this one cramped room had been home to the forty of us who did not have private quarters. Sandwiched between the upper deck and the cargo hold, it was a dank and airless space with its curved oak plank walls and a ceiling so low that the men had to walk with bends in their backs. The only light came from a row of five square portholes across from where I sat, and the only air came from the hatch that remained open when it wasn't raining.

There was a sturdy oak table in the center, which was where we took our meals, sought refuge from the scorch of the sun, studied our Bibles, and when it was too dark to read, told stories of our lives. When the waves tossed us about like beans in a basket, that table, bolted to the floor, became our anchor. Tonight, a group of eager women—including Goody Hammer—were already seated around it, gossiping and waiting for Governor Winthrop.

As THE SUN BEGAN ITS SLOW DESCENT, the Great Cabin grew crowded. Soon the air was abuzz with our chatter.

Papa, Mama, Michael, Noah and I took our places in front of the plum-colored curtain of our berth that Mama had drawn closed. She had already put Grace to her breast and tucked her to sleep between two bolsters on the mattress.

Through the portholes the flaming lemon sun was slowly slipping behind a formation of billowy clouds, dispersing a band of scarlet that for a moment hovered above the pointed pine trees of Cape Sable like a radiant crown. Soon it faded into a paler glow.

"Mary, light the tapers," a jolly voice cried. It was William Coddington, Mary's husband.

Mary rose from the table and scurried to their berth. A moment later she returned joyously waving two tapers above her head. She fit them into candle-sized holes in the tabletop, one near the head and the other near the foot, and returned to her place. Two circles of flame blinked, fluttered and overlapped at the center of the table. Within the dancing rings of light, the women's faces glowed golden.

The crowd applauded.

William took his place behind his Mary and squeezed her shoulders. Mary smiled tenderly up at him.

"Our Mary brought them for a special occasion," Mama whispered to me.

"He's coming! I hear him," Michael cried, gesturing toward the ladder.

I turned and watched for Governor Winthrop to appear in the light. I followed him as he wended his way through the crowd, his lean body encircled in a vast cape that swirled about him as he strode. He stopped to acknowledge Captain Milburne, and the men grasped hands in a jubilant knot of affection. He nodded at Thomas Dudley and William Coddington. When he espied Papa, he leaned into the crowd and gripped Papa's arm.

"Thank you, Gabriel. I am forever indebted to you for keeping us safe."

"It was the Lord's work, not mine," Papa replied.

"Aye, but it took a brave man to climb that mast in a storm."

I reached for Mama's hand beneath the folds of our skirts and squeezed it. Feeling the pride I felt for Papa, she squeezed back twice.

Governor Winthrop was shorter than Papa and less powerfully built. His face was slender and bearded and his thin eyebrows were arched more like a woman's than a man's. His heavily-lidded eyes were black as nuggets of coal. He carried himself rigidly, as did gentlemen of his class and profession. He seldom smiled. But tonight there was a lightness about him that made us feel all was well.

He set a roll of papers on the corner of the table. He lifted his arms and patted the air, signaling us to lend him an ear.

"My friends," he said. His voice was raspy. "Today we have reached Cape Sable off the coast of Nova Scotia. In three days we shall reach the shores of Cape Ann on the northernmost tip of Massachusetts."

"Huzza!" we cheered.

"We shall remain at Cape Ann several days to allow the other ships to catch up." He paused and raised an eyebrow. "I don't know if anyone would be interested, but Captain Milburne tells me the ship's boats will be available to tender us to shore for recreation while we wait for the others."

"Huzza!" Our shouts became deafening. The boys, including my brothers, were hooting and stomping their feet. I clapped my hands so hard they stung.

"We will go, will we not?" I looked up at Papa.

"We will, my daughter, and you'll be first in the queue, I am sure!"

"Mercy will be rowing the boat!" Noah added.

"I will row if they need me to!" I teased back.

Papa's throaty laughter resonated throughout the cabin. Mama just shook her head at our banter.

Governor Winthrop paused long enough for us to enjoy the moment. Then he patted the air again. The muscles in his narrow face tightened—a signal he now had more serious matters to address.

I took a deep breath to regain my composure.

"My friends," he said solemnly. "I have come to know

each of you well over the past months. You are godly men and women. But even among the most pious souls, conflicts shall arise. It is my task tonight to offer you a course of conduct for our lives in America."

"Amen!" we responded prayerfully.

He unrolled the papers and held them in the glow of candlelight. "Almighty God has created each of us in his image and likeness, but in our human condition, he has willed us to be different from one another. It is the Lord's will that some of you be rich, some poor, some high and eminent in power and dignity, and others mean and in submission. He has done this so you might have need of one another."

"Amen," we replied.

As Governor Winthrop spoke of our differences, I observed my fellow passengers—the people who would be part of my future. At the table, sitting close to the governor, was the highborn Lady Arbella Johnson. She and her husband, Isaac, were the most affluent passengers aboard, but they were never boastful of their wealth, which set them in high regard by the rest of us. Across from them was Thomas Dudley, our deputy governor, the second in command to Governor Winthrop. He was a broad-shouldered man with a thick face dominated by liverish lips and eyes that probed like judges. Whenever I felt his imperious eyes brush past me, I felt grateful my own father was a man of pleasing countenance and agreeable manner. Beside him sat his daughter Anne, a girl of about my age who was already married—to Simon Bradstreet, another prime man amongst us. Anne would have been pretty had the pox not scarred her face. She carried a journal with her everywhere she went. Goody Hammer let it be known that Anne wrote poems, which I could hardly believe, for what woman wrote poetry? Beside them were Elizabeth Aspinwall and her husband, William, a young couple from Lancashire who were by far the most God-smitten people aboard. Upon our first meeting Papa had asked William his occupation, and this man of bluster replied that he was a student of the Bible first, and then he was a surveyor. Since then, I've always thought of him as the Lord's surveyor.

Joshua stood across the room watching me. I should have averted my eyes from his gaze, but I did not. I knew it was a fault, but Goody Hammer was slouching in the shadows with her eyes closed—for once she was not watching me, so I teased him with a smile. I was glad I had worn the crisp, white collar Jane had given me to wear in America. When I touched the knots on its edging with my fingers, Joshua responded with a lopsided grin that stretched almost to his ears.

My hopes soared. Would he be taking a ship's boat to Cape Ann later this week? How I prayed he would be.

My eyes darted back to Goody Hammer. I stared into her pale face and tired eyes, and I waited for my heart to soften towards her. When it did not, I returned my attention to Governor Winthrop, whose words suddenly caught my attention.

Our governor was talking about love now—not love of God, but of the tender love betwixt a man and a woman. His voice was as hushed as a breath in the night. "Nothing yields more pleasure and content to the soul then when it finds someone to love fervently; for to love and live beloved is the soul's paradise both here and in heaven." I felt sad for him because he had left his own wife who was with child in England, and I knew he was missing her.

Through the corner of my eye I watched Papa drape his arm across Mama's shoulders and draw her close. I was surprised by this action because such behavior was to be reserved for private moments. But there was no one standing behind us, so Papa must have felt at ease with it. He looked down at Mama wistfully and rubbed his thumb upon the skin of her neck. I wondered whether Mama was embarrassed by his affection. When she shifted even closer to him, I knew the answer. Their love was the kind of love I dreamt of, perhaps with Joshua.

"We must entertain each other in brotherly affection," our governor said. "We must delight in each other and make others' conditions our own. We must rejoice together, mourn together, labor and suffer together, always having before our eyes our commission and community in the work, as members of the same body."

Then he paused. Except for the waves lapping against the hull, the Great Cabin was quiet. He turned toward the porthole and stared out at the dark silhouette of land in the distance—this mysterious land to which we were now bound. What did he see it in that flash of a moment? Was it hope? Promise? Danger?

He returned his gaze to us, and with outstretched arms disclosed the words of his heart. "We shall know that the God of Israel is among us when succeeding plantations say this in our praise, 'May the Lord make us like New England.' For we must consider that we shall be as a city upon a hill. The eyes of all people are upon us."

A chill crossed my chest at the loveliness of his words.

Then his voice dropped, almost to a hush. "But if our hearts shall turn away, so that we will not obey, but shall be seduced, and worship other gods, our pleasure and profits, and serve them; it is propounded unto us this day, we shall surely perish out of the good land."

"Amen," we replied solemnly.

I looked through the portholes and saw, drizzled in silver

moonlight, the faint outline of America. Others were staring at it too. While once we were strangers to each other, people separated by place of origin, wealth, manner, and dress; there was none of that now. We knew each other intimately after our long voyage. We knew each others' moods and heartaches, fears and foibles, losses and longings, scents and snorts in the night, and we were obliged now, all of us, to live in covenant with one another in this new land, or pay the price of our sinfulness.

That evening, I was overcome by a new sobriety. I made promises to myself: I will not be proud. I will not daydream of a future that is only God's to know. I will forget my grievances toward Goody Hammer. I will be a more pious, less critical girl in America.

Although my intentions were true, they were promises I knew I could no more keep than fly.

Chapter Five

———— ✦ ————

Papa stood on the beach of Cape Ann with his hands in his pockets and his back facing the sea. "Come, let us walk," he beckoned me with a nod. Many evenings in England Papa and I had walked and talked after supper, just the two of us. On our first day in America his was the finest invitation I could imagine, other than a stroll with Joshua, who sadly, I had not seen board a ship's boat. With my brothers occupied in a game of ball and Mama resting on a blanket with Mary, I had the liberty to take leave.

Earlier that morning, Mama had told me Mary would be delivering a child the following March, which pleased and frightened me because Mary was a tightly-wound woman with a history of loss. Her first son, Micah, had died three year earlier, and her little Samuel went to God the week our Grace took her first breath. It was good now to give Mama and Mary privacy to talk.

Papa and I headed north toward a massive rock that jutted into the sea. Papa had a long stride and I hurried to keep up with him. At one point, I stopped to tie my shoe and he continued to walk ahead. Even though I was too old for such child's play, I amused myself by stepping into the middle of his footprints, twice the bigness of mine, without creating new ones of my own. He smiled when he saw what I was doing. I smiled back and hummed softly to myself, not a hymn but a lively ditty I'd heard the ship's boys sing at night. With Papa I could be lighthearted. With Mama I learned about prayer and hard work.

Papa and I walked in silence a bit longer, and soon his demeanor changed. The set of his jaw told me he had something on his mind and was having difficulty speaking of it. So I asked questions and he answered them.

"When we settle, what ships will you build, Papa?"

"Ketches for fishing and transporting goods from one settlement to another. Without roads we will need them first. Then a bark smaller than the *Arbella*, but able to carry a burden of some thirty tons."

Papa told me the names of the trees in the dense forest to the west, and the uses of their wood. "White oak resists water and decay and will be used for hulls . . . tall pine for spars and masts . . . pitch from evergreens for waterproofing." He spoke of the richness of pine, the sweetness of oak, the earthiness of cedar. He pointed out maples, birches, blue spruce, and larch. To me, they were mighty trees swaying in the breeze. To Papa, they were unbuilt ships.

Papa stopped and picked up a branch that blew onto the beach. "Smell this, my daughter," he said. "Pine. The scent of heaven." I lifted the sprig to my nose and rolled its needles between my fingertips so its perfume would linger on my skin. I tucked the sprig into the pocket tied around my waist.

"The scent of heaven," I repeated.

"And what is on your mind, Mercy?" he asked.

I told him what I had kept secret until then. I told him

about Goody Hammer's rebuke at the ladder and about the humiliation I felt. He nodded, but I could tell by his pursed lips that he was reluctant to judge her.

People deferred to Goody Hammer because they knew they eventually would have need of her, whether delivering a baby or setting a broken bone. But I did not understand Papa's dependence on her. He consulted with her whenever he launched a ship. He met with her beneath nighttime skies to study the position of the stars and the shape of the moon. He also drank a tea each day that he brewed from mysterious herbs that she brought him in a jar.

"She is a useful woman," Papa said at last.

"She is always watching me," I complained. "Wherever I go, she is there. Always dressed in black. Black apron. Black gown. Black hat. She is like that bird, pecking at me," I said, pointing to an oily black cormorant that had just swooped into the surf in pursuit of an innocent fish. "She is one who could spoil heaven."

Papa smiled. I did not smile back.

We walked in silence. Soon Papa slowed his pace so his feet barely advanced, and I too slowed my steps.

"My daughter, you are a woman now, so I shall speak to you as one. Your mama is again with child. The babe will be born this winter."

"No, Papa. Not now. Not here!" I blurted. Immediately, I regretted my outburst because in my father's dark eyes I saw a fear that matched my own.

"Fret not, Mercy. By winter we will have a home, I promise you. And Mary and Goodwife Hammer shall be there to assist Mama." Then his voice softened. "I know you believe Goody Hammer carries a grudge against you, but you cannot deny she has been gifted with the healing touch and helps many cleverly, especially women giving birth. She helped Mama deliver you, the boys and Grace, and what a fine job she did!"

Papa smiled a smile that did not last long. He fixed his gaze on the ocean and furrowed his brow. "We must care for Mama tenderly. We must not lose her."

A sense of foreboding washed over me. There were not enough fingers on my hands to count the women I knew whom had died giving birth. Now Mary and Mama were in jeopardy. Both women were but shadows of the strong women they were in England. Worry and seasickness had taken a toll on their faces, sinking their eyes into their sockets and causing their cheekbones to protrude like shelves. "I promise I will do my best," I told him.

"As will I," he said.

Then he said something I shan't ever forget. He said, "Mercy, our eternal lives depend upon our devotion to Mama. We do not want to stand before God on Judgment Day and be condemned for neglect of our responsibilities, do we?"

"Surely we do not," I replied. Then I could not help myself. I began to cry, and my legs beneath me lost strength and I fell onto the sand. I cried at the thought of losing Mama. I cried because Papa brought us to this wilderness. I cried because of the responsibility he was placing on me. I cried because his talk of damnation was unnecessary. Did he not know I would give my soul to keep Mama safe?

He reached out his hands and pulled me up. He said not a word, but wrapped his arms around me and held me tightly. When my cries turned to a whimper, he wiped my damp cheeks with his handkerchief and studied my face. "You are so much the image of your mama."

I pulled away and looked into his eyes. In his tears I felt his love, not only for Mama, but for me. I also felt his need to be comforted. He pulled me to him once more and again we embraced. He kissed my forehead. We parted and walked in silence.

Just then three sea birds scurried toward the incoming tide, leaving their cross-stitch footprints on the sand. Through squinting eyes the sand appeared golden, like the flame from a host of candles. Then the image of a man walking toward us took shape. At first, in the glare I could see only his light shirt, tan breeches and sandy hair blowing in the breeze. But as he neared, I realized it was Joshua. At the sight of him, my heart leapt into my throat. As he got closer, I noticed that he held his overturned cap in his hand heaped with bright red berries.

"G'day, Goodman Goodhue and Mercy. Sample the fruit of Cape Ann! Strawberries!" Like a host at a feast, Joshua offered us some berries.

"G'day," Papa replied, taking a step backward to remind me that I was the one Joshua was eager to see.

I chose the reddest berry and bit into it.

"They grow wild," he said.

After Papa left us, Joshua and I locked step. He led me toward the periphery of the beach where people were gathering berries from a clump of low plants. Children were eating them as quickly as they could pick them, smacking their lips, licking juice from their fingers and laughing. How innocent they were. In ten years they would be like me, beset with worries about birth and death and God's judgment. I looked up at Joshua's beaming face and saw a lighthearted man reveling in the present. Did not the Lord give us these sweet strawberries to savor? I will put aside my worries, for surely the Lord will protect Mama.

That afternoon Joshua and I talked without pause—about our families (his mother, Clarissa Hoyt, had become unwell with fever and died before Joshua's first birthday), the friends we had left behind, where we might settle, and when we might encounter Indians. We had heard about Indians. The Narragansetts would cause us no problem. It was the Pequots we had to fear. Aboard ship I'd overheard horrible stories of the Pequots. "They'll flay you alive," Shrimp once told an innocent lad half his size. "Does flaying hurt?" the frightened boy asked. "Aye, it hurts when they rip the skin off your face, the hair off your head, and they gut out your insides while you're still alive." I chose not to repeat that gruesome story to anyone, and especially not now to Joshua, lest it spoil our day.

Joshua told me of his ambition be the finest cooper in America, "which should not be difficult because Papa and I are among the first," he laughed.

"Do you worry about where we will live?"

He pondered my question for a moment. Then he stood back, flexed his muscles and postured to show me his strength. "Take notice, Mercy Goodhue," he laughed, "We Englishmen are men of might. If your papa can build ships and right a mast in a storm, and I can build a hogshead, surely we can build homes."

"Will we have enough food?" I asked.

Joshua did not ponder that question at all. He tossed me a strawberry and gleefully told me the story of a minister named Francis Higginson who just a year ago had settled in Salem and wrote to friends in England of the bounty of America. "I do not remember much from that letter—everyone was passing it around quickly. It set everyone's mind favorably upon America. Perchance you read it too."

"I've heard of it."

"Well, Reverend Higginson wrote about strawberries, great ears of corn, green peas, turnips, carrots bigger and sweeter than those in England, radishes as large as plums, and pumpkins and cucumbers. He told of a fish called bass that is sweet and wholesome, of lobsters weighing as much as twenty-five pounds, and turkeys that are fatter than our English turkeys."

I studied his face with awe. I had never heard that many words come out of his mouth without him taking a breath. When I could fit in a word, I said, "You say you remember little from that letter, but you remember everything, Joshua Hoyt. Now I know why you came to America. You came to fill your belly!"

"Now you know my secret!" he exclaimed.

Toward the end of the afternoon, the wind gained strength and blew my coif off my head. On the strongest of legs, Joshua dashed faster than the breeze to retrieve it. He caught it in mid air and handed it to me with a flourish and a bow. That morning I had not taken time to braid my hair and now my hair blew around my head wildly. Modestly, I turned my back to him and tried to stuff it back into my coif.

"Watching you is like watching one stuff handfuls of silk into a teacup," he mused.

"You watching me makes me blush," I countered.

Then he gently touched my arm. It was the first time a young man had touched me. "I wish never to embarrass you, Mercy Goodhue."

By the end of the day I had forgotten about Papa and Mama and the dangers of carrying a new life in her belly, and I forgot about the Pequots and their flaying. All I thought about was Joshua.

Chapter Six

Boston, Massachusetts

In August of 1630 we settled on a peninsula the Indians called *Shawmut*, but at the suggestion of Governor Winthrop, we agreed to call our new home Boston after the village in Lincolnshire many of us had left. The Boston peninsula was a flat span of land with trees, but not too many of them, a broad meadow for a settlement, and generous fresh water springs. The peninsula was linked to the mainland by a long neck that was mostly swamp with marsh grasses and rushes. The land was level except for a high hill rising out of the midst of the peninsula, and three smaller mounds emerging from its top. We called those hills Trimountain.

The early months in New England had been marked by arrivals and departures. At last all eleven ships were anchored in our harbor. The *Talbot* fared least well with the loss of fourteen souls. Many of those traveling upon the *Success* arrived nearly dead, and most of the goats upon that ship died. Soon, praise God, the ships would be returning to England carrying my letters to Jane.

I assumed that everyone would be settling in Boston, but

dissension soon erupted amongst us. With eager ears, I listened to the people squabble around me. The blustery Thomas Dudley and his family decided to settle in Charlestown where the water was known to be good. A few hearty souls including Lady Arbella Johnson and her Isaac decided to settle in Salem, even though the town was besieged with scurvy, and even though it had become known to us that Reverend Higginson, whose letter had lured so many of us to America, perished there the previous winter when food was scarce and many starved. I prayed Goody Hammer would see it as her Christian duty to go to Salem to care for those in need, but she chose to settle in Boston with us. "I must be near the Goodhues," she firmly announced over a supper of dried meat and peas.

She followed me to America. She was settling in Boston. Would I ever be rid of her?

The good news was that the Coddingtons and the Hoyts were also settling in Boston.

Praise God!

It was during the building days of autumn that we labored to become the kind of community Governor Winthrop had spoken of—a community of people knit together to do God's work. Although many hands labored, it was with a single heart that we built Boston.

Our plan was to raise thirty dwellings before the first snowfall. We arose at daybreak to make use of every daylight moment. We all took jobs: felling trees, sawing, hauling timbers, hoisting, hammering, gathering reeds for roofs and rocks for fireplaces, gathering pumpkins to dry and corn enough to get us through the winter. To set an example, Governor Winthrop worked side-by-side with the lowest of servants. Joshua labored as a sawyer, sometimes working as top sawyer; other times inside the sawpit, guiding the wood for his partner. My job was to collect rocks for fireplaces in the hillocks of Trimountain.

Smartly, Papa had packed a tent for us to live in until we had a permanent dwelling. Our family was more fortunate than many—some lived in caves until they had cottages. One Jonah Miner made his home in an oil cask and could not be dissuaded from this notion.

DURING THOSE EARLY DAYS we formed ourselves, not into a church—for it was the Church of England and its popish ways we had left behind—but into a congregation. We called ourselves the saints of the Boston Congregation. To be accepted we were required to give testimony, to provide evidence the Holy Spirit dwelt within us. It was up to our ministers and magistrates to accept or reject our testimony.

We met outdoors within a circle of oak trees where, seated upon logs, we shivered for hours in the windy advent of winter listening to each other tell our stories of how the Lord had come to us. We assembled the way we had in England: The women's side on the right was a placid sea of white coifs; the men's side on the left was a spiky range of black hats.

Papa was admitted into the congregation first. I expected him to speak a long time, but his testimony was brief. He said that while he was always a believer, his real conversion came when he was invited by John Winthrop to join the Massachusetts Bay Company, a blessing that led him to renounce strong ale.

"I am a hater of sin," he said in a full, deep voice that resonated throughout the grove. With John Winthrop sitting in the first row vigorously nodding his approval, no one would challenge his testimony. For his bravery upon the *Arbella*, Papa was a man held in high esteem. He was welcomed into the congregation without question.

Mama, full-bellied with child, merely had to recite a Bible verse to justify her acceptance. Her good works and pious nature spoke for themselves, as did Goody's Hammer's good works when it came her time to testify.

When it was my turn, I stood up and clutched my hands together to stop shaking. I had practiced my testimony aloud while walking the hills of Trimountain gathering rocks for fireplaces. Even though I was beset with fear, I was able to speak the words I had memorized:

"I am Mercy Goodhue, the daughter of Gabriel and Hannah, and this is my testimony. When I was a child, my mama taught me to pray in secret places. She would send me into a small chamber behind our chimney, and in the darkness I would confess my sins and pray for forgiveness. One afternoon when I was eight, I prayed harder and longer than I had ever prayed before. I told God the truth. 'I am prideful. I am willful. I wish for things I do not have.' I recited my sins again and again so God would hear them and forgive me. Then suddenly, I felt His glorious light surround me, first as a brilliant flash appearing in the corner of my eye, and then as the light of a million suns. I fell to my knees and into a faint. That is where Mama found me. I knew then, I was a child of God."

My parents nodded approval as I spoke. Joshua smiled to give me confidence. Even Goody Hammer nodded beneath the shadow of her hat. Mary, who favored me as a daughter, said afterwards, "You are born of goodness, my child."

That day was one of the finest of my life. The assurance that I was a saint—that I had naught to worry about because I belonged to Him—was a taste of heaven on Earth. At that moment, I knew I was bound for heaven.

Chapter Seven

⁓

On the eve of our departure from England, Papa had given me a keepsake box that he crafted of pine. On the lid he carved an "M" for my name, along with flourishes that swirled like the four winds from the corners of the M to the corners of the box. He filled it with a stack of ivory writing paper; an inkpot, tightly corked; a stick of sealing wax; and four pens, two with quills from hawks and two from swans. Setting the gift before me, he said with a knowing laugh, "'Tis what you need to write to Jane of all you see and do in America. Like you, she will enjoy a good tattle."

I had written to Jane faithfully throughout our voyage, telling her about Joshua, the ship, and gossip about the passengers, especially my growing list of grievances against Goody Hammer. My letters were piled up nearly to the lid of my keepsake box by the time our ships began their slow returns to England. A thick packet of letters addressed to Jane was now in the hold of the *Talbot*, sailing somewhere upon the Atlantic.

Five months after we had settled, I wrote her this:

November 10, 1630

Dearest Jane,

I pray this letter finds you and your family well. After seven months of separation I miss you more than I can say. How I wish you were with me. Until now we have always seen the world together as if from one set of eyes. With so much new to see and learn, it does not seem right to be in America without you. I beg you to convince your Papa and Millicent to sail next summer so we all may be together.

I have much news to share. The most important is that Mama is again with child. I pray daily for her health and that she may have enough to eat. So far she is as fit as one can be in this wilderness. Although we are always hungry, we make do with clams we dig from the tidal flats, nuts, acorns, and pumpkins. In the spring we will plant seeds that with God's favor will bring us a plentiful harvest by summer.

The other news is that we no longer live in a flimsy tent.

We now live in a cottage of rough timbers, chinked with rags and mud, with one small room (eight paces wide, ten long), two small windows for light, and a hearth that provides some warmth in a winter that already has shown its cruel intentions.

Our floors are the cold damp earth. We are among the fortunate ones to have glass in our windows that Papa brought from England. Others must survive the winter with heavy oiled paper covering their open spaces.

There are paths that crook through Boston that the Indians had cut through the land. Although they are no more than crude dirt trails, we already call them streets, remembering the heavily traveled lanes in England. Isn't that a silly thing to do? The longest and widest of them is the High Street. The one that leads west toward Trimountain is Hill Street. The one that leads to the spring we call Spring Street, and the one that stops at a pasture is Milk Street. We live on Water Street, which leads to the Great Cove, which will be our harbor.

I am happy that Goody Hammer dwells across town. She lives in a squat cottage cobbled into the side of a hill I must pass when heading to our graveyard, already home to too many. She visits us only to bring Papa herbs for his tea, the same strong brew she provided him in England, the purpose of which remains a mystery to me. Papa is a healthy man of great bodily strength. He has no need of teas from such a woman. I also heard she is using charms and incantations in her healing—a practice of evil strictly forbidden by our ministers.

Joshua and his father have built a lean-to off the back of their cottage that will be their cooperage. Joshua is a man of even greater ambition than I credited; already he speaks of digging a well to provide a ready supply of water, which they need for the making of their thickest barrels for ale.

Our neighbors are Goodman and Goodwife Demsey, fine people from Suffolk, and Davy Person, a sad gentleman from Groton, whose wife, Caroline, died of scurvy a sennight ago. The scurvy is a ravaging disease. Before Caroline died her feet were as puffy as bread dough rising out of its pan. Her gums were so swollen that her teeth had separated one from another leaving great gaps between them. She had spit four teeth out of her mouth. I do not like to think about it.

But there is one story about Michael I wish to tell you.

Up until the end, Caroline had insisted on attending services in the grove. Davy is not a strong man—he is but a stack of bones hinged at the joints and held together by the thinnest layer of skin. But every afternoon he carried his Caroline within the scoop of his own frail arms from their tent to the grove. Seeing Davy's burden, Michael offered to assist him. So day after day he helped Davy set her on a blanket. He helped her drink water, covered her feet to keep *her warm, and after the sermon he helped Davy carry her back to their tent.*

Michael's ceaseless devotion toward Caroline had surprised me because—you know Michael—he is mostly concerned with joking with his friends, and never wanting to appear over-pious. Taking notice of his kindness, I praised him, but he looked away and said nothing. Days later, I again voiced my high regard for his actions.

"Caroline will see God soon," is what he said.

Then I blurted something I probably shouldn't have, "And you want her to put in a good word for you?"

"Maybe just a whisper of my name," he said, with a twinkle in his eye.

Oh, the goodness of him.

It is becoming difficult to write for the fire is dying, but I shall persist as long as my ink does not freeze. Soon there will be frost on our walls and ice on our sod floors that will not melt until we feed the embers in the morning. I am sitting at our table wrapped in my cloak, hood, and blanket, and I am wearing three pairs of woolen stockings that make my feet thick as sacks of grain. Snow has been falling for days, and the wind whistles through the timbers like the voice of Satan. Then follows the night, which is colder and darker than the darkest nights in England.

I live now in two different worlds—one of daylight where it is possible to be confident and go about my business with ease, and the other of night where I cower beneath my covers like a kitten. Outside our doors we know not what spirits, animals, or Indians lurk in the darkness, their appetites primed to devour us. At night the wolves howl wildly and the wind whistles through the cracks in our walls. Sometimes I cannot tell the difference from the screech of the wind and the mournful howl of the wolves for they persist, one upon another, in a frightening chorus. My only consolation is the nearness of Papa, who sleeps through the turmoil unbothered. He is a brave man, ready to protect us if he perceives a threat.

I have seen the Indians—the Narragansetts who live amongst us— and even though they are peaceful, they still strike terror in me. The women are kind, but the men with their broad shoulders and gruff demeanor are fearsome in appearance. Their skin is brownish and shiny as a polished coin. Their hair is glossy black and they fasten it behind their ears with cords decorated with beads, shells, and animal teeth. Papa says the Indians are of little threat to us because their numbers have been greatly reduced by the smallpox. Governor Winthrop tells us that if we deal with them fairly, the Lord will deal rightly with us. When fear overcomes me in the black of night and I imagine their faces hovering above me, I remember what the men say.

For all our trials, the Lord has treated our family with greater compassion than many who have already perished from the cold and the scurvy. Several days ago, Goodman Hiram Henshaw, who arrived on the Jewel, *lost his leg to the blade of an ax and bled to death. This fine gentleman left behind a comely carrot-haired wife, Catherine, and three sons and a daughter. Pray for the Lord's benevolence towards us to continue, for without his favor there is naught. I long to receive your letters, but I know I must wait patiently for my letters to traverse the sea and then wait again for yours to do the same. I pray all is well with you and your family.*

Mercy

Chapter Eight

1631

Throughout that autumn I managed to keep a good distance from Goody Hammer. But that changed in January of 1631, when in the midst of a howling blizzard a forceful rap came upon our door. Mama fumbled with the latch and pulled the door over the icy threshold. A gust of snow blasted in, giving us the trembles, and there she stood, bold as a chimney.

"Pray, mum, what brings you out on such a day? Gabriel has tea enough."

"T'day I come to see you," Goody Hammer replied briskly.

"Come in. Come in. You have brought a helper, I see."

A dog with half-closed eyes and snow on his mangy coat crouched beside her. She patted the cur's head with a gloved hand. "The Lord brought him to me this morning, my payment for helpin' a Narragansett woman birth a son. I'd rather have fish oil for my Betty lamp, or a shilling or two, but this mongrel is all they had to give."

The dog was scruffy with a gray and white coat and whiskers matted like sodden moss beneath his nose, a wintry animal, probably one even the Indians didn't want. One of its ears pointed upwards, the other was scalloped as if a wolf had nipped off a chunk. "Elijah, I call him. He smells naught and hears less, and he doesn't bark."

I stood at the table carving the meat of a pumpkin for soup. At the sight of her, I set down my knife and wiped my sticky hands in my apron.

Goody Hammer pulled a long arm out of her cape. Her gloved black fingers clutched a Bible that traveled through the tunnel of her garment like an appendage of her hand. She tucked her gloves into her apron pocket and set her good eye on Mama's bulging belly. "I've come at the behest of Reverend Wilson to do the work of the Lord. He bids me to speak t'ya about a matter of some urgency . . . your perilous physical and spiritual estate, Hannah."

"Children, be still while Goodwife Hammer and I speak," Mama said. "Mercy, give Grace a biscuit, will you?"

Grace, wearing two gowns and a bonnet, sat on the cold floor whimpering with her stockinged legs curved in front of her. At eleven months old she held anyone outside our family suspect. Noah, seeing her mounting tumult, lifted her by her arms and walked her to the mattress.

The wind outside howled and snow crept in through spaces in our walls, leaving peaked shelves of white upon the earthen floor.

"Let us sit," Mama said, leading Goody Hammer to the warmer side of the table. Mama sat with her back facing the drafty door. Ancient Elijah doddered toward the hearth, curled up and tucked his head within the circle of his wet paws.

I slid a wooden box off the cupboard shelf and gave Grace half a dried biscuit—one of two we had saved from the ship— and then seeing Elijah's sad black eyes following me, I set the other half on the hearth before him and tousled his wet hair.

"You offer my dog a biscuit but not a crumb to me?" Goody Hammer said.

Her accusation rattled me. "Of course. I intended to set one on your saucer along with a cup of cider," I lied. I poured two cups full and set them in front of the women. Begrudgingly, I gave the crone our last biscuit.

"Is the child active, Hannah?"

"Aye. Given its vigor, I am persuaded it is a son. He shall grow up as spirited as those two," Mama said, gesturing to the boys.

Michael and Noah did not look spirited at all. Their faces became frozen masks in Goodwife Hammer's presence. They stared at her withered eye and, like me, shivered as we listened with keen ears to the conversation between the women. I joined them on the mattress and covered our legs with a quilt.

"Let me feel the child," Goody Hammer said brusquely.

Mama turned so her belly was positioned away from us. Modestly, she separated her skirt from her bodice. Goody Hammer hobbled around the table, knelt on one knee and placed her veined hands on Mama's stomach. She closed her eyes and patted Mama's bare skin like a blind woman identifying an object by touch. "The head be here, and this be a knee," she said with authority. "The child must turn if it is to be born among the living."

"Is there time for the child to turn?"

"There is time and we will pray." Goody Hammer pursed her lips and retreated into thought. She reached into her pocket and removed a black velvet pouch drawn closed with a cord. She dug two thick fingers inside, spread it apart and pulled out a gray-red stone the size of an almond. The stone was wrapped in frayed twine and fashioned into a necklace. Carefully, as if she were handling a ball of golden threads, she unwound the twine and dangled the amulet in front of Mama's nose.

"Wear this around your neck. It has the force to turn a child." Then in a deep voice she chanted *"Vidi aquam egredientem de templo . . . et omnes, ad quos pervenit aqua ista salvi facti sunt, et dicent."* Her chant, full of rough edges and soft hums, made me tremble even more.

"'Tis an eagle stone. It has powerful virtues. Do not remove it or allow it to touch your skin, Hannah. Wear it until the child enters the world. Then at the infant's first cry we will quickly remove it so it does not draw forth your womb."

Mama backed away. "Doesn't Reverend Wilson disapprove of this magic?"

"Aye, our ministers claim to disapprove, but they'd be the first to reach for 'em when all else fails. The blackcoats are no different than us," she cackled. "They too do what they must. Come a plague, they'll wear 'em around their necks like the Papists wear their crosses."

Mama slipped the amulet over her neck and tucked it under her collar.

I longed to cry out loud, "No charm from a cunning woman can aid you." But I knew such an outburst would embarrass Mama and turn Goody Hammer even more against me.

Mama's hand shook as she lifted her cup to her lips.

"You know when you conceived this child, death entered into you, Hannah, and now your days may be numbered. 'Tis reasonable as you prepare to live, you must also prepare to die."

I ran my fingers over the knobby surface of the ticking covering our straw mattress. At the mention of death, I twisted a loose thread around my fingertip until it swelled thick with blood.

"I pray for deliverance," Mama said.

"If the Lord deems otherwise, are you prepared for

judgment as well?"

"I prepare for it daily."

"Your life is in more powerful hands then." Goody Hammer rose to her full height and straightened her back. "Come, Elijah. We must be off." She tucked her biscuit into her pocket. The mongrel raised his head off the hearth and then curled back into a ball.

"Elijah!" Goody Hammer stomped her foot. This time the dog rose on its twiggy legs, arched and straightened its spine and hobbled to her side. "He learns quickly as we all do," Goody Hammer mumbled, glaring at me.

"Thank you for your visit, Goodwife Hammer. Gabriel will fetch you when my time comes." Mama glanced at me and then at the hag. "I have a request to make before you leave. I would like Mercy to assist at this birth."

Goody Hammer scowled at me.

Her scowl reminded me of what had happened the morning Mama's travails with Grace began. While Papa was out fetching Goody Hammer, I had done all I could to make Mama comfortable. I prepared a pallet for her on the floor and eased her into a seated position against the wall. Each time a pain commenced, I soothed her with kind words. Fear overcame me but I did not show it. When Goody Hammer arrived, I begged her to allow me to stay, for I had done an exemplary job of assisting Mama and I wished to continue. But the hag glared at me with her good eye; her bad one spun off into the darkness of its socket. "Has your course begun yet, girl?" When I replied honestly, "It has not," she snapped, "Then you be unready." I stood there helpless and humiliated. To add to my embarrassment, she pressed the flat of her hand between my shoulder blades and pushed me out the door with Papa and the boys.

"If you say so, Hannah," was all Goody Hammer said now. She donned her cape, tucked her Bible inside her pocket, and with her cur she retreated into the wintry whiteness.

THERE WAS NO ONE I COULD TALK TO about my fear of Goody Hammer. Surely, I couldn't upset Mama or Mary with my worries, and Papa, with his loyalty to Goody Hammer would discredit me, so the following day I wrote to Jane. It was a single sheet I penned in haste.

January 14, 1631
Dear Jane,

I have been bothered by thoughts I can share with no one else, so after a sleepless night—when thoughts of the most terrifying matters consumed me, I write to you. I thank heavens you are a friend I can confide, whom I trust above all others.

My problem is regarding Goody Hammer. She called upon Mama yesterday, but it was a meeting that scared me. In England, when she visited Mama before Grace was born, she examined Mama and they prayed. That was all. This time she said that the child inside Mama has not turned, and she strung an amulet around Mama's neck—an eagle stone to make the child turn. As she did so, she chanted words so evil I should have covered my ears. The words were gibberish, words of magic that frightened my brothers and me. I felt as if badness had entered our home.

You and I know, Jane, that witches abide in all places—we have seen them do great harm in England with their potions and ill manners—so does it not follow that Satan might have sent her across the ocean to make mischief in America? There is no one to fear more than a witch, thus I want to have as little to do with that woman lest she is one. When I see her coming to bring Papa his tea, I grab my shawl and hide behind our cottage. Thankfully, she never tarries. She is one to do her business and be off. Now she is working her mischief on Mama. What must I do? I know I am given to letting my mind wander to fearful, imaginary places, but now the danger seems as real as night and I need your help.

I thought we were free of witches in America, but I fear we are not. Am I mad to think this? Tell me honestly what you think, my dearest friend, for it is you above all others that I trust. Also tell me true, what should I do?

Mercy

P.S. Have any witches been prosecuted yet in Lincolnshire?

Chapter Nine

As Mama's time approached, she became more self-absorbed. She completed household tasks, but did them slowly and silently. Her belly was heavy, so I understood her sluggish movements, but I did not understand her silence. Typically, Mama hummed as she worked, either her favorite Psalm or a string of random notes that clicked together merrily. Without her sounds, our daily life felt hollow.

Shortly after Goody Hammer's visit, Papa surprised Mama with a bolt of white wool that arrived from England, and also a spool of thick thread for tatting lace. We cannot eat wool and lace, I thought, but upon seeing Papa's pleasure in giving his gift, my disposition changed.

"'Tis more fabric than you shall need, Hannah, but it will make a gown for you to wear in the spring, and one for Mercy." Mama pressed the finespun cloth against her belly and twirled before him like a young girl.

Papa stepped back to admire her. "How handsome with your dark hair," he said. Then to me he added, "You will look as lovely in your new gown, Mercy, the perfect image of your mother you are."

Laughingly, Mama passed the fabric to me and I held it up to my body and twirled as she did, trying to catch a glimpse of myself in the windowpane. It was in the glass that I saw Papa standing behind me watching me. His look gave me pause, so I quickly stopped my preening and returned the fabric to Mama.

In the days that followed, Mama became obsessed with her sewing. She carefully cut the cloth for our gowns so there was nary any waste. With the remnants she stitched smocks and caps for the baby. I took pleasure in watching her slim fingers guide a brass needle through the cloth, pierce the soft wool, watching it disappear and resurface again until all that was visible was a row of precise stitches that looked like snowy footsteps to a mysterious destination.

One day I asked, "Mama, where shall you wear it?"

She did not reply.

"Where shall you wear it?" I asked again. It was not often she had new gowns, nor was it often she had destinations worthy of such finery.

"Perhaps soon, my daughter." At that moment, I understood. I heard of women laying out their own grave clothes along with the clothes for their newborn, but I never heard of a woman sewing such a splendid gown for such a purpose.

"No, Mama, you will not!" I cried, snatching the needle from her hand. White thread snapped and curled in the air. "There will be no need for it because you will live and the baby will live, and you will wear this gown when Joshua and I one day marry." Without thinking, I accidentally jabbed the needle into my palm and drew blood.

"Perchance there be no need for worry, but I must prepare in case the Lord calls." Mama picked up a scrap of wool from the floor and wrapped it tenderly around my hand. She pulled me close, and together we wept.

Chapter Ten

———— ❧ ————

February 16, 1631

Dearest Jane,

Mama said good things happened on the Sabbath. It was only fitting that on the Sabbath she went to God.

Mama died on the thirteenth of February and took her babe with her—my sister who never lived to take a breath or even a name.

T'day, beneath bleak skies Papa, Michael, Noah, and I carrying Grace in my arms, followed Mama's coffin to the graveyard. It was dusk when we trudged up the hill. Her women carried her coffin—a crude pine box pounded closed with iron nails. Goody Hammer and Goody Henshaw walked at her head, Goody Demsey and Goody Aspinwall at her heart, and Goody Dudley and her daughter Anne Bradstreet at her feet. Their arms bore a precious gift to God—the remains of a life led for Him.

Billy Bowdoin, our drummer boy, marched ever so slowly ahead of Mama's coffin beating his drum. Others joined in procession—Thomas Dudley, stern-faced and wrapped in his lugubrious cloak; Reverend Wilson, weary from too many such treks; William

Coddington; William Aspinwall; Ezekiel, and Joshua. Mary, who will soon enter her own travail, was so stricken that William insisted she remain at home.

There were no tears, no songs, no words. Just the crackle of footsteps in the frozen snow, the hiss of the wind, and the fall of snow upon our hoods. How I longed to hear the comforting sound of Mama's hum break the silence of our walk, but her voice is amongst us no longer.

As I pen this letter, some from the congregation are here consoling Papa. The neighbors have brought food, which he refuses to eat, and ale, which he willingly drinks. I have excused myself from our guests to take refuge on Mama's side of the mattress and have drawn the curtains closed around me.

Mama's travail began on Saturday afternoon, shortly after Papa left to do business on the Mystic River. He was not there when she cried out for him. I ran for Goody Hammer with such speed I do not remember my feet touching the path. But I do remember shouting the names of Mama's women and, like a madwoman, thumping my fists on their doors. When we returned, Mama was screaming—not for her own pain, but for someone to remove the boys and Grace from our home. Goody Hammer bid them to the Demseys next door and then she settled Mama on a blanket on the floor. I stoked the fire and lit all of our tapers so Goody Hammer might have good light.

Throughout the night the women supported Mama in their arms. Mary sang hymns softly. Elizabeth brought her a tea of tansy. Catherine Henshaw, who bore four children of her own, told stories to make her laugh, which Mama forced herself to do in gratitude. Still, as night transformed into morn, the babe within would not turn. The women recited Sabbath prayers, which provided her some comfort.

By midday conversation stopped, for Mama could not abide

her pain. I sat beside her, holding her hand, feeling her strength slacken. Then she released my hand and I could no longer call her to awareness. Mary sobbed tears that fell upon her own full belly. Wild with fear, I begged Goody Hammer to do something, anything. But her hands hung helplessly by her sides. She stared at me with those eyes. "I do all I know," she said. "Do more," I pleaded, pulling on her sleeve. "All I have to give is what you do not approve of," she said.

"Then you must do it. Use the charms," I commanded her.

Goody Hammer pulled out her pouch and spread the charms around the edges of Mama's pallet—another eagle stone, a crystal, a lodestone, a sharp hound's tooth, and a furry rodent's claw. One by one she rubbed them, chanting words of magic over each of them. A voice inside me said that using the charms was evil, but I would have tried anything to keep Mama amongst the living.

Throughout the afternoon, she adjusted the amulets around Mama's bare belly and felt for the position of the baby. She gazed into Mama's eyes to reach her with her powers. Her lips moved as if in prayer, but they were not prayers she uttered, but gibberish I could not understand.

After twenty-two hours—Catherine Henshaw counted the flips of an hourglass and marked them on paper—the babe turned and with a great deal of agony and cries and blood flowing onto Goody Hammer's arms, dripping upon the blankets, and seeping into the earthen floor that dutifully swallowed it, Mama pushed the babe into the world. Then with her work completed, her life went to God. Neither Papa nor a minister was there to give her a lift to heaven. I do not know whether Mama knew the child was born dead or that she had birthed another daughter.

Afterwards, I could not face Goody Hammer. Her amulets and gibberish did Mama nothing but harm. Her chant raced through my mind like a fiendish melody. I cannot rid myself of it. In the dark of night my mind reels thither and yon, and I try to fathom what is true. I know not what to believe. I know only that Mama is dead and she died at Goody Hammer's hand, and I urged Goody Hammer to use her magic. I knew it was wrong, but I told her to do it.

I helped Goody Hammer prepare Mama and the baby for the grave. When I met Papa at the door the next day I fell into his arms and sobbed out what had happened. He pushed me aside and would hear nothing of my account. "She is not gone!" he insisted. When he saw Mama holding the shrouded babe in her arms, clothed in her white gown, her dark curls arranged around her face, he took her hand and tried to pull her out of the coffin. Then he collapsed upon her, but Goody Hammer had the strength to lift him up. I could do nothing, say nothing, for mine was not the voice Papa longed to hear.

Today after the funeral, Papa is a wounded animal. He calls wildly to anyone who will listen—to God, to Mama, to me. I can do little to console him for there are no answers. It has been difficult explaining Mama's death to the boys, who are both as mute as rabbits cornered in a chase. Grace does not understand that Mama's absence is forever.

Jane, how do I go on? It is now that I fathom what you have had to live with—the loss of your own dear mother at birth, and the presence of Millicent, a stepmother—who is good and a blessing to you—but is still not the mother of your heart. If anyone should be able to advise me on how to live with such loss, it should be you. I wish you were here to guide me.

Mercy

Chapter Eleven

———— ❧ ————

In the weeks that followed, Papa took solace in the cups of ale he poured for himself from a firkin that Samuel Cole, a shipmate, left at our cottage. The quarter barrel sat wedged with wooden blocks on the end of our rough table, a fixture with a ready tap.

There was no consoling him. Guilt gnawed at him. He stumbled aimlessly, batting his arms about, wiping his tear-stained cheeks on his shirtsleeves. His fingernails were gritty. His eyes were bloodshot. He wore the same white shirt every day since Mama's burial. He even stopped drinking the tea Goody Hammer provided him.

"Mama would not want to see you thus," I said, gently. I guided him to his chair, but with all his weight he pulled free. After a while, his repeated laments became voices that echoed in my head: "My Hannah, I loved you too much . . . I took too much pride in your beauty . . . I forced you into this wilderness against your will . . . I was not there when you called out for me. Curse the ships I build and sink them to the bottom of the sea." Papa was referring to the bark, *Blessing of the Bay*, which took him to Mystic on the day Mama died.

"Papa, you have done Mama justice as a husband," I tried to reassure him.

"You know naught of my love for your mother," he would say, heaving his arms to heaven. In the flickering candlelight the veins in his arms throbbed like worms beneath his skin.

"You cannot know the mind of God, Papa. You must not question His ways," I offered, speaking words Mama would have spoken. Yet mine was not the voice he wished to hear.

"I should not have purchased that cloth. I only wanted to bring a smile to her face, to ease her worry, and for it I was punished. That gown became her winding sheet." Papa's drunken fingers quivered before my face like claws. The wind howled and beat against our walls. Its roar was the shriek of God chastising us from the outside while our consciences tormented us from within.

I CARRIED WITHIN MY HEART a hot and heavy ball of sadness. It was constantly there, except for the few gentle moments upon waking when snippets of dreams still claimed my memory. But all too soon the ball gathered weight and I became aware of the pain within our household.

It was during these months that Grace took her first steps. The child who had completely been Mama's now became mine. The Lord gives babies the gift of short memories. They recall the last face that smiles at them, the last hand that lifts a cup to their lips, and the last arms that hug them when their world is unlovely.

Each day I noticed small changes in my sister that caused changes within me. One day Grace gripped the bench and pulled her chubby body up. Pleased with herself, she laughed—with cheeks that flushed like plums and a voice that tinkled like a bell. This made the heavy ball beneath my heart lighten.

The next day Grace stood up longer before tumbling to the ground. And the next she stepped away every so slightly. "Grace, see you can walk," I encouraged. One evening Grace took two steps, still with a firm grip on the bench, and then she walked off balancing herself within the circle of her plump arms, grinning. The heavy ball inside of me lightened further.

Noah and Michael carried their own pain. They picked at their evening meals with downcast eyes. Their steps lacked haste and purpose. But as with me, Grace became their healer.

In the absence of Papa's affection, Michael took to lifting Grace above his head and kissing her silken forehead as he swung her down. "Tell me now, Grace, of your day," he would tease. Then Noah would answer in a breathy girl's voice, "I stirred the soup . . . swept the floor . . . led every cow in town to pasture," whatever described our activities, true or exaggerated. He would rock her in his arms like a baby, "And look how sleepy you are. Tomorrow you will slaughter a goat, fly like a bird to London and return with armloads of skunk cabbages." And that is how Grace took to falling asleep at night.

Papa did not respond to Grace. To him she was a reminder of the child he lost and the wife whose comfort he desperately lacked.

THERE WAS A PINE TREE IN THE WOODS that Joshua and I had taken to meeting beneath, a tree that was once struck by lightning. A giant limb had broken from its trunk and drooped boughs over the ground like a bountiful skirt of scorched lace. We called it our Meeting Tree.

To enter, Joshua lifted this massive bough like a curtain. Inside we felt concealed from the world, away from the gossiping tongues of Boston.

It was beneath the Meeting Tree that I opened my heart

to Joshua. One day, when the wind had teeth in it, he brought two heavy deer pelts his father had traded with Indians for a hogshead. We spread one on the pine needles and draped the other over our laps and sat facing each other.

I hadn't planned to unburden myself to him, but when he inquired as to Papa's welfare, my problems came tumbling out. I told him about Papa's unquenchable thirst and how he had stopped catechizing the children.

"When Mama lived, Papa would gather us at eventide," I told him. "He would have us repeat a Bible verse forty times for the forty days Jesus was tempted by the devil. Mama told us that memorizing the verses would arm us against Satan . . . throughout our lives we would have the verses to call upon. She selected the verses . . . marked the pages for him with leaves she pressed inside our Bible." My voice quavered at the memory of our family gathered together—Papa in his chair, Mama on her stool, we children seated on the bench beside the hearth—and my words poured out in spurts. Joshua reached for my hand, and I allowed him to take it, welcoming his comfort.

"When one of us was naughty, Mama selected verses to correct us. Sometimes she even picked verses to correct Papa when he became too spirited . . . too boastful . . . less prayerful . . . when he drank too much and fell asleep in his chair."

Joshua smiled.

I wiped my eyes with my apron.

"May I hold you?"

I nodded and he moved to my side of the soft pelt and wrapped his arm around my shoulders. "You're shivering."

"Hold me," I said looking into his gentle blue eyes.

"I will hold you forever," he whispered.

I sank my head into the crook of his neck, feeling his breath upon my cheek, wanting never to leave him. "I'm so ashamed."

"Why? What could you have done that was so wrong?"

I shook my head in embarrassment.

"Mercy, don't be ashamed. I shan't think less of you for anything you say."

I looked into my lap. "When Papa refused to catechize the children, I took over. It was bold of me. At first, I selected verses to provide them solace for they were so in need of it, but as the days passed I found myself getting angrier at Papa for deserting us, so I selected verses to correct him. I thought if my words could not heal him, Scripture might. Last night I resorted to Proverbs 20: 'Wine is a mocker and strong drink is raging and whosoever is deceived thereby is not wise.'"

"And your Papa, what did he do?"

"He did not wish to hear."

Joshua considered the problem. "I've no answers, Mercy. But perhaps you could ask Reverend Wilson. Surely, he will provide good counsel."

The thought of meeting alone with Reverend Wilson made my stomach tighten. What if he considered Papa's drunkenness such an abomination that he had him arrested, branded with a D on his chest, and tied to a tree in the grove for others to jeer at? There was a man in England who was made to wear a barrel around his body with holes cut out for his arms. He had to sit in the center of Market Square in the hot sun enduring the taunts of people who gathered around for the amusement of it, some of them hurling stones that clunked against the wood. I shuddered at the thought of Papa being subjected to such ridicule. He was my papa. It was my responsibility to protect him.

"Reverend Wilson will keep your confidence, I know he will," Joshua said, seeing my reticence. "He will understand. Perhaps he will even meet with your papa to set him right.

That is the work of a minister, is it not?"

Joshua left the Meeting Tree first that afternoon, and I remained alone for a short time so we would not be espied leaving together. When I stood up, my head brushed a branch, and a sprig of pine needles fell onto my shoulder. "The fragrance of heaven," I said aloud, remembering what Papa had said on Cape Ann.

I slipped out from between the branches and straightened up. When I turned around, there behind a scrub oak stood Goody Hammer. She stepped forward and grabbed my arm. "I just passed Joshua at the lip of the forest," she said angrily. "You must watch yourself with him."

"Not now, Goodwife, please not now," I said, shaking free of her and running home.

Chapter Twelve

———— ❦ ————

Mama used to say the days of our lives are like the weather—there could only be so many wintry days before the buds would sprout. That winter I kept watching for hints of spring, waiting for rebirth. But the hardness of winter continued to punish us.

It was during this bleak time that I heard a pitiful wailing outside our door. The children were asleep, and Papa, besotted with ale, was splayed upon his mattress. There came a crunching of shoes on our footpath. I peered through the curtains, fearful of Indians. But in the black of night I espied our neighbor Goody Demsey stumbling toward our cottage. The lantern she held high illuminated her distorted mouth.

At the door she collapsed into my arms.

"Oh, Mercy, our Mary has died! The baby too."

"My God, no! Not Mary."

As I gently guided her to Papa's chair, the trembling woman sobbed the story of Mary's travail, but I was not listening for none of it mattered. All that mattered was that Mary too was gone. Mary who was minutes away from holding a babe in her arms, and in a breath, even before her infant could see daylight, both their lives ended. And poor William, who so longed for a son.

That night I could not sleep. Why did God will this to happen? There would be another funeral procession, this time with William following the coffin into the bitter wind.

Papa coughed and I returned my attention to him. What would Mama tell me to do about his drunkenness? Be of good courage, she would say. Mary loved me like a mother. How would she counsel me? Trust in the Lord but confide in Reverend Wilson, she would tell me.

I must be strong; I must heed their advice. I closed my eyes and imagined Mama and Mary hovering above me, heavenly presences now—speckles, stars, mist and gentle shadows smiling down on me, guiding me. This image forced my decision. I would meet with Reverend Wilson.

Instead of meeting in the frigid grove the following Thursday, Governor Winthrop opened his home to us. His was the largest dwelling in our settlement—two floors of rooms set off by itself in a field of several acres. That afternoon I was but one of many cloaked and hooded worshipers bundled to our ears, heading in that direction.

I expected his manservant to greet us, but the governor stood at the door. He wore a bright blue shawl around his shoulders, which surprised me because until then I had seen him only in sad colors. Aside from his servants and a son, he lived in that massive home alone. He had built it for his wife and the rest of his family who would be arriving in the spring.

"Miss Goodhue," Governor Winthrop said, extending his hand and arching his eyebrows. "I was grieved to hear of your mother's passing, and I'm sorry I was in Watertown the day of her burial." I bowed my head to acknowledge his condolences, but his words reminded me of how important men always seem to be away at significant moments.

I followed the others into the common room. A massive fireplace dominated the heavily raftered room with timbers bearing the fresh marks of the woodman's ax. Inside the fireplace two sets of claw-footed andirons supported a massive stack of logs that blazed, crackled, and belched out heat. A continuous bench banked the walls on either side of the hearth and wrapped around the room. As in the grove, the women sat on one side and the men on the other. In the air hung the aroma of newly hewn wood, fruity tobacco, and damp wool.

I espied Joshua in the center of the room surrounded by a group of merchants. His hands were animated in the telling of a story. It pleased me to see him in society, for he too had been laboring hard building homes. Goody Hammer sat alone in a corner reading her Bible. I did not feel her eyes upon me.

I took a seat beside Goody Henshaw. Her head was bowed and she was writing in a small black journal on her lap with a quill so worn at the nib I thought it might expire before she committed her thought to paper. She looked up, saw me staring at her quill, raised it into the air and chuckled, "There's no excuse for this, is there, Mercy? In a land so full of turkey feathers!" Her eyes were soft and green, like twin ponds of emerald water. There was a gentle quality about her that put me at ease. If Goody Henshaw could be lightly disposed after the shock of losing her husband to the blade of an ax, surely I could handle my problems.

"I was recording a recipe for cornbread," she explained.

"Aye, we are all learning to eat cornbread," I said, thinking of the cornbread I took over to the Coddingtons days ago after Mary's death. "You were with Mary when she died?"

"I was," Goody Henshaw whispered. "Our Mary suffered

hard and died with the name of the Lord upon her lips." Then, as an afterthought, she added, "Even Goody Hammer's amulets could not keep her amongst the living."

I took a deep breath and imagined Goody Hammer circling them around Mary's belly as she had around Mama's. Perhaps they both would be alive were it not for those vile amulets.

"Did you know William is returning to England for a time?" Goody Henshaw asked.

"I did not."

"He decided this morning. He wishes to mourn in the company of his family. He will sail with Reverend Wilson on the morrow aboard the *Essex*.

"I didn't know Reverend Wilson was leaving."

"Aye, to retrieve his wife who would not travel with him a year ago. She said she would come only when there would be a home for her to live in. Now our minister must risk his own life to retrieve her. I don't understand such lack of confidence from a minister's wife."

"Nor do I." I would have participated in the gossip and said more, were I in the mood.

"How is your father?"

Goody Henshaw's question caught me by surprise. "He is fine," I lied.

"He cannot be fine," she whispered. "I know he cannot be. It will take years for him to be fine." She patted my hand gently.

Governor Winthrop entered the room and took a seat beside William Aspinwall, the husband of over-pious Elizabeth. Reverend Wilson followed him in and stopped in front of the hearth. Joist Brown, our newly appointed constable, stepped up to a small table and inverted the hourglass, signifying the lecture would begin. Joshua and I exchanged supportive glances.

For the next three hours I watched the grains of sand pass slowly through the narrow neck of the hourglass. I was so distracted during the sermon that later Joshua would have to remind me that Reverend Wilson exhorted on the Beatitudes.

Afterwards I lingered, talking to the women. My mouth seemed to work independently of my mind as I answered questions about my family, thanked people for their condolences, inquired of their health—all the while avoiding Goody Hammer and following Reverend Wilson's black skullcap as it circled the room, listening for the nasal pitch of his voice above the yammer of the others. I watched our minister's mouth form words, fingers touch shoulders, head nod, his scruffy body shuffle from person to person as they wished him a safe journey.

As the crowd thinned, I attempted to move closer to him, trailing him like an anxious child trails a parent in a crowded marketplace. I was almost beside him when he coughed, turned abruptly and ambled off. My heart sank as he moved into the shadows and entered a room off the hallway. It was my last chance. I followed him and boldly rapped on the heavy wooden door he had left slightly ajar. I would never have disturbed him had he closed it tight.

"Miss Goodhue." Reverend Wilson's usually high-pitched voice was a weary whisper. He waved me in. The room bore a reddish hue from a taper glowing on Governor Winthrop's desk. Shadows from the flame flashed around us, lighting a shelf of books behind the desk.

"Reverend Wilson, I'm in need of counsel. I know you are sailing on the morrow and I wish you safe travels, but today I have nowhere to turn."

He sighed—not a dismissive sigh, but a tired one—

scratched his unkempt beard, and sat behind the desk. "Let you close the door. I am sure Governor Winthrop would not mind us occupying his library for a few moments."

I lowered myself into the chair opposite him and took a deep breath. "Reverend Wilson, you know my mother died in February."

"Hannah Goodhue was a godly woman."

I took another deep breath. "My father suffers deeply from his loss."

"I understand your mother left you the burden of caring for your brothers and an infant."

His words made me wince. "It is not my responsibilities that trouble me, sir. I am coping with the household duties. My mother taught me well. But my father does not recover. Papa has become intemperate with drink, and he is no longer the same man," I said, looking up to measure his reaction.

Reverend Wilson fingered the broken spine of his Bible. His fingernails made a scratching sound on the leather. His eyes strayed from me to the book.

"Is this not a change one might expect of a grieving husband?" he asked.

I sank deeper into the chair cushion. He thinks of me as a child—a child who does not understand the pain of adult problems. "He drinks to excess," I said boldly.

He studied me with owlish eyes. "Does he do anyone harm?"

"To none other than himself. He takes little food. He does not go to the grove for prayer. He believes the Lord has deserted him."

"Perchance your father has deserted the Lord," Reverend Wilson countered quickly. "Does he fault the Lord for the death of your mother?"

"No, he blames himself because he was away at Mystic. He believes the Lord punished him for paying more attention to his quest for fortune."

"He takes rightful blame. The Lord punishes such sins, sometimes with severity. When your father is drunk with alcohol he creates a void in his senses that Satan can enter. Satan then takes advantage of his weakened condition."

Reverend Wilson tapped the cover of his Bible once more. "Your father is a stalwart member of the Boston Congregation. He is a hater of sin, and I believe God will provide him the strength to renounce the evil spirits threatening him." With clumsy hands Reverend Wilson opened the book and shuffled through the pages until he found the passage he was searching for. He moved his index finger down the center and read in his nasal voice: "'Whosoever is born of God doth not commit sin; for his seed remaineth in him, and he cannot sin because he is born of God.'"

"Your words comfort me," I lied. "But what am I to do now, sir?"

He looked at me straight. "You are a young woman, Mercy Goodhue. You must pray for his deliverance and strive to keep your home a place where the Lord resides. You must hold your tongue. You must show patience and act with prudence. You must not judge your father but instead weep at the condition of your own soul. Remember, Mercy, it is the role of the woman to give comfort to the man. The head of every man is Christ, and the head of the woman is man."

His voice grew irritable and more commanding, which caused me to press my back into the chair. I did not want to be there any more than he wished me there. He was leaving for England to fetch a wife who refused to travel by his side a year ago. She was inconveniencing him, and now I was inconveniencing him as well. I needed his kindness, not his judgment.

"You must practice good cheer and keep your mind on excellent things. You must resist complaining, for the burden you carry comes from God just as the joy you receive is from Him. Do you not recall what Job said to his wife when she cursed God for inflicting him with painful sores?" I nodded because it would be insolent not to.

Without hesitating, Reverend Wilson turned to a page of the Bible more worn than the others, and read, "'Thou speakest as one of the foolish women speaketh. What? Shall we receive good at the hand of God, and shall we not receive evil?'" He looked up, pleased with himself. My eyes focused on the short whiskers poking out from behind his oily collar, surely evidence of not being cared for by a wife. I bit the inside of my cheek and fixed my gaze behind him at Governor Winthrop's bookcase. My courage was ebbing. To distract myself I read the title of one of the books on the shelf: *The Trial of Witchcraft*. I counted five such books before Reverend Wilson spoke again.

"Remember, Mercy, God is testing you, and as He tests you, He watches you. The all-seeing eye of God is upon you, and there is not an act or word or thought that goes unnoticed by Him. You must fear the Lord. You must not anger Him, for He sees all you do and if you anger Him, His wrath can be great."

His gaze became more intense.

"You asked, though, what you should do now. You must declare tomorrow a day of personal thanksgiving. You must fall to your knees and thank Him for your tribulations, for they shall open your heart to His mercy. You must allow the Bible to be your delight, to make its words your own." Then he looked into my eyes with a force that burned. "What is your purpose on this earth, my child?"

"To be worthy of salvation," I answered with the words I had been taught.

"Aye. It is not this life but our eternal life that matters. You must use this life to prepare for the next." He closed his Bible and tenderly stroked the black leather. "Do you understand, my daughter?"

I stared at him, unable to speak.

"It is your eternal life that matters, Mercy, not this one," he repeated. "Is it not so?"

He would not release me from his gaze until I acquiesced. Reluctantly, I said what he wanted me to say. "It is not this life that matters, but my eternal life."

"Lay it to your heart then, and may God grant you grace."

He stood up, signaling the end of our meeting.

OUTSIDE, JOSHUA WAS LEANING against a hickory tree with his booted foot against the trunk. When he heard the door open, he hurried toward me. "What did he say?" He cupped his hand around my elbow to steady me as we made our way down the slippery lane.

My mind was befuddled. I did not know how to respond. I stuttered, gasping for clarity and fresh air. "He said I must thank God for my tribulations. He said with good prayers, Papa would surely recover."

"He is right. We must give him time. Things will get better at home, Mercy." He wrapped his arm around me. I told him more of what Reverend Wilson had to say, but then I could speak of it no longer, so rattled was I. I wanted to forget our minister's discourse on heaven or hell, salvation or damnation, the wrath of the Lord.

"Joshua, let's go where we can be alone."

I knew the risk of being alone with Joshua. Even in the dark people could be watching, and if they saw me, I could be accused of being a Jezebel. I knew I should head home, but home was not where I wanted to be. Grace would be asleep, having been tended to by my brothers. I wanted to linger with Joshua, to feel his comfort, to forget what happened with Reverend Wilson, to put off my responsibilities. "The Meeting Tree," I said.

SHELTERED BY THE SNOW-ENCRUSTED pine boughs, Joshua opened his cape to me and I stepped into its swath. He pulled me close. In the silence we spoke a language not of words but of feelings. I could feel him swallow. I could feel his breath and heartbeat. Nestled within his arms I mused about how breaths and heartbeats and swallows measured our lives, and how moments are marked by the flip of an hourglass, the beat of a drum, the tender love betwixt a man and woman. Reverend Wilson spoke about eternity and the condition of my soul, but now I wanted no part of what he had to say. I wished to dwell in the present. I smiled and breathed in Joshua's woodsy smell. His lips caught a twinkle of moonlight and I wondered what it would feel like to kiss them. Would his kisses be tender or rough? Would they send shivers through me as I imagined they would?

I stepped back and looked at him. Overcome with feelings, my eyes welled up with tears. His eyes rested gently upon mine. "From the first day I saw you on the *Arbella*, you've had my heart. I love you, my Mercy."

My heart beat faster. "And I love you, Joshua, and you have my heart," I whispered. My words felt natural, probably because I had repeated them so many times to myself. They were words I had oft spoken aloud as I had gone about my work, and I'd said them before falling asleep. "I love you, Joshua."

In the shadows I could see his eyes take on a new intensity. He kissed me and his kisses were soft and slow and warm. When his hands moved to my breasts and opened a button of my bodice, I knew I should have pulled away, but I did not. I could not. I longed for his touch. I wanted to feel these feelings with this man I loved.

I felt the stirring a woman feels for a man, but with it came the guilt of offering myself to him. I longed to lift my skirts to him. My desire was as powerful as anything I had ever felt, even as powerful as my longing for salvation. Yet, in the end, I did what I had been taught to do. I would not be a lightskirt or a Jezebel.

"We must wait, Joshua," I whispered in his ear.

And dutifully, he pulled away.

After Joshua hurried off after walking me to our cottage door, I felt alone, but I also felt like a woman who was cherished by a fine man. With my hand pressed against the door, I pictured Papa on the other side of it sitting at our table. It was then I realized my heart beat for two men, and I could no more dismiss Joshua's tenderness than I could Papa's melancholy.

Chapter Thirteen

The following evening I tried a new approach. I would not be a foolish woman unable to cope with life's upsets. I would be of good cheer and set a new mood within our home. I wrapped Mama's crimson apron around my waist and went to work.

After supper, I selected a joyful Psalm for our nightly recitation and motioned for the boys and Grace to take their places on the bench. Grace climbed up betwixt Noah and Michael. She was too young to recite verses, but she sat respectfully like a miniature woman with her back erect and her dimpled hands resting upon her knees.

Papa remained at the table watching us and drinking ale. From time to time, I glanced at him, then looked away.

I took a confident breath and read from Mama's Bible: "'The Lord is my rock, and my fortress, and my deliverer, my God, my strength in whom I will trust; my buckler, and the horn of my salvation.'" By the fifth repetition, Noah and Michael began to memorize the verse and joined in. By the fifteenth repetition, they memorized it well enough to take liberties, calling out "horn," and in each ensuing repetition yelling the word louder. Michael leaned across Grace and grinned at his brother. This was all the encouragement Noah needed. He started to sway from side to side. I could not scold them. This was the first time they've shown joy since Mama's death, and I did not want to disrupt their mood with correction. The mischievous twinkle that disappeared from Michael's eye months ago returned. Noah took to tapping the rhythm of the verse on the floor with the toe of his shoe. By the twentieth repetition Grace joined in the merriment. "Horn," she cried, and we laughed, and our laughter was like music.

By the fortieth repetition—Noah kept count by flashing his fingers—the four of us were giggling and swaying. Grace clapped her hands. I set her on my lap and drew her into a hug.

Papa watched us sullenly from his chair. Finally, he'd had enough. "Are ye heathens?" he bellowed.

I stepped forward. "No longer can we be sad. Mama wouldn't have wanted it."

Michael marched up to my side and said, bravely. "Mama would have taken pleasure in Grace's sweet prayers. In days gone by, you would have too, Papa."

While at one time Papa may have considered our remarks insolent, this time he overlooked them. His bulging eyes stared into the smoky air as if he were trying to penetrate a wall blocking him from the person he longed to see.

"Boys, prepare for bed," I whispered. They nodded and began to lower their cots from where they hung on the wall.

Papa poured himself another tankard of ale and I stoked the fire.

The flames leapt. *Remove this cup from Papa*, I prayed.

Suddenly, Papa thundered, "I know not any of you!"

Michael did not look up from the blanket he was unfolding. Noah kept his eyes on his task. They were used to our father's anger. But Grace began to cry. I kissed her forehead and carried her to Mama's rocking chair and rocked her. I sang her Mama's favorite song, purring the words as Mama once did, "Give thanks to the Lord, for he is good. His mercy endureth forever." In Mama's place, I would be a good mother to her. I would raise her as Mama would have wished. Noah and Michael would help, as surely would Papa when he came to his senses.

When Grace was calm, I settled her on our cot and stepped outdoors for air. Snow was falling gently. Fresh and pure, it glistened on the pasture in the moonlight. Soon it would be spring.

I took a deep breath and recalled Reverend Wilson's words about God sending tribulations to test me. I lifted another log from the pile outside the door and returned inside, kicking the door shut behind me.

Immediately, I noticed a change in Papa. He was engaging the boys in conversation.

"You grow tall," he slurred, pointing an unsteady finger at Noah.

Noah responded by standing straight as a rod and stretching his slender body to show he was becoming a man. "Papa, would you mark my height on the door, for I've grown since my last mark." He wanted to be as tall as his brother. He flashed us a hopeful smile.

"Not t'night," Papa replied, but then he reached into the pocket of his breeches, and with fumbling fingers pulled out his small silver knife and tossed it to me.

I motioned for the boys to stand against the doorframe and dutifully made their marks in the soft wood, carving their initials into the doorframe, as well as the date, 4.1.31. I felt Papa's stare on my back as I stood back to admire my handiwork.

"Ye must record such things, my Hannah," he said, calling me by my mother's name.

Much toll the mighty ale takes.

Humming the hymn's refrain, I tucked the boys into their beds, then made my way to the rocking chair and quietly eased myself into it.

The unexpected silence in the room agitated Papa. While most people are jarred by a sudden noise, he, in his stupor, became more rattled by silence. He stumbled to the door, opened it and left, probably to relieve himself.

Cool air blew inside. I drew its freshness into my lungs and exhaled, finding relief in the simple act of breathing. Breathing was the one thing I could control.

I was relieved that Papa left me alone. I had done a fine job that evening and now I was free to think about Joshua. I closed my eyes and remembered his kisses, the warmth of his breath against my cheeks, the strong feeling of his forearms beneath his shirtsleeves, and the longing I felt when he opened the buttons of my bodice and whispered, "I love you, my Mercy." How I ached for him.

IN THE LIGHTNESS OF DREAMS I felt myself rising from my bed, floating into the heavens. It was summer and the air was fragrant with jasmine. Pillows of white clouds caressed me. Familiar voices whispered soothing words. *I'm with you, my child.* It was Mama. Her smooth face was close to mine. Her breath smelled of fresh apples. I stared into the pool of her brown eyes, into the gentle smile that had for so long been lost to me. I smelled her sweet scent and felt her beating heart. *Now you belong to another. Go to him.*

"Joshua," I heard myself say. At the sound of his name, Joshua's manly hands, stronger than Mama's, caressed my cheeks and moved down the length of my neck to my breasts. "I love you," he said.

"And I you."

"Do you know how much I love you, how much I cherish you? Come." His strong arms lifted me and carried me away. Cool air drifted across my toes.

"Joshua?"

"I have need of you. Come . . ."

He lowered me into his bed. Flaxen sheets pressed into my back. I felt the thickness of a pillow beneath my head, and then the weight of him descending upon me. A firm hand stroked the sharp bones below the neckline of my smock, then reached beneath the thin cloth.

"Come to me, my lovely."

Joshua's presence faded.

I opened my eyes. It was Papa.

There was desire in his face. He was looking at me the way he once looked at Mama. Fear overcame me. I tried to pull away, but his legs pinned me down.

"Papa, no . . ."

"Hush, you are mine." His breath was sour from drink. His hands pressed me into the mattress. I tried to move out from under him, but he held me there tighter and tore my smock to below my breast. A calloused thumb moved in circles around my nipple. I forced his hand away.

"No!"

My heart beat wildly. I squirmed to free myself from beneath him, but I could not move from under his weight.

"No!" I cried. "I cannot . . ."

"Hush," he said, raising his head and staring at me. "We must not wake the little ones."

"Do not . . ." My voice rose, but before I could say more, his lips, shiny and moist in the moonlight, descended onto mine. The pressure of his face pinned me deeper into the mattress. I tried to cry out but couldn't.

He yanked up my smock to above my waist. The thickness of him was between my legs.

I tried to scream, but fear blocked my words. My voice caught in my throat and only feeble sounds came out.

"Be still. Do not wake the children."

"I am your child, Papa."

He puffed hot breath into my face. His damp hands stroked my hair. "Such beautiful hair," he slurred.

"No!" I cried. As he mounted me I caught sight of the cleft in his chin, a gouge, black and deep as hell. *A dimple in chin, a devil within.* He pushed himself into me—he pushed in and out in a place where I had never even touched myself. My body stiffened and there was pain. His face was hot and contorted and heaving and grimacing.

He lifted his weight off me. He rolled onto his back and stroked his chin. He closed his eyes, took a deep breath, then slower, shallower ones. I wanted to run, but could not move— not until he was asleep. In fear, I watched his massive chest rise and fall until the strain on his face settled into the softness of a satisfied man surrendering to sleep.

When he began to snore, I rolled out of bed, pulled down my smock and stumbled to the door. A flash of moonlight struck the looking glass in the cupboard, claiming my attention. I turned and caught a glimpse of myself in the silvery glass. My eyes were wild. My mouth was contorted. The dimple in my chin was a gouge as black as a chunk of coal. I ran outside and pulled the door closed behind me.

In the darkness, I ran to the cistern and tore off my smock. My thighs were splotched with blood. My legs were trembling.

I reeked of his sweat. My insides throbbed as if crushed glass was coursing through my veins. I cleaned myself with icy water, wiped myself with my smock and dressed again in its wetness, for it was all I had to cover myself.

Wild with fear, I stumbled into the night. I leapt over snow-crusted rocks and frozen grasses, sharp as needles. Ice crackled beneath my bare feet, yet I felt not its sting. Moonlight spread over the pasture like a coverlet and I ran toward it, for I believed there I could rest unmolested.

Then a terror—greater than my own Papa's lust—struck me. In a blink, I was outside of my body. I was watching another girl weave across the field. This girl was as frail as a reed, chestnut-haired and long of limb. Her smock was torn at her breast and hung to her ankles, slapping in the wind. At the place of her privities, the garment clung to her body with the wet seal of blood. She ran with one arm flailing wildly off to her side and the other wrapped across her chest to protect her modesty.

I considered for a moment that the girl was a phantom—a specter haunting the night—but she could not be one for she left her marks behind her: jagged footprints in the snow and clouds of breath trailing at her back. She stopped in a slash of moonlight—not gracefully, as a maiden might upon reaching her destination, but abruptly, as if she had encountered a wall.

I was this creature. Yet I could not be her. I am a good girl, not one to have been sullied in such a manner.

"Help me!" the girl cried to the heavens.

"Help me!" I cried in the same voice.

And then we were one.

The lust in his eyes flashed before me. The weight of his body pressed into me. My womanly parts throbbed. Terrified, I fell into the snow. No one would bother me here.

The wind stilled. The snow cooled the fire of my skin. The only sound was the panting of my breath.

The sky was a dome studded with stars that pricked the darkness. One star burned brighter than the rest and behind it I discerned the eye of God peering through, watching my every action as He has watched me from the day of my birth. He has been privy to my goodness, but also to my sins—every kindness begrudged, every immodest sway of my hips, and tonight He witnessed the gravest of my sins.

I closed my eyes to His judgment and curled into myself in shame.

Chapter Fourteen

———— ✦ ————

It was our neighbor Davy Person who found me in the pasture.

"I thought I saw a wolf in the snow," he stammered when Papa pulled the door open. "But it was your Mercy. A mongrel ran off as I neared. His heat kept her warm."

Papa breathed down on me. The stench of alcohol on his breath found its way into the pit of my stomach. When Goodman Person set me in his arms, I puked on his shirt. Then I returned to darkness.

For the next several days time ceased to exist. I remember awakening, if only for flashes, to dizzying sensations: the feel of a cool cloth upon my forehead, the pressure of a hand smearing a gritty decoction onto my chest, pain stabbing my throat, the sound of deep voices intoning Scripture, the rack of my cough, a swirling burst of sunshine across my eyelids, the lap of something rough and wet like a tongue upon my hand. Exhausted, I slept again, returning to a frightening place of dark and twisted passages, of ascents and terrifying falls where the smell of Papa, transformed into snakes, slithered inside me. It was Satan burrowing deeper and deeper into me.

Then one morning, awakening from a nightmare, I heard myself cry out, "Be off with you. Do not bite me." My throat pained as if I had swallowed a blade, and my mouth was as dry as dust. There was yellow light behind my closed eyelids.

A hand brushed across my cheek and fingers separated a plait of my hair. "Mercy, 'tis I, Goody Hammer. Nothing bites you."

Terrified by what I would see, I opened my eyes. "Go away!" I cried at the sight of her.

"Be still, girl. You are safe. There's no need to speak." She stroked my cheek with a damp cloth and rinsed it in a pail of fresh water beside my bed. The tinkle of water droplets sent a chill over my body. She pulled the quilt up to my neck. "You know me. I am Goody Hammer and I come to care for you. You have been ill, my child."

"I'm not your child and why are you here?"

"Your Papa summoned me. I come in the morning and leave when he returns. Grace is with Goodwife Demsey. Your brothers are at the harbor with your papa."

The hag's spidery eye hung inches above me, and her thick breath poured down on me. I thrashed my head and rubbed my cheeks in the pillowbear. The picture was becoming clear: Papa had sent his emissary to minister to me—one who, like him, is evil.

"Witch. Go away," I shouted. "You've come to trick me."

"You speak nonsense, girl, but thank the Lord you speak at all." She wiped my brow with a corner of her apron. "Go ahead and close your eyes. I know my countenance is a fright to behold to one not 'customed to looking at it. But I'm no witch and I have no tricks, and ya need not gaze directly at me. Set your eyes on the air behind me and we'll get on well together." Goody Hammer lifted the pail, stood to her full height and turned toward the door. "I'm going to the spring for water. Use your time to settle yourself."

Trembling, I propped myself up on my elbows and examined the room. Our dwelling was tidy—not tidy the way Mama had kept it, nor tidy as I kept it— but tidy from the hands of another woman. On a bench sat a stack of shirts, breeches, and tiny gowns carefully folded and ready to place in drawers. Shafts of light streamed in through the green bottles Mama had brought from England and cheerfully set on the window ledge. The blue and white striped sheet on Papa's mattress was clean and tautly drawn. I flinched and looked away. The table was clear except for a ring of jars and vials surrounding a tall bottle in the middle. Some contained translucent liquids; others were packed tightly with weeds, seeds, and herbs. I thought of the tea she brought Papa and the evil in it. How many bitter drops of those liquids had she forced down my throat, and what gritty salves had she rubbed on me?

All too soon, Goody Hammer returned. She lumbered past me and hung a damp cloth on a hook on the mantel to dry. She picked off a stiffly dried sheet with a dark stain in the middle, breeches, gowns, and wee smocks from a line strung across the hearth.

"Your Joshua comes every evening to sit with you."

"That is good," I croaked. My throat hurt as if I had swallowed pins.

"With the thaw, he and Ezekiel are digging their well. None too soon, I say. This morning I saw old Ezekiel pushin' his water cart up the lane and he looked 'bout ready to expire. A hogshead of water be a heavy load, and I worry for the burden of it on him. He needs a horse, he does. About that well, the stars say 'dig' and I told 'em so. Already they've dug ten feet."

I sighed, irritated by the grating tone of her voice.

"Do not look so annoyed, girl, for you may benefit from the Hoyt's well, if y'know my meaning." She watched my face for a reaction. "What goodwife wouldn't want fresh water behind her cottage? Me? I'd marry a goat for a well," she cackled.

I sunk back into bed and drew the quilt over my eyes. What man would want me now? Hidden beneath my covers I wondered how much Joshua knew, what he suspected, what he was thinking every evening he sat beside me. What had I mumbled? What had he heard from the gossips? There was always gossip.

Goody Hammer continued babbling, but the quilt muffled her voice:

"Goody Demsey came . . ."

"Goody Aspinwall brought a vegetable stew . . ."

"Reverend Phillips came to pray sweet prayers for your recovery . . ."

"Everyone inquires 'bout your health . . . why you were bleedin' . . . perhaps from your course, they say."

Stop! I wanted to shout. I could hear the clatter of their voices, like crows, one more eager than the next. It was embarrassing. And Reverend Phillips. I pictured his long face, the humorless set of his jaw, his black tunic arched over me in prayer.

"Soon your father will return with your brothers. Grace, y' know, has slept by your side every night since you took ill. Even the croak of your cough didn't drive her away."

Stop!

"I know about your father's drinkin'. Aye, he confessed it to me and he confessed it to Reverend Phillips. He is a changed man now. The morning I came to care for you, he met me in the doorway, tears comin' down his face, saying if he were not besotted he could have kept you safe indoors. That morning he rolled the cask into the field and dumped the ale into the ground. He is again taking the physick I bring, a strong tea of white dittany, St. John's wort, and other secrets. The Lord is pleased with his contrition and is healin' him. And today, He heals you too. Oh, the ways of the Lord!"

UPON ENTERING OUR COTTAGE and seeing me awake, Papa ran to my cot the way he had once run to Mama's lifeless body in her coffin.

"Mercy," he sobbed, sinking to his knees. "Thank God, you live!"

My body trembled beneath the quilt. I could not look at him. Instead I pinned my gaze upon the comforting smiles of Noah, Michael, and Grace standing behind him.

My father reached for my face. He stroked my cheeks with his clammy fingertips. I shut my eyes. He ran his fingers down my hair. I held my breath. He fussed over me. I turned away. He tucked my quilt around my body. I recoiled. "Mercy, I'm your papa," he gently chided, plumping a pillow behind my back. The salty scent of the sea that followed him everywhere made me want to puke.

After Goody Hammer left for the day, Papa sat on the stool beside me and fed me spoonfuls of stew. He fed me as he would feed a baby, lifting the spoon from Mama's silver porringer, blowing on the hot vegetables himself before moving the spoon to my mouth, signaling me with his eyebrows to open wide, and when I did, nodding approval. I found myself staring at the cleft in his chin—*A dimple in chin, a devil within.* I wanted to spit the food in his face.

Joshua came, and he too reacted with delight upon seeing me. But his approach was gentle and reticent. To my relief, he assumed no liberties. He merely whispered words to cheer me and in return I forced myself to smile, which Papa saw as an invitation to continue the merriment.

"Everyone! Gather around Mercy! Let us cheer her recovery!"

Joshua stepped forth offering a princely smile. Michael scurried to my bedside from across the room. Noah sat on the corner of my bed, and Grace, her mouth smeared with supper, bounded onto my lap. I pulled her chubby body close.

"Huzza!" Papa cheered.

"Huzza!" the others, including Grace, joined in.

"The Lord has granted us a mighty deliverance. Let us settle down and pray," my father said, pressing his palms in the air for decorum.

Mama's Bible sat on the table. I watched this man who for so long had refused to pray, who called us heathens, lift the Bible as if it were the body of the Christ Child. He sat in his chair, and with fervent fingers flipped through its pages. The image of him pretending to be a pious man turned my stomach.

His hair was combed and he was wearing a clean shirt. My eyes followed the line of his well-cut nose to his unclosed lips, stopping at the cleft in his chin. "You are my Papa," I gasped. He looked up and nodded lovingly. He patted my hand and resumed turning pages. A crimson maple leaf that Mama once had pressed inside the book marked the page he was looking for.

"Psalm 108," he said solemnly. "'My heart is steadfast, O God; I will sing and make music with all my soul. Awake, harp and lyre!'"

I studied his every action: The earnest movement of his lips, the corrective raise of his voice when he noticed Michael becoming distracted, and his indulgent smile when Grace mispronounced a word. He was behaving as if nothing had happened. Hadn't Mama always said I was an imaginative girl who even in the best of times saw profiles in shadows and images in clouds. Could it be my mind was playing tricks on me? Was Satan twisting my thoughts? Perhaps nothing had happened. Perhaps, as the gossips said, my course had begun and I ran out to clean myself and in confusion I ran into the snow. Perhaps it was a hideous dream?

Papa moved his hand across the page of the Bible and he rubbed his index finger in small circles on the maple leaf, around and around in the same spot—just as he had rubbed my breast. It did happen! I wanted to snatch that leaf and set it in a place where it would remain safe. He had no more right to it than he had to me.

Voices rang out in cheerful exultation. Papa intoned in a baritone so powerful that one would think it could only emanate from the Lord's mightiest archangel. I did not join in. No one would fault my silence tonight.

I was accustomed to letting my mind travel during prayer, and as the others prayed, I began piecing together the events of that horrible night.

What did God see as He looked down on me then? An overbold girl who had taken charge? A girl who had the imprudence to tie her dead mother's apron around her waist, to rock in her mother's chair, to sing her dead mother's song? A girl who remained mute when her father miscalled her by her mother's name? I had not intended to seduce Papa, yet then I believed that with every movement of my hands and every turn of my hips I had. When he forced himself upon me I had not the courage to scream, to shake him from the false world he had entered, nor had I cried out for help. I was a participant in his sin.

As impassioned voices intoned their fortieth repetition of the Psalm, I remember recalling another Bible verse from the First Epistle of Paul to Timothy: "And Adam was not deceived, but the woman being deceived was in the transgression."

A sweat, cold as frost, washed over me and a bead of moisture slid down between my breasts. I am even more culpable than my father.

Chapter Fifteen

Papa had arranged for Goody Hammer to care for me until I was fit to resume my household duties. During the weeks that followed, she and Elijah arrived at dawn and remained until dusk when Papa and the boys returned from the harbor.

Her habits became predictable. Every morning she would set her heavy canvas bag on the table and lumber over to me to examine my throat and feel my forehead for fever. Then she'd unpack her bag, always setting her mortar and pestle near the edge of the table; and her vials, jars and bottles in the center with the tallest jar in the middle.

One day, when I felt well enough to sit at the table, I asked her. "Mum, what is in those potions you create, and what have you given me?"

The crone straightened her back and flicked a flea off her shawl in the direction of Elijah. "This comes from you anyway, ya bag of bones," she chortled. The crotchety dog lifted its head with such effort that it might have been a bag of rocks. He scratched himself and returned to his nap.

"Girl, 'tis many secrets in these vials that I do not readily share, but with you I will share them drachm by drachm as long as your curiosity prevails." She had that look of complicity on her face I had come to associate with others who dabbled in quackery. There were many such women in Old Boston who used to gather at the foot of the Witham Bridge to read from their almanacs and exchange herbs. What a silly and dangerous woman she is!

She extended her broad arm so that the folds in her sleeve shed a pall over the glass vials, jars, and bottles. "This is dried mustard seed," she said, tapping a glass bottle with a thick yellow fingernail. Awakened, the golden grains inside the glass shifted and the steep hill of grain collapsed into a gentle hillock. "It brings down the courses. I used it on you that first night when you bled. A fine poultice it makes when mashed smooth as silk."

"And this one?" I asked, pointing to a wide-mouthed jar.

"Ah, a real treasure," She lifted the jar that was stuffed to its brim with a white powder speckled with dark flakes. "Laudanum. From the poppy. Some call it the plant of joy. It has the power to rob pain of its sting. I blend it from the seed of the opium poppy, add saffron and drachms of cinnamon, and dissolve it in red vinegar. 'Tis useful to give before extractin' teeth or drawin' blood." She shook her head. "But you had no need of it."

"What had I need of?"

She pointed to a slim jar. "This one I gave you. Summer savory to expel phlegm from your chest and lungs. Your cough is abating, is it not?"

"Aye."

She tapped the jar's flat lid as if it were the head of a child who had done a good turn.

My eye stopped at the largest jar in the middle. During the past week, I noticed whenever the old lady gave me a tea to drink, she made it from the leaves in this jar. It was a bitter tea she mixed with honey, and after I drank it I would sleep for a long time.

"And that tall one?"

Goody Hammer lifted the tall bottle to eye level. The light from the window behind it gave the wooly leaves a dark green tinge. "Henbane. I brought it from England. It grows under the dominion of Saturn. Some call it the hog's bean. With nightshade it is the most powerful plant I learned of from Ol' Mim."

I had no idea who Ol' Mim was and had no desire to ask. It was the henbane that fascinated me. "What does it heal?" I asked cautiously. I had heard of it before. It was a plant associated with danger.

Goody Hammer arched her eyebrows and lowered her voice. "What it heals is less important than how it heals." Both her eyes looked larger with her eyebrows raised. To avoid the sight of her grotesquely withered eye, I stared beyond her out the window. A slick black crow flapped by and cawed sharply, causing me to flinch, a movement the old woman noticed.

"You are a jumpy one."

"Aye," I admitted.

"A tea of henbane allows a good sleep, and a sleepin' body heals itself of infirmities."

"Then why didn't people use it to cure the plague in England? Or scurvy? Obviously it's not powerful enough to cure the deadliest of maladies."

"Ach, you are also a clever one," Goody Hammer mumbled. "There be limits to what even henbane can do for you. The croup it'll help, the plague no."

"Do you have magical powers?"

"None other than what comes from God. 'Tis from Him

all power flows." She held high a hand of five thick fingers and stiffened them until they trembled.

"People say you have magical powers."

She leaned back on her bench and cackled. "Ha! People have always said that about Ol' Mim and me. Ever since the plague in Loughborough they claimed it."

"What was their claim?" I asked.

"Do you really want to know?"

"Aye."

"'Twas a long time ago. When I was fifteen, your age, the plague took half the villagers in Loughborough, including my parents, Ruth and Abisha. My grandmother, Ol' Mim we called her, came to care for us. She was a widow woman and a healer. 'Twas with Ol' Mim that my sister Eloise and I cared for the sick. We wandered from cottage to cottage, cleanin' bodies, lancin' boils, soothin' buboes with the poultices and salves and an ointment of angelica that Ol' Mim concocted. We wrapped the seepin' flesh of the sick ones in rags and prepared 'em for the limestone pits that became their graves. 'Twas a miracle, everyone claimed, that the three of us remained untouched by the plague. So people thought of us as magical women."

"You have become like Ol' Mim," I said.

"Aye, that I have, and it was a gift from God I did. I was no beauty. You can see that with your own two eyes. But neither was Ol' Mim. She had the gift of healin' though. So I learned it from her. I watched and copied her. She taught me the workings of the body . . . about the humours that are blood, phlegm, bile, yellow and black." Goody Hammer pursed her lips as if she were remembering something. Her voice slowed and softened.

"On warm evenings, Ol' Mim would take me by the hand and walk me out into the field to study the heavens. You know it. There's a time for every action under the heavens . . . for havin' a bath . . . for cuttin' your fingernails . . . for lettin' blood. It's the stars that affect the course of a ship at sea and the course of blood passin' from a woman's body. On nights when the moon was full, Ol' Mim taught me to curtsy to the moon. Outa respect. She'd pinch the fabric of her skirt on both sides and lift it so her ankles would show. Then she'd place one foot exactly behind the other and she'd curtsy like the Queen's handmaiden . . . and I'd do the same." Goody Hammer reached up and tapped the crown of her black coif. "Ol' Mim had wild gray hair she would let blow wherever the wind would take it. In the moonlight her hair glowed. She looked like she had a halo around her head. When I was with Ol' Mim I did not feel ugly. I did not think of my cursed eye. Ol' Mim would say to me, 'You'll be a healer like me, won't you?'"

"Are you a thornback?" I interrupted.

Goody Hammer bowed her head. From across the table, the tight white skin on her cheeks took on a shine. She looked at me straight. "I'm no spinster. I'm a widowed woman. I married a good man from Old Boston, but he pegged out too. 'Twas so long ago I can't remember his face. Not that he had a face you'd want to remember, if ya know what I mean. Lost most of his teeth but still had enough of 'em on the right to chew. But it was the inside of him that mattered." The old woman tapped her breast.

I felt myself smiling.

"Luke Hammer was his name. Ol' Mim brought him to me. 'Ya need a man,' she said, but what I think she was really tellin' me was, 'Ya need a daughter,' cause Ol' Mim could see into the future and that sweet girl Luke and I made, she was our pot a gold. But even gold don't last forever."

The old lady's stare pulled me in so I could not look

elsewhere. And I did not want to. Her milky spider eye was becoming easier to abide. I relaxed and listened.

"Luke's features I can't remember. But my daughter's, hers I can't forget. I see her in my dreams. A beauty she was, like you, with dark hair and eyes. You remind me of her, with your questions and your smarts. But she had my height, and she knew a thing or two about healin'. Took to healin' like me and Ol' Mim, she did."

"What was her name?"

"Faith. Faith Hammer," the old woman said soulfully, as if the mention of her daughter's full name could bring her back to life.

"How did she die?"

"Consumption."

"I am sorry for your loss," I said meaning it.

"I, too. But I don't let it get the best of me because a thing like that could ravish your soul if ya let it get t'ye. You just got to walk orderly on the path the Lord sets in front of ya. Sometimes it feels like there's glue on your shoes, if you know what I mean."

I nodded. I considered telling Goody Hammer I was lonely too, but I could not find the words, and furthermore, this woman had hurtful losses of her own. "I know you live alone," I said, changing the subject. "Isn't it unlawful for a woman to live alone?"

Without breaking her gaze, Goody Hammer propped her elbows on the table and tapped her fingers together in the position of a church steeple. "'Tis unlawful for most, but the governor granted me liberty to do so," she boasted. "My days you can't predict 'em. One day I'm delivering a baby, the next I'm yankin' a rotten tooth from a jaw, or giving a clister. I'd be a disruption to any family."

"How is it you have time for me?"

The old lady leaned forward. "I shall tell you a secret. I have always been fond of ya, girl, though you mayn't think it. When your Papa summoned me, I made you my priority. I'd do anything for Gabriel Goodhue. Your papa has been like a son to me, looking after me when no one else cared a mite, and now I look after him too. 'Twas because of him I came to America, y'know. And look at you, girl, you're up and talkin' and a few minutes ago I saw a smile cross your face. Your Papa will be glad to hear of it. Your smile is like a pot a gold to him."

The mention of Papa jolted me back to reality. I had been talking to Goody Hammer as if she were a sympathetic grandmother. But she was not a grandmother. She was a cunning woman.

I willed myself to look away. How could I be so ignorant? How could I believe the crone's stories? The signs of a witch were all around me: the loathsome amulets, the potions and the incantations, the physick she prepared for Papa that he was once again taking in tea.

The truth had become clear: In his drunkenness, Papa had allowed Satan to enter into his body, and through his seed Satan had entered into me as well. Then he brought a like-minded one into our home to conjure me.

LATER, WHILE GOODY HAMMER WAS OUTDOORS, I poured every last leaf of her henbane into a napkin and hid it inside my keepsake box in the bottom drawer of the cupboard. Then carefully, I filled the jar with an equal amount of a harmless herb that had lost its fragrance. No longer would I let myself fall under her spell.

Chapter Sixteen

When I awoke the following morning, Goody Hammer had not yet arrived. Papa left me a slice of bread slathered with butter on the table, and beside it a thin package. Instantly, I recognized Jane's graceful script. My friend has come when I needed her most. I brushed my fingers across my name on the wrapper.

Miss Mercy Goodhue
Massachusetts Bay Company
Boston, America

As I pried the wax seal on the package with my fingernail, the reality of my situation became painfully clear. The letter I was about to read was written by the Jane of five months ago, just as the letters I sent her told her nothing of the sad woman I had become. Yet I took strange comfort in this, for during the short time it would take me to read the letter I could pretend I was the innocent girl that Jane once knew.

I pressed her letter to my chest and imagined her seated at her father's writing desk, her skirt pulled up to reveal her slim ankles. She dips her quill in the inkpot. She presses her lips together as she does when she concentrates, and she writes. I can almost hear the nib of her pen scratch the paper.

December 24, 1630
Dearest Mercy,

You have been in my thoughts since the day we parted, and your marvelous letters have helped bridge the miles betwixt us. Letters, of course, are no substitute for having you beside me.

I think of you always, picture you and remember your ways. When you are the sprite, your eyes dance and tease. When you are sad, you are inconsolable and neither heaven nor earth can deliver you from your melancholy. When you are pious, you are so silent that I imagine you listening to excellent sermons delivered by angels in your head. But, when you are excited, your words leap breathlessly over each other. Everywhere I go it is as solemn as an empty church since your departure.

I shall now respond to the many points from your letters. First, and most important, I hope your Mama is in good health. Papa, Millicent, and I pray for her daily.

Second, I am delighted you have found companionship in Joshua, and aye, I too believe he is a suitable match for you. The trade of a cooper is a respected one. Coopers are strapping men—all the better to protect you in the wilderness. With him you shall have what every woman dreams of—an endless supply of vats, pails, and buckets that never leak.

At that moment, I felt as if I were living in the past and the present at the same time. While Jane's letter spoke of hope, in my world there was only fear.

I hope by now our shipments of lemons have reached New

England and eased some of the pain of the dreadful scurvy, etc.
Reports from Mister Coddington of disease and deaths have
discouraged my father and Millicent from thoughts of emigrating.
Papa now forbids me to speak of it, but I know I cannot hold my
tongue. Why not go to America? I say. One day is exactly like the
last here—so why not embark on an adventure? Regardless of my
appeals, his answer is no, and it appears you and I must remain
sisters across the ocean a trifle longer. Of course, I must respect my
father's wishes, but I do vow with my hand on the Bible and my
eyes fixed on the heavens that the man I agree to marry must be
eager to live in America. He must also be handsome and not too
godly, for I believe men who are too pious are men of weak parts.

As much as I longed for Jane's companionship, I knew
having her with me now would cause even greater problems.
Even though she was my most trusted friend, I could never
tell her what happened. I could never say the words. I want her
always to think of me as good.

I have been thinking about your fear of Goody Hammer, and
I have only one response: What you suspect may be true. She may
indeed be a witch, so my advice to you is to stay away. There is little
you can do to keep your Papa and Mama from her power—for they
have already invited her in— but you, you must keep your distance.
This may seem like harsh advice, Mercy, but it is all I can think of.
Of course, you must pray for them, as will I.
You inquired about the latest happenings in England regard-
ing witches. I've taken the liberty of investigating this subject
through eavesdropping and sly interrogation of Millicent, who
knows as much gossip as any woman in Lincolnshire, and from her
I've learned this:
Do you remember Goody Suzanne Fowler, the mother of Sol-

omon Fowler, the blacksmith from Pulvertoft Lane? She is now under suspicion of sorcery. Millicent learned of this from Solomon Fowler's wife, Rebecca, who together with their newborn infant, live under Goody Fowler's roof. Their child refuses to suckle and Rebecca is of the mind that Goody Fowler has tampered with the milk in her breast and turned it sour.

We also know Goody Fowler has the mark of a witch upon her leg, for Rebecca has seen it. Rebecca has confided to Millicent that one night when her mother-in-law was asleep, she lifted the woman's skirt and pricked the mark with a needle, and the hag was neither disturbed by the prick nor did her leg bleed. I have heard this is a true sign of a witch. Rebecca intends to make this known to the ministers who will confront the old woman and attempt to convince her to right her ways through fasting and prayer. If she is not contrite, she may face death by hanging for it is illegal for a person to consort with Satan.

Rebecca Fowler has also claimed that the old lady had cruelly bewitched her in the night. She has told many people this story, which Rebecca swears is true:

She says she had awakened in the night from a deep sleep. When she opened her eyes, she could see her mother-in-law's bed was empty. She tried to say to her husband, "Solomon Fowler, your mother has disappeared," but she could not speak. She tried to nudge him, but she could not move her limbs. In fright, all she could do was stare into the room. Then, in the space above her mother-in-law's bed, a specter took shape. A band of fog? A creature? She knew not which. Fear gripped Rebecca, the likes she had never known. Then the specter glided closer to her and gained definition. Aye, it was a creature, an old woman hovering above her, a crone with silver hair and curls flowing down the sides of her cheeks—her face floating like smoke within the loose fabric of her coif. The creature sat on her chest, pinning her hard to the mattress, stopping her breath. Rebecca tried to cry out, but she could not. The creature puffed hot breath on her face and made sounds she knew came not from her own throat but from the creature's. All she could do was pray for deliverance from this witch who came to take possession of her. "Depart, cursed devil. Lord, deliver me from evil," she prayed. Eventually she slept, and the witch, who Rebecca believed was her mother-in-law, released her from her spell. By morning she recovered the use of her body, but the hag had left her milk sour.

Millicent says the true signs of a witch are the following: Does she harm others through her sorcery? Does she bear the mark of the witch upon her body—a stain on her skin, a mole or blemish that cannot be washed off, or perchance a third teat? Does she apply infusions of henbane and nightshade, which is called the devil's herb? Does she use amulets in her healing? Does she chant gibberish? Does she have a familiar—a cat or dog or even a ferret she sends forth to work her mischief? If so, she may be in consort with the devil.

I heard footfalls outside the door. Goody Hammer was arriving. I stuffed the letter beneath my pillow and held myself to stop trembling.

Chapter Seventeen

In the weeks that followed, I forced myself to resume my household duties. The sooner I could demonstrate to Papa that I was well, the sooner he would pay Goody Hammer a stipend and send her on her way. It was with a fury that I cleaned, scrubbed, cooked, churned, sewed, planted, and cared for Grace, chasing after her wherever her curious legs might take her. The more I felt Goody Hammer's eye upon me, the harder I labored, moving about the cottage and garden with a covetousness of task intended to make her feel unnecessary.

Goody Hammer knew something was amiss. I felt it in her sideways glances. She tried to speak of it, but always I rebuffed her.

On the last day of her employ, she came to me in the garden behind our cottage. I was kneeling on the ground planting the parsley I started from seedlings indoors. She crouched beside me and made simple talk.

"You know it, Mercy, I can read a person like a book. Ol' Mim taught me to do it. You watch the blink of an eye, the twitch of an eyelid, the knot in a person's throat, and you learn about 'em that way. These things tell ya as much about a person as the coatin' on his tongue or the clouds in his pee."

Her knee touched mine and I moved away. "What are you saying, Goodwife?"

"What I'm sayin', girl, is that I must ask you about that night. Had your father left you alone in the house for a time?"

I bit the inside of my cheek.

"I ask for a reason."

The trowel trembled in my hand and I covered it with my other hand, but I knew she noticed, for she noticed everything.

"He left only to pee," I mumbled.

"Was another present?"

"My brothers and Grace."

Goody Hammer studied my profile. I gripped the trowel tighter. The parsley. I just want to plant the parsley, those sweet young stalks, barely sprouted with new spiky leaves nurtured from seeds.

"I know you're fond of Joshua, for I've watched you together."

I swallowed and closed my eyes.

"I know about such things. Even ol' Luke and I had our secrets. I understand the burnings of the young."

She was embarrassing me.

"Did you run off to meet him that night, and are you nursin' a wound of guilt over it?"

"I did not. I am not," I snapped.

"Did he take up your smock?"

I felt the heat in my face.

"Mercy, when I examined you that first morning, your gown was drenched in blood like your course began, but the flow did not continue past a day. Your course has returned since?"

"Aye," I said sharply. She knew my course had returned for

she had been watching my every move like a guard in a gaol. She saw me scouring the breeches and rags I wore those days.

"'Tis good," she tapped the top of my hand. "Sometimes men cannot keep their privities inside their breeches, and too many unready girls become mothers. I've seen it happen to the godliest of women." I glanced at her and she gripped me with her good eye, holding me in place with such power I could not look elsewhere. "You know where I live, Mercy, on the path to the graveyard. I leave my Betty lamp burnin' all night for those in need of me. Come when you are ready to talk. I only wish to help you."

"Shut it, please," I said, breaking her gaze.

"Mercy!"

"Just shut it, Goodwife!" I stabbed the trowel into the ground and ran.

Inside the cottage, I slammed the shutters and through a slit in the wood I saw her kneeling on the ground staring into the air that held my secrets. She reached for the trowel, gripped its handle and yanked it out of the ground. As I watched her, I wondered: What if through magic and alchemy, she could read me like a book?

Chapter Eighteen

———— ❧ ————

With the advent of warm weather, the building of cottages resumed with a prayer-like zealousness. The crack of the ax was always upon us.

Election Day in May passed with predictability. The General Council of selectmen that had formed during that first year to make and enforce the laws had reelected John Winthrop governor, and Thomas Dudley deputy governor.

Ships from England arrived in the harbor weekly, increasing the population of Boston and the communities of Watertown, Dorchester, Charlestown, and Roxbury by the hundreds. During these days I did not write to Jane. I had neither the energy nor the inclination to put pen to paper.

Papa and the boys spent most of their days north of Boston in Mystic working on the *Blessing of the Bay*, the first bark to be commissioned by the Massachusetts Bay Company for coastal trade. With the timely delivery of sailcloth and cordage from England, it would take to the sea in August.

At home, I settled into the comfort of repetition. Whereas once I might have longed to experience more of life, now I wished for less. I required less of everything—less food, less sleep, less attention. Although we worshiped in the grove, another sizable plot within sight of the grove had been designated for a meetinghouse—and another for a pillory pit—for as saintly as the members of our congregation were, some souls required admonishment. During our first year in America, Governor Winthrop told us we had suffered enough on the passage over, and he had been lenient. But this year things were changing. Our magistrates believed a firmer hand was needed to keep us orderly and pious, and public punishments were doled out to those who exceeded the bounds of moderation.

Sadly, we were becoming more like England. Transgressors were made to wear the letter of their crime on a red cloth upon their clothing. A for adultery. B for blasphemy. P for pilfering. Goody Whitmore, an ill-mannered woman was fined eight shillings for uttering three profane oaths to her husband. One Jane Peters was fined for disorderly singing. A merchant deemed guilty of usury by the General Court was given ten lashes—stripes well laid with a cat-o-nine tails. Jeremiah Faircloth was found guilty of gambling with cards and finding amusement in Satan's picturebooks, and for this his eyes were bound shut for a fortnight. Roger Scott was fined for sleeping during services and for striking Joist Brown who awoke him from his slumber with a poke. Even sad Davy Person, who was still mourning the loss of his Caroline, was fined ten shillings for missing three Sabbath services without good reason. Noting he was a habitual offender, Governor Winthrop, who reacted harshly to those in whom he saw a diminishing holy spark, reminded him that had the pillory been constructed, he might have been clamped inside it till nightfall.

Still in America we had not persecuted a witch. Perhaps that too would be in our future.

Chapter Nineteen

One Sunday afternoon, not long after Goody Hammer left our household, Papa took Noah and Michael to the stream for a wash, and I settled Grace down for a nap. These were the rare times of solitude I treasured. No sooner did I sit in my chair than I heard Joshua's eager knock on the door.

"Am I interrupting your Sabbath?"

"Oh, no, please come in," I said, feigning cheerfulness.

He removed his straw hat and set it on the table. His cheekbones were tanned from outdoor work, a tan that ended an inch above his eyebrows where his hat rested.

"I promise I shan't stay long."

"No. No. Please stay. I was just going to read the Bible," I lied, gesturing at Mama's Bible on the table, "The Book of Job," I said, not thinking.

"That explains your sadness," he laughed. "At first, I thought it was me."

Since Papa had his use of me, my joy at seeing Joshua had diminished. It was not that I did not care for him, for I did, but now I wanted to take a step backwards in our love rather than take the leap forward that he expected.

Joshua lowered himself into Papa's chair, stretched out his legs and locked his arms behind his head. His forearms were sinewy and strong, and he had girth on his bones he had not had in the early days when food was scarce. A bowl of strawberries sat on the table and I invited him to eat, which he did, picking the red berries off one by one.

He was in a conversational mood. He told me about a letter Reverend Wilson had written from England to one of his parishioners. "His wife is still balking at coming to America . . . again she decided not to return with him. A preacher's wife should be of greater faith, don't y' think, Mercy?" I agreed. In better days, I would have added to the gossip. But now I believed the woman was better off in England—away from a husband who understood so little about a woman's needs. I had no more stomach for gossip.

Joshua told me of his progress digging their well, offering details on the methods of digging it. When he saw me lose interest, he changed the subject.

"There will be a fest to mark the harvest, and I'd be honored, Mercy, if you would accompany me. It'll be on the first Thursday in September, after the lecture."

"September is three months away."

"Then we have three months to anticipate it," he laughed.

I was not ready to venture into society. I did not want to face the gossiping women's whispers and stares. But how could I decline Joshua's sweet invitation or squelch his enthusiasm? "Joshua, I shall still be in mourning then."

His smile dissolved. "Mercy," he said earnestly, "More than two hundred people have died since we arrived. Everyone is mourning someone."

He caught me unprepared, so I agreed.

"All you must do is come," he smiled, reaching for my hand.

He kissed my fingertips, and I allowed this familiarity. Then taking assent as invitation, he stepped around the table. My heart raced. *Don't.* He placed his hands upon my shoulders and rubbed them. Their warmth penetrated my gown and smock. I wanted him to stop, but instead I tilted my head backwards and smiled into his upside down face. *Remember, it is Joshua who touches you, Joshua who means you no evil.*

He bent over and kissed the tip of my nose. His sandy hair flopped over my forehead creating an airless cocoon in which he lingered for a moment. His breath smelled of strawberries. His hands moved down my chest ever so slowly, stopping at the top of my breasts where my skin began to thicken. *No, Joshua.* But how could I tell him no when I had said yes so eagerly before?

"Today is the Sabbath and we must withhold our affection," I said softly, placing my hands over his and holding them in place so they could advance no further.

Most nights I lay in bed loath to move or sniffle for fear my sounds might attract Papa from across the room. Sometimes I'd reach for Grace's warm hand in the dark and clutch it to feel protected. I was alert to Papa's every sound.

When Papa got up in the night, through squinty eyes I'd watch his shadowy form rise from his mattress and wend its way toward me. My heart would pound. Then, to my relief, his wide hand would slide the bolt across the door and he would leave the cottage to pee. Minutes later he would slide the bolt back and lumber to his bed. Sometimes his hip would nudge the corner of the table and he'd grumble. Sometimes he'd gulp water from the tankard he kept on the floor beside his bed. The slurp of it rekindled memories of the ale he had once consumed so liberally. It was only when I would hear his snores that my heart could rest.

One night in the heat of August, when the air weighed on me like a sopping coverlet, I could stand it no longer. The terror lurking outside our walls was less fearsome than the terror abiding inside my head.

I ventured outdoors. I took a few steps, batting my arms about in the dark like a blind women feeling for obstacles. After a few moments, I was able to discern the shapes of the trees and the dips and swells of the landscape surrounding me. I circled our cottage. Then emboldened, I ventured farther and made my way across the High Street and up the well-trodden path to the graveyard. Clusters of stars twinkled above me, and the moon cast enough glow through fields of bloodroot to light my path up the hillocks of Trimountain.

I had to pass Goody Hammer's cottage on the way, but that did not deter me. At the crest of the first hill, I saw a pinpoint of light emanating through her window, the flame of her Betty lamp. I heard her voice in my head—"Come when you are ready." I will never be ready. I looked away so her flame would not conjure me. At the edge of her property I pulled my cloak tightly around my body and ran toward the graveyard.

Two boulders marked its entrance. I turned between the markings and followed a path of rutted earth that branched off like guiding fingers toward jagged rows of glistening tombstones. In the moonlight I found Mama's grave. I knelt upon the spongy ground and traced with my forefinger the words Papa had carved into her wooden marker:

Hannah Goodhue
Died February 13, 1631
Age 34

"Mama, do you hear me?" I whispered. "I'm sorry. I didn't will it to happen. Please help me. There is no one else I can tell."

I waited for an answer, but none came. An owl hooted. A field mouse scampered across pine needles. Thousands of stars studded the sky, each a pinhole into heaven.

"God, I know You are watching. I know You are listening. But I no longer feel Your presence." In desperation, I fell onto Mama's grave and pressed my body into the soft earth. I closed my eyes and tried to rekindle the warm feeling of her arms soothing me, telling me everything would be fine and if I prayed with my heart and soul and voice, the Lord would hear me.

I squeezed my eyes shut and tried with all of my mind and heart to pray as I prayed as a child in my closet when the Lord had come to me. I prayed for the light I saw that day to return. "If I was at fault, forgive me."

But there was no light and there was no forgiveness. The owl and the crickets were mute. Not a blade of grass moved. Then the sounds came, but they came from me. A moan, then a doleful cry that started in the hollow of my throat and trembled off my lips in sobs. I wept on Mama's grave until my insides felt as dry as bone. I looked up into the vast sky once more. The stars seemed farther away now, and I heaved one final plea to the God I loved who had turned His back on me.

Chapter Twenty

On the day of the fest I nervously braided my hair, tucked it inside a clean linen coif and pinned a fresh white collar around the plain neckline of my black gown. I fastened a dry cloth around Grace's bottom and slipped a fresh smock over her wiggling body. When I heard Joshua's knock, I set a grin on my face and opened the door. His smile widened at the sight of me and he handed me an abundant bouquet of bittersweet tied with a cord. "For my love," he beamed.

At the grove, we nodded to each other and took seats in our respective sections. I took a space on a log in the third row next to Jennifer Henshaw, the eight-year-old daughter of Catherine.

"You are here with Joshua, I see," Jennifer giggled as she slid closer to her mother to make room for me. "We passed you on the lane. He is a handsome one."

Before I could reply, Reverend Phillips strode down the center aisle. He did not smile, even to the children. Upon reaching his destination—a broad clearing encircled by oak trees—he turned to face us.

I spread Grace's blanket on the grass at my feet and sat

Grace upon it. I handed her a cord of brown buttons I brought to keep her occupied.

Unlike the scruffy Reverend Wilson, Reverend Phillips was as fastidious as one could be in the wilds of America. He stood tall, shiny-faced and humorless in his black tunic that dropped to the top of his leather boots. A long white stole hung around his neck and fell to his knees in equal lengths on both sides. The tips of his boots pointed slightly outward, like pelicans' feet, one toward the women, the other toward the men.

"Let us pray," he said solemnly. He squinted into the blue sky. It was unseasonably hot for September. He stepped out of the sunlight into a patch of shade and wiped his brow with a handkerchief.

I loosened the laces of my coif and billowed the fabric of my black skirt. Jenny, also wearing black, imitated my actions, making enough show of it to get a finger scolding from her mother.

"Let us give thanks for the window glass, lemons, and gunpowder that arrived from England yesterday on the *William & Francis*. We also received seven hogshead of twine for herring nets." His voice was a monotone.

A gleeful chorus of "Praise the Lords," filled the air.

Reverend Phillips waved his arms like busy oars rowing a boat. "What a joyous sight it is to see this grove of saints." He looked up into the sky and smiled approvingly, as if the heavens had opened. "The eye of the Lord is watching. He is smiling down upon us."

I glanced over into the men's section. Predictably, Noah was taking our minister's words literally and was examining the sky. Michael was staring straight ahead, as if in a trance. He did not relish Thursday lectures and was fond of escaping into daydreams. Papa glanced at me and looked away.

"Our members are growing," Reverend Phillips bellowed, eyeing the people standing at the periphery, in some places two-deep. "All of Boston is becoming a noble army of God, and our legions are indeed vast when we include settlements in Salem, Watertown, Dorchester, Charlestown, Roxbury and the rest!"

That afternoon we began with a cheerful hymn of thanksgiving.

"Now thank we all our God, with heart and hands and voices, Who wondrous things has done, in whom this world rejoices . . ."

As our voices rose in praise, it occurred to me that while so much had changed from England, so much remained the same. As in England, the men and women sat separated from one another, the deep male voices on one side, the high-pitched female voices on the other. But on both sides of the ocean we were an impossible flock to lead in song. Each of us took the tune exactly where we wanted it to go with no two people beginning or ending at the same time or on the same key. Behind me Goody Aspinwall gave her version a pleading tone. Anne Bradstreet trilled her endings into a musical curl. In the men's section, Papa's robust baritone overpowered every other voice. And Joshua? His steady voice wove in and out of the fabric of the others, and I harmonized with him.

"That was heavenly," Reverend Phillips said, managing a tightlipped smile. He moved closer to us.

"I wonder who he will call up today," Jenny whispered.

"What?"

"Admonishments."

I did not expect admonishments, not on a day of celebration. I expected the lecture to be brief with most of the afternoon set aside for recreation. But that was not to be.

Reverend Phillips extended his arms and let them drop

to his sides. Beads of sweat dripped from his sharply cut nose and spread into a watermark on his stole. "Saint Paul wrote of submitting yourselves one to another in the fear of God, to be united in holy walking," he said. I knew what he would say next, for I had heard those words before. His next sentence would be about disorderly walkers. Perspiration formed above my upper lip, and I reached into my pocket for a handkerchief, but I had forgotten one. Seeing my peril, Jenny pulled a white cloth out of her sleeve and offered it to me.

Grace lost interest in her string of buttons and began tugging at my skirt. I lifted her into my lap.

"In every community we have disorderly walkers. They are missteppers who deliberately swerve off the path of righteousness and fall into sin. They have no place in our community of saints until they publicly repent and gain forgiveness."

I tightened my arms around Grace.

"Martha Purdy! Come here." Reverend Phillips bellowed.

A gasp came from somewhere behind me, followed by the rustle of cloth and heavy footfalls. A fleshy, broad-hipped girl of about my age shuffled forward.

I leaned into Jenny. "What could be Martha's sin?"

"She went after her father with a rake. A neighbor saw her do it."

"Shhh, Jenny," her mother scolded.

Grace began to whimper.

I swallowed hard. I knew Martha only by sight. Each Sabbath she and her father, Joseph Purdy, walked to the service together, but Martha always kept her head bowed, never making eye contact with a soul.

Grace climbed up my chest and started playing with my lips.

"Not now, Grace."

She smiled sweetly, so I allowed her to continue. The child was teething and her plump chin was moist with saliva, as was the bodice of her gown.

"Look you at the congregation," Reverend Phillips commanded Martha.

Martha lifted her head sheepishly.

"Martha Purdy is the daughter of Goodman Joseph Purdy and the dearly departed Lucy Purdy, who left this earth a year ago."

Tears welled up in my eyes. Grace was studying my face. She had long ago pulled off her tiny coif. She nestled her curly head into the crook of my neck and patted my back gently, comforting me as I had so often done to her.

"Her sin?" Reverend Phillips asked. "She lifted a hand to her father," he answered his own question.

Dressed in a heavy gown of brown prunella, Martha stood in a swath of sunlight staring down at her dusty square-tipped shoes. She folded her arms across her amble breasts.

Reverend Phillips stepped closer to her and held his wide hand up above his head like a paddle. "She struck blows at her father with a rake," he thundered.

Reverend Phillips lowered his voice and spoke to us as if in confidence. "I have investigated this matter and I have found the claims made against Martha to be truthful." He glanced at Martha, then at us, allowing the silence that followed to make a statement of its own. Nervous coughs filled the air. Elizabeth Aspinwall cleared her throat. Jenny reached for her mother's hand and squeezed it until her knuckles whitened. Then there came a hiss from somewhere in the front row of the men's section—a cruel hiss that made me want to leap to Martha's defense and run with her into the forest, away from fathers and ministers and magistrates.

"She hangs her head in shame," Reverend Phillips

asserted, pointing an accusing finger at her. I located Joseph Purdy slouching in the second row. His head was bowed. He was not looking at his daughter. Purdy was a fishmonger by occupation, a gruff, noisome sort who was known to provoke arguments over trivial matters.

Martha sobbed softly.

"Let you speak, Martha," Reverend Phillips ordered her.

Martha's lower lip trembled. "I am guilty," she whimpered.

Grace started to cry. I rocked her but could not console her. I rocked her harder, which only caused my sister to wail and kick her bare feet into my stomach.

"Grace, hush, please?" I pleaded.

Catherine wrinkled her eyebrows in sympathy, and before I could object she switched places with Jenny. "Mine were babies once," she whispered. "May I try?"

"Thank you."

Catherine's practiced hands lifted Grace over her shoulder and she rubbed her back. Grace quieted and stared at me with soulful eyes.

"The constable will shackle Martha Purdy to a tree where she shall remain throughout the afternoon and where she shall be shunned. Neither man nor woman shall minister to her." Reverend Phillips nodded to Joist Brown who reeking with sweat and self-righteousness hoisted himself off the purple cushion he sat upon at the end of the first row. Too eager to perform his duty, he planted his feet on the ground like two massive tree trunks. It occurred to me that the hiss I heard earlier came from this despicable creature.

"Remember Martha Purdy's transgression and judge it accordingly, as is our earthly right to do," Reverend Phillips intoned. "But withhold your ultimate judgment, for it is God alone who knows whether Martha is a saint or a sinner. Saints must do everything to prove themselves worthy of God's forgiveness. Sinners can do naught but await their just doom." His words resounded in my head like an echo in a cave. Sinners can do naught but await their just doom. I looked away from him—at Papa sitting across the aisle and beyond him at the newly dug pillory pit shimmering as if the earth were on fire in the heat. By next spring the sinners of Boston would be languishing in it, locked in cages, whipped at the whipping post, or slammed into the stocks. Dizziness overcame me. I blotted my brow with Jenny's handkerchief.

"Are you all right?" Catherine whispered.

"Only the Lord knows the truth," I whispered back.

Catherine's green eyes studied me curiously. She reached over and patted my hand.

Off to the side I watched Joist Brown, chains and a ring of keys rattling at his side, lead Martha to a clearing where a huge oak tree had fallen years ago. He picked this spot for its suitable distance from us and for its place in the sun. As he walked his fat fingers dug into the sleeves of Martha's gown. By his angry demeanor and the movement of his jaw I new he was taunting her.

I looked into my lap, but my eyes would not remain there. I could not help but keep Martha in my sight. With a clink of metal Joist Brown shackled her wrists together and made a great show of locking the chain around the tree trunk. Tears streamed down Martha's face as she stood in shame, knowing we were watching her.

THE GOODWIVES HAD SET UP two long tables near the entrance to the grove, which they covered with crimson tablecloths and weighed down with buckets of flaming red maple leaves and pinecones and platters of food. With hungry eyes Joshua watched them uncover trays of pork pies, cornbread, roasted turkey, crab legs, salmon and more, but my eyes kept bouncing to Martha who stood in the sun watching us, whose woeful expression pained my heart.

Joshua took my elbow and led me through the crowd where more tables had been set up. Goody Hammer was sitting at one of them with her almost-dead Elijah napping at her feet. She nodded and I returned her acknowledgment. I waved to Anne Bradstreet who, along with her Simon, was conversing with Reverend Phillips and his teenage daughter Abigail. Abigail was animatedly telling a story and her father was smiling at her pridefully, the way Papa had once smiled at me when I was being amusing. I recalled the warm feeling of it, as if I were the most special girl on earth. As we got closer, Reverend Phillips laughed a deep laugh—so untypical of him that I saw a number of people take notice. He was now a man away from his profession and at ease with himself in the society of his family and friends.

I spotted Papa on the other side of the crowd. His booted foot was propped up on a log and he was puffing on his pipe. He was in spirited conversation with Goodman William Blackstone, Boston's earliest settler. I hoped to move through the crowd without having to salute him, but Joshua, who earnestly sought his approval in courting me, thought otherwise. When Papa was alone, Joshua heralded him with a wave and pressed a warm hand on my back, guiding me in his direction.

"Good afternoon, sir," he said cheerfully.

"And t'ye, Joshua." The men clasped hands like brothers.

"My daughters are no trouble?"

"Both are well behaved today, sir."

"May I join you for the meal?"

"We'd be honored, sir."

I flashed Papa a look of disapproval that said I was not honored.

Disappointment darkened his face. "I understand," he said, giving me a knowing look. "You want to be alone with your Joshua. There is work I must do at Bendall's dock."

Joshua's face reddened. "Goodman Goodhue, please stay, sir," he insisted. Determined to make him feel welcome, Joshua plied him with conversation. He complimented him on the successful launch of *Blessing of the Bay* and inquired about his future endeavors.

My eye shifted to Martha across the grove. I made brief eye contact with her, then not to cause her embarrassment, I looked away. Martha was meant to be invisible to us. Men, women, and children were to keep their distance from her, forgetting—or trying to forget—she was amongst us. At afternoon's end, Joist Brown would release her from her chains and she would walk home alone.

Papa reciprocated, telling Joshua about Goodman Blackstone's grievance with neighbors whose errant cattle roamed freely throughout our settlement.

"They frighten the children, and just last week the appearance of one of Goodman Purdy's grazing bulls almost caused Goody Aspinwall to fall backward into her lye cauldron."

Papa laughed at his own story.

"Old Blackstone wants to corral them in a common area for the sanity and safety of everyone. He's making his case to whomever will listen, so if you wish not to be held hostage until dusk hearing about our gamesome cattle, you'd better keep your distance."

Joshua laughed.

I stared at Papa coldly.

Disorderly walker, a voice inside me said.

Papa looked up and checked the position of the sun. He tugged at the taut brim of his hat and said, "I must take leave now."

When he was out of earshot, Joshua furrowed his eyebrows. "Why did you want your father to leave?"

"Because he is a disorderly walker," I uttered. Sometimes I did not know what came over me. It was like another person was living inside me, a creature unknown to me speaking words I would never speak, acting in ways I was not proud of. I chuckled so Joshua would think I was joking.

Joshua's eye jumped to Papa who was zigzagging down the crooked path, wending his way, this way and that, through clusters of people. "Disorderly walker," he mumbled, and then laughed. "Now that's what I've been waiting to see. Your humor has returned!"

JOSHUA WENT OFF TO FILL our plates, and I was grateful to have a moment to compose myself. I settled Grace on a blanket to nap and joined my brothers who were seated on a log sharing a trencher of food. In the distance sad Martha Purdy stood hunched forward, her wrists fettered to the fallen oak.

Noah handed me a gourd of cider. I pressed the cool cup to my cheek and glanced at Martha. The voice inside me spoke again. *Go to her.* Immediately I knew what I had to do. I wove my way through the crowds, past the table of food where Joshua espied me and waved, toward the clearing where Martha stood, her body bowed like a dampened loaf of bread. A map of sweat had spread across the broad back of her heavy prunella gown. Martha's eyes widened as I advanced upon her.

"Go away. Someone will see you," she warned. "I am to be shunned."

"I care not." I held the gourd to her mouth.

The girl drank until it was empty. "Thank you."

With the back of my hand I wiped the droplets of sweet cider off the corners of her lips so flies would not vex her.

Martha looked exhausted. "My shoulders ache, as do my wrists," she said, not in a complaining tone, but in a manner simply reporting her condition.

Martha's wrists were chafed so I squeezed Jenny's handkerchief between the chain and her tender skin. "Soon it will be over," I said softly, turning to leave.

"Mercy," Martha called.

I gave her a backward glance.

"He came upon me first in lust. Then I took out after him."

I looked straight into her eyes. "Did he defile you?"

"I fought him off. Do you not believe me?"

"I believe you," I replied. "You are a good girl. You did no wrong. Now you must put what happened out of your mind forever."

I STIFFENED MY SHOULDERS and strode back to the fest, my eyes pinned on the pine needles blanketing the path. It could have been me up there. It should have been me since my sin was greater than Martha's. She rebuffed her father. I had not offered a peep. And I had the impudence to tell Martha to put it out of her mind! How could she forget? Every time she walks down the lane, people will point to her and behind cupped hands whisper the story of her offense, each time making more of it.

Many eyes were watching me.

Elizabeth Aspinwall's mouth was agape. Anne Bradstreet whispered to Simon and pointed a delicate finger in my direction. Reverend Phillips, somber again, looked over his shoulder, met my gaze and shook his head in consternation.

Goody Hammer, still seated with Elijah sleeping at her feet, followed my every move. I knew what they were thinking: What an overbold girl is Mercy Goodhue to interfere with a minister's punishment. Who does she think she is?

A great flock of birds flew overhead, and I quickly looked up. How I wish I could fly away with them . . . back to England, anywhere. But step-by-step, I made my way back to Joshua.

Joshua, balancing a trencher heaped with food and two gourds of cider in his hands, was also watching me. His eyes were wide, his mood composed. I feared what he would say, for the approval of the community was important to him.

"You did right to help her," he whispered in my ear. "That's why I so cherish you."

I was spared that day. There were no repercussions. It was probably because I had been severely ill that Reverend Phillips showed me leniency.

Chapter Twenty-One

————— ❧ —————

I had not written to Jane since Papa had his use of me. I could neither reveal what happened nor could I be false in my correspondence by feigning all was well. Instead, I wrongly chose to avoid putting pen to paper. Eventually my avoidance prompted Jane to write this letter.

June 12, 1631
Dearest Mercy,

I shall get right to the point. I have not heard from you in months and I am fraught with worry. Word of your illness has come to us from others. Elizabeth Wilson said you were found nearly frozen to death in the snow. She believes an Indian was at fault, or perhaps the young man you have been seen with has led you astray. This I can hardly believe. Reverend Wilson says you have been distracted since your Mama's death and are troubled over matters he cannot discuss. An acquaintance of the Dudleys says you are recovering under the hand of Goody Hammer, which frightens me, for she is one who has ne'er done you good. What am I to believe? I wake up every morning hoping a letter will arrive. I watch through the window for a messenger to stop at our door.

I close my eyes at night lamenting that nothing has come. Forgive me if this urgent letter is meaningless and I receive a letter from you tomorrow , but I know not what to believe and I shall not rest until I see your firm and reassuring hand on one of your letters. I could not bear it if any evil has come to you. If hurt has come to you, it has also come to me.

Jane

Ashamed of the worry I had caused my friend, I responded at once. Finishing this letter gave me little consolation, for it would be months before she would receive it.

August 1, 1631
Dearest Jane,

    I received your letter of concern today and I write back immediately with my apologies for not having written of my illness.

    I write now to set your mind at ease. 'Tis through the care and prayers of many that I am, at last, fully recovered. I cannot tell you exactly what happened that night, for much of it I do not remember, although I can say that neither Joshua nor an Indian was to blame. I have been distraught over Mama's death and my increased responsibilities at home, and I will confide in you this: In his own melancholy, Papa had taken to drink again which put an extra burden on me to set him right as well. As for that night, aye, I was in the fog of a confusing dream when I wandered off into the snow, and it was only through God's providence that our neighbor, Goodman Person, found me still breathing. Even sorrow brings sunshine, does it not, Jane? Seeing our family was spared of still another death, Papa has thus given up strong ale. I am now fully recovered, my days unfold joyfully, and you are not to worry.

Mercy

Chapter Twenty-Two

1632

It was March of 1632 that baked goods started arriving mysteriously on our doorstep. Every Thursday morning a new treat appeared—a mincemeat pie, a half-dozen corn muffins, or a plate of sticky biscuits. At first we thought they came from a goodwife who had prepared extra, but there was no stopping them. By the first Thursday in April—with the arrival of a bowl of creamy custard covered with a blue cloth, a generous gift in itself—curiosity got the best of us.

Michael believed the treats came for me. "A carpenter at the shipyard asked me about you," he teased.

"Carpenters do not bake custards," I groaned.

Noah believed they came for Papa. "Goodwife Henshaw watches you in the grove. Whenever I look her way, she's leaning forward staring at you with her eyes bugged out."

"She nearly falls off the log doing it," Michael added.

"They come not from her or any other woman," Papa replied sharply. But I could see by the glimmer in his eye that he was flattered.

"We have a plan to find out," Michael said, brushing a dark shock of hair off his forehead and nodding at his brother.

"We have no such thing," Noah countered.

"But we will, won't we, Noah?" he said nodding vigorously.

Noah smiled. "Aye, definitely we will have a plan."

Papa shook his head and sipped his tea.

THE FOLLOWING THURSDAY before dawn, Michael took his gray blanket outdoors and lay in wait beneath the window, crouched and covered to look like a woodpile cloaked with canvas. Noah and I sat on the bed watching through the corner of the window. Just as a sliver of orange light lined the horizon, a childlike figure clad in black appeared. It crept past Michael and as silently as midnight deposited a package wrapped in a blue cloth upon our doorstep.

The sly creature hurried off and Michael took chase. "I've got you now," he shouted, nabbing the younger boy and tackling him to the ground. He wrestled the child and the child fought back until, eventually, Michael got the better of him and turned him on his back to take a look at his face. The child's hood fell away from his head and a long strand of yellow hair whipped across Michael's arm. "You're a girl, you're wearing a coif!" he exclaimed, releasing his grip on her shoulder.

"I'm Jenny," she whimpered.

"I knew it!" Michael said, leaping up and brushing himself off.

"Now help me up, you ruffian, will you?" Jenny fussed.

"Your mother sends the food, I knew it," Michael said, extending a hand to give her a lift.

"It's true, but it's a secret. She sends me because I'm quick-footed."

"And sly."

"It's a strawberry pie," she said, brushing dust off her gown.

Just then, Noah stepped forward and offered Jenny his

arm. "Come with me. I'm no ruffian," he laughed as he led her toward our cottage. In passing he winked at his brother. At first the girl hesitated, but Noah urged her forward with the gentle pressure of his arm. That morning I noticed an awkward gallantry in Noah. It was only right, his being fourteen.

Until then, Michael, the firstborn twin—by half the sand in an hourglass—had taken the lead in all things. That morning, however, Noah decided to compete for Jenny's favor.

"Meet the baker's daughter, Jenny Henshaw," Noah announced at the door.

Facing us, Jenny, with her sky-blue eyes blinking nervously and her coif dangling from her fingertips, looked like a stunned and ruffled rabbit.

I WAS NOT SURPRISED it was Jenny. Catherine, a comely woman, was also lonely. It had been more than a year since Mama's death, and it was customary for widows and widowers to couple after a year, sometimes sooner. Yet I was not prepared for it. I wanted to dismiss Jenny with a swat, but those around me were merry, so I forced myself to be merry too, for Mama would have expected that of me.

"Now that we have pie, let us enjoy it," I suggested gaily. "Will you stay, Jenny?"

Jenny's fear passed and she became as lightsome as if she were invited to a party.

I carved a wedge for Grace, the largest slice for Papa, and passed out trenchers of pie and spoons. Having no appetite, I set my piece aside for Joshua who would devour whatever I put in front of him. Papa held out his tall chair for our small guest.

We ate in silence until Noah blurted. "I was right, Papa," he said, winking at Jenny.

Papa blushed.

"Right about what?" the girl chirped, flicking a yellow wisp of hair off her brow. Her lips were shiny from strawberry syrup and her blue eyes darted innocently from face to face, wordlessly repeating her question to each of us. The men, especially Noah who could hardly take his eyes off Jenny, were overtaken by her charm.

Suddenly there was a knock on the door. Michael, seeing his brother's preoccupation, answered. "Goodwife Henshaw, how nice to see you this early," he greeted her as eagerly as if he had been expecting her arrival.

The carrot-haired woman in a blue cape and hood crossed the threshold and stood before us. "Is my Jenny here? I had begun to worry," her voice quavered.

Noah splayed his arm out playfully toward Jenny.

"Would you like pie?" Papa asked.

Blushing, Catherine took a seat near Jenny.

Papa bowed his head and led us in prayer. "Thank you, Lord, for the gift of pie and for the hands that made it."

I wanted nothing to do with any of it. Although Goody Henshaw was a fine woman, I was unready to welcome any woman into our house to replace Mama. And truthfully, I did not want Papa to be happy. But the mischievous smiles on Jenny's and my brothers' faces made me take measure of myself. I couldn't spoil their fun by pouting. I would force myself to be gay.

Thus, that Thursday morning everyone, including me, talked and laughed and teased one another as if we were family.

As it came to be, Goodwife Henshaw was not alone in her pursuit of male companionship. Soon that I received another letter from Jane filled with her romantic notions.

January 15, 1632

My Dearest Mercy,

I rejoice that you are well. You will never know what burden your letter of reassurance has lifted from my shoulders. As young women, we are meant to be light of heart and full of enjoyment of life, are we not? It is my prayer that you are of good cheer and merriment.

I have the greatest news to share. Last week I met the man I am destined to marry. His name is John Allen Loring, and he is the son of Millicent's elder brother, Edward Loring. He is older than I am. He is twenty-two. He came to deliver a waistcoat he had completed for Papa. I nearly slipped on the ice when he turned the corner with the bundle in his arms. 'Twas one look and I was smitten. He is taller than me, has dark hair that curls over his forehead and eyes so brown they look black. His mouth is stern until he smiles. Then his teeth shine as broadly as a row of white tapers on the altar of St. Boltoph's. He does not yet know he will marry me.

This was our conversation.

JAL: "G'day. You must be Miss Perkins."

JP: "Jane Perkins."

JAL: "I'm pleased to make your acquaintance, Jane. I am John Allen Loring, Edward's son. I'm delivering this." (He handed me the package.)

JP: "Papa is not home, but I shall see he receives it. Thank you." (I accepted the package.)

JAL: "Goodbye, Jane. Perchance we shall meet again." (My heart leapt!)

That was it. What do you think, Mercy?

I have so many things to ask Goodman Loring. "Do you have prospects of making money? Do you wish to sail to America?" My better judgment told me it was improper to ask these things upon our first meeting. But without asking, Millicent told me that he is a skilled man, and that he just returned from London where he apprenticed as a tailor. You know, I am not one to pray excessively, but in this instance I have given myself over to the habit. For the past five nights I have prayed like a Papist on my knees for God to persuade John Allen Loring to show interest in me. Nothing has transpired yet, but I trust that with good prayers something will.

I beseech you to write when you are able. I pray for you and request you pray for me in return, for my need at this time is for a husband who is ambitious and willing to travel. How I look forward to embracing you. I dream of us meeting again in grand celebration with our handsome husbands, Joshua Hoyt and John Allen Loring. Oh, how I take pleasure in writing his name on paper.

Jane

Chapter Twenty-Three

That summer had been good to Joshua. He'd made fast progress digging his well, and in compensation for his labor, the muscles in his upper arms and shoulders plumped and hardened, the skin of his face tanned to bronze, and the fine hairs on his forearms glistened like silk threads. He was a man any woman would be proud of, and I was fortunate to have him by my side.

One sweltering evening in late August Joshua walked me to his cottage to show me the progress he had made on their well. He opened the low gate made of twigs and branches and led me into a sizable garth where he and Ezekiel stored and hewed their wood. The Hoyt's newly acquired mare grazed greedily the back of the property, hardly noting our arrival.

"Papa is asleep now. We are alone."

Joshua's complicit grin made me uncomfortable. I knew he would try to kiss me in the manner we once kissed. I wanted to welcome his advances, to once again feel the reckless joy of encouraging him, but now there was only apprehension.

I followed him across mounds of silvery wood shavings, around a tree stump slashed by the blade of an ax still stuck into it, and past a heap of thick white oak logs waiting to be quartered. He led me to the edge of the well.

"It is but a pit now, but eventually there will be water and it will have a wellsweep and a stone wall around it for safety. We dug another three feet today . . . about twenty more to go. The challenge is to shore up the sides with timbers to keep it from collapsing inward."

"Let me see," I said, stepping as close to the edge as I dared. Joshua gripped my elbow when I leaned forward. There was only mud and darkness below. I picked up a pebble and tossed it into the pit-hole. I heard a plop, but saw nothing.

"The mud is temporary. 'Twill be a grand day when we strike water."

Joshua put his arm around my waist and drew me close. I pulled away.

"What is it, Mercy? No one can see us here."

"It's just . . . it's hot tonight and I'm sticky. I cannot imagine you wanting to touch me," I said, wrapping my arms around my chest.

"You didn't mind me touching you before."

"But it was winter then."

"So you say I can only touch you in winter?"

"Don't be silly."

He took a step backwards, turned away and stared into the air. Every muscle in his face tightened.

"Joshua," I whispered.

"What?" he pouted.

"I'm sorry. I've been scrubbing dirty clothes all day long and sweating." I considered telling him my course had begun and I felt I was stinking, but I was too embarrassed to say that.

"I spent the day laboring beneath the same sun as you."

"Aye," I said, looking down at my dusty shoes. It took

everything within me to keep my feet planted where they were. "It will never happen again, I promise you." I tugged on the cloth of his sleeve. "Joshua," I pleaded.

He turned slowly and gave me a start of a smile. Then he reached out for me, put his hands on my hips, and pulled me toward him. He was giving me another chance.

It is Joshua who holds you. I watched his lips, shaded by the frayed rim of his straw hat, descend upon me. There was a longing in his eyes I had come to know.

"You are lovely," he whispered. The warmth of his breath and the gamey scent of his body engulfed me, and the pressure of his lips pressed into mine. I felt suffocated. *It is Joshua. Allow it. Do not flinch.* Every muscle within me longed to pull away, but I forced myself not to move, for if I moved a hair's breadth, I knew he would notice and become angry.

"Don't be shy, Mercy, for my love is true."

I willed my body to lean into his. "As is mine," I said. I focused on his features—on the thin lines of his eyebrows and the ruddiness of his cheeks, and the soft curve of his lips. I thought about the hardworking man he was and how esteemed he had become in our community. *Relax. Relax.* I moved my hips from side to side desperately trying to emulate that girl who once gave herself to him so eagerly.

"Now that's my old Mercy," he said, satisfied.

Chapter Twenty-Four

B y the first week of September the weather had cooled. A breeze carrying the omen of winter wafted in through the window, fluttering the curtains. We had just finished our pottage and Papa set his spoon on his trencher, leaned back and settled into his chair.

Michael stood to leave, but Papa reached for his elbow. "Stay," he said.

Something was afoot; I sensed it. I folded my arms, stared at my father and waited for the inevitable. Since he began courting Catherine, he'd been in unusually high spirits—telling animated stories of incidents at the shipyard, expelling deep belly laughs over trifles deserving nary a chuckle, finding humor even in the messes Grace created. Several weeks ago, he announced that starting that evening we would recite our Bible verses twenty times rather than the customary forty. "I am persuaded that twenty repetitions will deliver us to heaven as speedily as forty," he decreed. But my brothers and I knew the truth. Twenty repetitions would deliver him to Catherine's door in half the time.

"I have news," Papa said, focusing his attention upon Grace

who would give him the least resistance. "Last night I asked Catherine to become my wife, and she agreed."

Michael nodded and said nothing. Noah looked down at his empty trencher.

Grace's small fingers plopped the kernels of corn she hadn't eaten into her milk cup.

"Catherine will be your new mother. Your stepmother," he corrected himself.

"No new mother is necessary," Noah said. "We've done well without one for the past year. Mercy does the work and we help."

"I help. You're lazy," Michael said.

"You'll both do better with a stepmother."

Papa said he and Catherine planned to be married later in the month, and the day after the ceremony we would move into Catherine's house on Sudbury End, which was "larger . . . has floorboards . . . a spinning wheel . . . a garret for sleeping . . . featherbeds . . ." His voice droned on.

He rolled up his shirtsleeves. His forearms were tanned and muscular. A few plaits of gray streaked through his bronze hair, which he had let grow and had taken to pulling back and tying with a cord at the nape of his neck, in the fashion the younger men of Boston now favored. He was a gentleman courting a lady.

I listened with my arms folded across my chest. It shall suit Papa, not us. We had removed ourselves from England for him. And now we were removing ourselves to Catherine's for him. Again, like the tail attached to the dog, we had no choice but to follow.

"And Mercy, what do you say?" Papa asked.

I shrugged my shoulders. "Nothing." I picked at the cuticle of my thumb, and when a bubble of bright red blood appeared,

I wiped it on my apron.

"I seek your approval," he said almost pleadingly.

I would not look at him.

"Mercy, you know Catherine. She is a woman of merit who has suffered a loss with forbearance. For the two of us to meet and unite, well, the Lord's hand must have been hard at work in bringing us together."

"Where will I sleep, Papa?" I stared at him and did not blink.

Papa looked stunned by the question. "You and Grace shall sleep with Jenny in the garret," he said quietly. "You may have my mattress, the best bed. That should put a smile on your face," he said.

Clenching my fists, I stared out the window at an early autumn fog rising over the far edge of the pasture, creeping in our direction. Surely the fog within Papa would one day lift, and then he would have to face the truth.

IN LATE SEPTEMBER PAPA AND CATHERINE married in the grove.

The afternoon of their wedding had a chill in it. The oaks, hickories, red maples, sugar maples, and black maples were shedding an abundance of red, russet, brown, yellow, orange, gold and scarlet leaves that dropped like feathers upon us. It was upon this autumnal carpet that Governor John Winthrop stepped into the clearing, smoothed the front of his black silk waistcoat, and peered into the congregation with his dark eyes, motioning Papa and Catherine to step up.

The governor wore a dense ivory ruff around his neck that he reserved for the most celebratory of occasions. From where I sat in the first row, it looked as if his head was resting on a thick fluted platter. He signaled the eight of us to come forward—Jenny, Grace, Ralph, Caleb, Peter, Noah and Michael and I. We formed a half-circle behind our parents to show assent, but I was keenly aware of the significance of such a show.

PAPA BUTTONED THE LOWER silver button of his waistcoat and adjusted his stance. Catherine smiled at him with shy eyes. Unlike Mama, who was half a head shorter, Catherine matched Papa in height. She was a handsome woman with her red hair blazing out of her coif like the petals of a marigold. That afternoon she wore a green gown that in the sunshine looked brighter than its deep hue.

Governor Winthrop spoke briefly about how he met Papa in England, and how he became acquainted with Catherine here in Boston. He did not mention Mama or Hiram Henshaw, but he did not have to. Among those who knew them, theirs was as strong a presence as if they were here in flesh and blood. The congregation had only to look at the eight of us to be reminded of them.

Michael, who had our Mama's chestnut hair, had sprouted up visibly since he last wore those brown trousers at her burial. Were it not for Papa's long brown kersey stockings, two, perhaps three inches of his bare legs would be showing. Noah, though he had grown fond of Catherine and was visibly charmed by Jenny, appeared dazed. His body was present, but his thoughts seemed elsewhere. Grace, with pink cheeks and dark hair, stood like a little lady. Her smile was Papa's but the curl of her upper lip belonged to Mama. I had sewn an extra hanging sleeve onto the shoulder of her pale blue gown so I could tether her from behind, but Grace was well behaved and I had no need of it.

Catherine's three boys stood with their bodies slightly touching, as if for support. A family resemblance also linked them: their mother's carrot-colored hair and, I assumed, their father's sharp nose, for Catherine's was small and straight. Ralph, at seventeen—my age—was lanky and ill at ease in his too-long breeches and tan waistcoat belonging to his deceased father. Caleb, taller than Ralph but as lithe, was fourteen. He had the habit of tucking his chin into his collar to hide his pimply face. Peter, a cheerless boy of nine, stood sternly beside him, his mouth a thin line that looked drawn on his face by chalk. To his left stood Jenny, who along with Grace, grinned throughout the ceremony. Silly Jenny, I thought. Surely Catherine had told her the same stories Papa had told us about how splendid it would be when our families combined. Didn't they know that a family doesn't mend as easily as a hole in the heel of a stocking?

"And the Lord God said, it is not good that the man should be alone; I will make him a helpmeet for him . . ." Governor Winthrop began. "And they shall be one flesh."

I studied this woman who was a word away from becoming my stepmother. She was attractive and quick and helpful and had a way of getting what she wanted, including Papa. I prayed a quick prayer that she would find happiness.

"Catherine, will you have this man for your husband?" he asked.

"Aye," Catherine replied.

A golden brown hickory leaf sailed through the air and lit upon Catherine's shoulder like a protective hand. It was a brittle leaf with edges curled upward, a leaf whose season had passed. Images of Mama lying in her coffin still and cold flooded my mind. Do you see Papa with Catherine? Do you feel replaced by this woman who in life was your friend? I knew I should be happy for them. I knew I should be happy for my life would only become easier with Catherine in it, but all I felt was sadness. My heart was breaking. If I were alone

I would have sobbed, but I could not do that, not in front of Catherine whose shattered heart was today being reborn.

Governor Winthrop asked Papa, "Will you have this woman . . .?"

Papa appeared hale and sturdy, the kind of man any woman would have admired and wished to marry. That was the man Catherine and the congregation saw, but I saw a different man.

"I will," Papa said.

Then there came a hum. *Shhh* . . . Then the *Shhh* became louder. I could not tell where it was coming from. The breeze rusting through the trees? A swarm of insects? The hum of someone in the congregation?

Shhhaaame. The voice seemed to be coming from behind me.

Before I had time to turn, the voice clipped, *Shame!* Was it a mother admonishing a child? I looked over my shoulder and quickly swept my eyes across the faces of our people. I saw the Aspinwalls whose faces held the smiles of saints; Martha Purdy, who caught my eye and nodded reassuringly; and Goody Hammer whose face was bent into her Bible. Nothing seemed amiss.

Shame! This time the voice was as sharp as rock scraping granite. Again I turned, and again all was as it should be. And then in the silence came a gust of many voices coming from everywhere, echoing around me in varied pitches. *Shame! Shame! Shame!* A ghastly choir of judges it was. I knew not what was happening, who was crying out, where the sounds were coming from. There was a dazzle of light behind my eyes and a dirgeful hum inside my head. The voices were coming from inside me. My heart beat rapidly. Heat rose into my face, followed by an icy chill of awareness that brought me to a sweat.

"By the laws of God and this commonwealth, I as governor of the Massachusetts Bay Company, declare you, Gabriel and

MERCY GOODHUE | 141

Catherine, husband and wife."

There was a rustle in the congregation, and the lone voice spoke to me again. *Shaaame.* Then all was silent. I was stricken with fear. I longed to run, but I was so possessed by fright that I could not move. Was it Satan inside me speaking? Was it Goody Hammer working a spell? Or was it the harsh voice of God judging Papa . . . and me?

Papa and Catherine turned to leave the platform. He noticed my upset and took my hand. "You are unwell," he said.

"I am fine, Papa," I replied, forcing a smile. I pulled my hand away.

As quickly as the voices came, that is how speedily they left. The only sounds I heard now were the merry voices of the jabbering congregation, the joyous chirp of female laughter, the hearty banter of the men.

AT THE CELEBRATION, I obliged myself to laugh with Catherine's children, to accept kind wishes from Goody Demsey and Davy Person and Anne and Simon Bradstreet, who traveled from Charlestown to Boston, as they do, for anything important. I avoided Goody Hammer, but all the while I could feel her watching me. Was it she who was bewitching me?

For the rest of the afternoon, with Joshua at my side, I strolled beneath the lush canopy of trees that shed leaves upon us like an autumn rain. I ate the bride's cake. I sipped the cool berry punch. And I smiled and spoke glowingly to our guests about the beauty of the day and our family's newfound happiness.

But inside, my stomach was clenched into a knot of fear.

Chapter Twenty-Five

The following morning I stood in the doorway watching Papa and my brothers hoist our pine cupboard onto Ezekiel's wagon and watched our possessions wobble down Water Street toward Sudbury End.

After the men left, I sat alone at the table surveying the items I still needed to pack. I set Mama's silver porringer aside so I could enjoy its beauty while wrapping everything else.

The sun was fickle. One moment threads of dusty light flashed through the window and danced upon the porringer's smooth surface. The next moment the light dimmed, transforming it into a cold utensil. I recalled the many dinners my family had eaten with it on the table. I pictured Papa sternly dishing up food, Mama wiping her brow and settling onto the bench, Michael hunched over his plate, and Noah charming me with a smile. Then I remembered the night Papa fed me stew, the disgust of him blowing on the steaming vegetables.

I lifted the porringer and studied my misshapen reflection in it. My eyes were grotesquely far apart, a wisp of hair hung over my forehead like a leather strap, and the dimple in my chin was a dark pit below my stretched lips. Were my memories as distorted as the image of my face in the curve of the silver? Were memories not also combinations of light and dark, truth and imagination? When does one bleed into the other? Does it happen as quickly as a cloud passing before the sun? Or does it happen as slowly as scurvy that begins with an ache or spot before it ravishes? I thought of the voices. Is it possible to mark the precise moment when a person crosses from sanity to madness, piety to depravity, saved to damned?

I hastily wrapped the porringer in a napkin and set it in the crate. Then I looked across the room at the task I had been dreading: stripping the sheet off Papa's bed.

I intended to quickly be done with it, but when I raised the sheet above my head, Papa's scent—sea salt, perspiration, and ale—washed over me in a wave of memory. *Please Lord, help me forget.* I forced myself to stare above the bed into the sunlight beyond Mama's three green glass bottles on the window ledge. I shook the sheet and shook it again, this time with such force that the fabric billowed and snapped loudly in the empty room. Then, as if time slowed its pace, the corner of it curled in the air and upon descent caught the lip of one of Mama's emerald bottles. The bottle tipped end-over-end through the air and shattered on the earthen floor.

"No!" I shouted at the particles of glass scattered around me.

Heat flooded my head and as if some invisible force guided my hands, I yanked the pillowbear off Papa's pillow, wrapped it around my fingers and retrieved the largest shard of glass from the floor. With the razor-sharp glass in my hand, I spun around and slashed the sheet and the canvas cover on Papa's straw mattress. I stabbed the coarse cloth again and again with a force I did not know myself to possess.

"My own Papa!" I yowled. "Why?"

Satan's bed! the voice shouted. Again the voice came from

inside me. It was not my voice. It was deeper and stronger, as if an unknown creature was abiding within me, telling me what to say.

"Satan's bed," I repeated out loud.

I flung the shard across the room and tore at the mattress with my bare fingers, yanking out handfuls of straw and throwing them about, sobbing. I scooped up another handful of straw and spun in a circle not knowing what to do with it, moving here and there, not knowing where to go.

Burn it! the voice demanded.

An ember in the hearth caught my eye and I ran toward it. I threw the straw into the hearth and a fire ignited instantly. I gathered more straw in the well of my apron and back and forth I ran, dumping straw and cloth into the ravenous blaze.

Satan's bed! Let it burn! the voice cried. In a wild fury, I followed its instructions. *Let it burn!* I could not feed the fire fast enough. The blaze sputtered and crackled. Its frenzy became mine as I fed the fire.

"Let you burn! Burn in hell!" I cried.

"Mercy, what are you doing?"

I looked over my shoulder and there was Joshua at the door. He rushed toward me, batting away the smoke. "Lord in heaven, what has gotten into you?" He gripped my shoulders tightly and held me at arm's length. His eyes searched the room and me for answers.

I fell into him and sobbed.

He held me, but there was tension in his grip.

"I broke one of Mama's bottles!" I stammered, pointing to the glass on the floor.

Joshua took a deep breath and exhaled. "Is that what this is about? A bottle? A bottle can be replaced."

"Other things can't be," I stammered, watching the flush

on his neck rise into his cheeks.

He released me and kicked aside a glass shard with the tip of his boot. His eyes followed the path of straw from the empty bed frame to the hearth. "What were you thinking? You destroyed your family's best bed. You could have slept on it—"

"I could never sleep on it."

His eyes darkened. "There's more to this, Mercy. There must be. Is it about your father and Catherine? Did he once bring her here?"

"No, this is not about Catherine!"

He stared at me without blinking, awaiting an explanation.

For a moment I considered telling him the truth. I felt my lips part but the words remained like bricks upon my tongue. What would such a revelation accomplish? Then he would know I was a tarnished woman and he would not want me, and I could not bear that rejection. If he knew, he would take revenge upon Papa, and what end would that serve other than upsetting Catherine's newfound happiness by making a torrid story public?

What is it, Mercy?" His arms enveloped me and his flushed cheek was cool against my own. "You are so thin, I am afraid to squeeze you for fear you might break."

"I am breaking, Joshua." I closed my eyes and pictured the bits of shattered glass. I was as broken as Mama's bottle. I willed my mind to journey to a safer place. Without Papa. Without voices. Without memories. Joshua rocked me and wiped my cheeks with his handkerchief.

"I need you, Joshua."

"I'm here," he soothed.

"Joshua, we must marry," I blurted.

Joshua loosened his hold on me and took a step backwards. He looked stunned.

"What?"

"I love you, Joshua."

I held my breath waiting for him to speak, knowing my earthly future depended upon what he would say. I watched his lips part. The moments were torture. I wanted to hear—but was afraid to hear—the words of his heart.

"Mercy," he said firmly, "This is not the time to discuss marriage." He took my hand and led me out of the cottage and into the sunshine where we were enveloped by a swarm of giddy children. Once they scampered past we resumed our talk.

"First, Mercy, you must tell me what is troubling you?"

I took a deep breath. I knew he deserved an answer, a truthful answer, but even as I exhaled I knew I could not tell him. "What is troubling me is in the past and I have put it behind me," I said.

He studied me with doubtful eyes. "Was there another? Is there another?"

"No. There could never be another," I said. "I promise you. There is no one else." I gave him an innocent smile—one that I knew had power over him. It was trickery, but I could not help myself.

He studied my face.

I lifted my chin and tried to look brave.

"Then I have no choice but to accept your word."

"Then we will marry?"

He looked at me straight. "Mercy, I'm confused. You burn a bed to ashes and then you propose marriage. This is not the time for a proposal."

I looked at him sheepishly. I did not know what to say.

"When that time comes, Mercy, I want to be the one to ask for your hand, after speaking with your father."

I studied a thread of straw that clung to the stitching in my shoe. "Not Papa," I said quietly. "This is none of his concern."

Joshua stood firm. "Mercy, I love you. You must believe me. Since the day we met, you've owned my heart. Have I not made that clear to you? But whether you relish it or not, when the time comes I will speak to your father first, for that is our way and you will have no part in that conversation. It is mine to handle. Not today, nor the morrow, but in my own time."

"Aye, Joshua."

The hollow clop of horses' hoofs came closer. Papa, Noah and Michael were returning for the final load of furniture. I wiped my eyes in my sleeve and ran into the house to clean up. Joshua followed me in to help.

LATER, WHEN JOSHUA AND MY BROTHERS were off delivering another load of crates, Papa entered the house. He rubbed his palms together and surveyed the bare room. I was sweeping away the last of the straw on the floor.

"The mattress, Mercy. Where is it?"

I glanced over my shoulder just as he stepped into a band of sunlight that made his hair shine reddish bronze. He was a new husband freshly returned from his first night with Catherine. He stuffed his hands in his pockets and postured in front of me like a rooster with a puffed chest. He was much too sure of himself.

"Where is the mattress?" he asked again.

"I burned it."

"You burned it? Why? There was still use in that mattress."

I stood up and faced him. "You know why I burned it!"

Papa stiffened. "I know not what you mean," he snapped. "I know not what you mean about anything anymore, Mercy! When you deign to speak to me, it is with the sharpest of tongues. You treat me as if I'm an animal primed to harm you, as if I'm someone who cares not a whit for your welfare, when in truth I wish you every blessing a father could wish his flesh and blood." He was closer to me now.

I was stunned by his outburst and knew not how to reply. How could a father not remember what he did to his own daughter?

Papa was so close I could feel his breath. "What devil has gotten into you?" He stared at me, waiting for an answer.

"You know what devil has gotten into me!"

"Shut it, Mercy!" He turned to leave.

"You have no memory of it, do you, Papa?" I said to his back. He turned. "What did you say?"

"Or is it you do not wish to remember?"

"Remember what?" he snapped.

"There, Papa." I pointed to the empty bed frame in the corner. "What you did to me in that bed. In the bed I burned!"

"What I did to you?" A shadow of horror crossed his face. "I would never—"

"You did, Papa. You were besotted with ale. You came to me in the night and carried me to that bed."

Papa's ruddy face turned to chalk and his jaw fell slack. He took measure of me and then looked away. Beads of sweat formed on his forehead. He did not blink or swallow or seem even to breath. He stood with his mouth agape for a long time. But then, like a man coming out of a trance, he shook himself and left whatever place in his mind he had momentarily fled to, slowly returning to our empty room. His eyes darted about, studying the space with the look of a man who took no comfort from what he saw. He was seeing things honestly for the first time. The stark, roughly hewn walls. The uneven earthen floors. The corner where the mattress had been. That night.

He knows it happened.

With heaviness, he staggered and slumped to the ground, and like a mourner at a grave onto which the last spade full of earth had been tossed, he sobbed. I walked past him soberly, sadly, out the door and into the autumn afternoon to find Joshua.

DURING THE DAYS THAT FOLLOWED, I waited for Papa to speak of our encounter, to make amends, to ask for forgiveness, but he made no such overtures. He acted as if I were not there. When he was forced to address me, he locked his eyes somewhere above my head, as if the vision he preferred of me resided elsewhere. To him I was the transgressor. There came to be a devil's agreement between us. I had the perverse satisfaction of knowing I was now no longer alone in my memory of that night, and in it I held power over him. Surely he was wondering whom else I had told. A minister? Jane perhaps?

There were other changes: Papa's clipped response to questions; his tendency to divert his eyes too quickly away from me; and at supper, his haste in leaving the table, as if he were uncomfortable sitting in the circle of our family longer than he had to, as if the chain formed by our touching shoulders would snap at any moment under the tension of its weakest link—either himself or me—and he had to remove himself before, with a confession of a guilty tongue, that fatal break would occur.

FOR MONTH AFTER MONTH my mind was a house of many chambers, each of them devoted to a particular person in my life.

I kept a chamber in which Papa dwelt darkly, allowing

myself to enter it only when necessary, then retreating on swift legs. With more work and people to attend to now, it became easy for my eyes to sweep past him in conversation and to engage him only when necessary.

The chamber in which Joshua dwelt was one I approached with caution. There was a side of me I would not allow him to see. My words became measured and my actions and affection toward him became that of a player on stage. Where was the charming, passionate girl I had been before Papa had his use of me? I tried desperately to find her again, but inside my fear pulled me back.

The chamber in which Jane dwelt was one I visited periodically, but then—although I knew it was wrong—it was on my terms and only after I composed exactly what I wished to tell her, presenting myself as the unsullied creature she had once known. After my actual betrothal to Joshua, I took pen to paper and wrote her this.

Dear Jane,

Joshua asked Papa for my hand in our parlor yesterday. He was nervous but Papa put him at ease. It was with merriment later that Papa announced our plans at dinner and poured us all cups of hot cider to which Catherine added cinnamon and dollops of thick honey. Our wedding banns will be posted on a tree in the grove for three consecutive Sabbaths for all to see. At last, Jane, I will be that embarrassed girl in the congregation with blushing cheeks. For our wedding I shall wear the white gown Mama and I sewed before she died. My greatest sadness is that you, my most trusted friend on earth, my sister from afar, will not be here with me. I await your every letter to hear the news from England.

Mercy

Unlike the chamber in which Jane dwelt, the space I reserved for Catherine was bathed in easy companionship. This chamber was a safe one I ventured into freely, lingering there comfortably. What I once feared—that Catherine would be a meddlesome stepmother, good only for demanding more work of me and prying into my affairs—did not come to pass. Catherine was tireless. She accomplished more in one day than most women did in two, and she had a gift for making work seem enjoyable. I felt my spirits lift when we were alone together, for then we were occupied in easy conversation about household matters and my wedding.

Late one afternoon in early October, on Killing Day—when the men in town slaughtered the cattle, swine and lambs they had fattened for the winter—Catherine had returned from the cellar with a jug of vinegar best for pickling, and set it on the table. Her jaw was set. Something was bothering her. Then, halfway betwixt the door and the table, she turned to me and asked, "Mercy, do you know what's troubling your father?"

"I know not," I lied, setting a vat on the table. "Perchance he is occupied with work." I couldn't believe I was protecting Papa.

"That's what he says," she said softly. "He tells me not to be concerned, that it will pass." Catherine poured the vinegar into the vat and turned her head away, blinking her eyes from its sting. "I don't mean to worry you. I ask only because no one knows his moods better than you."

"Papa has his moods," I said, knowing it was really Catherine I was protecting.

Chapter Twenty-Six

As a young girl, I imagined that on my wedding night my beloved would woo me with soft words. I imagined that he would slowly unbutton my gown and lower me onto his bed to prepare for love. But that is not what transpired.

After our marriage in the parlor, Joshua and I walked back to Joshua's cottage. Suffering the effects of too much sack-posset, a rich concoction of thick cream, spices, egg yolks and beaten whites, mixed into strong ale, Joshua's unsteady hands wrapped my cloak around my shoulders. "Thank you!" he waved to Catherine and Papa as we headed out the door. "God be with you all, and a good night to us!" he slurred and laughed out his words as we departed.

To give us privacy, Ezekiel had moved his bed into the cooperage and was snoring by the time we arrived. Joshua unsteadily stoked the fire his father had started, and then left to wash himself in a trough behind the house. I also washed, but in a bowl of tepid water Ezekiel had left on the table along with a fresh white cloth and two sprigs of sage for cleaning my teeth. Hurrying so that Joshua would not see me naked, I slipped out of my gown and into bed.

Throughout the evening's festivities I had managed to distract myself from my fears of my wedding night. But now alone in bed, fear overtook me. I wanted to run, but I had nowhere to go. I was bound to Joshua. He was entitled to my body. As my husband, he owned it. I turned my head and prayed into the clean pillowbear. *Let this night be Joshua's and mine. Let no other memories or voices come betwixt us.*

As I lay in wait of my husband, I forced myself to recall images of the evening: Joshua greeting his friends heartily; the pretty bride's cake; Ezekiel wearing the same breeches and shirt he had worn to his own wedding, swaying back and forth like the pendulum of a grand timepiece, gracing us with a long-ago promised wedding song in his rich baritone; Catherine flittering around the room lighting tapers; merry faces illuminated by candlelight; Governor Winthrop solicitous of his wife, Margaret, newly arrived from England; William Coddington winking as he introduced his own new bride whom he wed during his sojourn in England, another Mary— as vivacious as the first and now visibly with child; Reverend Wilson fluttering about like a scruffy old owl; Goody Hammer at the window locked in serious conversation with Papa, the moon hanging behind them, bright as a polished pearl.

Joshua sauntered into the room singing, not as forcefully as he sang in the grove, but loud enough to announce his presence. His run of the tune was not unpleasant. The sack-posset had improved his voice and set him in the jolliest of moods.

Lord, let this night be Joshua's and mine alone, I prayed pulling the quilt tightly around my neck. *The scent of ale on his breath is his, not Papa's.*

He blew out the taper. Metal buttons clanged as he dropped his waistcoat on the chair and fumbled with the laces on his breeches. His naked body approached the bed and when he flopped down, the mattress shook. I took a deep breath and closed my eyes. I waited for him to touch me, but he did not reach for me. We lay there for so long a time I thought he had fallen asleep.

Just as I was beginning to relax he turned on his side and faced me. "Mercy, as it is for you, this is my first time. If I'm clumsy, please forgive me."

Joshua offered his innocence to me for the taking. He confessed his inexperience as if it were a fault, yet I could not confess the fault of my experience. My heart softened with love for him, a love so overwhelming it brought tears to my eyes. Again, I considered telling him the truth. Perhaps he would not remember it in the morning because of all he drank. Perhaps the sack-posset would dull the pain of my words, but most likely it would not. Joshua was wobbly in the feet, but his ears and brain still functioned well. This was not the time for such a revelation.

I reached over and took his hand. "Do not worry, my husband. I know you wish to please me."

"I do, my darling. I always will."

Then he rolled on top of me and the rest happened quickly.

THE DAY AFTER OUR WEDDING, Joshua removed my belongings from Papa's home and set them on the floor of our cottage. I brought a small bundle of clothing, a handful of table and wearing linens, Mama's green bottles, my keepsake box, and Mama's rocking chair. With Ezekiel's blessing and Joshua's encouragement, I set up the Hoyt cottage to become my own. Their dreary dwelling, absent of color, was greatly in need of a goodwife's touch.

Joshua and Ezekiel had finished digging their well the

previous summer, so I was now one of the few women in Boston to have water available outside her door. The wellsweep had become a village attraction, with people strolling behind our fence to examine it.

Now surrounded by a squat wall of stone, the well sat in the center of the garth. Five paces to its right was the wellsweep, a contraption that lowered a bucket into the well for the drawing of water. The wellsweep's frame—a wooden structure shaped like a Y—was taller than me. In the nook of the Y, Joshua had centered a timber the length of a small shallop's mast. To the end of the pole closest to the well he had hooked a chain and bucket. To the other end he attached a wooden handle, which he weighed to the ground with a large flat rock.

On my first day as his wife, he took my arm and led me through the cooperage and out the back door to teach me to draw water. He stood behind the handle and then quickly moved aside so I could stand in his footsteps.

"Shove the rock aside with your shoe and slowly raise the pole above your head."

I kicked aside the rock and lifted the pole. "Is this high enough?" I asked.

"Aye. You see the bucket dropping into the water . . ."

"Aye."

"Now wait for the bucket to fill, then pull on the pole and bring it back down . . ."

"It's heavy," I laughed.

"Aye, water is heavy. Now set the rock on top to hold it, then walk to the well and unhook the bucket from the chain."

"It is that easy?" I laughed.

"Aye. Now, Goodwife, you'll always have fresh cool water."

EZEKIEL JOINED US FOR MEALS, but had taken to reading

his Bible and falling asleep on his bed in the cooperage. When I objected to his exodus—I felt I was displacing him—he assured me it was where he preferred to sleep. He was a man of privacy who understood the privacy a newly married couple required.

I came to learn Ezekiel was also a man of economy. He took from life only what he needed and no more. Unlike his son, he ate sparingly and paid little attention to food. He was equally as parsimonious with words. Ezekiel spoke only what was important.

Mama had said that a wife never really knows her husband until years after their marriage, if at all. In the early days, I learned that Joshua was a man of large appetites—for food, for family, for respect within our community. He confided that he one day aspired to be a selectman, to be more than a freeman, to be leader in our community. "I came to America for prosperity, Mercy, and I look to you to be my helpmeet in achieving it. A man is deemed in equal esteem to the virtue of the woman he marries, and to the children she births," he said more times than I could count. In exchange for this man of value, he expected me to become a wife and mother respected by all.

Another thing I learned of quickly was Joshua's appetite for love. Pleasing me was a talent he fell into quickly. When I found myself recoiling when he touched my breast or my thigh with intentions of lovemaking, Joshua was patient.

"Love is new to you," he'd say. "I know not much about women, but I know about mares," he'd laugh, attempting to turn my skittishness into humor. Then, in his gentle way, he would calm me. "First, let me stroke your muzzle," and his voice would trail off as he glided a finger down the ridge of my nose so gently I could barely feel it. I'd close my eyes and breathe deeply. "And your hair," he'd whisper until the soft repetition of his movements sent me to the deepest edges of sleep. "Your throat," he'd soothe, stroking me ever so lightly under the chin, his touch like a feather. When I trembled in contentment, he'd respond with a firmer hand. And when I would smile dreamily up at him, he'd tickle me, at first as gently as a kitten's fur brushing against the silky-smooth hairs of my arm, and then with a more deliberate touch meant to provoke me into friendly retaliation, and then with an even rougher hand which would send us frolicking on our featherbed until our play became lovemaking. During those moments I had no problem reminding myself it was Joshua I was with, it was right that I offer myself to him, and he meant me only pleasure. When I did this I was able to give him pleasure, for he told me there was no other women in the world whose body and spirit could satisfy him as completely.

Although I loved Joshua, I did not feel the kind of thrill Jane spoke of, nor did I feel that heightened pleasure Jane told me was necessary for a woman to feel in order to conceive. I was grateful I did not. Joshua longed for children immediately and inquired about the state of my womb monthly, so with him I feigned disappointment and told him it was not yet the Lord's will that I conceive. Childbirth was a perilous business. Until I attained forgiveness, until I knew there was a place for me in heaven, I could not risk hastening my leave of this world in childbirth.

Chapter Twenty-Seven

1633-1634

Our modest settlement of a few hundred souls burgeoned into a community of nearly nine hundred by 1633. If you counted the people in the surrounding settlements, the numbers were well in excess of that. The population of the Massachusetts Bay seemed to swell daily with the arrival of new babies sprung from fruitful wombs everywhere, and immigrants pouring out of ships sailing into the harbors weekly from England.

Those years there was no relaxation of our zealotry. The sights we set upon heaven—with America as a mere stepping stone—became even more vivid because the Lord continued to reassure us of our status as His elect. We only had to think about it, our ministers told us. Had the Lord not delivered us from tribulation upon tribulation? Had He not willed us to survive the brutality of the sea, the ravishing scurvy, bitter winters, near starvation? Had He not delivered us through bouts of smallpox that killed off most of the Indians but left us unscathed? Aye, He did these things and more. It was in this mood of hopefulness that 1633 began.

We, the saints of Boston, were counting off the months

until the grandest of all blessings would be delivered to us: the arrival of John Cotton, the most highly esteemed of our ministers.

Governor Winthrop had attempted to lure Reverend Cotton to New England even before we sailed, but the will of God had kept him in Lincolnshire a bit longer. For a year and a half he had been ill, hovering betwixt life and death. Then his wife died from the same ague that had laid him low. Only during the past year had the Lord restored him to health and good fortune that included marriage to a widow named Sarah Storey, whom everyone declared a virtuous woman.

For a long time Reverend Cotton had been a thorn in the crown of the Church of England because he resisted conformity to practices like kneeling at the sacraments and wearing a surplice over his cassock like the papists. Finally last year, having had a belly full of Reverend Cotton's defiance, the powerful Archbishop Laud commissioned his arrest. But again the Lord delivered Reverend Cotton and allowed him to escape into hiding where friends kept him safe and arranged for him to reunite with his new bride, Sarah.

The townsmen of Boston labored to finish the meetinghouse so it would be ready for Reverend Cotton's arrival. Because Reverend Cotton was a realist who believed that even in the most well-ordered towns sinners abide with saints and must be chastised, our men also worked to complete the pillory. The men built a home for the Cottons on Sudbury End on property nestled in the shadow of the smallest dome of Trimountain, which long before his arrival we began referring to as Cotton Hill.

In September the Griffin arrived carrying its saintly cargo: John Cotton, his Sarah, and their new son whom they named Seaborn for his having been born at sea. We met his family with a volley of cannon shots reserved for only the most celebrated of Englishmen.

At first we feared that our new meetinghouse—a long and low structure that resembled a barn more than it did a place of worship—would disappoint him, but we were mistaken, for Reverend Cotton was a man of humble heart, and he took to our modest place of worship as easily as an angel takes to a cloud.

I shan't ever forget the first morning he preached to us in America. I was sitting on a bench in the center of the meetinghouse, my fingers knotted together in anticipation.

The final beat of Billy Bowdoin's drum struck and Reverend Cotton glided down the aisle. His eyes were soft and tearing in recognition of the many friends he never expected to see again in his lifetime. He was as I remembered him: A man of about Papa's age, short in stature, with blue eyes, an aquiline nose, and generous pink lips. He wore a simple black tunic with small buttons descending from bib to hem and a black skullcap that covered all but a fringe of graying hair that surrounded his round face. By the time he ascended the two steps to the pulpit and turned to face us, not an eye including his own was dry. There was a single arched window behind the pulpit. It, like the other windows, was set too high to look out, lest the views distract us. That morning a veil of buttery sunlight glided in through the glass and spread across his shoulders like a translucent cape.

Reverend Cotton was not frightening like Reverend Wilson or tiresome like Reverend Phillips. My grandmamma used to say his tongue was silver, and she was right. Often he had spoken of "God's caress"—how God tenderly touches those He had chosen.

That first morning he preached from the Gospel of John, Chapter One, Verse Sixteen: "'and of his fullness have we all received, and grace for grace.' Grace is a gift freely given by God to his faithful. It causes our souls to trust in Him and to say, He has delivered me out of six troubles, will He not deliver me out of the seventh?" It was in this spirit of hope that I prayed this godly preacher could aid in the healing of my fractured soul.

THE YEAR AFTER REVEREND COTTON'S ARRIVAL flew by as I labored to make a clean and comfortable home for Joshua and Ezekiel, which was an endless chore given the dust blowing in off the street and in from the cooperage. A dust cloth became my constant companion.

Mama had taught us that every good work was another rung climbed on the ladder to heaven. So it was with this imperative and Joshua's desire for a perfect helpmeet that I made myself a useful woman in Boston. I regularly scrubbed the meetinghouse windows from the high steps of a ladder until the glare of the sun upon the glass stung my eyes. I shared my household goods with others, and helped Joshua deliver bowls, vats, and buckets to customers while always adding a gift of cheese or bread neatly wrapped in paper. This was the year I earned the reputation of a woman of good fame who would never withhold assistance to a soul who required it, who was indeed an ideal helpmeet to her husband, Boston's ambitious cooper.

The restless, work-filled pace of my days provided ballast to my moods, which like the sea, changed from moment to moment. But by filling my hours with work and prayer I was able to keep the demons inside me at bay. The light of day was kinder to me than the dark of night. On those nights when I was jolted awake by menacing dreams, when the voices spoke in my head reassuring me one moment, admonishing me the next, I would become agitated and Joshua would wrap his arms around me and soothe me with tender words of comfort. "I shall love you forever," he would say. "I'm here, my darling." Protected in his arms I felt calm, and neither demon nor devil nor witch nor sorceress could claim me. I was able then to quash the voices, and I was at peace.

Mama told us, "Just about when your days start feeling the same one upon another, and just when you take comfort in it, the Lord will send around something to stir your pot. It is His way of reminding you that He is in charge and not you."

Again she was right, and again the unexpected arrived, this time in a letter from Jane that would change my life. I opened it and a dozen red rose petals sprinkled into my lap.

February 15, 1634
Dear Mercy,

Within this small letter you shall find a handful of dried rose petals that come from a glorious vermilion bouquet my handsome John Allen brought me a week ago. This is my way of telling you that aye, John Allen Loring and I will be wed on March 16. I will soon become a married woman! I have saved some of the petals to wear in my shoes on my wedding day! We are truly sisters now, for we continue to walk the same path into marriage. We have already made our intentions known to the town clerk and they will be published on the door of St. Boltoph's starting the Sabbath of February twenty-third.

JAL is very aggressive in his pursuit of me. It is good we marry, for marriage will save us from the trouble I sense brewing. I know you understand my meaning. Papa has taken pains not to leave us

alone together. I can barely contain my longing for him, and he is of
the same desires. Certainly, the devil has taken hold of me!

So, like you, I am to be a wife with wifely duties. You may
think me foolish, but I am anxious to scrub my own floors, mend my
own clothing—JAL's and mine, and serve cider to the goodwives
in town. Millicent says I will tire of these activities, but I intend
to prove her wrong.

I spoke to JAL about America, and he says perhaps one day our
future may hold just that!

Extend my best wishes to Joshua and to your family, and give
sprightly Grace a kiss for me.

Jane

"Jane is to be wed!" I shrieked into the empty room. Then
in fumbling with the wrapper, I noticed another letter tucked
inside, one dated almost two weeks later than the one I had
just read. A rush of fear coursed through me. I hoped nothing
had transpired to undo my friend's joy.

February 28, 1634
Dear Mercy,

I shall get right to it. JAL and I are coming to America! It took
me but two weeks to convince him that he could be as successful in
Boston as he could be in England. We will sail upon the Griffin
and will arrive in September. At such time I will be appearing at
your doorstep requesting a cup of tea.

I have four months to pack. I request your advice on what to
bring, and, of course, tell me what you need from England, what
necessities and trinkets you have been longing for. If you write
immediately, I will surely receive your request before I leave.

Mercy, our dreams are coming true!

Jane

Naturally, I wrote back immediately.

April 15, 1634
Dearest Jane,
My heart is dancing! Soon we will be together again. I will welcome you on the Griffin *the day of your arrival. You can be assured I will be there, and I promise everything will be in perfect order when you arrive. EVERYTHING! In response to your kind offer to bring me items I need, I am listing them here. Joshua is watching this list grow as I write, and he is teasing me that no ship's hold is large enough to stow them all.*

writing paper
ink
cloth for gowns and doublets
chocolate
combs
two dozen hooks and eyes
spices
ribbands
leather gloves for Joshua (his hands are large)
silver buttons
Of course we will reimburse you for the cost of these items.

Mercy

Chapter Twenty-Eight

While I prepared for Jane's arrival in September, the town, by its steady growth, seemed to be preparing for her as well.

In March of 1634, a market opened north of the meetinghouse in the square behind the pillory pit. In anticipation of the increased demand for their products, Joshua and Ezekiel spent their evenings sanding staves for the pails, fruit bowls, tankards, vats, and vessels they planned to sell. Also in March, Samuel Cole opened an inn that had four rooms to rent.

In May, Governor Winthrop, who served as governor for four years, was defeated on Election Day by Thomas Dudley. Many of us were disturbed by the upset because we feared the governance of Boston would become even more rigid under the imperial Mister Dudley. A good number of freemen who voted for the governor and his eight assistants were discontented with Governor Winthrop's leniency, which I did not perceive as lenient at all, given the harsh discipline inflicted on rule breakers. Most freemen believed Thomas Dudley would provide a firmer hand. As it turned out, not too many men opposed Governor Winthrop because he was elected deputy governor.

As the weather warmed, I adjusted my day's routine to suit the longer hours of sunlight and make good use of every daylight moment. I took to rising earlier to complete my chores—setting a fire, fetching water from the well, preparing meals, scrubbing, laundry, gardening, butchering, making deliveries for Joshua, milking, and on Thursdays, marketing. Then at midday, I would hurry to the bluff above the Great Cove. Of course it was much too soon for Jane to arrive, but fixing my attention on the sea she was traversing made me feel closer to her. When I returned home, there was still daylight enough for more work.

Toward the end of spring, Joshua received a letter from John Allen Loring requesting his assistance in finding them a home. In a swirling script that rivaled Jane's in embellishment, John specified that the dwelling be in the center of town. He also specified that the cottage have a well-lit room where he could work as a tailor.

Within a week Joshua located a cottage in the center of town that once had belonged to a young couple, a man and his bride who both died of an ague the previous winter. The cottage had a small room behind the chimney intended for the children the couple never had. The distance between Jane and I now would be the same as it was in Old Boston. We could run to each other's homes in minutes.

One night several weeks before their arrival, I lay in bed making a mental list of the items Jane would need to set up housekeeping. The house came furnished with a table, bench, chair and a bed, but there was so much more I needed to do. Jane would need trenchers and pitchers and cups, and I'd have to arrange for bins of flour and sugar and ale and a tin of salt. I'd have to plant a garden, scour the cottage until it was spotless, provide tapers, baskets, barrels for rainwater, spoons, a iron cauldron for making soap, curtains and linens, and diverse dried meats. There would be endless preparation.

It had to be perfect: The trenchers . . . sugar . . . ale . . . baskets . . . barrels . . . scatter seeds for flax . . . drinking mugs . . . a warming pan . . . dry wood . . . a kettle . . . a ladle . . . The voices in my head echoed everything I had been telling myself.

It must be perfect.

Nothing can be amiss.

Everything must be perfect.

Then it occurred to me that while I had been spending all my time preparing for Jane's arrival—her table, her food, her tapers—I had given no thought to the days that would follow. Jane was a chatty one. She would demand conversation about everything. She would want to visit Papa, and upon seeing us together she would sense the breach between us. I could continue my charade in letters, but in her presence I would have to prove that the years had not changed me at all.

Shadows of dancing leaves flickered on the rafters. There was just enough moonlight to detect the sheeted mound of Joshua's bare chest, arm, and face. Like his father, Joshua was able to sleep through the fiercest thunderstorms. But then, did not sound sleep come to those with a clear conscience? My heart thumped wildly. Not only had I deceived Jane, but I had deceived Joshua. It was only because of the sack-posset he drank that he did not realize I was not a virgin. I told him I had laid a towel on our bed and buried the bloody thing behind the house the following morning after our wedding because my grandmother had said the practice meant many children. I did not want children and prayed they would not come. I am a Jezebel, piling sin upon sin.

Tormented by guilt, I pushed those thoughts out of my mind and forced myself to review once again the items I needed to prepare for Jane—tapers, salt, spoons, a ladle, baskets, a supply of grain and sugar, kindling, dried meats, linens, napkins, a warming pan. *Everything must be perfect,* the voices in my head commanded.

It was afternoon when the far-away beat of Billy Bowdoin's drum captured my attention. I dropped my dust rag and ran into the street. Halfway to the Spring Gate, I espied Billy's boyish figure and the triangles of his gaunt arms working his drumsticks. My heart pounded madly as I raced toward him.

"The *Griffin* has arrived! The *Griffin* has arrived!" he was calling. "She now rounds Castle Island!" I raced back to the cooperage, shouted the news to Joshua and Ezekiel and sped back down the High Street. At the crest of the hill I sighted the *Griffin* entering the outer harbor, its sails cupping wind, a flash of gold bouncing off its prow in the September sunshine. I ran furiously, speeding down the incline, depending upon angels' wings to deposit me onto the dock safely. On the beach, the wet sand slowed my pace to a lumbering gait that made me feel like the weight of all the sand on the beach was inside my shoes. I was running inside a familiar dream in which I could see my far off destination, but could not reach it. Tension gripped my muscles, sweat streamed down my neck, my heart pounded wildly, time was passing, yet I was covering no distance at all.

By then I had prepared exactly what I would say to Jane, how I would respond to her inquiries, what I would have to do to convince her I was still the same. I had rehearsed our reunion so carefully that nothing could possibly go wrong.

The dock was crowded. I elbowed my way through clusters of yammering women and stern gentlemen whose bodies, thick as doors, blocked my access to the high posts at the end of the dock where the ship's boats would hitch their lines. As I pushed forward—madly, recklessly—I stomped upon something hard.

Goody Hammer spun around. She glared at me, crouched down and rubbed her heel.

"I . . . beg your pardon, ma'am. Believe me, I did not see . . ."

Gripping my arm for support, she pulled herself up, grimacing and making a grand show of it. "Mercy, I will be fine, but you must learn to put forth less speed and greater wisdom."

"Aye, ma'am."

"The *Griffin* shall disembark in the Lord's time, not yours," Goody Hammer scolded. Her words beneath the ladder on the *Arbella* came back to me, and I snapped, "Why are you here, ma'am?"

"As if 'tis any of your business," Goody Hammer huffed. Then the old woman's tone changed. "If you must know," she said in a kinder voice, "my sister Eloise sent me bundles of herbs—betony, henbane, and feverfew and I am here to retrieve 'em. But I am sure with your urgency your parcel is more important than mine."

I took a deep breath to calm myself. "Jane arrives today . . . Jane Perkins . . . Jane Loring now. She is married."

"Jane, of course. Now there's a girl I'll never forget." She tossed her head back and chortled. "She was a lively one, like you, a colt in need of breakin'. But in any case, girl, step ahead of me. She is your friend and t'day your parcel is more important than mine."

Appreciative of her kindness, I nodded and did as I was told.

By then the Griffin was anchored in the harbor and two ship's boats were gliding to shore. Each was packed with about a dozen passengers in browns and blacks, stuffed together like pinecones in a basket. Jostling from foot to foot, I squinted into the sun trying to espy Jane, but she was not amongst them.

The first boat carried what seemed to be members of a single family, for their slender faces had a commonality. There were three rows of boys and girls and each row was a larger version of the one in front of it, definitely sprouts from the same rootstock. The children dragged their cupped hands in the water and jabbered at each other. Oblivious to their chatter, their stern parents scanned the faces of the people on the pier.

"The Hutchinsons," Goody Hammer mumbled into my ear. "That one there is the mother of the brood," she said pointing to the woman craning her neck behind the children. I remembered hearing about the Hutchinsons. At the previous week's Sabbath service, Reverend Cotton had announced that another midwife named Anne Hutchinson would be arriving on the *Griffin* with her family. I took this to be good news for our growing population.

"Now you will have help," I said over my shoulder to Goody Hammer.

"The kind of help I need not," the crone mumbled. "I hear she is a troublesome one."

The husband, a tall broad-browed man with a black beard bobbing against his collar, stepped onto the dock first, then offered his hand to his wife, the stern woman. The woman was birdlike in her movements and barely taller than her two eldest girls, who were already on their feet. She straightened the high collar of her loose-fitting gray gown. Surprisingly, she did not accept her husband's hand but leapt out of the boat unaided with the quickness of a seed blown out of a straw. Her black eyes darted about. She was searching for someone in the crowd.

"She's seekin' Reverend Cotton," Goody Hammer mumbled. "Everyone knows she worships the ground he walks on. When he left England, she couldn't find a preacher who would satisfy her. So she begged her husband to follow him here, and being a weak man, he complied. 'Tis a fault for a wife to wield such power over her helpmeet."

I ignored her.

"She thinks John Cotton is the Blessed Lord Jesus Christ Himself," Goody Hammer grumbled. "Watch her. She is trouble."

We were not the only ones watching Anne Hutchinson. Every eye seemed to be following her. When she and Reverend Cotton met, he accepted her outstretched arms in fond reunion. It struck me that the two resembled each other—not so much as kin, for he was light-complexioned and she more olive in coloring—but as kindred spirits. But they were both grand in gesture, which made them seem larger than anyone else in the crowd. He stroked his beard and nodded cordially as she pumped his arm with a familiarity that seemed inappropriate for a woman to exhibit to her minister. Words seemed to flow from her mouth like cream from a pitcher. When she stopped talking, the words poured out of his mouth with an equal facility.

I glanced back at Anne Hutchinson's bearded husband who was crouched low to the ground pointing out the hillocks of Trimountain to a squirming child, who in her eagerness and intensity seemed a miniature of her mother. Jane would tell me about them later.

By then the passengers from the second ship's boat

disembarked and a third boat was approaching the dock. I strained my eyes to see the faces in that boat.

"Aye, there she is!" I cried. "Jane! Jane!"

Jane was seated at the stern beside a man in a flat purple hat with spiky brown feathers. She caught sight of me and I cried back, waving furiously.

"That's the girl I remember," Good Hammer cackled. "Giddy as a goose!"

With a jaunty manner, the man with the feathered cap helped Jane out of the ship's boat. Surely he wasn't John—her John would be a man of our kind, dressed in a dark doublet, breeches, and a conservative peaked hat. This fellow, with his celadon shirt, feathered hat and green woolen stockings, was not her type. When both her feet were planted on the deck, she ran past him toward me. Just as I was feeling relief, she turned and called, "John!"

"A peacock," Goody Hammer mumbled into my ear.

Jane fell into my arms.

"Praise God," I cried out. That moment I didn't have to pretend. Jane's cheek was damp against my own, and I could detect the familiar scent of flowers and smoke about her. My arms trembled as I hugged her, or maybe it was Jane's trembling arms I felt. We stepped back to take a close look at one another. More than five years had passed and she was more beautiful than ever. Her golden curls billowed out of her coif like the petals of a daffodil. The other women were dressed in their sad colors—probably the same gowns they toiled, prayed, and slept in throughout their voyage. But Jane was not one of them. She chose a yellow gown with tiny cloth buttons and a fresh white coif. Although I knew it was impossible, I wouldn't have been shocked to hear she found a way to bathe aboard ship.

OTHER PASSENGERS JOSTLED ABOUT, embracing their loved ones, shrieking tearful greetings and thankful prayers. Impatient elbows nudged us. We were blocking the passage of others, but we didn't care. I looked over my shoulder to see if Goody Hammer was observing us, but she and Elijah had disappeared.

When Jane introduced me to John, I felt my face redden. "I'm pleased to meet you," I said, wiping my cheek with the back of my hand.

John was taller than Joshua and more solid than I expected him to be. He had short black hair that curled out from beneath his cap, and eyes as blue as the sea. In every way, he was a comely man. I feared for how the magistrates, so fixed on simplicity, would deal with his carefree manner and flamboyant garb.

By then Joshua arrived with his cart and the four of us stood on the pier, surrounded by bundles and crates. "I can see you've not packed lightly," he said.

"We packed for a lifetime," trilled Jane.

"How was your crossing?" I asked, pulling Jane close and walking behind our husbands.

"We prayed a lot," Jane sighed. "Every day was like the Sabbath."

"I know your meaning," I giggled.

"There was this minister aboard, a Reverend Zachariah Symmes, who preached night and day. See him . . . yonder." She pointed to a hefty man with lots of cheek and no chin who was scolding a young lad. "He's as fearful a preacher as I've ever met. He shouts his sermons because he is deaf, and speaks of naught but damnation. Fortunately, he is settling in Charlestown."

"And the crossing itself? Were you frightened?"

"Reverend Symmes frightened me more than the storms. But John calmed me and kept me occupied with activities other than sermons, didn't you, John?" she called ahead to her husband.

"I did my best!"

"He kept me so occupied, I believe I'm with child!"

"You art not."

"I believe I am," she said, tapping her belly.

I looked around to make sure no one else overheard such private news.

Jane was unabashed. "Next spring," she laughed.

I stopped to embrace her. John was walking backwards, grinning from ear to ear. Jane took my hand and pulled me aside. "I met the most fascinating woman aboard," she whispered. "When we are alone, I shall tell you about her. Her name is Anne Hutchinson."

THE FRINGED LEAVES ON THE LOCUST TREES outside Jane and John's cottage had melted into dusk by the time I flung open their front door.

Jane scurried in first and nearly ran into the table, at which point she yanked at both sides of her gown as if to slow down. She flittered about looking everywhere at once.

"Mercy, it's perfect," she squealed. "Thank you."

"My Jane has been anticipating this moment for six months," John said with mock exasperation. The speckled feathers in his hat swayed slightly as he set bundles on the floor.

"As have I," I said calmly. Everything was perfect, and I was proud of my work. The curtains. The pewter trenchers. The pitchers. The tapers. The cups. The bins of sugar, flour, and salt filled to generous levels. The cauldrons. The kettle.

The linens. The barrels. Nothing was amiss. It pleased me that Jane approved.

Jane ruffled her gown as if giving it permission to move again, and with quick steps flittered around the room. She stopped to admire every object that caught her eye. On tiptoes she lowered an oval pewter platter from the roughly hewn mantle and pressed it to her bosom. At the bed, she ran the flat palm of her hand across the knobby weave of a blue and white-stripped pillowbear. John smiled as he watched her glide from chair to stool to bench, trying out each piece of furniture, claiming it by sinking her bottom into its seat. She noticed the doorway leading to the room behind the chimney and ran toward it. Although it was too dark to see much, she pointed out to John exactly where he might set up his worktable and store his bolts of cloth.

Joshua arrived a few minutes later carrying a metal firebox with a red glow bursting through its crosshatched slats. At the hearth he scooped the burning embers beneath a tent of dry kindling he had set there a week ago. Instantly the wood burst into flames and John, who came to his aid, set three larger logs onto the fire.

As I poured cups of cider, I watched my husband and friends. In my mind, they were painting a portrait of how our lives would be, each adding the brushstrokes of words and movement. For the first time in years, I felt hopeful about the future. For the first time, I did not wish to be back in England, for those I had been pining for had come to me. I watched Jane sip her drink, set it on the table, and begin flapping around the room once again, prattling on to whomever would listen, admiring everything. I prayed her lightheartedness would extend to me, and that in her company I would be able to live now with a joyous heart.

John removed his purple cap, carefully righted the feathers in the headband and set the cap on a stool. He seemed keenly aware of every move Jane made, smiling at her with delight as she drifted past. He hummed a cheery tune, a melody he probably learned on the *Griffin*. The jolliest tunes people hum now are the tunes they learned from seamen and not from the Psalms. I was glad for that melody and listened hard to memorize it. In Old Boston we had songs and fiddlers. Here we are deprived of such gaiety.

Joshua joined John at the hearth and before long the two of them were engaged in jovial conversation. John was telling Joshua a humorous story about Jane misspeaking the word "porpoise" for "purpose" in addressing Reverend Symmes. Hearing John tell the story, Jane began lumbering around the room, belly out, like the rotund Reverend Symmes, which brought us to laughter. This led to another story and to another until our voices reached such merriment that Joshua closed the window, lest the neighbors hear.

Jane pulled me toward her and swung me into the circle of her arms. "Praise the Lord we're together again," she squealed.

I took my lead from her. The two of us began to sway and then to swing in a dance, fast and then so fast that Jane's saffron skirt and my gray one blended into a whirling wheel of motion. When we released hands, I twirled by myself, but with Jane's joy inhabiting me. I felt like a young girl in England again, unbound and free. I swayed and hitched my skirt above my ankles as Jane did, and I grinned and blinked, and the men hooted and clapped—John slapping his hand against his thigh, Joshua beating the table with such zest the taper in its center jiggled in its candlestick. They clapped in rhythm, sipped more cider, eyed each other for encouragement, and stomped their boots, urging us to dance faster. I took Jane's hand and

swung her in a circle to the music of the phantom fiddle in my
head, and Jane giggled as if she heard it too. In no time I was
dancing even faster and wilder than Jane, and I was the one
encouraging her to quicken her step.

The forbidden joy of that evening so enveloped us that
before the last log in the hearth had completely burned,
the men had risen from their chairs and the four of us were
dancing a spirited ronde of our design, crossing one foot over
the other, moving in a circle to whistling provided by Joshua
and a bawdy seaman's ditty sung by John. Soon we were all
bellowing in ear-deafening voices: "We be three poor mariners
newly come from the sea . . . We spend our lives in jeopardy."
Jane made no concessions to the child she was carrying. If
I ventured to read her mind, I would have wagered that she
determined such playfulness was exactly the armor her child
needed to enter our solemn world. The four of us danced and
sang, "we spend our lives in jeopardy" until our hair was damp,
our toes ached inside our shoes, and our voices grew hoarse.
Outside the window, a sliver of moon hovered above us like a
smile. That would be the most joyous evening of my life.

Chapter Twenty-Nine

The next day, a Thursday, I invited Jane to visit before the lecture so we could stroll to the meetinghouse together.

Jane arrived before midday carrying a plate of cornbread. "Sarah Cotton brought it this morning. She is a lovely woman. When I told her I was with child, she allowed me to hold her Seaborn. A lusty boy he is, with a nose like a berry. On the way here I stopped to introduce myself to Margaret Winthrop, who was heading to the Spring Gate with the new Mary Coddington. The women gather there for a wash and gossip, you know."

"My goodness, I promised to show you Boston and already you know the prime women in town and their habits," I said, showing irritation . . . and jealousy.

"Don't worry, there are plenty more women to introduce me to."

I watched Jane's eyes dance around the room.

"I thought it would be impossible to make a cozy home in the wilderness, but I was mistaken," she said.

"Joshua helped. He made much of what you see."

"And mark your Mama's bottles! I remember them from England."

I swallowed hard, remembering the shattered fate of one of them.

"It is an oven here in Boston," Jane said, changing the subject. She flew hither and thither in her conversation like a bird unable to settle on a single branch. She flopped into Joshua's chair, pulled down the collar of her gown and blew into her bosom to create her own breeze, unfastened the buckles on her shoes and kicked them off so they landed near the door, then sat back in feigned exhaustion fanning her pink cheeks with her hand.

"You're flushed," I said.

"It's stifling in here," she replied, fanning faster. She pulled her skirt and smock above her knees and sat with both legs fully exposed.

"This cider was on the doorstep all night and it's cool," I said, setting the jug on the table, and then reaching for cups on the top shelf of the cupboard.

"Stop there and let me look at you. Yesterday was such a blur and I want to slow things down today so I can remember every moment. Mercy, you are as lovely as ever, but you're not eating enough. I noticed it yesterday, but I didn't want to embarrass you."

I knew I had become thin. My gowns hung heavy, as if they were made of too much fabric. Even my shoes felt too large for my feet. When I'd caught a glimpse of myself in the looking glass, I thought I was seeing a stranger who bore only a vague likeness to me. My cheekbones were more pronounced, my eyes looked larger and darker within my face, and my hipbones protruded like the arched wings of a stork. Joshua had noticed it as well and had been encouraging me to eat, but in anticipation of Jane's arrival I had no appetite for food.

"I'll plump you up. Here, eat this," Jane said, whisking the napkin off Sarah Cotton's plate of cornbread and handing me a crumbly chunk. "Eat."

I took a bite and forced myself to swallow. I felt every gritty grain travel down my throat, and focused all my attention on keeping it down.

"Tell me about Boston. What must I know about life here?"

Outside the window behind Jane, two women arm-in-arm were heading for the meetinghouse. "Well, Sabbath services start at nine of the clock every Sunday and the Thursday lecture is at one, and after it the marketplace is open. Billy Bowdoin is our drummer boy and the beat of the drum alerts us to make haste. At the first beat, we must hurry," I said, gesturing toward the door. "Our ministers and magistrates are serious about attendance. If you miss for other than sickness, you'll be fined."

"How sick must one be?"

"Near death."

"How much is the fine?"

"A shilling or two, more for a repeated offense."

"I've enough shillings tucked away for a number of absences!" she laughed.

"But if there are too many, you could find yourself in the pillory—in the stocks or in the cage where they lock up sinners."

"You fret too much. They'd never lock up innocents like us. I'd find a way to outwit them. I'd scuffle like a cat," she said, clawing the air with her fingers.

I laughed, but then thought the better of it. "Let you not tempt them," I said sternly. "Order is the rule in this town." In a firm voice I told Jane about the fines many have received for minor infractions, about Martha Purdy, and about a dishonest baker whose arms and legs were locked in the stocks and had to wear a lump of dough on his head. I told her about the heartless Joist Brown, and about how a yeoman had been locked in the cage for drunkenness for an afternoon. "For the next year the fellow must wear a cloth stitched with a red letter D on it around his neck whenever he ventures outdoors."

Jane's face became serious. "Which reminds me, how is your Papa?"

"He's remarried, you know. You'll meet Catherine at the meetinghouse, and of course you'll meet her children."

"—Aye, but how is your Papa?" she interrupted.

"He's well. He's currently building—"

"—No, Mercy, it doesn't matter to me what he is building. Has he stopped drinking?" She pressed her lips together waiting for my answer.

"He's sober now," I said, convincingly.

"Then good for him."

"Tell me about Anne Hutchinson," I asked.

"Ah, yes. Mistress Hutchinson! Where do I start?" She leaned closer. "I can speak of virtue upon virtue that she possesses. She is unlike any woman I have ever met. She is a mother, a midwife, and a prophetess. Zachariah Symmes preached twice a day, but it was Mistress Hutchinson's ministry that we preferred, which, of course, set Reverend Symmes against her. She knows Scripture better than any minister, but she speaks to our hearts. Do you know the best of it? She promised to open her home to us in Boston so we could meet without men and discuss Scripture together. Can you imagine? We will have liberties here we never had in England. I can hardly wait!" Her voice raced with enthusiasm.

A drumbeat boomed in the distance. "Jane, we must go," I said nervously.

Jane scowled. "No!"

Through the open window, I had been watching people pass. What began as a trickle was now a steady flow with all the cottages of Boston emptying themselves of the women, men, and children, offering them up to fulfill their mid-week obligation. The passersby wore their sober meetinghouse faces. After the lecture the same people, suitably chastened, would make the return trip. Many—especially the women—would have that saintly look about them I had become expert at noticing—that guileless, glassy-eyed, transfigured look that transforms them into creatures more of heaven than of earth.

"We must go," I repeated.

Jane arched her eyebrows. "What if we don't?"

"I told you what happens if we don't."

Jane spun around and snapped the curtains shut. "Not today. Today is for you and me." She grinned impishly. "No one shall know. You're always there and they'll assume you're there today. All those white coifs. They'll not notice you're missing. And me, they've never seen me anyway."

"What if Joist Brown comes pounding on our door?"

"Let's hide beneath the window!"

While in England I would have risked my soul for pleasure, now I was not so sure. But I succumbed to Jane wishes because I did not want her to think I had changed. Abandoning decorum, we set the jug of cider on the floor between us, leaned against the wall and spent the afternoon drinking, laughing, and talking until the service was over. Jane told me that Anne Hutchinson had fourteen children, eleven of whom traveled with them. She counted them off on her fingers: "Edward, Richard, Faith, Bridget, Francis, Samuel, young Anne, Mary, Katherine, William the younger, and, I've run out of fingers for Suzanna, who is but a year old. Anne's William is a quiet man, completely devoted to her, who enables her to go about her work and studies. He gazes at her as if she just stepped off a cloud! There's gossip that he is unduly in her service, but I see it differently. He is a manly man, if you know my meaning."

"Fathering fourteen children is evidence of it!" I pointed out.

Jane nodded vigorously, pondering my comment. Then she giggled. "I cherish my John, but I shall never aspire to such devotion."

ONCE WE WERE SURE the lecture was over, we strolled to the marketplace. It had rained the previous night and we sidestepped mud puddles and skirted the ankle-breaking gouges made by wagon wheels. Busy black mosquitoes swarmed around us with the zealousness of winged preachers, and in the jolly spirit of the afternoon we swatted them away.

Jane's curious blue eyes took in everything. She examined a merchant's table heaped with fabric. She fingered the scarlet stammel for petticoats, the swanskin flannel for sheets, even the black prunella for clergymen's gowns and mourning clothes. She held her nose as we passed Goodman Purdy's fish stand, which I found fitting given his abuse of Martha. When he waved a slab of cod in front of our noses and gestured toward a knee-high rack of birch limbs upon which rows of silver-gilled bass, bluefish and cod were drying out, I turned my head on him. Farther down, Jane playfully thumped the head of a tar-haired Indian boy wearing no more than a strip of leather over his fundament, and laughed when he dashed between our linked arms to join his father, a stone-faced Narragansett selling blankets.

As I led Jane toward Joshua's booth, I told her details about Goody Hammer I had not written in letters: how during a terrifying storm on the *Arbella*—when the timbers of our ship shuddered so loudly I feared we would break into a million pieces, when the ship rolled so wildly we couldn't tell up from down—Goody Hammer was the only one walking about. "She bent into our berth where the six of us were huddled, and she fixed her evil eye upon each of us in turn. 'T'night the Lord hears us naught,' she said. Then she reached into her pocket and pulled out chips that resembled black Communion wafers. 'Press these beneath your tongues, all of ya, 'Tis broomwort and chamomile for dizziness.' I accepted her herbs, but when Papa was not looking, I crumbled them in my pocket."

"Did you puke for lack of them?"

"Everyone puked. Her herbs made no difference."

"'Twas the same on our crossing. Nothing gave us relief, although John would say differently," she laughed, tapping her belly. I laughed with her.

"I meant to ask you, Mercy, does the crone have a dog?"

I told her about Elijah.

"The cur may be the hag's familiar," Jane said seriously.

"I have thought of it."

Jane slipped her arm around my waist. "You're not alone anymore, Mercy. I know her as you do, and if evil is at the bottom of her, the two of us will find it. I promise you."

"Whatever became of Rebecca Fowler whom you wrote about, who accused her mother-in-law of being a witch?"

We stopped walking. Jane looked around to make sure no one else was listening, then she whispered: "Our Rebecca did the most courageous thing imaginable . . . a deed I could not conceive myself doing even if all the angels of heaven were perched upon my shoulders urging me on. After a year of living in fear under the old woman's thumb and gathering evidence of her malfeasances, Rebecca took her evidence to the court."

"To court? She did?" I exclaimed.

"Aye. Then one day, after enough time passed and another neighbor had stepped forth, two inquisitors from the king's chamber of inquisitors descended upon their cottage and searched it for evidence. I know not for sure what they found, but some say it was burnt feathers and amulets. They shackled the old lady's wrists with rope, and shoved her into a cart bound for the gaol near the Barditch, where she languishes now in the foulest of cells awaiting inquisition. Every day she is visited by women who press her to name other witches in town . . . to clear them from our midst."

"What about Rebecca?"

"Not only is Rebecca free to manage her own household, but also she has the satisfaction of knowing she has helped remove an evildoer from town, and for this she surely will be assigned a higher throne in heaven."

"Rebecca is a brave woman."

"For this one act she is sure to rise straight to heaven when she dies, for those who snare a witch are instantly saved, you know."

"I know it."

"So that is the story of Rebecca Fowler," Jane said solemnly. "But that is England and this is America. There are no such opportunities here, I am sure."

My thoughts turned to Goody Hammer. *Perhaps there are.* But just then, Joshua called to us, "Mercy, Jane, over here!" He was ambling toward us, and behind him were Catherine and Papa, with Grace eating a sticky cinnamon bun trailing behind. And following them were Caleb, Noah, and Michael.

"Look who has come to welcome you," Joshua cheered, pointing to the procession of Goodhues behind him and waving them forward.

Jane ran toward Catherine with her arms wide open, and

the two women embraced. She squatted down and scooped Grace into her arms. "You don't remember me, poppet, but I am Aunt Jane." She planted kisses all over the child's sticky face. "You are a tasty morsel," she giggled. Little Grace's face tightened, and she looked to Catherine for reassurance.

Wrapped in the flurry of reunion, Jane turned her attention to the boys. "You are fifteen, is that correct?" she asked, embracing them as one and carrying on about how handsome Noah was and how much Michael resembled his father. She pumped Caleb's hand as the shy, pimply-faced boy fumbled, visibly abashed by the whirlwind of a woman who descended upon him. Finally she turned her attention to Papa, who had stepped to the side of the lane and was nervously fingering the brim of his hat. He was neither smiling nor frowning. His eyes bounced between Jane and me as if he was assessing how much Jane knew and how much I had revealed. When Jane ran to him with outstretched arms, his demeanor softened and he fell into easy conversation with her, inquiring about her trip, her new husband, the health of her parents.

I stepped back and removed myself from their circle. Catherine, sensing my discomfort, took my elbow and walked me a few steps away from the group. "You have been absent from us too long, dear Mercy. We miss your companionship. Grace misses you. Can't you see it in her eyes? I know you were busy preparing for Jane but now that she is here, that will change, will it not?"

"Aye, Catherine," I mumbled.

Catherine studied my face curiously. "Are you unwell? You're pale as a lily."

"I am quite well," I said, forcing a smile.

Until then, I felt in control of my dealings with Jane. But at the sight of Papa that changed. Had I some forewarning, I could have prepared what to say. I would have even given Papa a daughterly embrace to maintain my charade. Had Jane seen me freeze at the sight of him? Soon I realized I had nothing to fear. Jane was so engrossed in her own pleasures that she was oblivious to my behavior. As we strolled out of the marketplace and towards the meetinghouse, she wrapped her arm around my waist and jabbered about how fit Papa looked, how marriage seemed to agree with him, how all men are better off married, and how delightful Catherine is. By the time we reached the meetinghouse I had composed myself and was able to resume my role as Jane's guide to the sights and ways of Boston.

"The men laid the footings for this meetinghouse about six months before Reverend Cotton arrived," I heard myself say confidently. "The building is eighteen feet by thirty-six feet . . . in the summer it gets so hot inside we melt . . . in the winter it is so cold we can see frost on the walls . . . we can see our breath . . . can you imagine? Some people bring their dogs to warm their feet . . . but still it is better than meeting in the grove . . ."

We walked in step with each other, just as we had in Old Boston. I was beginning to feel more in command.

Rounding the corner of the meetinghouse, Jane espied the pillory pit and her tone changed. "There it is, hell on earth," she said.

"Aye. Perhaps we should save it for another day?"

"No, it's best that I know the worst of Boston, so I know what's facing me."

The pillory pit was empty, but the sight of it was nearly as foreboding as it would have been filled with sinners.

"It is the devil's stage," I said joylessly, remembering the raised platform in Old Boston, upon which performers swaggered about in gay costumes, their voices straining to be heard over flute and dulcimer. This stage was but a stage burrowed into the ground, a place of correction for sinners. I led Jane along the narrow footpath encircling it.

Four devices were inside the shallow pit: the pillory itself, where offenders stand on a stool with their neck and arms clamped into a scissor-like device; the stocks, a low-to-the-ground structure where sinners sit on the ground with their ankles shackled; a whipping post; and the cage, where sinners are held captive.

Jane pointed to the pillory. "How long is a person locked inside?"

"An hour, two hours, an afternoon, but never overnight because of wolves. The purpose is not to kill, but to humiliate and shame. They say we will have a gallows one day, and that will be for killing."

"That cage is gruesome!" Jane shrieked. "It's for animals, not man."

"They lock women in it too."

"I thought I'd seen the last of that in England."

"Those in power take discipline seriously here in Boston." I pointed to the grassy knoll surrounding the path around the pillory pit. "After the service, people gather to witness the punishments. Some bring blankets and their lunches. The cruel ones taunt the sinners. They throw rotten eggs, fruit, stones, and more."

"They might have arrested us for dancing last evening," Jane said grimly.

"They might have. Let's move on. I've seen enough."

"As have I."

Chapter Thirty

———— ❧ ————

John transformed the empty room behind their chimney into a well-appointed workshop, and before long, everyone in Boston knew he was open for business. It was impossible to miss the rectangular sign hanging perpendicular to his doorway, painted with green lettering: John A. Loring, Tailor. And it was impossible to attend the meetinghouse without hearing John's name mentioned, for he had become a broadside for his finery. To him, the meetinghouse was where he could exhibit the latest men's fashions, and where Jane could introduce the women to a variety of laces, bows, and embroidery from England.

Every Sabbath John was festooned in a new outfit he made himself. Sabbath last, he wore a doublet with three slashes, two more than the magistrates deemed acceptable, and beneath it a purple shirt that blazed through the three diamond-shaped cutouts in his doublet. Inside the meetinghouse, every eye was locked upon him. I watched people's lips count the number of slashes—one, two, three—nudge one another and point to him with their eyes. Yesterday he strutted into the meetinghouse wearing breeches tied beneath the knees with pointed ribbands, and leather boots with cambric tops—all of this with the assistance of a walking stick he needed for affectation only. When Jane bounced onto the bench beside me, I noticed she had stitched a two-inch border of golden lace onto the edge of her coif. When I pointed to it, she crossed her knee to reveal an identical band of lace on the hem of her gown.

That day Reverend Wilson preached on the sin of vanity. At first, I thought it a coincidence he selected that topic, but as it turned out, it was a theme well planned between him and Governor Dudley. After the sermon Governor Dudley rose to his full height, puffed out his barrel chest, and with heavy feet stomped onto the platform. He asked us to remain seated for two announcements. The first was that Reverend Wilson would be leaving once again for England in October to attend to family matters. Everyone knew he would be making another attempt to convince his uncooperative wife to come to America.

Then Governor Dudley focused his bulging eyes directly on Jane and John and announced that it was by an order of the General Court that an immediate ban would be in effect on all gold and silver laces, and on all embroidered caps, great veils and great sleeves with many slashes worn in a flaunting manner. Their faces reddened as the governor read the decree, for they felt his censure and the sting of every eye upon them. Although I thought of John as foppish, I knew his goodness and his love of Jane, and I was embarrassed at the public upbraiding they received. They would be wise not to violate the court order, for their next correction was sure to be more public and painful.

On the way home, John walked ahead of us with Joshua. He was sullen. But Jane carried on as if nothing had happened. She told me John had begun teaching her to sew for the wealthier women of Boston, who of course were much too modest to allow a man to measure their bodies.

"How will this ban on finery affect you?"

"Not at all," she laughed. "Even before Governor Dudley finished speaking I came upon a solution. What I cannot attach to the outside of a garment, I will sew on its inside. This shall make my garments mysterious and desirable, and the ladies will choose their braids and laces, and if they cannot flaunt them on the outside, I will conceal them on the inside of their hems. And without a word said, we will pass each other on the lane and know each others' secrets."

I marveled at Jane's rebellion, but doubted whether I would be brazen enough to participate as I already had enough troubles of my own. From the sly smile on her lips I knew the idea had piqued her imagination. When we met our husbands on the corner, Jane could not restrain herself. In a giddy whisper she told them her scheme, explaining with every embellishment she could conjure up. "Purple braid for Mary Coddington . . . seven inches of scarlet lace for Goody Hammer . . . Psalm 22 embroidered on Elizabeth Aspinwall's petticoat." For the first time that morning, I laughed—an intemperate laugh I could not contain. Our husbands looked at us as if we were crazed, but after checking and seeing no one else was watching us, they joined in. We swayed with humor, our faces flushed and tears streaming down our cheeks.

"Ours shall be the first thriving shop in Boston," John predicted. I knew he was speaking defensively, but I also knew that with his flair and Jane's determination their business would be a success.

JANE WAS TROUBLED when we met to walk to the meetinghouse the following Thursday. She was nervously tapping her hand on the quilt of beaver pelts hanging over her arm. When our husbands were sufficiently ahead of us— John, this time dressed in sad colors—she murmured, "Goody Hammer asked me to sew her a gown."

"She what?"

"This morning I opened the curtains and there she was sitting on the bench beneath our window waiting for me. She had a package on her lap."

"What did you do?"

"I opened the door, of course. It was cold and she was shivering."

"Did you bid her in?"

"Aye. We have a shop and we do allow our customers to enter," she said, annoyed.

"Tell me exactly what she said."

Jane took a deep breath. She pursed her lips the way Goody Hammer did and mimicked her voice. "'My sister Eloise wishes me to have a new gown,'" she said in a tone as low as her toes, "'and I wish ya to sew it for me.'"

Her imitation made me smile in spite of myself. "What did you say?"

"The truth. I told her I'm all thumbs and surely I'd ruin her cloth."

"And what did she say?"

"She said every apprentice needs practice."

"And what did you say?"

"That I'm busy stitching a cloak for Reverend Cotton, which is God's holy truth."

"What did she say?"

"She said if I have thumbs enough to sew for the saintliest man in town, I have thumbs enough to sew for her, and she would wait until I am able."

"Surely you're not going to do it?"

"She was persistent. I told her I would be finished with Reverend Cotton's cloak a week from the morrow, and she said she would be back then. That's next Friday!" She threw her hands up in exasperation. "Before I could think of an excuse, she handed me the cloth and was off."

"What will you do?"

"That's why I'm telling you, Mercy. You must advise me. You have more experience with her than I do."

John was holding the meetinghouse door open for us. Reverend Cotton was beside him clearing his throat. I released Jane's elbow and we hurried inside.

THE MEETINGHOUSE WALLS GLISTENED with a thin layer of frost. Jane spread the furry quilt over our laps and lifted a corner of it to cover her stomach. I elbowed Jane and gestured at Goody Hammer who was slouched on the bench in the first row with Elijah asleep on her feet. The dog's tail extended into the aisle and thumped on the floor like a heartbeat. Jane shook her head.

That afternoon Reverend Cotton exhorted on loving ones enemies. From the pulpit, his blue eyes swept over our faces as he quoted from the Gospel of Matthew: "'But I say unto you, Love thine enemies, bless them that curse you, do good to them that hate you, and pray for them which despitefully persecute you.'" Unlike the others who dutifully flipped through the pages of their Bibles to find the verse, I kept my Bible closed and stared into the air, half agreeing with our minister, half refuting his words. I pulled the quilt tighter around myself, and drifted deeper into thought. What if, like Rebecca Fowler, I could prove Goody Hammer is a witch? What if I could perform an act of such overwhelming importance to our community, the likes of which had never been seen in New England, then surely the Lord would take notice of me. Surely then there would be no question about my salvation. As Reverend Cotton exhorted, I lit upon a plan.

Later, heading up the High Street, I told Jane my idea. "When Goody Hammer arrives a week from the morrow, you will measure her."

Jane stopped walking. "I cannot touch her. There is danger for me in it. If she is a witch, I must keep my distance."

I knew she would argue with me, but I would have none of it. I was so convinced of the rightness of my plan that I could hardly get my words out fast enough.

"I've thought it through, Jane. If she is a witch, you are in greater danger if you refuse to measure her. She may put a curse on you. You have no choice."

Jane shook her head.

"You must pay her tribute so she does you no harm."

"I cannot . . ."

"All you must do is measure her. When you're finished, you will invite her to linger for a cup of tea into which I will have added an herb that shall make her sleep. In my possession I have such an herb. When she is asleep, you will be done with her and I shall step in. I will examine her body for the mark of the witch."

Jane looked at me as if I were mad.

"Are you not afraid, Mercy?"

"I am afraid, but the idea came to me while the sainted Reverend Cotton was speaking, so it must have merit."

"You would touch her body so?"

"I must. I've had my suspicions ever since Mama died. Now I must act." I told her about the henbane leaves I kept hidden in my keepsake box. "The hog's bean. She used it on me to make me sleep. Now I shall use it on her."

Finally, Jane relented. "I'll measure her. But then, you must take over and I shall have nothing more to do with it."

Jane realized there was one more obstacle. "What about John?"

I figured that out as well. "You must remind him that Goody Hammer is a modest woman who will be more comfortable in your presence alone. He will understand."

That Friday was crisp and sunny, hardly the kind of dark day one might choose to perform the mischief we were up to.

As it came to pass, Joshua had asked John to accompany him, Noah, and Michael to Spectacle Island to chop firewood for the winter. Supplies in Boston had been so exhausted by the incessant building of homes and we had to import firewood from the surrounding islands.

After Joshua left and I finished my chores, I set my mind on preparations. I opened my keepsake box, carefully lifted out the napkin full of dark-green leaves, and slipped the packet into my pocket.

"I thought they'd never leave," Jane fussed upon greeting me at the door. "Joshua and your brothers were also here. They each drank three cups of cider and ate all the pottage left from supper, and they got to telling stories and laughing. You'd have thought it was a celebration. Michael is so handsome, just like your father. If I were unmarried and younger, he's the one I'd have my eye on. And Noah, he is so tenderhearted. He speaks fondly of young Jenny. Don't you expect the two of them to marry when they're older?"

Jane was blathering on and on. I oft had the same thoughts about Noah and Jenny, but now was not the time for them. "We have work to do," I said, removing my cloak and tucking my gloves into my pocket. With fingers stiff from the cold I dug into my apron pocket and produced the packet of henbane.

It was almost midday and Jane kept peeking out the door to see if Goody Hammer was in sight. When she spotted her rounding the corner, she handed me my cloak and pushed me outdoors. I hid along the side of the cottage. After Goody Hammer entered, and when through the window I saw that the door to the tailor's room was shut—our signal—I quietly reentered the house. As I prepared my infusion, I listened to their muffled conversation.

"My cloth. It is linsey-woolsey, very costly. We must make good use of it."

"Aye, mum. Soft."

"Let me unfold it. You might snag it with those snips you're holding."

"Aye, mum. If you will step behind that curtain, mum, and remove your gown. You may keep your smock on."

"Ah, by all means."

I heard the curtain slide on its rod. A moment later Jane appeared in the kitchen.

"Are you ready?" she whispered.

"Aye," I replied, pointing to the tray on the table set with two cups and a plate of biscuits. "The tea is steeping. All I must do is pour it," I said, rubbing my hands together.

"Which cup is mine?"

"The blue one. It will be cider. Hers is the white one."

"Be still. Not a cough or a sound."

Jane returned to the tailor's room. In her haste she left the door ajar, just enough for me to peek in.

Goody Hammer's back was toward the door. She had removed her peaked hat and coif, and her hair—silver and dark strands—cascaded over her back and fell beyond her waist.

I cringed at the sight of her thick bare arms, the texture of chicken flesh, wrapped across her chest to conceal her ample bosom. Her unevenly cut smock touched the floor in places, and the hem was soiled from dragging on dirt roads. Her dingy stockings sagged in folds above bulky black shoes.

"We shall begin," Jane said. She knelt down and removed the cloth measuring tape from around her neck. For the sake of modesty, John had taught her to always begin measuring a woman at the bottom and work upward toward the bosom.

"From hem to waist," she called out, "thirty-five inches."

Jane's flint scratched on paper.

"Waist, forty inches . . . Waist to neck, eighteen . . . neck, thirteen . . ."

Jane's fingers trembled not at all, which I admired.

"Shoulder to wrist, twenty. Wrist eight . . ."

Finally, she said, "We are done."

Goody Hammer let out a deep sigh. "'Twas quite an ordeal. I am lightheaded . . . but I shall recover once I'm outdoors. She fanned her face with both hands. Jane offered her an arm to help her off the stool.

"Let us rest a moment, mum," Jane suggested.

"Aye, let us rest. N'er have I been fitted for a gown. Verily, I am nervous as a puss." She fluttered her hands as if she were stirring up a hornet's nest.

"You look pale. Sit and I shall fetch you a cup of tea."

"Jane, you are a capable helpmeet to your John, who would do well to follow your example." When I heard you took to sewing, I knew the Lord sent you hither for a purpose."

"Aye, mum, but as I said, I'm a handful of thumbs."

"Now, tell me about your husband. Is he a fussy man? He looks as if he might be that sort, and others say . . ."

"No, mum, my John is quite easy."

"Prideful, some say he is."

"He takes pleasure in color. That's all. And fine cloth."

"Then he is a vain man," she interrupted. "D'y' know what the Bible says about vanity? The prophet Zephaniah says the Lord shall remove the prideful from their city, and n'er again will they be haughty on His holy hill."

"Aye," Jane said coldly.

"From the look of you, your child should be coming mid spring?"

"April."

"Then I shall call on you as your time nears."

"Let me fetch the tea now."

When Jane entered the kitchen, her face was as red as a cooked beet. "Did you hear what she said about my John? She thinks she is going to be my midwife! I'd sooner have a barber or that insipid Joist Brown deliver my baby! Thank God Mistress Hutchinson is amongst us."

I handed her the tray.

"Not now. It takes time to pour tea and set a plate with biscuits," she said, fluttering her fingers in the air.

We stared at each other without speaking, and I knew we were both thinking the same thing. What if she didn't fall asleep? What if she recognized the taste of the henbane? I'd added enough honey to hide any bitterness, I was sure.

After sufficient time passed, Jane lifted the tray. The cups jiggled against each other and the deep golden liquid rocked inside them. "White for her. Blue for me," she mumbled.

"Aye, and don't spill it," I whispered.

Jane took a deep breath and backed out the door, and I remained behind listening.

"Aye, there's a refinement about you," cooed Goody Hammer. "And biscuits. Do you offer all your customers such a treat?"

Spoons clinked against china.

"'Tis a new brew," Jane said.

There were sipping sounds.

"Sweet."

"Tell me about your sister who gave you the cloth."

"Ah, yes, Eloise, a godly woman, a lover of true religion."

There was a pause long enough for them to sip their tea.

"She's remained in Loughborough where we were born, where our parents died in the plague, where she now labors in the cottage of Reverend Hempstead. She never married, a thornback, you'd call her," she said with a snicker. She blathered on about Ol' Mim who had the healing touch and gave her the gift of it. "Marigolds, dandelions and plants with yellows flowers cure the jaundice, and plants with heart-shaped petals cure heart problems, not love problems but heart problems. You only have to look as low as your ankles to find . . ."

"You appear tired, mum," Jane said slowly.

"I'm feeling..."

"Would you like more tea?"

"I . . . I . . . I must gather my things and be off." She was slurring and fumbling and trying to stand up. "I am unsteady."

"Rest here on the bench," Jane said. "Rest before you leave. It is quiet here and no one will interfere with you," she said reassuringly.

I cracked the door and peeked in. Jane had her arm around Goody Hammer and was helping her swing her corpulent body around to recline on the bench. She helped her lift her thick legs up so they were centered with her shoes pointing toward the rafters. She tucked Goody Hammer's bundle of cloth beneath her head for a pillow, then folded her arms on top of the fleshy mound of her chest, but abruptly both of her arms slid down and her fingers, thick as sausages, dangled above the floor.

Jane gasped.

Goody Hammer's breathing gradually slowed. Jane lowered herself to the bench beside the old woman's feet. Once she was soundly asleep, I stepped in.

The henbane did its job. Never had I seen Goody Hammer in such repose. Even when she sat napping in Mama's rocking chair the days she nursed me, part of her was always on guard, her foot on the floor ready to leap to a need. Now she was as close to dead as a living person could be. Her cheeks looked like pillows punched in. Her breasts drooped on either side of her chest like mounds of bread dough.

I placed my hand on my collar and felt my heart racing. "I will do the rest now, and you will leave."

Jane glanced at the door and hesitated.

"Be off now . . . 'Tis best," I said, shooing her away.

Her blue eyes locked into mine. "How can I leave you? I said I would, but I've changed my mind. I shan't let you do it alone."

Arguing with Jane was futile, so I nodded assent.

I untied the ribband on one of the Goody Hammer's shoes; Jane untied the other. I pulled one shoe off gently; Jane removed the other, but nervously dropped it on the floor. I arched my eyebrows in annoyance, but Goody Hammer did not flinch and together we pulled off her threadbare stockings.

Jane lifted one leg and examined its underside. "Nothing," she said.

I did the same with the other. "Nothing."

Suddenly, Goody Hammer snorted a hollow snort that erupted behind her nose. We jumped. Then she raised an arm over her chest and attempted to roll over.

"Catch her!" Jane cried, flapping her hands in the air. "She's falling toward you!"

I caught her weight and hoisted her back onto the bench. After the scare of it, I paused. "We must pray," I said.

"Mercy, are you mad? This is no time to pray. We must finish." With two fingers Jane pinched the edge of her smock at the hemline and signaled me to do the same on the opposite side. Together we lifted the thin cloth until it loomed above our heads like a tent. In the dim and airless cavern underneath, we could see her bare body up to her neck. "Nothing," Jane said, dropping her side of the cloth. There was no evidence upon her of a third teat on her chest, a sure sign of a witch.

"We must check her fundament," I said. Never had I seen the private parts of another woman, but I knew I must inspect those most intimate parts on Goody Hammer. Gently, I separated the sticky skin of her thighs. Between her legs, on her left thigh was a mark, a red and knobby mark with a shape to it. "Look here," I whispered to Jane. My eyelids pulsed like heartbeats. It was definitely there.

Jane peered under the gown. "I see it. It is small with red bumps in the shape of a claw."

"A claw?" I said, my voice trembling.

"That is what I see."

"Give me a pin, Jane."

"No, Mercy, you can't do that."

"Give it to me."

Nervously, Jane picked a pin up off the floor and handed it to me.

I pricked the mark. Nothing happened. The crone did not a flinch or murmur or groan or shriek to show she felt pain. Nothing. Not even a drop of blood.

I had my proof. Goody Hammer was a witch. She had been able to keep her secret because she was a midwife. She examined everyone else's body, but no one ever examined hers.

"Who will you tell first?" Jane whispered.

"John Winthrop," I said, remembering the books in his library on witchcraft. I took a final look at the witch's mark and tried to memorize its shape and hue.

"I shall stand before him, and I shall be brave but not proud, and I shall quote Exodus: 'Thou shall not suffer a witch to live!' Then I shall calmly speak my evidence. I shall . . ."

"Mercy," Jane said, snapping her fingers in my face. "This is no time for Scripture. I'll wash the cups and you tidy her up."

I sat alone on the bench beside Goody Hammer. The sun streamed in through the window. Reflecting off the snow, it was blindingly white. A comforting sense of victory settled over me as I listened to the rhythm of the witch's breathing and watched her chest rise and fall. I felt the blissful tranquility the Lord affords to those who have been mightily tested and delivered.

The rest would be easy. I pulled up Goody Hammer's stockings. I slipped her shoes on her feet. I felt as if an invisible shield of protection had fallen upon me that enabled me to touch the witch without harming myself.

I had been blessed and I needed to give thanks. When I was a child, Mama would say, "Pray aloud, for the Lord will hear you twice. He will hear your words, and He will know your mind." So I prayed in a full and clear voice. "Oh, Lord, give me the strength of King Josiah who destroyed all the mediums and spiritists and cleaned his household of evil." I repeated my prayer louder. I would pray it forty times. Surely then the Lord would hear me, and the light of a million suns would enfold me.

In the recesses of my mind I heard a knocking, and I felt the walls shaking about me, which at first I took to be the work of Satan trying to thwart me. But I feared not because I knew that not a legion of devils could harm me now. I continued praying. "Give me the strength . . ." I was concentrating so deeply on my prayers that I would not have flinched even if Lucifer and his minions were flapping like bats above my head.

Just then, Jane ran into the room. "Your papa is pounding on the door."

I PEEKED THROUGH A CRACK in the shutters and saw him. "Mercy, come!" he commanded.

"My God!" I cried, hurrying into the kitchen.

"Lift the latch and see what he wants," Jane said.

I would do no such thing. Witches had the power to summon their cohorts, and in her sleep, surely Goody Hammer's spirit had traveled to Papa and now he was seeking revenge. Satan is a crafty creature and surely it was the Satan within Papa pounding.

"Mercy, let him in!" Jane's voice rose.

The pounding grew louder. Papa was wailing. "There's been an accident, Mercy! The shallop capsized! You must come!"

Jane shoved me aside. "It could be John or Joshua," she pleaded, yanking the door open.

Papa keeled forward and would have fallen into Jane's arms had he not grabbed the doorframe to steady himself. His cheeks were streaked with mud. His breeches were drenched and hung from his body like wet sacks. "We took the skiff out . . . too far . . . it capsized."

I pushed myself forward. "No," I screamed in his face. "Not Joshua."

"Who was in the accident? Was it John?" Jane begged.

Papa looked at Jane soulfully. "John lives." Then his eyes settled on me. "'Tis your brothers," he sobbed. "My sons . . . I was there . . . I tried . . . the current pulled them away. Joshua got caught in it, but John swam out and saved him. John swam out again, but it was too late . . . Michael and Noah, they are gone."

I gasped.

"Joshua and John are searching. They refuse to stop." He trembled and clung to me as if I were his tether to life.

"They cannot be gone," I pulled away and screamed, "You must find them!"

He stared at me helplessly.

"FIND THEM!" I grabbed him by the shoulders and shook him.

He did not react.

"Then I'll do it," I cried, pushing him aside. I ran into the snow. On the High Street, bystanders turned and gawked at me. At the sea I flew down the embankment, over rocks and frozen marsh rush, not feeling the mud seeping into my shoes or the cold. I expected to see a commotion at the shore, but everything there was eerily silent, except for the pounding of the waves on the beach and the cracking of ice shards one upon another. In the black waters outside the harbor, in a skiff that bounced wildly in the churning sea, I could see Joshua's red cap and John's blue one.

Papa was running behind me. At the surf he put his arm around me and, out-of-breath, panted, "Now we can do naught but pray."

I broke away and looked at the dirty muddled skin covering the sharp bones of his face, his hollow brown eyes. I took measure of the man he had become. The man who could have been at his wife's side the day she died, but was not; the man who should have kept his lusts from me, but did not; the man who now spoke of prayer, but was unworthy of it.

"You were with them yet you did naught," I screamed. "You are a seaman, yet you allowed the sea to snatch your sons."

"Mercy, you were not there to see the horror of it." The words trembled from his lips.

I was not listening. All I knew was that I had lost my brothers. The Lord's wrath is great and He was not done punishing me yet.

When darkness turned the ocean as black as ink and they could no longer continue their search, the men plaintively rowed back to shore. Exhausted and nearly frozen, they staggered onto the beach. I ran into the choppy waves to meet my husband. "I'm sorry, I'm sorry," Joshua kept repeating. I clung to him as if he were my life. Catherine, who ran down to the beach several times to bring us blankets and hot cider, descended again, this time to insist we follow her home.

I HAVE ONLY DREAMLIKE RECOLLECTIONS of that evening. Brooding faces hovering above Catherine's kitchen table, a sober Reverend Cotton mouthing words of consolation that meant nothing to me, the muffled weeping of Jenny and her brothers from the garret above, raps upon the door and piercing wails from friends who heard the news, Papa sitting with his back toward me, keening, his eyes fixed on the fire snapping like demons in the hearth.

Upon returning home with Joshua, I gave no thought to Goody Hammer. It was only in my dreams that I saw her standing alone on the deck of a ship staring into still black waters.

THE BODIES OF MICHAEL AND NOAH were lost at sea. I imagined them floating to places where life had never taken them. Perchance adventurous waters carried Michael to the

West Indies where he had dreamed of traveling. Perchance gentler waters washed over Noah like a satin coverlet, stroking his forehead, tousling his golden hair. Noah would never marry Jenny, but I knew she was his heart's desire.

So little evidence remained of them in Boston. They left behind their clothes, shillings in their pockets, chisels, hammers, and their fishing boat. But even those possessions would soon be assumed by others who had need of them. A stone falls into a pool creating ripples that become larger ripples. A life ends and there is memory, but even memory is a thief. What was the shape of Noah's eyes? I did not remember. Did Michael's lips curve upward when he smiled? Did his laughter rise up from the depths of his belly or the crook in his throat? I thought I knew these things, but I did not. I hadn't paid enough attention the hundreds of times we sat across from each other at the supper table, nor had I studied their features sufficiently when they recited Scripture and I had endless time to observe them.

Although there were no bodies to bury, I insisted that Papa pound granite slabs into the graveyard to mark their existence alongside Mama's grave.

Chapter Thirty-One

1635

In January of 1635 an enormous snowfall shut down Boston. It was as if a flannel blanket had fallen over us, covering the cowpats, transforming the bushes and fences and dwellings into a single, swelling mound of white. Trimountain was sheathed in snow, except for a few barren oak trees, their gnarly branches rooting out of the hillside like witches' fingers reaching out of snowcapped graves. Were it not for the flame of a taper in the cottage across the lane and the forked footprints of a wolf outside our gate, I would have believed all of Boston had disappeared.

It was during this ceaseless downpour of white, when we were confined to our homes, that Joshua found Ezekiel dead in the cooperage.

I had been shaving a cone of sugar into a glass bowl, watching the sparkling grains cover a hairline crack in the bottom of the bowl, wondering whether the Lord was controlling the placement of each grain of snow upon Boston as I was the sugar in my bowl. I nearly dropped the scraper at the sound of Joshua's soul-piercing cry.

I ran to the cooperage. He was bent over his father's cot

trying against the resistance of the old man's dead weight to raise him up by the shoulders. Ezekiel's head fell back and he caught it, cradling it in the palm of his hand as he would an infant's.

I fell to my knees beside them. Ezekiel's thin lips, already colorless, were parted ever so slightly as if he were preparing to speak. As I stared into his vacuous eyes, I prayed the Lord would judge him kindly and listen to the gentle song that was his life.

"The Lord is not done punishing me," is all I could say.

THAT AFTERNOON, AS SNOW PUMMELED our windows and darkness pressed in on us, Joshua and I washed Ezekiel's body and dressed him in his grave clothes—the clean gray breeches and shirt he had worn to his own wedding thirty years ago. He had told Joshua he wished to be buried in them because he wanted his wife, Clarissa, to recognize him in heaven.

"He died peacefully," my husband said after a long silence. Joshua was right. For some, the journey from this world is prolonged with shouts of regret and pleas for mercy, and for others it comes in the terror of an accident. For Ezekiel, his passage was as peaceful as a child's dream on a snowy winter night.

As I listened to Joshua pound slabs of oak together for a coffin, I recalled first meeting Ezekiel upon the *Arbella*. It was our first evening aboard ship, and after we had finished our meal a group of us remained at the table to become acquainted. In the midst of our conversation, Anne Bradstreet looked across the table at Ezekiel. "Goodman Hoyt, I hear you are a gifted singer," she chirped in a voice as smooth as buttermilk. "Perchance in the course of our voyage, you might entertain us with a hymn?"

Ezekiel smiled at her through his ample white beard. His blue eyes glowed joyfully in the amber candlelight that made all our faces glow. "The next time I shall sing alone, my dear, will be at my son's wedding." That was when Joshua and I first made eye contact.

Ezekiel did sing at our wedding, but it was not the hymn everyone expected, but a lively ballad. I know not where he learned it. I remember just a few lines.

> *He took her by the lily-white hand*
> *And begged her company;*
> *He took her by her apron band,*
> *Says, "Follow, follow me."*

That night of our wedding, Ezekiel sang with a twinkle in his eye, his gaze moving from Joshua, to me, and back to Joshua, of whom he was so proud. The windows were open and all of Boston was privy to Ezekiel's rich tones. Indoors, amidst the candlelight, amongst family and ministers and magistrates of much higher position than we, there were tears and smiles between the couples in the room—Governor Winthrop and his Margaret, William Coddington and his Mary, Papa and Catherine, and me and Joshua. Ezekiel's song had united us in the loving way Governor Winthrop had spoken of on the *Arbella*.

In the flickering candlelight Joshua and I lowered Ezekiel's body into his coffin. Joshua kissed his forehead and stroked his snowy beard; I patted the wrinkled flesh of his entwined fingers and bid goodbye to the deep voice we would ne'er hear again. Afterwards, I watched my husband pound iron nails into the hard oak lid. Joshua's cheeks were damp and the skin around his eyes was puckered, as if the agony that was too painful to bear inside was finding its exit through his eyes.

IN THE WEEKS THAT FOLLOWED, I became as silent as if the cloak of repose that had settled over Ezekiel during the last year of his life had fallen over me. Noah and Michael's deaths and now Ezekiel's had made me imagine my own, and for hours I sat motionless in Mama's rocking chair pondering mysteries I could not understand. I could die in childbirth. I could be plucked into eternity as I walked down the lane. Or, like Ezekiel, I could die old and used up in my bed. We are droplets of water sliding off leaves. Some slide quickly, others get tangled in a vein and settle in the narrowest of crevices. But the end is always the same. Leaves dry and crumble into dust, and in the end we stand before God to be judged.

Just weeks ago, I had renewed hope of redemption. Forgiveness was within reach, but now it had been snatched away. What a fool I was to think I could force God's mercy by outing a witch. The Lord had taken notice of me. He took away three people I loved, and in so doing told me I had not been forgiven, that I was unworthy of His love.

As the days passed, I felt the tepid waters of life drain from me. I ate even less food, uttered fewer words, walked fewer steps, inhaled fewer breaths. My fingers were all that moved. I became so troubled that I picked at the skin around my cuticles until they bled. Joshua gently admonished me to stop, which I would do for a moment, but then I would pick again, as if I were trying to destroy the body that life had so befouled.

I knew Joshua had need of me, that his pain was as great as my own, that his heart had also been shattered. He went about his life with forbearance—he was a man not to succumb—but his spirit was dulled and his energy depleted by the absence of his father. Only half his heart seemed to beat in the days after his father's death. His eyes begged me for tenderness. I knew I should have reached out to him. I know I should have listened to him speak of his own hurt, to hold him in my arms, but I had nothing to give. I sat motionless in Mama's rocking chair for hours. I told myself to be of courage. I tried to lift myself from my chair to approach him tenderly, but I could not. I was as good as dead. Surrendering to my melancholy, I allowed myself to float farther away from the hands of Joshua, who at first reached out to me, but then began to pull away.

AGAINST JOHN'S COUNSEL, Jane, who had no business venturing out on icy lanes in her pregnant state, called upon me daily. At midmorning I would hear the crunch of her shoes upon the crusted snow and then two hasty raps on the door. No matter how unresponsive I remained, Jane continued to call.

Joshua was grateful. His shoulders relaxed the moment Jane appeared in the doorway. Her presence meant his burden of watching me would be lifted for an hour, during which time he could work in the cooperage without worrying about the harm I might do to myself.

Joshua endeavored to cheer me as best he could. At first he begged me to resume my care of the house, and if I was not ready for that, at least to open my heart to him and speak of my pain.

"Where is it you go in your head, Goodwife? If I know, perchance I could go there too and take you by the hand and pull you out." But I could not respond. When he spoke of his love of me, I found his declarations shallow. If you love me, you should know how to heal me.

Over meals, Joshua seemed unsure of what to say. So he

had taken to studying my countenance, which proved more intrusive than talk. What did he see in me? Perhaps he was imagining the cheerful girl he might have chosen for his wife, and the children he should have had by now. As much as I longed to be that wife, I could not find a way out of the murky waters that drew me down.

While Joshua grew silent in my presence, Jane did not. From the moment she crossed our threshold, she chattered. Sometimes she spoke as tenderly as if she were soothing an infant. Sometimes she scolded me as if I were an adolescent. In desperation, she tried to coax me with food. Every day her offerings became more aromatic and abundant: Apple pudding, a generous hunk of pungent cheese, a pot of venison stew and boiled beans seasoned with sage, a loaf of warm bread. The sight of her offerings made me want to puke. Joshua barely touched the food either, which was a marked change for him. Through all her talk, I sat as stiffly as a woman sitting for a portrait. But I was listening. I listened to every word she said, and in my mind I created elaborate rebuttals.

When Joshua was beyond earshot, Jane would tell me things she would not say in his presence. The first time we were alone after my brothers' deaths, she told me what had happened to Goody Hammer that afternoon.

"I remained with her until she recovered," she said, staring at me helplessly. Jane's hand was in her pocket and she was fumbling with something inside. The movement of her hand stretched the green woolen cloth across her middle and accentuated the bulge of her stomach, now large as a melon.

I said nothing.

"I could not have left her unattended," she added defensively.

Still, I did not respond.

"What else could I have done?" She yanked her hand out of her pocket and spread her palm out flat, as if offering me a hand heaped with explanation. "When Goody Hammer awoke, she was confused and unsteady on her feet, and it was dark and the lane was slick. Surely she would have fallen, and I could not be responsible for that. So I helped her home."

Part of me thought how brave Jane had been, navigating the pitch-black lanes of Boston carrying a baby in her belly while supporting a witch at her side. Jane instantly accepted her responsibility, venturing into the frozen dark of Boston as cavalierly as she had, just months ago, conceived her child upon tempestuous seas. But I thought her a fool. She could have neglected the witch, allowed her to crack her bones on the ice, or she could have even given her a push along the way.

"I have something to show you," Jane said, reaching into her pocket again. She pulled out the object she had been fingering, a black velvet pouch tied with a drawstring. "Her amulets. I found them on the floor behind the curtain where she changed her clothes."

Recoiling, I pressed my back into the chair. Jane had had those amulets within her possession for more than a month. They were beset with danger. With every bounce of her step, every sway of her hips, she allowed them to rub against her stomach, to release their evil powers upon her. Jane was as aware as I was of monster births, babies born with deformed lips and withered legs, or worse—infants born wild with the voice of Satan shrieking from their lungs.

"Pray, what were you thinking?" I cried.

Jane jumped in her chair, surprised by the sound of my voice. "I'm thinking I want to be rid of these things," she answered.

With determined fingers, she spread the drawstring and

dumped the amulets on the table betwixt us. An almond-shaped eagle stone tumbled out first—perchance the same one Goody Hammer had given Mama. A sharp yellow wolf's tooth followed. Then a golden bullet, a thistle, a hunk of matted hair, and a corked vial of cloudy yellow liquid, probably urine.

"Begone with them!" I cried, sweeping them to the floor with the back of my hand. "I want no part of them. And pray, are you mad? You carried them with you . . . near your belly where your child grows?"

Jane's face tensed and I knew I had gotten to her.

"The Lord protects my child, I know it. All the charms in the world aren't powerful enough to change the life God has created within me," she said, tapping her stomach. "But I don't want them. We must destroy them."

I stared at the amulets strewn about the floor. I wanted nothing to do with them, yet I wanted everything to do with them. My mind was here, my mind was there—batting from wall to wall like a fly in a closet, settling on nothing. Another change of heart overcame me. "We must keep them. We must hide them."

"You're the one who is mad! What we must do is put an end to this madness."

"If we destroy our evidence, we'll be allowing a witch to go free!"

"Then you do it. I wish no part of it."

"I thought you were of the same mind as I!"

Jane took a deep breath. "I've changed my mind," she said calmly. When I walked with Goody Hammer that night and saw her confused and disheveled, something changed inside of me. I could not harm her then, and I cannot harm her now. I will not be a party to it."

"Then I shall do it without you. I shall do it myself."

Jane leaned across the table and fixed me with a stare. She spoke slowly, without meanness or accusation, and she tapped her finger on the table to mark her points. "If you accuse Goody Hammer, no one will believe you. You've been ill. Everyone knows that. You've been distracted. You are not thinking clearly. No minister or magistrate would credit your claim regardless of the evidence you present. If I were to do it—which I am not about to—they would give me no credit either because being pregnant is as good as being distracted. They'd deem us both crazy."

"I'll keep them nevertheless," I said firmly.

"Then so be it," Jane said, shaking her head in frustration.

We broke eye contact and shifted our stares to the amulets scattered on the floor like an ill humour between us.

That evening when Joshua was busy with his accounts, I excused myself to go outdoors. On the way I grabbed a trowel from the cooperage. Out back, I dug as deeply into the frozen earth as I could and buried the bag of amulets beneath the rock that held down the handle of the wellsweep.

Chapter Thirty-Two

As much as I pleaded to be left alone, Jane would not release me from the promise I had made to attend to her at the birth of her child. In my despair, my desire to abandon my friend was greater than my loyalty to her, but I had no choice but to assist her. On the April morning that her travails began, John raced up our path to fetch me.

Before I could object, Joshua pulled me out of Mama's chair, wrapped my cloak around my back and pushed me out the door. "Do her the service she deserves," he said sharply.

John ran ahead giving no mind to the ice underfoot. At the corner he spun around and called out that he would race ahead to fetch Anne Hutchinson and Catherine, and that I should hurry to Jane. But once John was out of sight, I slowed my pace. Another child would be born in Boston. Another saint, perchance a woman. What a misfortune it is to bring a woman into this unforgiving world.

Jane's house was still when I entered, which seemed unusual. I expected to hear groaning and screaming. She was propped up in her bed, covered from toes to chin with a white coverlet, except for her arms that rested demurely outside the covers on either side of her expansive womb. Her white hands dangled gracefully from the lacy long sleeves of her ivory flannel smock, a new smock she had stitched for the occasion.

"Ah, you've come. I'm so relieved, Mercy. I was beginning to fear no one would arrive in time and I'd be left to handle things myself. You know the bungle I would make of that," she smiled weakly.

"I'm here," I said.

"Now I have no worries." Jane closed her eyes and sank deeper into her mattress.

I looked around the room. Everything was in its place. Cups and trenchers from breakfast had been washed and stored on the shelf. The table had been cleared of any trace of clutter. A pitcher of water and a cup sat on the smaller table beside her bed. Two cedar logs snapped in the fireplace and imparted a sweet aroma. "Do you have pains?" I inquired.

"One just before you arrived. They are becoming more frequent. That is when I started to worry you were not coming."

"I'm here."

"Hold my hand . . . another," she gasped. Her hand was as small as a child's inside mine. I squeezed it and felt the fan of her frail bones. Jane held her breath and exhaled. "Mistress Hutchinson should arrive shortly. She'll know what to do."

Just then the door opened and a blast of cold air carried Mistress Hutchinson inside.

Anne Hutchinson's eyes found Jane. "Ah, you're comfortable, I see." Her voice had the clarity of a bell pealing in the air, and her calmness was reassuring. She set an overstuffed bag on the table. She glided over to Jane and pressed her cheek to Jane's forehead.

"You are warm, my daughter."

"And you are cold," Jane managed to tease back.

Jane told her about the duration of her pains and Mistress Hutchinson nodded. "'Tis as it should be." Then she shifted her attention to me.

"You are Mercy Hoyt," she said, smiling kindly. "I've heard of you from Jane."

I felt myself blush. I was sure Jane had told her about the deaths of my brothers, about my melancholy, and probably much more. "I'm pleased to meet you," I said, extending my hand.

I had observed Anne Hutchinson in the meetinghouse and at the marketplace, but we had not yet spoken. She was a sparrow of a woman, and I found myself looking down at her. She had a thin, prominent nose and penetrating eyes, black as peppercorns. But they were not cold like Governor Winthrop's or judgmental like Thomas Dudley's. I felt them light upon me and melt.

She took my hand and squeezed it. "We'll have a chance to become acquainted today. Waiting is a large part of attending a birth."

"Is there anything I should do now?" I asked.

"Is this your first birth?"

"My second, counting the stillbirth of my sister when my mother died." Instantly I regretted my words, especially with Jane overhearing.

"God willing, today we'll have a different outcome," she said. "Aye, there is something you can do." She reached into her bulging bag and from a side pocket pulled out a stained piece of paper. "Here is a recipe for a wine cordial. Jane has the ingredients on her shelf—sugar, cloves and nutmeg, and here is the wine," she said, handing me a heavy jug. "Make a pitcher full, and set it there." She pointed to the small table beside Jane's bed.

While I worked, Mistress Hutchinson gripped Jane's elbow and helped her stand. Then she walked her around the room. Jane had hemmed her smock with an edging of white lace that trailed on the floor behind her.

"Walking is the best medicine for you now," she told her tenderly. "Walking and praying. As we walk I shall remind you of what Jesus said to his disciples about childbirth. He said a woman has pain because her time has come, but after her baby is born she forgets the pain because of the supreme joy that follows, that is unlike any she has ever experienced."

"I cannot believe it now," Jane said, bending forward to accept another contraction. She held the weight of her belly in both of her hands and grimaced.

"With the grace of God, it shall be so, my daughter." She rubbed Jane's forearm. "These are the grinding pains, so breathe deeply and they shall pass. They prepare you for the forcing pains. After the baby arrives, you shall feel the grumbling pains . . . when you grumble to everyone who will listen about your discomfort," her voice carried a chuckle. She was speaking to Jane, but every once in a while she glanced at me. When Jane winced and Mistress Hutchinson saw me wince along with her, she bid me to join them, and she wrapped her free arm around my waist and drew me close. She was the mother Jane and I had both lost, and she was offering her strength to us. "You young ones have the future ahead of you," she said, caressing us.

"It is not the future I fear, just the next few hours," Jane moaned.

"We can tell it is her first, can we not?" Mistress Hutchinson whispered to me, as if in confidence. She released me. "When you finish the wine cordial, my daughter, look inside my bag for an hourglass."

I was reluctant to leave her embrace, but I did as she instructed.

"Mercy, you will time Jane's travail," she said, instructing me to set the hourglass on the table, watch it carefully and mark each hour. She reached into her apron pocket and handed me a flint and a scrap of paper wrapped in twine. "As we wait, you will remind Jane of joyous memories, and when a pain seizes her, be silent then and think only pleasant thoughts so they might become hers."

I took a deep breath to prepare.

Jane looked as frightened as a deer facing the barrel of a musket. "Will you remain with me throughout?" she asked Mistress Hutchinson.

"Throughout," she answered.

Just then Catherine rapped on the door and rushed in. "Has the baby come yet?"

Jane stepped forward and held her protracted belly out for Catherine to see. She attempted a laugh but a contraction gripped her, causing her to double up.

"Aaaah," she cried.

"I see it's time to get you settled on the floor," Catherine said.

Mistress Hutchinson and I supported Jane by the elbows and guided her to the spot Catherine was preparing for her beneath the window, where the light was good. Catherine laid several soft quilts down and covered them with an old sheet Mistress Hutchinson handed her. The sheet had been washed many times, but no amount of scrubbing could have removed the purple blot—blood from a previous birth or death—that rested like a storm cloud on its middle. Catherine yanked up her own skirt and sat on the quilt with her back against the wall. Just as another pain came, I helped Jane position herself between Catherine's legs so that Jane's back rested against the pillow of Catherine's bosom. The window was open, and the corners of Jane's sheer blue curtains fluttered in the breeze. A wedge of sunshine cast a golden glow over the bodice of her white smock and pale arms. It shone through the lace trim on her sleeves and created an intricate pattern of squiggles and ovals upon her hands. Mistress Hutchinson closed the window so Jane would not get a chill and closed the curtains, which made the lace patterns dance and disappear. When the pain subsided, I straightened Jane's smock to cover her knees.

"Let there be no need for modesty amongst us," Catherine chortled. "By the time my Jenny came, I didn't care whether I was naked as a whale in front of my women."

"Nor did I," Mistress Hutchinson said. "All I cared about was putting an end to the misery and putting a cup of wine to my lips."

I was shocked to hear such talk from two godly women. Seeming to read my mind, Mistress Hutchinson set her gaze upon me and said, "There are many sides to a woman, my daughter, and you have just seen sides of me only my sisters and women friends would understand." I felt honored to be included in this select group.

Throughout the afternoon, Mistress Hutchinson did not take her eyes off Jane for long. She made it a point to touch her in some manner whenever she felt Jane required it. She brushed her perspiration-soaked hair with a cloth, stroked her arm, lifted her smock and gently brushed her belly with oil of almond and cloves, which made the stretched skin on Jane's stomach shine like an oiled turkey on a spit.

When Jane was gripped by a contraction, she held her hand and braced her for the duration of the pain. "Cry out if you must. Let the heavens hear your screams!"

And cry out Jane did. She let out screams all of Boston

could hear.

Mistress Hutchinson remained calm. To distract her, she told the story of a young woman in Alford who was giving birth to her first child. The woman's husband was so concerned with his wife's safety and so distraught when he heard her screams that he refused to wait in the tavern, but instead sat in a chair outside the front door listening to her every cry and sobbing so loudly he became a nuisance. "Finally, we could abide him no longer and we chased him away with brooms!" she said. "Only then was the woman able to push the baby out."

"That is not my John," Jane tried to laugh with tears rolling down her cheeks. "He's content to wait at the inn."

After I'd flipped the hourglass three times, Mistress Hutchinson bent over to her and whispered. "Your travail grows smart now, as it should."

By nightfall the agony was almost too much for Jane to bear. Her sweaty hair created a dark band across Catherine's bosom and in the dim shadows her face was contorted in a lizard-like expression. In Jane's face I saw Mama. In her anguish I heard Mama's cries. And suddenly Goody Hammer was in the room, crouched beside Jane, setting her amulets in a circle around her stomach, chanting her sorcerer's chant in a tone as low as hell: *Vidi aquam egredientem de templo . . . et omnes, ad quos pervenit aqua ista salvi facti sunt, et dicent.* The harshness of the words, seductive and eerie, resounded in my head—a pulsing, piercing voice that rose above Jane's cries and Mistress Hutchinson's words of comfort.

Vidi aquam egredientem . . .

"No!" I cried.

Mistress Hutchinson studied me curiously from across Jane's enormous belly. "All is well, Mercy," she said, trying to calm me.

I found her dark, reassuring eyes. Goody Hammer is not here, I told myself.

Jane's smock was up around her chin. The skin of her belly, slick with oil, was stretched tighter than I could ever imagine skin stretching. Beneath it the creature inside her was moving—I could see it. I thought of monster births. What creature was twisting inside of her? Those amulets Jane had kept close to her belly. What harm had they caused? *Keep the child safe,* I prayed. *Let the Lord's power be greater than the witch's.* Forty times I must repeat it. I kept count on my fingers. *Let the Lord's power be greater than the witch's. Let the Lord's power be greater . . .*

Mistress Hutchinson scooted over to Jane's splayed knees. "Let me have another look."

"Please, please, God, let this be over," Jane moaned.

I kept praying, knowing that Mistress Hutchinson's next words would reveal the Lord's decision. *Let the Lord's power be greater than the witch's . . .*

Finally, Mistress Hutchinson looked up. "All is as it should be," she said with composure. "Ready yourself now to push."

Jane took a deep breath and gripped my hand and pressed herself back into Catherine's bosom. "Aaaah!" she howled.

"Again."

"Aaaah!" she yowled, gritting her teeth.

"Keep pushing! Again!"

I kept praying. *Let the Lord's power be greater than the witch's.* I kept count on my fingers. Twenty-five. Thirty. Forty.

"It's coming now," Mistress Hutchinson said calmly. There was blood up to her elbows.

"A boy?" Jane gasped.

"In a moment, my daughter. I've not come to that end yet."

Catherine chuckled. Even Jane smiled weakly.

"Good . . . Wait . . . Relax," Mistress Hutchinson said. "And now, once again, push as hard as you can. It is almost over."

"Owww!" she screamed.

Mistress Hutchinson's face took on a radiance I had never seen before, not even on a minister. She had the look of one who has seen God.

"The Lord has been good," she said finally. "He has pleased you with a fine daughter. She is as fair as an English rose." She held the baby—sealed in mucus and bloody liquid—upside down by her feet, and the infant let out a piercing cry.

"Thanks be to God," I said, feeling the tension drain from my body.

Mistress Hutchinson laid the wiggling baby on Jane's belly and covered it with a clean cloth. As she cut the umbilical cord with snips, the tension in the room turned into gaiety.

"You mustn't cut too long, lest the girl become immodest," Catherine teased. Tears streamed down her cheeks into Jane's hair.

"My daughter," Jane said, trembling. She tried to sit up but slipped back into Catherine's bosom. Jane could not keep her eyes off her baby. She slid her baby finger into the infant's palm. "She squeezed my finger," Jane giggled in astonishment. "My strong daughter. God's miracle." In another breath she said, "I think I shall call you my Miracle."

"What a fine name," Mistress Hutchinson said.

Then Jane handed the baby to me.

"I cannot," I said.

"Aye, you can. You are her godmother and next to me, you'll love her the most."

Reluctantly I accepted the warm bundle and after a few moments it felt natural in my arms. I smiled at Miracle's shriveled face and gently stroked her feathery hair. I cautioned myself not to get too attached to the baby, as it was possible that this child like many others would not live a year, a month, or even a week. Miracle whimpered and I returned her to Jane, giving her up as reluctantly as I accepted her.

I remained with Jane throughout the night. Unlike any birth I heard of, this one was a celebration. There was laughter and there were stories and after Jane was clean and settled in her bed with Miracle at her breast, there was wine. And we drank of it freely.

AT THE FIRST BLUSH OF DAYLIGHT, I accompanied Mistress Hutchinson to the door. "Thank you for caring for Jane and for your kindness to me," I said emboldened by the wine. I longed to continue my connection with her.

"Birthing is my work," she replied, examining the knot our entwined fingers made. "'Tis not I who gives them life but the Lord working through me." I remembered how Goody Hammer once said the same thing, but there was goodness in this woman that I did not believe Goody Hammer possessed. She was a woman I longed to learn from.

"Will you join us on Monday?" Anne Hutchinson asked me with a quickness that made me think she read my mind. "We women gather to discuss the sermons of the previous Sabbath and to extract greater meaning from them."

"Perhaps," I hesitated, unsure if Joshua would allow it.

"I think you shall find our discussions helpful to your soul, my daughter."

When I released my grip on Mistress Hutchinson's fingers, I continued to feel her power. I promised myself I would convince Joshua.

Chapter Thirty-Three

The following day Joshua was sweeping sawdust out of the cooperage when Reverend Symmes called to him from across the fence. I was indoors listening to their conversation.

"G'day, I say. That's some contraption you've got there!"

Joshua continued sweeping as if he had not heard. My husband was irritable and not in the mood for idle chatter, especially about his wellsweep. It had become a novelty in Boston, being the first of its kind in town.

When Joshua failed to respond immediately, Reverend Symmes beat his walking stick on the fence to gain his attention. Having no escape, Joshua propped his broom against the doorframe and strode over to him.

Reverend Symmes was a stout man, jowly and chinless, who walked with a wobble. Although he was not ancient, he was nearly deaf, so he strained to hear through a tarnished silver horn that hung around his neck. He was a man of large appetite for Scripture, food, and gossip.

"Reverend Symmes, you've come to check on us in Boston," Joshua greeted him politely. "Good morning to you."

"What is it you say?" He held the horn to his ear.

"You've come to check on us," Joshua spoke louder, cupping his hand around the corner of his mouth.

"That's right, young man. I have come from Charlestown to hail John Wilson who arrived today with his wife. At last the good woman has deigned to honor us with her presence." His tone softened. "From all appearances she seems a useful woman."

"We can use useful women," Joshua mumbled.

"Fifteen ships are in the harbor today . . . Too many new arrivals . . . A blight on us." Reverend Symmes waved his walking stick toward the ocean. "All the opinionists not tolerated in England are coming here," he growled.

Joshua inquired about his crossing, which I knew was meant to remind him of his own newcomer status, but Reverend Symmes either did not hear, or did not make the connection. Instead he took it as an invitation to discourse on a topic about which he was relentless: Mistress Hutchinson. Jane told me that throughout their voyage Reverend Symmes had filled whatever ear was nearest him with the failings of Mistress Hutchinson, and the closer to America they sailed, the more inflamed his diatribes became.

"Opinionists like that Hutchinson woman," he shouted.

"Aye, Goodwife Hoyt met her at the birth of the Loring child."

Reverend Symmes kept railing. "A brazen one she is. She sailed on the *Griffin* with me, y' know. If I did not hear her say it with her own tongue, I never would have believed it." He beat his cane on the fence again. Then he repeated the story that had been circulating around Boston for the past eight months. "We stood on the upper deck near the forecastle, she and I, and do you know what she said to me?"

Joshua shook his head.

"She said we would arrive in New England on September the eighteenth."

"And that is when you arrived," Joshua finished the story.

"Exactly."

The fix of my husband's jaw told me he was losing patience with the minister.

"The eighteenth of September," Reverend Symmes rapped his cane again. "And I said to her, 'How do you know this, ma'am?' 'I know because the Lord speaks to me,' she said."

Joshua stuffed his hands in his pockets and swayed from leg to leg.

"'Then you are a prophetess?' I asked her." He spoke in the low interrogating tone he probably had used with her.

"And what did she say?" Joshua asked quickly, trying to hurry him along.

"She said, 'The Spirit speaks within me.' She said that nothing of significance has happened to her in her life that has not been revealed to her beforehand. Can you believe the arrogance of that woman?" he barked, causing two women who were strolling along the fence to take notice. "She claims God speaks directly to her . . . gives her messages as if the two of them are neighbors. The boldness of that woman. She must be reduced!"

"Reverend Symmes, we all know the Lord speaks only to ministers. He would never speak directly to a woman."

The two of them nodded in agreement.

I gulped.

"Do you know what she's up to now? She's preaching to the women in her home. Not only does she deem herself a prophetess, but now a preacher!"

"Her husband does not curtail her?" Joshua asked, indignantly.

"What was that?" he asked, holding his horn to his ear.

"Her husband. Does he not stop her?" Joshua repeated louder.

"He does not," Symmes shouted. "Her William is a man of weak parts. But mark it. In time it will be the will of the town to reduce her. If her husband cannot do his job, it is left for us to do it. I feel it in my bowels." He tapped the fence with his cane. "I have said enough. I must be on my way."

Joshua nodded and returned to his sweeping.

Reverend Symmes hobbled a few steps, then looked over his shoulder at Joshua. "I have watched her pray—with her eyes pointing up to heaven, posing like one in a trance, waving her arm like a lover of true religion. The woman is a fraud if I've ever seen one. Our women are in worship of her, as if she were a Sarah. But she is a Magdalene. Do you know what the Bible says about false prophets? It says the sun will set for them and the day will go dark for them and they will all cover their faces because there is no answer from God? Now I've said enough, I must be off."

Joshua took a deep breath and waved.

Reverend Symmes took a few more steps, stopped and slapped the fence with his walking stick. "You wish to find a devil? Look no further than that woman!"

It was not long before the entire town was gossiping about Anne Hutchinson. Because of the grumbling, there was no opportune time for me to ask Joshua for permission to attend her meetings. By then I knew his opinion. My husband had become so strongly influenced by the prime men of Boston that he began repeating Reverend Symmes's story to every man who came into the cooperage. It did not please me that my husband had become a gossip.

Finally one Sabbath, after pleasing Joshua with a well-prepared meal, I risked vexing him. As I expected, he refused, and the following day he refused again. But on the third day, he relented. "You weary me, woman. Go then, if it gives you peace, but I like not the smell of it."

THE HUTCHINSON HOME was almost as sizable as the Winthrop's. It was a gabled house of two levels built to accommodate their vast family, several other relatives and two manservants.

That first Monday, I arrived early to get a seat. I'd heard from Jane that the room fills up quickly—so quickly that many of the women come carrying their own stools.

Jane was already there when I arrived and I slid onto a bench beside her in the second row. Miracle was napping with John keeping watch. "He dotes over our girl beyond reason. I fret he will never have the heart to discipline her," Jane said, shaking a head of curls that had darkened slightly since she gave birth.

I listened with half an ear, but watched the preparations at the front of the room with two eyes. Mistress Hutchinson's lanky husband William was spreading a clean white cloth on the tabletop. He set his wife's Bible with well-fingered pages on top of it, and positioned her chair behind the table. The chair's smooth spindles rose from its high back like massive tapers.

"It's good you've come," Jane whispered.

"I've been awaiting this day."

"Ah look," Jane said, turning and waving. "It's Elizabeth and Mary and Catherine and Jennifer and Goodwife Demsey and Mary Coggeshall, the wife of John the silk mercer; and Elizabeth Hough, Atherton's wife. And there's Mary Dyer, the milliner's wife entering," Jane whispered into my ear. "Mary is

Mistress Hutchinson's closest friend. I see them strolling arm-in-arm up and down the lane. She always sits there," she said, pointing at an empty place on the bench in front of us. "Mary would be a comely woman, if only she would smile, don't you think?"

"Aye," I said, noting Mary's sternness.

As Jane prattled on, I took notice of the women who were not present: Margaret Winthrop, Sarah Cotton, and Elizabeth Wilson. But I knew every word Anne Hutchinson uttered would get back to them, and through them to their husbands. By eventide the following day, even Joshua would be supplied with more than enough kindling to toss upon the fire of his arguments against her.

Mistress Hutchinson made her way through the crowd, nodding warmly at those she recognized, including me. My heart fluttered at the compliment of her attention.

With raised hands she called upon the Holy Spirit to bring us wisdom. Then she bade us to close our eyes and imagine the peace of the Spirit descending upon our heads. Jane took a deep breath and I did likewise. The room became silent. At first I was aware of the sounds around me—coughs, the rustle of cloth, muffled voices, the clatter of iron pots somewhere in the back of the house—but soon those sounds faded and all I could hear was the hum of my own breath.

"Sabbath last," Mistress Hutchinson spoke softly, as if she were arousing sleepy children to wakefulness, "Reverend Cotton preached on the Covenant of Grace and the transformative value of grace in our lives. He said that in our quest for salvation, all the good works we perform are not as important as the grace the Lord bestows freely upon us." She pulled a notebook out of her apron pocket and opened it to the notes she had taken of his sermon.

"All our ministers, except Reverend Cotton, preach a Covenant of Works," she declared. "They teach us that good works pave the road to heaven. But there is another covenant which binds us even more solidly to the Lord." She entwined her fingers and locked them together. "That is the Covenant of Grace." She looked into the sea of our faces. "We watch each other, do we not? In the marketplace, at the meetinghouse, even here today, we watch. Do we not?"

Heads nodded around me.

"And what do we watch for?"

At first we were silent. But then a brave, high-pitched voice coming from back spoke. "We watch each other's actions. We watch for good works. We watch for signs of salvation in one another."

"Ah, that is very well said, Goody Oliver," Mistress Hutchinson said. Goody Oliver was the wife of Boston's surgeon, Thomas Oliver. "Indeed, we watch each other's actions. We watch to accertain whether that person is behaving righteously or is up to evil, and we judge, do we not, whether that person is amongst the saved or the damned?" She nodded as she spoke, signaling us to agree.

"Aye," we murmured.

I thought of a game Jane and I had played as girls in England. It was a simple game. Wherever we were in a public place—in Market Square, at St. Boltoph's, or in her father's shop watching him sell gloves to customers—one of us would point to a person and the other had to decide, by their demeanor, whether that person was saved or not. We'd based our judgment upon that person's reputation. Some people were known for their good works. Others were simply affable sorts we thought the Lord would favor . . . people who curled their lips a certain way when they smiled, or who had that particular hue of bronze hair we admired. The poor souls we damned were the criminals, the degenerates, those of ill temper, those who had been cursed with madness, warts, or derangement.

"And who are we to judge?" Mistress Hutchinson asked. "It is written in Romans 2 that at the point you are judging others, you are condemning yourself."

From behind came a ruffling of skirts and the scrape of wood against the floor. Wending her way between the stools and benches was the one I had just been thinking of. A chill crept over me as I reached for Jane's hand.

"Goodwife Hammer, I'm pleased you are joining us," Mistress Hutchinson said respectfully, bidding her forward. "Come, let you sit here." The women in the first row squeezed together to make room for her.

Terror coursed through me. Jane's body tensed and she squeezed my hand tightly. Mary Dyer turned and glared at her. Nervous coughs clipped the air. Mistress Hutchinson rose from her chair and stepped in front of the table.

"Thank you, I shall stand," Goody Hammer said curtly. She stopped directly behind me and set one hand upon Jane's shoulder and the other upon mine. Her fingernails pressed into my skin. I could not flee if I wanted to. Had Goody Hammer realized we had given her henbane? That we lifted her smock and explored her body? Had she come to publicly accuse and embarrass us?

"I've been listening in the back and I can no longer remain silent. Mistress Hutchinson, you criticize the women in this room for watchin' each other and passin' judgment unfairly, but are ye not at this moment passin' judgment on Reverend Wilson and all the other fine ministers of the Boston Congregation? The only one you defend is your pet, Reverend Cotton!"

Gasps filled the air.

I was relieved that the crone had not come to castigate us, but I was shocked by her attack. Mistress Hutchinson looked stunned, yet she did not lose her composure. She took a breath—deep enough to suck up the scant amount of air remaining in the room—then leaned into Goody Hammer.

"You suggest I judge our ministers, and I do, Goodwife Hammer. But I do so not to discredit them. I wish only to point out the error of their ways and shed a glorious light upon our understanding of doctrine. A matter as significant as doctrine cannot remain unclarified, for it is our sacred beliefs that guide us to heaven."

"Our ministers instruct us in error, you say?" Goody Hammer complained.

"Not so much in error as incompletely."

We were breathing quicker now, and I smelt the pungent odors of our bodies.

"Let me tell you," Mistress Hutchinson continued. "Good works are not enough. The Covenant of Grace is more important than the Covenant of Works, and our ministers, with the exception of Reverend Cotton, do not teach that as they should."

"What say you? That works are unimportant?" Goody Hammer snapped. She pressed her fingernails deeper into my skin. "Do you claim the hours we spend nursin' the sick, comfortin' the bereaved, buryin' the dead, are unnoticed by the Lord? You know the Beatitudes, and you are a performer of good works yourself, ma'am."

"As does every woman," Mistress Hutchinson agreed. "We do good works because we are filled with God's grace and can do no other. It is God's grace working within us that enables our good works. But it is the acceptance of the Covenant of Grace that will bring us salvation. God's grace is a glorious light. It is the Spirit of God that enters us in our quiet moments of prayer, and it is in those shining moments that we know we are saved!" Mistress Hutchinson's frail hand patted her own heart, and I could not help but pat mine. "When the Spirit possesses us, we become more than mere creatures. We become one with the Spirit!" Other women placed their hands upon their hearts as well.

"Grace is not something we can bargain with God for: 'Lord, if you assure me of my salvation, I shall give my last shilling to the poor.' Then good works become merely a legal transaction. Grace is given to us freely. It is not earned."

"May I speak, Anne?" Mary Dyer came to her friend's defense.

"Of course, Mary."

The earnest-minded woman glanced at Goody Hammer with furrowed eyebrows. "I have oft thought of the trickery that can be performed by the unsanctified who do good works only for the show of it."

"You speak the truth, Mary. The unregenerate perform their good works out of fear. Those who have been sanctified perform good works because they are filled with the Spirit and can do naught but good." Mary nodded.

I had considered my own behavior since the night my father had his use of me. I had embraced the Covenant of Works because I had been taught that good works were all that mattered, that they were my steppingstone to heaven. If I laid them out carefully one after another in the neatest of order, if I shined each of them to a gloss that pleased the Lord, surely then I would be among the saved. But from Mistress Hutchinson I was hearing there are two rungs on the ladder to heaven: good works and grace.

"What does grace feel like?" The sound of my own voice

speaking up in the room surprised me.

Mistress Hutchinson was pleased with my question. She gave me her full attention. There was not a furrow in her forehead, not a crease in her smile that did not belong to me now. In her next words she would impart her wisdom to me and it would flow upon me like baptismal water.

"God's grace is a feeling of ravishing joy," she said with her dark eyes pinned on me. "It's the feeling of being consumed by the fire of the Spirit, my daughter. It is so overwhelming that you cannot restrain yourself from shouting! It's the feeling of being so on fire with the Lord that you know without a doubt you are saved! It cannot be taken from you."

"Never?" I asked without shyness.

"Never, Mercy. What door the Lord enters, He will never exit!"

"What if you—"

"What if . . ."

"What if . . ."

"What if . . ."

I was one of many women asking questions. But the shrillest, most persistent voice belonging to a young girl in the rear prevailed. "What if a person afterwards performs the most evil deed imaginable? I don't mean stealing a goat, which the Lord would surely forgive. Nor do I mean being unkind, which we all can be. What I mean is killing another person, practicing witchcraft, or participating in a sin of a carnal nature with man or beast."

Gasps shot through the room.

I was annoyed that the girl diverted Mistress Hutchinson's attention from me; but I realized it was just as well. Coming from my mouth, such an inquiry would have raised suspicions in people who had been watching me, people like Goody

Hammer, whose grip on my shoulder was becoming painful.

"Then I would be persuaded the person was never saved in the first place, but merely imagined that the Spirit of God dwelt within her. A person with such sins could be among the damned," Anne Hutchinson said.

I felt the floor fall out from under me. The air grew hot. A chill raced through me, as if icy water had been poured into my head and was trickling down my body. Mistress Hutchinson's image became a shimmering blur of black against the white wall. I watched her lips move and tried to concentrate upon her words.

"When Satan has you in his grip," she said, clasping her hands together tightly, "naught but God's grace can free you."

The room whirled. Goody Hammer's fingers squeezed my shoulder tighter, as if in claim of me. Pinned by her grip, I couldn't move, couldn't breathe. Mistress Hutchinson's words echoed in my head: "The person was never saved in the first place."

"I've heard enough." Goody Hammer released her grip on me and I exhaled. I turned and looked into her pale face. For a moment our eyes connected, then she swung about and stormed off.

When the meeting ended, Jane bid me a hasty farewell for Miracle was waiting to be fed. I remained seated on the bench, head in my hands, too stricken to move. When I looked up, Mistress Hutchinson was sitting beside me.

"You are troubled, my daughter, I see it in you."

I swallowed hard.

"Perchance it is something I said?"

"No, ma'am," I lied.

"If you're not in a rush, I would like you to stay and have a talk."

Before I could protest, Mistress Hutchinson took my hand and led me through the parlor and up a narrow flight of stairs. It was only her tight hold on me that kept me from collapsing. The steps creaked under the pressure of our footfalls. When we reached the top, she led me down a dim hallway and into a sunny chamber. From one wall to the other, the spacious room was crowded with two large beds, more bedrolls on the floor, a chest of clothes, and a bench set beneath the window. Sitting on the floor, playing with a basketful of acorns, was the bleary-eyed girl I had seen at the dock.

"Mary, Bridget could use your help in the kitchen, please."

"Aye, Mama."

The child moved with quick birdlike motions. She collected her acorns and tiptoed out of the room.

Mistress Hutchinson pointed toward a stool near the open window. "Let you sit."

I settled myself on the stool and glanced out the window. Below, outside the front door, Mary Dyer and four other women lingered saying their goodbyes. Across the street was Governor Winthrop's house. It was said that Governor Winthrop kept an eye on who and how many people entered the Hutchinson's. There was a crack in the shutters and a flash of movement behind. Aye, someone was watching.

"Mercy," Anne Hutchinson whispered. "Tell me what is troubling you, for I know something is amiss." She set her hand upon mine.

"The Spirit has not been within me for years," I murmured.

Anne Hutchinson said nothing.

"I was once saved, ma'am. The Lord came to me when I was a child and told me so. I made my testimony in front of the others."

Mistress Hutchinson smiled knowingly.

"And what has transpired since then, my daughter?"

I looked into Mistress Hutchinson's dark eyes that seemed to melt into my own. Her presence was like Mama's, and as with Mama I could not remain silent. "The Spirit is absent from me now," I said, feeling my eyes tear up.

Mistress Hutchinson listened.

"I have sinned grievously, and for it the Lord has punished me severely. He has taken my brothers and Joshua's father, Ezekiel."

"We are all sinners," Mistress Hutchinson whispered, "and for our transgressions the Lord punishes us accordingly. Six years ago, I lost my Susanna and my Elizabeth to the plague that ravished Alford. Susanna was but fourteen when the Lord took her."

"Almost the age of my brothers."

"And Elizabeth was merely eight. And my own Joshua, the Lord took him as an infant some thirteen years ago." A mist of sadness crossed her eyes, darkening and deepening them.

"When they died I was as distracted as you, my daughter, and I too believed the Lord had taken leave of me. But I prayed every waking moment and I did my duty as a wife, and as time passed the Lord blessed me with children enough to fill this house. The Lord so willed another Susanna and Joshua to be born to us, and . . ." she hesitated and looked at me straight, "I have only told my William this, but I will tell you now. I am again with child. This one shall be my fifteenth. So the Lord's blessings continue."

"I shall keep it secret."

"I know you shall, my daughter."

I blotted my eyes in my apron. "When you spoke today, I realized I too had been living under the Covenant of Works. I've tried to do good and I've prayed the Lord would take notice and credit me for my deeds, but He has given me no sign of it."

"God will regenerate you, my daughter. If there is a flicker of the Lord's flame within your heart, which I believe is there—for it was truly once there—with constant prayers it will burst into an abundant flame that the Lord shall fan."

"You said the Lord does not withdraw a gift that has been given?"

"That is true. You must wait for that burst of radiant flame, and then the Spirit shall speak to you. He shall, my daughter. In time He shall speak to you."

"And when the He speaks, how will I know the voice is true?"

"You will know, just as Abraham knew, that it was God speaking when He bid him to offer up his son, Isaac."

When Mistress Hutchinson helped me up by the elbow and walked me down the steep stairs, the chatter of her children and the aroma of roasting chicken engulfed us.

"You will be with us next week, my daughter?"

"Aye."

As I walked to our cottage, I could not stop myself from repeating, "The Lord will fan that flame. The Lord will fan that flame. The Lord..."

WHENEVER I RETURNED HOME from Mistress Hutchinson's, I could hardly wait to tell Joshua what had transpired there. For the first time in my life I had information of the finest kind to share. It pleased me when he lingered at the table after supper to hear my discourse.

I told him everything I knew about Mistress Hutchinson and her family: That her father was a deacon who, much like Reverend Cotton, defied the Church of England; that she

read all her father's books, some in Latin and Greek; that
when she was newly married, she and William would travel
all day from Alford to hear Reverend Cotton preach. I told
him about a discussion Elizabeth Aspinwall had initiated. I
tried to copy Elizabeth's whiny voice and manner in telling it
to Joshua, standing up and kneading my thighs as Elizabeth
had done at the meeting. "'Some say a woman has no business
preaching, that such pious endeavors are to be solely the work
of a man. What do you say, Mistress Hutchinson?'" Then I
assumed Anne Hutchinson's quick, confident tone. "'In Saint
Paul's letter to Titus, he counsels the older women to teach the
younger women.'"

After several weeks Joshua grew impatient with me. At
first he became inattentive, staring not at me but at the cider in
his mug or the blackness on the other side of the window. He
did not silence me, thus I believed I had permission to speak.
Then one day, without explanation, he rose from his chair and
left, leaving me with only the walls to hear my stories. Another
evening, when I was telling him about my mistress's belief that
every person has the Lord's ear if only he would claim it, he
interrupted me.

"Goodwife, I have no patience for this harridan who steps
outside her boundaries," he said, slamming his spoon on the
table. "She is a woman of unlimited opinions, of dangerous
opinions. She knows not her place, and her husband does
naught to put her in it."

Stunned by his harshness, I hung my head, allowing his
stare to bear into me like the craftsman's mark he affixes with
a hot poker onto the lid of a finished barrel.

"There's been talk about the Hutchinsons," Joshua clipped.

"There's always gossip," I countered.

"It's more than gossip, Goodwife. Today John Winthrop

stopped in to order several hogshead, and he had a few things to say about William Hutchinson."

"What did he say?"

"He said William Hutchinson is a man of mild temper who is wholly guided by his wife."

"He is not!"

"And you, Goodwife. Do you know more about this man than does John Winthrop?"

I gulped. "He is her helpmeet," I pleaded softly. "I have watched him prepare the room for her and carry his grand chair to behind the table for her to occupy."

"You said it yourself. He trails after her like Grace follows a kitten," he chided.

"Mistress Hutchinson is a better teacher than any of the blackcoats behind our pulpits."

Joshua glared at me, "Your audacity riles me!" He slapped his hand on the table so hard that it nearly toppled the taper.

"I mean no disrespect, my husband," I whispered, attempting to placate him.

Joshua burned me with disapproving eyes. "You've just insulted the fine ministers of Boston who studied Scripture in England's finest universities."

What could I say to convince him that Mistress Hutchinson had a right to teach? "If you recall, Titus of the New Testament allows that older women instruct the younger," I said with as much authority as I could call up.

"If you recall, Goodwife, that is not how the verse reads." He reached across the table and picked up the Bible. "Titus, chapter two, verses three to five," he said loudly, jabbing a heavy finger at every word. "'The aged women likewise, that they be in behavior as becometh holiness, not false accusers, are given to much wine, teachers of good things; That they may teach the young women to be sober, to love their husbands, to love their children. To be discreet, chaste, keepers at home, good, obedient to their own husbands.'"

I gripped the edge of the table in embarrassment. Joshua was superior to me in many ways, but until then I did not consider knowledge of the Bible to be one of them.

"She is a lover of true religion," I said softly.

"She is a nimble-tongued woman who twists Scripture to suit herself. She has influenced your thinking beyond reason. You have made a false idol of her, and that shall bring its own repercussions, mark it, woman." Angrily, Joshua pushed himself away from the table and stomped into the cooperage. I lingered, pondering our conversation.

A short while later, a calmer Joshua returned and we sat across from each other, exchanging not a word. Until the taper betwixt us flickered and died, Joshua recorded numbers in his ledger, and I reread the letters of St. Paul.

Chapter Thirty-Four

1636

Spring exploded with a profusion of white and blue violets, wisteria and bluebells, and all of Boston rejoiced. Election Day, which was always a celebration, had in 1636 resulted in the election of a new governor, Henry Vane, a handsome newcomer to Boston. When Vane arrived the past October, I was among the many who stood on the bluff watching the pageantry of his welcome with a volley of cannon shot.

At twenty-three-years-old, Henry Vane was a man of aristocratic blood, impressive bearing, and extraordinary idealism. He was of the notion that government had no business interfering in religious matters, which of course, suited Anne Hutchinson and her supporters. He infused new optimism into the blood of so many of us who had for so long felt starved of the color and aroma of new ideas.

It was under this bold umbrella of security that Mistress Hutchinson opened her home on Tuesdays as well as Mondays for Scripture study. On Tuesdays, men were welcome. The Coddingtons, Bendells and Aspinwalls attended these meetings, as did handsome Governor Vane. As Joshua refused to attend, I only frequented the meetings on Monday.

I kept my ears open to the gossip blustering in from the cooperage. I overheard Innkeeper Samuel Cole tell Joshua that John Winthrop was bemoaning the fact that his influence among the people was declining while Henry Vane's star was rising; and I heard that old lion Thomas Dudley posit that Anne Hutchinson was feeling her power with a minister of her own in John Cotton and now a governor of her own in Henry Vane. Joshua, of course, agreed with them.

IT WAS DURING THIS TIME when new ideas sparred with the old, that a change came over me as well. Desperately, I wanted a child.

Jane assumed that the arrival of sweet Miracle swayed my fancies toward motherhood, and I allowed her to think it. But I knew differently: It was Mistress Hutchinson who affected this change in my heart. In March, Mistress Hutchinson delivered her fifteenth child, a boy they named Zuriel. Anne believed that in return for enduring many births the Lord rewarded her, not only with the assurance of salvation, but with the gift of prophesy. I had come to believe that if I followed my mistress's path, perchance the Lord would similarly reward me.

One night, I could not sleep for all that was on my mind. I lay in bed imagining myself with a child, nestling it to my breast and stroking its cheek. I pressed my hand into my stomach and imagined the flutter of life inside me. No matter how hard I forced myself to rest, I could not lie still. I yanked the sheet off and pulled it up again, wrapping myself in it. Every movement in our narrow bed created a ripple that engulfed Joshua as well.

That was the night I announced my desire to my sleeping husband. "Joshua, it is time we have a child."

Joshua groaned. "Surely this can wait. I'm trying to sleep."

I ignored him. "Do you desire a child?"

"It's not whether I desire a child or not, it is whether the Lord wills it," he grumbled.

"Perhaps we need to give the Lord greater assistance."

Joshua raised himself into a patch of moonlight. He sat back on his elbows, yawned and studied me curiously. "We've been married two years, Goodwife. I have wanted children from the start, but not once have you spoken of it. Now you wake me in the middle of the night to remind me of my unfulfilled desires and to discuss your change of heart!"

"I've just been thinking of it. I had a dream of having fifteen children, each of them a jewel in my heavenly crown."

Joshua slouched back into the darkness. "Can we not get through the night without talk of that Hutchinson woman?"

"You're raising your voice."

"You are raising my temper!" he barked in words that bit the night. "I pray when the Lord grants us children, it is because He sees you are prepared for motherhood and not because of some whim or folly in imitation of another." He spit out the word, another, and turned his back on me.

ABOUT A WEEK LATER, after we had gone to bed, I reached for Joshua's hand and placed it upon my thigh. There had been strife betwixt us, but that evening at supper, for the first time in a week, we had spoken without animosity and even laughed over a story he told me about a flock of wild turkeys running through the meetinghouse as Reverend Wilson practiced his sermon.

Finally, my husband responded to my touch, as I knew he would. "Let me soothe you," he said, taking up my smock little by little, touching my waist and breasts. Those were familiar motions that usually struck fear in me, but that night I responded eagerly.

"'Tis so unlike you, Goodwife,"

"Perchance you now have a new wife," I whispered softly.

In the darkness we persisted in our lovemaking, but I knew that Joshua and I were not alone. The Lord hovered above us and His arms joined us as tightly as two hands folded in prayer. The flex of every muscle, the sweetness of every word, the rise and fall of our bodies were acts performed in His service.

Almost every night that spring I awakened Joshua for lovemaking. As summer advanced and the nights warmed, our contact became more intense. In the darkness I moved in ways that in the light of day would have embarrassed me. Joshua welcomed whatever new form of lovemaking my excited body proposed. My longing for a child directed every movement of my limbs, every shift of my hips, every kiss I delivered to every part of his body.

Those months my needs could not be satisfied. Lovemaking became my prayer of the night.

DURING THE DAYTIME the voices inside me told me to pray. *Pray. Pray.*

When I was kneading bread dough, shaking the bed linens outdoors, weeding the garden, I prayed out loud. The more rapidly I prayed, the purer I felt my soul becoming. Eventually, prayers were not enough. The voices told me to clean. I needed to cleanse the space in which we lived, to make it spotless. So I scrubbed every surface, every corner and cranny of our dwelling with soap and water, and when that was done, I began anew. I prayed aloud as I scrubbed the tabletop and each of the trenchers and cups in the cupboard. I prayed as I scoured the windowpanes and floor, as I wrung steaming water from Joshua's gritty breeches and shirts in the bubbling cauldron outdoors. "Purge me with hyssop, and I shall be clean. Wash me, and I shall be whiter than snow." My hands reddened and blistered from the scalding water, but I forced myself to ignore the pain. Flinching from it, I believed, would have spoiled my prayer.

One crisp afternoon in late October, Joshua found me on my knees scouring the same patch of floor I had scrubbed the day before.

"The floor is clean enough, Goodwife," he said firmly, extending his hand to help me up. I did not reach for his hand. I continued scrubbing.

Joshua's eyes narrowed. "Listen to me."

I willed the prayers in my head to overpower his voice, but his voice was like the roar of the ocean, swallowing every sound but its own.

"Purge me . . ."

"Enough of your constant praying! You awaken each morning mumbling to the Lord, but you say not a word to me. Would it be so hard to say, 'G'day, my husband. What orders must you fill today?' You continue this way until night, then you only stop when we are occupied in bed."

"And you wish not to be occupied in bed?"

He stammered. "Well, no . . ."

Then he won't be from now on, the voice inside me said. *There's no need for it anymore, at least for the next nine months or so.* But Joshua did not have to know that yet. Mistress Hutchinson was the one I intended to tell first.

"Now look you, stop your scrubbing and listen!" he cried. "I hear you speaking verses when I am with customers in the cooperage. They must think you are distracted out of your wits, and I am beginning to think it myself."

"Dear Lord, help me."

"I say shut it, Goodwife."

I focused on a sticky spot on the floor and tried to raise it with my fingernail. "Pitch," I muttered.

I wished for Joshua to leave me alone, but he planted his feet solidly before me. His brown stockings were clotted with dust from the street, and I reached over to brush them with my rag. Later I would boil more water and scrub them.

"Stop, woman, and look up at me," he said lifting me up with both of his arms so I was standing in front of him. His blue eyes turned gray as granite. His clothes smelled like dust and sweat.

Mama had been right. The verses I would need for life would come to me. Without malice, I spoke to my husband. "'I will sprinkle clean water on you and you will be clean. I will cleanse you from all thine impunities. I will giveth you a new heart and put a new spirit in you.'"

"Mercy!" he cried, shaking my shoulders.

Do not flinch. Not until you finish the verse, the voices said. "'. . . I will remove from you your heart of stone and give you a heart of flesh.'"

"You are deranged, woman. You have the gall to quote from Ezekiel, the prophet of the Lord, the holy man whose name my father carried. What madness has overcome you?"

"I pray for inner light, and I pray it surrounds you as well."

"Inner light. Free grace," he spat out the words. "This Hutchinson woman is filling you with her nonsense."

"And you have filled me with a child. Now we, like Anne and William, are amongst the blessed!"

Joshua's face turned ashen. "My God," he cried, letting go of my shoulders. He paced around me in a wide circle. "My God, woman, you are unfit to become a mother. What have we done?"

Chapter Thirty-Five

From the moment I knew Joshua's seed had rooted inside me, I rehearsed over and over in my mind how I would tell Mistress Hutchinson. She was to have been the first to know, but Joshua had bespoiled that.

So, the following morning, I wrapped myself in my cloak and hurried down the High Street to Mistress Hutchinson's. I ran as fast as my legs could transport me—past the stoic brown cattle grazing in the Aspinwalls' pasture, past the corner where I caught a fleeting glimpse of John polishing his green sign, and across the street to the Hutchinsons.

Out of breath, I rapped on the door. There was no answer. I stepped back and looked up at the gables of the two-story house ascending before me like the Temple of Jerusalem. The windows were frosted with ice and shut, but I could hear the chirpy voices of children within. I stepped up to the door and pounded impatiently.

Young Bridget opened the door. Her hands were covered with cornmeal, and she wiped them in her dark apron, leaving a coating of yellow dust and clumps of sticky dough on her apron that I reached out to brush away.

"I've come to see Mistress Hutchinson," I gasped.

"She is here, Goodwife, but she is occupied with Zuriel." She took a step backwards.

"It is a matter of some importance," I beseeched her.

"You are Mercy Hoyt, are you not?" Bridget inquired, wiping a film of sweat from her forehead. "Excuse me. I've been kneading dough."

"Cornbread. It leaves its grit everywhere, does it not? I am Mercy, and I come to bring your mother wondrous news," I said in my most charming tone. "I beg you to tell her I am here, and when she knows it, surely she will see me."

The voice spoke in my head. *When Mary heard Elizabeth's greeting, the baby leaped in her womb, and Elizabeth was filled with the Holy Spirit. In a loud voice she exclaimed: "Blessed are you among women, and blessed is the child you will bear!"* I smiled sweetly.

"Pray, come in then, and I'll fetch her." She regarded me cautiously.

I watched the slim shape of the girl retreat and disappear behind a door. I stepped into the hallway and closed the front door behind me. The room was dim, so it took a moment for my eyes to adjust. Except for the muffled voices of children playing upstairs and their footfalls on the ceiling, the house was still. To my left was the parlor, that great room that had become my sanctuary. The room was deserted. I longed to step inside.

Boldly, I entered.

The furniture had been rearranged. The long oak table that usually was set away from the far wall had been pushed against it, with the benches stowed beneath. The table beckoned me like an altar, and I scurried toward it with my hands extended, eager to touch its smooth center, the sacred spot where my mistress sets her Bible. As I pressed my palms into the cool wood, a choir of sparrows chirped in a tree outside the window; and when I turned to acknowledge them, a beam of sunshine blinded my eyes. I blocked the light with my hand, but then purposely lowered it to gaze into the brilliant light. Surely, it was a sign from the Lord. When Jesus spoke again to the people, he said, "I am the light of the world. Whosoever follows me will never walk in darkness, but will have the light of life."

"Mercy!" It was my mistress's commanding voice.

Startled, I turned toward her. "Mistress Hutchinson," I said, stepping into the shadows. I was relieved she did not reprimand me for venturing into her parlor, however, I did note a look of surprise on her face.

"What is it, my daughter? Bridget tells me you are in a frenzy and you come bearing news."

"Oh, is that sweet babe your Zuriel?" I exclaimed.

Anne Hutchinson smiled lovingly at the infant in her arms. "I was just beginning to feed him. I pray you do not mind if I do so as we speak." She glided toward the darkest corner of the parlor and gently lowered herself into her husband's tall chair. The baby was loosely wrapped in a tan blanket and an oft-washed green gown. She nestled Zuriel within the crook of her arm and with her free hand opened the buttons of her bodice. The infant rooted for her breast and latched on to it with a practiced tenacity.

"Now, what is it you've come to tell me?"

I fell to my knees, clutched at my mistress's skirt, and gazed up into her eyes. Mistress Hutchinson stared back at me in bewilderment. She wasn't smiling as I expected her to be. She should have been smiling. I tugged at her gown and thought of Mary's visit to Elizabeth and how she had fallen at the feet of her cousin, her heart pounding like mine, overflowing with joy as the child leapt inside her womb.

"No, Mercy," Mistress Hutchinson gasped, clutching Zuriel a little tighter. "It's not necessary that you kneel before me. Stand up, my dear."

I did as she instructed.

"Now, what is it you have to say?"

"I am with child!" my words rushed out. In the torrent of excitement tears streamed down my cheeks, and I could hardly wipe them for my fingers trembled so. My whole body vibrated with joy. "You are the first person I am telling, except for Joshua who knows, but I didn't intend to tell him first, I promise you."

She looked at me curiously. "So that's what this is all about." She searched beneath Zuriel for a handkerchief in her apron pocket and handed it to me. "That's what you have come to say? That you are with child?"

"Aye, ma'am."

"Well, that is a relief, for at first I thought something was amiss. The Lord has truly sanctified you, my daughter. This is a time to rejoice."

"I've come to receive your blessing, ma'am."

"And you have it," she whispered. "Blessed are you among women, and blessed is the child you will bear." Her dark eyes smiled tenderly at Zuriel and then at me.

"This babe shall be my first of many if the Lord answers my prayers," I said. "I pray for fifteen babies, as you have. I pray that through the pain of bearing them, I shall be cleansed. I pray that you will assist me through my births, that you will be a mother to me and guide me and say, 'my daughter' when the grumbling pains begin." I clutched my stomach and pushed inward, wishing to feel the life inside me but knowing it was much too soon for that.

Mistress Hutchinson's smile faded. "Pray, calm yourself. Sit for a moment in my chair while I fetch you a cup of water."

When she left the room, I eased myself into the tall chair that still held the heat of my mistress's body. She deems me worthy to sit here. She wishes to provide me nourishment. Cool, fresh water. I rubbed the smooth wood of the chair's arms until my palms warmed. In my imagination the room was full of women crowded shoulder-to-shoulder, all of them focused on me with rapt attention. Elizabeth Aspinwall's worshipful eyes bore into me. Mary Coddington's high-pitched voice resounded with questions and praise. I imagined myself strong and confident, ministering to them.

Be silent no longer, the voice said. "I shall be silent no longer," I whispered aloud. "The Lord has filled me with child and also with His words, and I shall speak them. If my mistress speaks for the Lord, why shouldn't I?"

My mistress returned without her Zuriel. She handed me a cup of water and watched me gulp it down. I expected her to sit, but she did not sit. I expected her to be joyous, to ask questions about my health and my spiritual estate. I expected her to request to stow my cloak, to invite me to pray, to welcome me into her kitchen to pour loaves of cornbread into pans, to suggest a time when she might call upon me, but she did not. There was something in my mistress's face I could not identify—a face behind a face, impatience behind the stretched line of her lips. I told myself not think about it because, surely, I was imagining.

The water refreshed me. I lifted myself from the chair and remembered the work I needed to complete before nightfall. The cleaning, the preparation of a meal, the new work that beckoned me outside my mistress's door. In the short distance between Mistress Hutchinson's home and my own, there were people eager to hear from me, some inflamed with the Spirit, others awaiting enlightenment. "I'd best be off," I said abruptly.

"Be off then, and take care of yourself and the blessed life within you. I shall see you next Monday with the others?"

Her invitation was like a sweet fig tossed my way, and again I was jubilant. "Aye, ma'am. Next summer you shall attend at my child's birth?"

"If the Lord wills it," Mistress Hutchinson replied.

I fastened the hook on my cloak and skipped down the path, stopping to look back to see if Mistress Hutchinson was watching me from her parlor window, as I hoped she was. The shutter was cracked open, and through the frost I could see a sliver of her face observing me. But the face was not smiling.

On the High Street people everywhere blocked my passage. But I ran through them. I broke through a cluster of girls who had nothing better to do than twitter like song sparrows. I shoved a boy who carried a younger lad on his shoulders and nearly made him drop the lad. Flustered, I waved an apology and kept running. What would Mistress Hutchinson do now? I must instruct them, raise my arms as she does, think of a proper verse for each of them. But the verses did not come.

With my mind on Scripture, I collided with a cart carrying a load of straw. It tottered on the ridge of a rut, and then bundle upon bundle of straw toppled over in an ungainly barrage. I ran off. "Now see what you've done!" old Doctor Oliver called to my back.

Up ahead was Elizabeth Aspinwall. When I caught up with her, I saw she was carrying a load of apples in the hollow of her cloak. Their sticky sweet aroma repulsed me as I darted past. *Lord, send me the words,* I prayed.

"Have an apple, Mercy," Elizabeth called out merrily. She extended her apron to me. It was at that moment that the words came. I stopped running and addressed her boldly. "I shall not eat of forbidden fruit nor should you partake of it," I admonished. "Be not like the temptress Eve!" The voices in my head spoke through me.

Elizabeth's jaw dropped. Her lips disappeared into her fleshy face. "What possesses you, girl?"

"I speak in the name of the Lord," I called to her, running backwards. "And in the name of another who is more sanctified than I. John the Baptist prepared the way for the Lord, and I prepare the way for Mistress Hutchinson."

Elizabeth shook her head and shook a correcting finger at me, releasing the corner of her cloak just enough for a brilliant red apple to tumble onto the road. It rolled into the wheel of a pushcart and bounced in the path of a jaunty lad who bent to retrieve it for her, but when he noticed that Goody Aspinwall had no intention of recovering it, he wiped it in his sleeve and took a bite.

"Mark it," I called to Elizabeth. "The men of Boston are the transgressors, for they have chosen to eat the forbidden fruit. If they were of stronger parts, they would abstain from such temptations, would they not?"

I spun around and ran like a fitful wind. To everyone I passed, I shouted a prayer. The verses Mama had taught me spilled from my lips like water spilt from an urn. The voices spoke to me and I became the instructor. Mirium, Deborah, and Noadiah were prophetesses, and I was amongt them.

To Goody Dyer, who was guiding her children away from a barking dog, I shouted from Exodus. "'But among the Israelites not a dog will bark at any man or animal!'" Mary Dyer lowered her eyes, appreciative of the message.

To two vagrants whose wrists were tied behind their backs and were tethered with a rope, I cried, "Sinners, sinners!" And to slatternly Joist Brown who led them, whose ditchwater eyes never wavered from his captives, I called out from Psalm 69: "'Let them be blotted out of the book of the living and not be written with the righteous.'"

To a group of five ruffians who sat on a bench outside of Samuel Cole's inn, I preached the words of Saint Paul, "'In the name of the Lord, we command you, brothers, to keep away from every brother who is idle and does not live according to the teachings you received from us.'" I had seen those boys before outside the meetinghouse, never entering, just gathering in the shadows talking balderdash and blowing puffs of smoke from reeds they held to lips that bore the disgusted smirks of youth. They needed a prod and a verse, so I stomped over to the bench. "Harken, lads," I scolded them soundly, shaking my finger into their faces. "Find your way inside the meetinghouse Sabbath next, and use your tongues for prayer and not merrymaking. Satan will find work for you if you are not at work for God." I raised my hand above my head and held it high, in the manner Mistress Hutchinson did when she invoked the Word of the Lord. "Let the Bible be your delight!"

Sweating profusely and looking everywhere but straight ahead, I then collided with John Winthrop who was striding purposefully down the lane. "Excuse me, Governor," I stammered when I saw who it was.

He stepped aside and with a gallant flourish extended his black-cloaked arm, granting me liberty to pass. "Be on your way, Goodwife Hoyt, since you deem your mission more urgent than mine," he said indulgently. I looked up into his bullet-black eyes. I had his full attention then as he waited for me to pass, but a twitch of his arched eyebrow told me impatience lurked behind his courtly manner.

I was breathing so heavily I could hardly speak, but I knew I must speak up for the Lord allowed us to meet for a reason. I took a deep breath and forced myself to say the words that heretofore had been confined to my mind.

"There is a witch among us, John Winthrop," I said boldly, using his full name and my strongest voice. "One among us trafficks with Satan. She bears the mark of the witch on her leg. A claw. Right here it is," I blurted, nervously rubbing the spot on my gown where Goody Hammer's mark was. "I have seen it myself."

"You have seen what?"

"The mark of a witch she bears," I repeated. "I've seen it."

"There is no such woman among us," he said, whipping his cape around his angular frame. "You must silence yourself." His breath puffed white plumes into the frosty air.

"I speak the truth and I shall take you to her," I pleaded, grabbing for the edge of his cape. He pulled away before I could grasp it.

"I am late for an appointment," he muttered, spinning away. His broad cloak spread around him in a flurry and he fled, leaving a strong whiff of tobacco in my nostrils. Hah! On the *Arbella* he had boasted that he had been cured of the habit of tobacco. But he had been cured of nothing. He was as deceitful as the rest of them. Then he turned and called out to me. "Who is she? Who is this woman?" He stepped closer and waited for an answer, stinging me with his coal-black eyes.

I looked around to see if anyone was listening, but what did it matter if someone was? "She calls herself a midwife, but she is a sorcerer and a conjurer," I stated. "There are others who conspire with her," I said, thinking of my father who drinks her evil tea, of the women who welcome her amulets.

John Winthrop arched his eyebrows and nodded knowingly. I saw gratitude in his eyes, not the kind that comes from receiving a temporal gift, but the gratitude one feels when he has been given the gift of knowledge.

I smiled and bowed my head. My mission was complete. I turned on my heels and bounded up the High Street. After running several steps, I looked over my shoulder to see if John Winthrop was watching me. He was.

By now, all activity on the lane stopped as enraptured people centered their attention upon me. Goody Dyer gathered the children close to her along the side of the lane. The lad with the apple stopped chewing and stood motionless. Was this how Jesus felt when he encountered the gamblers outside the temple? Was this how Mistress Hutchinson felt upon the *Griffin* when her prophesies caused such a commotion? The fire of the Lord lit my soul and suddenly I was ablaze with the Spirit.

"Mark it! I shall be watching you Sabbath next," I admonished the boys sharply. "Remember, the eye of God watches you always," I said glaring up into the pewter sky.

I continued running up the High Street. William Coddington, clutching his peaked hat, loped toward me. "Mercy, come here. Let me help you." But with a shimmy of my hips and a wink of my eye, I scurried past him, reciting Scripture and marking the pace of my steps with the rhythm of my prayers. "Thank you, Lord, for my deliverance, and for once again listing me among the righteous."

BY MID AFTERNOON, I was just beginning to make good on scrubbing soot stains off the hearthstone—stains that had been there for years but I had not noticed—when Joshua flung open the door to the cooperage and stormed in.

"You have been speaking your foolishness around town!"

I looked up but did not stop my scouring.

"Your rubbing can wait."

"I've simply been going about my work," I answered softly, as not to rile him, for those days he was as prickly as a thorn.

"There's nothing simple about what you've been doing. There is nothing simple about being told by those who do not know me that my wife is distracted out of her wits."

I spread my rag over a clump of charred wood and rubbed harder.

"Pay attention, Goodwife!" he shouted. With both hands he lifted a corner of the table off the floor and let it drop. A stack of bronze coins he had set there after breakfast tumbled to the floor. One rolled toward the doorway and stopped. Joshua stomped another with his boot. "You weary me. Have you no mind of the effect of your behavior on our business, for our reputation in this town, for my own aspirations?" He was shaking and red-faced, and his anger was so intense that it stirred sympathy in me, for no godly man should have to resort to such anger. Yet I wouldn't allow his rebukes to affect me. I was on God's mission. I stood up and straightened my back. "My husband, this is not about your barrels, but about the more serious business of salvation," I said most calmly.

Joshua scowled. "My wares are our livelihood! They put food on our table and gowns on your back." He pointed an angry finger toward the cooperage door. "John Winthrop was just here."

"Did he wish to speak to me?" I asked, running to the window. Perhaps I could hail him, I thought. Surely, he wished to probe me for information about Goody Hammer.

Joshua grabbed my elbow and stopped me. "What business

would he have with you? He came to see me, Mercy, to tell me that Anne Hutchinson is befouling your mind with heresy, and that you are party to her religious incontinence. He suggested I take control of you—for my own reputation and for the good of the community!" Joshua took a deep breath. "He said I should keep you away from her meetings."

"Surely, you would not prevent me—"

"I will and I am. You shall no longer go to her. Do you hear me?"

I did not respond.

"If you disobey me, I will have no choice but to call upon Reverend Wilson."

Tears welled up in my eyes.

Seeing the tears, Joshua took a deep breath and lowered his voice. "Look at me, Goodwife. I love you. I want what is right for you. I want what is right for us. But I know not what to do. Please, stop your crying and your scrubbing and move away from the fire." He offered me his hand and I took it and allowed him to lead me to the rocking chair where I sat. He sighed from exhaustion and offered to fetch me a cup of water.

While Joshua was drawing water, I considered my role as his wife. Just as God stood above Him, he stood above me. He had authority to command me. But he had no authority to stop me from praying. Nor would he prevent Mistress Hutchinson from being my midwife.

As the cool liquid slid down my throat, I remembered the misadvice Reverend Wilson had given me the night I went to him for help. "It is the role of the woman to give comfort to the man. The head of every man is Christ, and the head of the woman is man."

"You are right, my husband," I said to appease him. I bit the inside of my cheek to keep from saying exactly what I was thinking. From now on I vowed to follow my inner light.

WITH THE EXCEPTION OF GOING to the meetinghouse, Joshua forbade me to leave our cottage. The following Thursday, the Boston Congregation observed a solemn day of fasting and humiliation for reconciliation within our community. Mistress Hutchinson's bold ministry was tearing us apart, and even Governor Vane who was hoped to be the arbiter of our dissension, was proving ineffective in mending the tattered cloth of our religion. Our community of saints, once held together by the Bible and our quest for salvation, was being split, not by a shift in destination—for heaven was still every saint's goal—but by a map of how to travel there and whose leadership to follow.

I CAME TO BELIEVE that Joshua had enlisted the aid of others in his conspiracy against me. John became his confidant, and Jane his helper. I came to distrust Jane's sweet and searching glances—with a benevolent hand she would set bread and soup upon my table, and with a critical eye she would assess my state of mind.

Her visits came with benefits though. The talker Jane was, she freely dispensed information about the happenings in Boston. John's gregariousness and Jane's charm had made the bench outside their tailor shop a popular gathering place for the gossips of Boston where even on the snowiest of afternoons two or three people could be found sitting awaiting an appointment or passing time. "I simply crack my window to hear their gossip," Jane confided.

Joan told me that one evening Mistress Hutchinson had been summoned by a messenger to appear at the home of Reverend Cotton at Sudbury End, and when she arrived, she was confronted by a legion of ministers who had traveled from Watertown, Charlestown, and other places to interrogate her. What a shock she must have felt when she found herself encircled by a panel of blackcoats: the grim-faced George Phillips; the babbling Zachariah Symmes, who even with the aid of his silver horn had probably misunderstood every word she uttered; the pouting John Wilson, whose ministry she had most severely criticized. Thank goodness her defender John Cotton was there to temper their assaults. Although Jane did not know the outcome of that meeting, she, like half the town, was persuaded that Mistress Hutchinson's troubles were just beginning.

That afternoon I told Jane about my encounter with John Winthrop and how I believed it was the Lord's intention to put us together so I might enlighten him.

"Tell me exactly what you said," Jane insisted.

I glanced at the door to the cooperage to make sure it was closed and Joshua could not overhear. Then I revealed the exact words I said, for they were words I would never forget. "I looked into John Winthrop's eyes and said plainly, 'There is a witch amongst us, Governor. She is the midwife and sorcerer.' That is what I said, and by the look on his face, I know he understood."

Jane looked aghast. "You did not."

"I did," I replied proudly. "'Tis true. There is a witch amongst us, and you and I have proof of it."

"What we saw happened two years ago, Mercy, and there has been no other indication of it since. In fact, last winter Goody Hammer sent over a vial of fig syrup for Miracle's raspy cough, and later a salve for sticky-eye that provided her good relief."

I stared at Jane with disbelief. What a false friend she had become. Miracle received two worthless remedies and Goody

Hammer became a heroine in her eyes. "You are the one who told me about Rebecca Fowler's bravery and how you believed she earned a high place in heaven for it, that she was been saved for it, and when I . . ."

"Let me just say that we are older now, Mercy, and I think you'd best forget it."

"You saw the mark of the witch on her as did I."

"Besides," Jane shook her head, "I am sure John Winthrop has other worries now. These days he is more concerned with snaring heretics than witches, and from the sound of it he probably thought you were referring to Mistress Hutchinson when you said, 'a midwife and a seducer'—for that is what he thinks of her—and that is what I find truly distressing."

"Nonsense," I muttered. "He knew exactly who I meant."

Chapter Thirty-Six

1637

Every week my belly grew fuller and the life within me more active. Sometimes at night I'd lift my smock and press the swelling skin of my stomach, hoping to arouse the baby, but it seldom responded to my touch.

As the life within me grew, the world about me changed. While the previous year began with promise, the year 1637 was filled with peril.

I had been completely out of touch with Mistress Hutchinson except for seeing her in the meetinghouse. But even there, Joshua monitored me closely. After services, when people gathered in small groups to partake in conversation, his arm firmly steered me away from whatever circle she was part of. Whereas once he might have been inclined to linger and converse with men in society, now there was none of that. He seemed in a hurry to return home, eager to contain me behind bolted doors where I could not embarrass him. He seemed more concerned with his status in the community than with me. The only time he did linger was when a transgressor was punished in the pillory pit following the service. Then, with a forceful grip on my elbow, he would say, "Come along now,

Goodwife," and lead me around the corner and down the serpentine path to the pit's edge to watch the spectacle.

The discord within the Boston Congregation over religious matters and the desire to repress Mistress Hutchinson caused ministers and magistrates alike to be more severe in doling out discipline, especially to women. I believed it was just a matter of time before Goody Hammer would be brought forth. For weeks I had been waiting to hear her name bandied about in gossip, waiting to see it posted on the meetinghouse door in the list of names of those to be chastised. But that did not happen. Every week Goody Hammer took her usual seat, flaunting the same air of self-confidence she flaunted the week before. I was sure it was just taking the magistrates longer to investigate her case, as witchcraft is a more complicated offense than most.

That spring, Election Day, once so full of optimism, had turned into an angry contest pitting the people of Boston against the people of the other communities. Most residents of Boston would have been content with the reelection of Henry Vane as governor, but those in the outlying towns—who had cast a harsh eye upon the activities in Boston and favored a return to more conservative governance. So on Election Day, the freemen—after having had resorted to fisticuffs and having had to be called to civility by Reverend Wilson who climbed up into a tree to be heard—reelected the community's original leaders, John Winthrop and Thomas Dudley. In terms of leadership, we were back to where we were in 1630; but in terms of unity, we were far removed from being the "city on a hill" that John Winthrop had envisioned upon the *Arbella*.

In addition to the religious and political upheaval that consumed us, a frightful Indian uprising was developing to the south. The Pequots, who had up until then kept to themselves, had viciously attacked settlers in Connecticut, and we feared that after hacking every pink scalp there, they would advance upon us in Boston. Unlike the Narragansetts, the Pequots were a warlike tribe, stout and proud and born with the taste of blood upon their tongues. Already they had murdered a man in Watertown, a trader named John Oldham whom everyone called Mad Jack. His death was mourned not because the good people of Watertown were sad to see him in the grave, but because the murder had occurred so close to their homes. There was also a rumor that the Pequots had snatched two servant girls and taken them into captivity. The thought of being dragged away and scalped by those savages made me wake up in the night and check the bolts on our doors, which I knew offered little protection against their sharp axes. I was no different than most of us who would lay awake for hours listening for their sounds, wondering whether in an attack they would creep up upon us barefooted, or whether there would be a noisy forewarning with whoops and hollers before they flayed us alive.

Each day through our window I watched Boston's militia, composed of our town's youngest boys, march in cadence up and down the High Street beating their drums and brandishing their gleaming swords, pikes, and muskets, preparing for the attack that next to damnation we feared the most. These frail young boys, nearly one hundred in number—for I had counted them—seemed no match for the brawn and bluster of the Indians.

It was upon this landscape of fear that my child grew inside me. No matter how I tried to reassure myself that the Lord would protect me in my travail as he had protected Mistress Hutchinson, I could find no peace. Now the Lord had broadened His dislike of me to encompass our community.

ABOUT A MONTH BEFORE THE BABE was due, I announced to Joshua that Anne Hutchinson, with whom I felt safe, would be my midwife. As I expected, Joshua responded angrily and commanded me to make other arrangements. It was unheard of for a husband to deny his wife the midwife of her choice, so later that day he relented, as I expected he would.

"So be it. Afterwards we shall be rid of her." Then he added, "Who are your other women?"

"Jane and Catherine."

He looked relieved.

As my time grew near, I expected my mistress to call upon me just as Goody Hammer had called upon Mama. I imagined that moment. Mistress Hutchinson would knock on the door and inquire about my spiritual estate. I would fetch her cider and would pour my heart out to her, disclosing my sins in full confession.

"She isn't coming," Joshua said whenever he caught me staring out the window.

"She will come. I am like one of her daughters."

"Goodwife, she has daughters of her own, and you are not amongst them."

The voices assured me. *She will come. Your husband is a man of little faith.*

I considered the Gospel of Matthew and the mustard seed. I turned my back to my husband and fixed my gaze out the open window at two women slogging past. The oppressive heat and weight of their dark gowns had slowed their pace. I scurried over to the window and leaned my head out. "Goodwives, dost ye not know that faith as small as a mustard seed moves mountains? That everything is possible for the believer?" The women stopped their chattering and looked wide-eyed at me. "Faith as small as a mustard seed," I called to them.

"Stop it!" Joshua yelled.

I shouted, "And ye too can move mountains!" One of the women looked over her shoulder and stared at me with her mouth agape. I waved to her. It pleased me that she received my teachings with such awe. "As small as a mustard seed!" I called to their backs, pinching my thumb and forefinger together to remind them of the size of that powerful seed.

Joshua ran toward the window, pushed me aside and slammed it. The redness in his neck rose into his face. "Shut it, woman. It is embarrassing enough that you deliver Bible verses to me all day long. I shall not have you delivering them to strangers. I forbid it, yet you defy me."

"You are my husband, but the Lord is higher than you, and it is to Him I bow. Do you not know that the Spirit resides within me, that I have been chosen to spread the Word?"

His eyes narrowed and darkened. "Subdue yourself, woman."

"She will come," I said, turning my back to him.

"I have work to do," he grumbled.

I turned and grabbed his sleeve. "What grudge do you have against her?" This time it was I who needed to rekindle our old argument.

"She is a noxious weed, Goodwife. I spoke to your father about it. Even he, a compassionate man in all respects, believes she should be rousted out of the congregation and sent to Connecticut. Let the Indians have her!" He stomped off.

"Joshua!"

He turned around.

"What does my Papa know of Mistress Hutchinson other than the rubbish that John Winthrop and the blackcoats stuff inside his head?"

"Look at the dissension she has caused in our town!"

"Look at the damage Papa has caused me!"

Joshua glared at me. "Now you blaspheme your father? What has he done to deserve it?"

I stomped my foot so hard that the heel of my shoe left its mark in the wooden floor. "It is time you know, my husband. The man you so revere took use of my body." I pressed my fingers into my eyelids, as if to darken the memory.

Joshua took a step backwards. "What was that?" he asked in a near whisper.

"He had use of me," I said less boldly. "He took me to his bed and had use of me."

Joshua's eyes were two hard stones. "You lie, woman," he said in disgust. "Now you befoul your father's name. Does your tongue not tingle with the telling of such a falsehood?"

"I speak the truth. I swear it on the Bible."

He was not listening.

"It happened after Mama died," I tried to explain.

"What . . . what has entered your mind, woman? Has Satan now taken control of your thoughts? I suppose next you shall tell me the child you carry in your belly is not mine!"

"I carry your child," I said calmly.

There was no room in his heart for understanding. He tromped around the table and stopped and glared at the thick Bible on its center. With one quick and angry swipe he flung it to the floor. "That's what I think of the Bible verses you recite wherever you go. If this is what they bring, I want nothing of them." A dried red maple leaf flew out from between the pages and hovered in the air.

"My husband," I pleaded, stooping to retrieve the book. When I looked up Joshua was gone. The door of the cooperage slammed.

I stumbled over to the rocking chair and fell into it. Mama's maple leaf lay on the floor. The once scarlet leaf had long ago faded into a dull bronze.

Joshua doled out wild and incessant blows to his wood. The hours passed and the pounding did not abate; in time the frenzy of it became one with my thoughts, my breath, my heartbeat, the pounding inside my head. I thought of all that had happened since we left England—my meeting Joshua and my love for him, my sin with Papa, the deaths of those I loved. What sins did the Lord forgive? What sins were unforgivable? My thoughts became so jumbled that I could no more attach myself to a single one than I could to a whirling wind.

It was dark before Joshua returned, and I had gone to bed. At the sound of him fumbling about the room I tensed up, dreading another confrontation. But at the same time I longed for him to pry the details of that horrible night out of me so we could cleanse the poisoned air between us. But he didn't utter a word. I listened to the clink of his belt buckle falling to the floor, and felt the flop of his body into bed, and the swoop of him kicking off the bedcovers in the night's sweltering heat.

My PAINS BEGAN ON THE FIRST DAY of August, the hottest in a string of fifteen days that scorched the residents of Boston with the fury of hellfire itself rising out of the earth.

Early that day, Jane came to check on me. Miracle followed her in by the hand, and they did not stay long. She set a loaf of bread and a basket of ripe plums on the table and inquired whether any signs my travail had begun. I shook my head. Jane shrugged her shoulders and turned to leave.

"Mercy, if you need me, I shall be at home. Just send Joshua."

Later, Joshua came in and ripped off a hunk of Jane's bread for lunch and grabbed two plums. He dashed out the door.

When I was alone, I brushed the crumbs from the table into my hand and threw them out the window to the birds. That was when I felt the first pain.

In a while another followed. I looked out the window for Mistress Hutchinson. They say a mother is oft aware of her daughter's pain without being told of it, so at any moment I expected her to come scurrying up the lane lugging her tapestry bag, heavy with wine jug and hourglass. At any moment she would rap on my door.

I must prepare, I thought. Supporting the heft of my belly with one hand, I opened the cedar chest, yanked out a stained quilt, and spread it out on the floor beneath the window. I lowered myself onto it and sat with my back against the cedar chest waiting for her.

An hour or so later, the pains became unbearable. I called out for Joshua, but there was no answer. He was just like Papa—running off to do business when I needed him the most. The pains gripped me and I needed help. I pulled myself up, staggered to the front door and pulled it open. The light was blinding and the heat was like the blast of an oven. Another pain made me double over. I felt something inside of me tear and suddenly my skirt and legs were sopping wet. Panicking, I stepped out into the lane to stop someone for help. I grabbed for the first skirt I saw.

"My child is coming. Please help me," I cried to the woman I stopped. When I followed the folds of dotted calico up to her face, I was staring into the terrified eyes of Jenny, who was not a woman at all, but an incompetent girl. With one look at my belly she exclaimed, "I know nothing about birthing. You know I do not."

I took her by the shoulders. "Listen you, Jenny. Go fetch Mistress Hutchinson, your mother, and Jane. Tell them to hurry! Find Joshua!"

"My mother is away!"

"Fetch the others then!"

Pain gripped me and I staggered into the house. I fell against the table board and knocked it off its trestles, dumping to the floor Mama's Bible, the plums, and the pitcher of water I had set out for myself.

"My God, Mama, I need you!"

Just then Joshua hurried in. "Jenny told me!" In one quick motion, he carried me to our bed. "Jenny is fetching Mistress Hutchinson," he said.

Through a haze of fear, I looked up into my husband's eyes, and remembering the strife betwixt us, I tried to read his heart. They were no longer the steely eyes I had come to know, nor the gentle eyes that once had comforted me, but they were soft eyes that said he was my ally, at least for the moment.

He wiped my forehead with his handkerchief. "What can I do?"

"Stay until she comes, please."

He held my hands through many more gripping pains.

Finally, a door swung open. Jenny ran in with Jane, and behind them hobbled not Anne Hutchinson, but Goody Hammer.

I glared at Jenny with disbelief. After the clearest instructions, I could not fathom that she brought the wrong midwife.

"Go away," I shouted at Goody Hammer.

Jenny cowered in the corner wringing her hands. "Mistress Hutchinson was not at home," she squeaked. "And my mother is at Mystic with Papa."

"Please send her away," I pleaded to Jane.

"But Goodwife Hammer is a midwife," Jenny interrupted.

"Do you not know that is her occupation?" she insisted, as if I was the newest resident of Boston. Goody Hammer stood behind Jenny listening, but saying nothing.

"Be still," Jane said sharply to Jenny. "Of course Mercy knows that." She looked at me hard. "I'm afraid you have no choice now."

Goody Hammer instructed Joshua to go to Cole's Inn and have a drink of ale. She told him Jenny would fetch him later. My husband departed on eager legs.

Goody Hammer's white face bore into me, and every fear I had multiplied. "Go, you! Mistress Hutchinson is coming," I cried, forcing words to rise above the knot in my throat.

"She is not comin'. She was summoned to Wollaston this morn to tend to her sister-in-law, Mary Wheelwright, who is lying-in with her own child and needs her. She will be there for several weeks. She asked me to come in her absence."

"Never!"

"Let us take a look." She reached for the hem of my gown.

I grabbed her wrist and held it. "I know what you are . . . you shall not bewitch me!"

"You speak craziness." Goody Hammer's damaged eye danced in its socket and the room spun in my vision. Her eye was drawing me in. I felt myself rising off the bed and floating into its twisted depths. She was casting a spell on me.

"Allow her this," Jane said firmly.

A pain like the stab of a knife overtook me. I lost my strength and released my grasp on her wrist. Goody Hammer stepped back. "Mercy, I would rather not be here also. I am aware you prefer another, but the one you prefer is not here."

The child inside me bore down again, this time with urgency, and I had no choice. I would have welcomed Satan himself if he promised to unroot the child from me. So I allowed her to settle me on the floor. When she checked my privities, I fought her off by batting and kicking, but as my strength dwindled, hers increased. Every touch brought new torture.

"Your child has not turned and I must right it," Goody Hammer said looking straight into my eyes. She called to Jane and Jenny. "Stand ye on either side of her and hold her down tight." Like dutiful handmaidens of Satan, they held me firm.

"This will pain you as nothing you have ever felt, but when it is over, it will be over. Take a deep breath now."

Instead, I held my breath knowing the witch would do to me what she did to my mother. "My God, Mama!" I screamed when her hand entered my privities. It was the sharp-claw of Satan reaching into me, claiming my child. Consumed by a terror greater than pain, I yowled. As long as I could hear my voice, I was alive. I could not die and face my judgment.

Goody Hammer chanted, *"Vidi aquam . . ."*

"Shut it!" I cried, covering my ears. You speak Satan's words."

Her face was a grimace. "Settle down, girl. These be words of healing—."

"You speak words of a sorcerer. Witch!" I screamed.

Goody Hammer's face relaxed. "The child has turned. The Lord has delivered us," she said, withdrawing her blood-soaked hand from inside me and wiping it on her apron.

"'Tis now time to push."

I pushed as she commanded, for I had no choice.

It was within a caul of blood and fear that a daughter was born to me. She entered the world with a piercing cry and flailing limbs that bespoke the passion and pain I had infused her with the nine months she grew inside my womb.

Chapter Thirty-Seven

A gainst my objections, Joshua arranged for Goody Hammer to stay with me during my lying-in. Jane offered to help, but Joshua thought otherwise. He trusted Goody Hammer would keep him completely informed of my behavior, whereas Jane might try to protect me.

Some hours after my child was born, Catherine arrived. Through half-shut eyes I watched her. A whirlwind she was, her carrot hair disheveled and dampened to bronze from rushing, her green eyes twinkling with the anticipation of seeing the baby. I pretended to be asleep. All I longed for was silence.

"I was in Mystic," she explained to Joshua, her hushed voice swelling with apology. "Gabriel wished for me to see the *Trinity*. I should have stayed at home. I didn't think the baby would come so soon."

"All went well, Catherine. There were no problems."

I turned my head away.

"Ah, there she is. Let me take a look at our sweet angel."

"She sleeps like a kitten," Joshua said.

"This world agrees with her," Catherine cooed.

I heard her tiptoe closer to the crib beside our bed, the crib Joshua had crafted from half a firkin and Jane had cushioned with a swan's-down pillow she painstakingly stitched.

"Bless the Lord, the babe is lovely. So pink and tiny. Joshua, she has your nose, and look, she has a dimple in her chin. The kiss of God. Gabriel will be pleased to hear of it."

"She bears the mark of the Goodhues," Joshua chuckled.

"And our Mercy, look at her. She's exhausted. I had better take leave now."

At the door, I overheard them whispering.

"Please come often, Catherine. Mercy is in need of a mother's love and can learn from your example."

Catherine sighed. "Oh, Joshua. So often I thought of it, but I did not want to intrude. Mercy has turned from me so. I know not what I had done to warrant her coldness."

"'Tis the same with me, Catherine, and with Jane who has done nothing to offend her, and Goodwife Hammer who only wishes her well."

"Gabriel says we must give her time and the Lord will show her the way."

ON THE SECOND DAY OF MY CHILD'S LIFE she shrieked incessantly and could not be comforted. I tried to nurse her, but she would not suckle. I held her close, but the more I attempted to soothe her, the more she kicked her scrawny legs into my engorged breasts and pushed me away. Even the slightest weight of cotton on her skin seemed an irritant, so I allowed her to lie naked in her crib. Even then she batted her arms and legs wildly, as if the air were her enemy.

On the third day, I rose up from bed, pressed my hands against the wall for support and stumbled toward the window.

"Where'd ya think you're going?" Goody Hammer asked.

I did not reply.

"On your feet t'day and t'morrow you shall pay."

I nodded my head. The sooner I did for myself, the sooner I would be rid her.

It was another day of sweltering heat and the High Street was deserted. The lane was dry as ash, and the leaves on the trees drooped from the weight of the merciless sun. Nary a bird or animal was present.

I tried to ignore the infant's piercing cries; the *chink, chink, chink, chink* of Joshua's mallet against his chisel; and Goody Hammer's never-ending prattle. She carried on a conversation with herself as if she had a phantom companion in the room. While I was weak and worn from the heat, Goody Hammer clattered about, from one chore to another, as if the inferno agreed with her: boiling water and speaking of it; scrubbing clothes and discussing the origin of each stain; rocking my infant and reminding me of her unselfish devotion to her; lugging pails of cool water inside and speaking of the pleasures of a drink and a wash; patting the cur, Elijah, who lingered half-dead on the stone hearth. Throughout all of it, I remained silent.

Occasionally, to be rid of her, I would step into the cooperage where neither she nor her mongrel would venture. Joshua nary made eye contact with me. With a set jaw he went about his work. So I stood at the window and looked past him, past the pole of the wellsweep and the bucket hanging motionless from its chain.

Late that afternoon, when Goody Hammer and I were alone, I found the voice I lost.

"I'm in hell on earth."

"What did you say?" Goody Hammer stepped close to me to hear over the pounding from the cooperage. I waved my hand in the air for her to leave.

"You speak not for hours, and then you mumble. What did you say?"

"I am in hell."

"Mark it, girl, all new mothers are in hell for a time. What makes you think you're different than the rest? Stay in bed with your legs shut and you'll mend, and in a month or two you'll be frisky enough to do it over again. 'Tis girls like you who keep me in business."

"You are my hell," I said, flicking her away.

Goody Hammer stepped closer. "You talk nonsense. Soon I'll be off and you'll have your wish. You'll be alone carin' for your babe, scrubbin' her linens and fetchin' water from that fancy well of yours. The stretchin' alone will lay you flat till Sabbath next, and then you'll credit me for helpin' ya." She snatched the broom from the corner and swept with a fury, stirring up clouds of dust.

"If the Lord was so against you, would He have given you this comely child?" She gestured toward the infant whimpering in her crib. "If the Lord was so out of favor with you, your babe would have been born dead, not the lusty girl she is." She opened the door and whisked the dust into the blinding light, then set her broom against the wall and her hands on her hips. "I have witnessed the Lord's rage and He has not delivered it to you. In England I once delivered not a human but a handful of clumps, a monster it was, blobs of deformed flesh. And you bore this healthy child," she said. "The Lord has not deserted you, woman."

"But I am not saved."

She shook her head. "You know your eternal destiny no more than I know mine. 'Tis blasphemy to expect answers no woman on earth is privy to."

"I suspect I am not saved."

"You suspect nothing."

I squinted into her spider eye. The black of it expanded like ink spilt on a blotter. "Why should I listen to you?"

"Because I care about you."

The infant's whimpering turned into a shrill cry and Goody Hammer broke my stare to attend to her. She set the babe upon her shoulder, tapped its arching back, cooed until she stopped crying. Then she looked at me straight. "You have been distracted ever since your mother died. What black bile consumes you?" She waited for an answer, stinging me with her strong eye.

"Ask Joshua, for he knows. Or Papa."

Goody Hammer raised her eyebrows. I made my way past her to the window and stared into the haze that hovered above the dirt lane like a spectral blanket.

THROUGHOUT THAT NIGHT the baby cried with colic. Occasionally Goody Hammer brought her to me. Giving suckle was natural to some women, but to me it did not come easily. I would attach the child's lips to my breast and allow her to gulp until I could no longer abide the pain. Then in agony I would return the child to Goody Hammer. Soon the child would cry again—short, sharp cries that felt like razor cuts upon my skin. She would quiet only when Goody Hammer hooked her again to my breast. After a few swallows, I would pull the child away from my bosom in agony.

"'Tis pain new mothers must endure. Giving suck will toughen your nipples," Goody Hammer kept repeating. To alleviate the pain she pressed compresses of violet leaves seethed in boilt milk and wheat bran onto my breasts. "It must be as hot as you can stand it," she said, kneading the salve into my raw nipples with untender fingers. Her salve did me no good. By the middle of the night I was writhing in pain.

While Goody Hammer labored over me, Joshua rocked the infant, walked her in circles and sang tunes in his off-key manner. When Goody Hammer was done with me, humbled by my husband's devotion, I opened my arms to the child. As I stared into her face, partially hidden by the mound of my engorged breast, I remembered something Mama had said: "The babe who sucks his mother's breast, loves his mother best." I must endure the pain to gain my child's love.

It was nearly dawn when the infant finally slept, as did Joshua and Goody Hammer, both of them worn from the ordeal. Goody Hammer made a place for herself in the rocking chair where she slept with gnarled fingers knit together across her stomach, and feet still buckled inside her shoes, propped upon a stool. I eased myself beside Joshua on the edge of our bed. There was just enough light in the room to see the hillock of white cotton covering the infant's body. A wet breeze weighted with the heat of the previous day fluttered in through the weave of the curtains.

I slept fitfully. My breasts burned. At first I refrained from scratching them for fear of waking Joshua; but as it became clear by his deep breathing he could not be roused, I scratched my chest gently and then more forcefully. But the scratching brought me no relief; it only compelled me to scratch more. My fingers became sticky with milk and with droplets of blood that in the shadows looked like gray smears on my skin. In desperation I tucked my arms beneath my hips, closed my eyes and prayed for deliverance.

Eventually I began to dream. I was in a parched field, a vast field where I was surrounded by a multitude of people. A line had been drawn in the dust, separating the field in two. It was a crooked line, as if drawn by a stick. A signal had been given (although I knew not what it was) that started the people scurrying about. They took places I knew to be preordained, on one side of the line or the other. Everything was orderly. Everyone but me knew where to go.

Then came a loud voice, as if through a trumpet.

Heaven or hell?

"I know not my place," I said in confusion.

'Tis blasphemy to expect answers no woman who walks this earth should know, the voice bellowed.

I awoke in a sweat. When I opened my eyes, Goody Hammer's face—bloodless and disembodied—was hovering above me, her lips parted, as if she had more to say. My heart beat faster. Then the specter disappeared.

I sat up and searched the room. In the gray haze of morning, Goody Hammer was asleep with her lips parted in the same fashion as they were in my dream. She plays with me. She jumps here and there, bewitching me. Then she disappears.

I prayed. With good prayers, surely the Lord would comfort me. "Silence the voices," I pleaded, repeating my prayer forty times, counting the repetitions and then beginning again. Then I saw it. It was the same as it was when I was a child, when Mama sent me into the closet to bare my soul to the Lord. A flash of light illuminated the entire room like a million suns.

You are forgiven, my child . . . You will walk in the light, and all will be well . . . All will be well. You are forgiven . . . forgiven.

There were many voices. They were melodic—like the blended voices of the godly people I had known, but who died—Mama, Noah and Michael, Ezekiel, all of them speaking in sweet chorus, and I felt safe in their midst.

"I am forgiven," I said aloud and in saying the words I felt the waters of peace wash over me like baptism. It was as my mistress said it would be. I only had to wait for that burst of radiant flame, and for the Spirit to speak to me. Cleansed of my most grievous sin, I sank back into my bed and closed my eyes. Life would be different now. I would no longer fear hell and judgment for I heard the words. I knew I was forgiven. I knew I was saved. With Joshua and my precious daughter, I would live in the light.

Barely had sleep overcome me, when I was awakened again, this time by the rush of water. I opened my eyes to see leafy shadows flickering upon the wall. Then the leafy patterns became pallets of mist sweeping away from the walls and curling across the room, moving like water toward me. My body tensed as the misty islands congealed into a dingy mass above my head. I felt a different presence now, the presence of evil. A harsh voice coming from the center of the specter growled.

Don't be a foolish woman. How can you be sure you have been forgiven?

I awoke in a cold sweat. "Who speaks?" I asked aloud.

There were many voices and they became noisome, arguing over each other in torrents of good and evil.

You are forgiven my child . . .

Fool! How do you know?

Hell is where you belong . . .

You are a good girl, Mercy. You walk in the light . . .

Listen not to such nonsense. You shall crackle like a leaf tossed upon fire. Day after day . . . you shall burn forever and ever . . .

The choir of grisly voices echoed off the walls and into my ears, resonating like screeches and drumbeats inside my head.

Heaven or hell? It matters not a speck where you go, woman. What matters is that you know your fate and know it now. For only then will you find peace in this life.

"Who speaks?" I asked aloud.

Joshua snorted and turned his back on me.

"Who speaks?" I asked again.

The voices repeated: *Do you seek assurance? Do you seek peace of mind?*

"I do. I must know," I answered.

Then knowing is all that matters . . .

I covered my ears.

A motion near the window caught my attention. A viscid breeze ruffled the curtains. A lone bird chirped out the first peep of morning. Another responded, and a choir of birds chattered wildly at the approach of dawn.

You are forgiven, the gentle voice soothed. But it was silenced by a mightier voice that cackled over it, and another that cackled over that voice, and soon waves of ear-deafening voices one upon another enveloped me and I could not tell one from another.

You shall have no peace until you know where you belong. Are you God's child? Or do you belong to Satan? You must know. You must know it now. Knowing is all that matters.

"I must know," I said.

Do you wish to end your uncertainty?

"I do."

There is a way, the voice said. *Remember that Abraham had no assurance until he sacrificed Isaac.*

The voices stopped and there was silence. I knew what I had to do. A firm hand pressed into my back and raised me up. I set my feet on the floor and looked down into the cradle. The infant was asleep. Her limp arms were raised in surrender above her head. Without hesitation I bent over and scooped her up. A muscle in her eyelid throbbed ever so slightly. Her body twitched, then relaxed. On tiptoes, I scurried into the cooperage, past Joshua's workbench and the pyramid of barrels stacked floor to ceiling, and into the garth, mindful not to disturb my husband or Goody Hammer whose overlapping snores gave a dissonant pulse to the lifeless morning. The heralding birds stopped their chatter.

I stood at the edge of the well and stared at the silhouette of the wellsweep against a sky splintered with red behind the smoky outline of trees. The long arm of the wellsweep pointed diagonally towards the new light, and against this landscape hung the water bucket on a chain.

"Now I shall know for sure," I said aloud. I kissed the soft pillow of the baby's forehead, unwrapped her from her sheet, held her up as if in offering, and placed the infant inside the bucket.

"Now there can be no doubt," I muttered.

I stepped to the handle of the wellsweep and bent to release it from the rock holding it to the ground in the spot above where I had buried Goody Hammer's amulets. With both hands I lifted the handle of the wellsweep above my head, let go, and in one quick motion the bucket fell into the well. In the stark silence of dawn, the wood tapped the still, dark water.

"Now I know what God has planned for me," I cried, raising my hands toward heaven. "It is done. Now I know I am damned." A feeling of relief washed over me. In knowing that hell was my eternal destiny, predestined by the Lord to be such, I could now go on living.

I fixed my eyes on the brilliant band of crimson light fringing the horizon—the presage of a new day, a day that would be unlike any other, and a day closer to my eternal fate that now was no longer in question.

A rooster crowed. A horse clomped by. A cart bumped past. The man who pushed it hummed a simple tune. The

High Street was coming to life.

I tromped through the cooperage into the house, and not caring whether I disturbed anyone, I slammed the door behind me. Goody Hammer was the first to awaken. Her body jerked in the rocking chair, sending her feet clunking to the floor. At the sound of the noise Joshua turned and stretched his sleep-swollen body over the width of our mattress, patting it to feel for me. He squinted into the light and closed his eyes.

"Now I am sure I will be damned," I shouted, "for I have killed my child!" At the sound of my declaration, I looked at my hands. The insides of my fingers still bore the white indentations of the wellsweep's handle, evidence that what I had done was not a dream.

No one responded, and I waited for my words to be understood. An eternity seemed to pass in a blink.

"My God!" cried Goody Hammer, sitting straight up. "WHAT ... HAVE ... YOU ... DONE?" Her veined fingers gripped the arms of the rocking chair and her body sprung from it. She hobbled towards me with her arms out and her fingers hooked like claws. She grabbed my shoulders and shook me. "What have you done?"

"Now I am sure I will be damned, for I have drowned my baby," I said.

"God, have mercy," Goody Hammer cried, running to the infant's crib. Seeing it was empty, she nearly fell on top of Joshua and shook him awake in a flurry so awkward that it struck me as comical, and I laughed.

Chapter Thirty-Eight

———— ❧ ————

S hut it!" Goody Hammer screamed.

The world moved slowly, as if time halved its speed and every motion was labored. Slowly, Joshua pulled up his breeches and tied them. Ponderously, he stepped toward me and probed my face with the harshest of eyes. Goody Hammer tugged twice on the cloth of his breeches and pulled him out the door.

Alone, I ran to the corner nearest the fireplace and huddled into a ball on the floor, wishing to disappear, ruing the day I was born. I stared at my guilty hands and willed the movement within them to cease. I willed the muscles in my arms and neck and cheeks to turn limp; I willed my eyelids to stop blinking, the world to turn to black. Then in the blackness I saw my image passing through the gates of hell, which had been my eternal destiny as preordained by God at the moment of my creation. Ashes to ashes, I thought as I watched my finger draw a line through the dust on the wooden floor. Elijah hobbled over and licked my knuckles with his rough tongue. This time I allowed him to do it, for what did it matter? I glanced across the room at the half opened cooperage door. The blazing red sun spilled onto the kitchen floor like a toppled cask of blood. Beyond the bloody sun, the witch was chanting the words of mystery I had heard before. Words wilder than the rage of the wind, shriller than the screech of angels.

"Vidi aquam egredientem de templo, a latere dextro, alleluia: Et omnes, ad quos pervenit aqua ista salvi facti sunt, et dicent, alleluia, alleluia."

"Hush you," I cried.

Her chant was a plea, a prayer, a proclivity. The words, guttural and harsh, gained force as they roiled in her throat and out her lips, like a wave onto the surf, into the swelling madness of the morning I created.

THE HOUSE SHOOK when they pushed the door open.

"She sleeps," Joshua said.

"It pleases the Lord she knows nothin' of it," Goody Hammer murmured.

Through a slit between my sooty fingers I saw her black shoes. They tapped quickly across the floor and stopped in the middle of the room beside the table leg. I looked up, above the hem of her white gown, her wide belly, her black collar, into her good eye. It was a beacon in search of me, flashing from bed to chair, from window to door, and finally to the corner of the fireplace where it stopped, pinning me where I was crouched.

"Drop your hands and show your face, woman."

"Go away," I muttered.

"Look up," she commanded. "You peek through your fingers like a woman gazin' through the bars of the cage. Stand and explain yourself."

I scooted against the wall away from her. Out of the corner of my eye I could see the jagged hearthstones, and beyond them a cool pillow of ashes resting in the bed of the fireplace. I blocked out Goody Hammer's wrath and focused my attention on the ashes. It was there that I longed to lay my head, where I would wait for a fire to ignite and reduce my body to a silvery heap. Joshua would scoop the small and weightless pile up with his shovel and toss it into the street. In them I would live on.

I would drift through Boston rising and falling on the breeze. I would twirl in small whirlpools of dust, skimming upon the white tips of the fitful waves slamming the shore. I would complete the unfinished business of my life. On the Sabbath I would fly to the meetinghouse and hover above the pulpit in wait of Reverend Wilson. When he intoned the words of Isaiah, "Surely wickedness burns like a fire; it consumes briars and thorns," I would release one silvery ash of myself upon him and watch it settle on his skullcap. I would hasten to the home of Anne Hutchinson, fly through her open window and up the stairs into her chamber where she would be sitting straight-backed in her chair reading St. Paul's Epistle to Titus and rocking the leg of Zuriel's crib with a motherly foot. I would drop a gray ash onto her exposed white stocking to remind her of her desertion of me. On the sharpest of winds I would take flight across the street and wait outside John Winthrop's door. At the precise moment he stepped out and squinted into the sunlight, I would blow a prickly ash of myself deep into his narrowed eye. His vision would blur and he would rub his eyelid with his knuckle as he walked, pondering what miniscule sin had warranted such a correction from the Lord. In a flurry I would seek out Papa at the shipyard and deposit a blanched ash, no larger than a teardrop, upon his cheek. Like the kiss of Judas it would cling to him, leaving a mark that would remain burnished there forever to remind him of the depths to which he had sent me.

In a single motion I swung my knees behind me, and like Elijah, I crept toward the fireplace. I crawled but two paces before Goody Hammer stomped one dusty black shoe in front of me, and then the other, stopping me with her girth.

"Mercy!"

"You shall thwart me no more, witch," I snarled. "Now I am like you. You shall burn in hell, and I along with you!"

"You speak nonsense!" With cool, wet hands she reached down, grabbed me by my elbows, and raised me up.

"You have accused me long enough, woman. Aye, there are witches, but I am not amongst 'em. They swarm the shires of England. We know it. But here we have purged ourselves of 'em. Here we are God's people, His saints."

"Rubbish! You bear the mark of a witch for I have seen it," I exclaimed.

"You've seen nothing, and if you know every blemish on my body, 'tis you not I who is a witch."

"Now you shall have new gossip to tell everyone," I hissed, "about how Mercy Hoyt killed her child, and about how you tried to save the infant but failed, just as you tried to save Mama and Mary with your charms and chants!" Now I could unbridle my tongue, for I was beyond heavenly censure.

Goody Hammer pulled me toward the chair and pushed me into it. "Your child lives. The Lord wills it. I know not why He has spared you this, but . . ."

"You trick me," I screeched, looking beyond her into the cooperage, through the open window at the wellsweep. "It cannot be. I lowered her into the well."

"Aye, you did it, but in the heat the water level receded enough to spare her. The water in the bucket rose up to her neck. It covered all but her face. You had one motive, but the Lord had another."

I stared at the woman in disbelief.

"The Lord intervened, Mercy."

Goody Hammer stepped aside and Joshua, who had been listening from the cooperage, came forth with the baby cradled in his arms, sound asleep. He had wrapped her in Goody Hammer's apron. The infant's miniscule shoulders were beaded with water and her wispy blond hair was as damp as a christened babe's.

Goody Hammer turned to Joshua and lowered her voice. "'Tis best we summon Reverend Wilson to pray with her, for it is his higher prayers we must call upon now. He is due home today from Connecticut."

"Not Reverend Wilson! That blackcoat is a worthless fool!"

"Fetch him," Goody Hammer said firmly. "If he is still away ministerin' to our militia, find Reverend Cotton. You give me the child," she said to Joshua. "I'll tend to 'em both."

While Joshua was gone I paced the floor, moving in and out of a bar of sunlight that slashed the room in two. As if I were invisible, Goody Hammer sat in the rocking chair rocking my child, her dusty shoe tapping the plank floor with each roll of the rocker.

Exhausted, I fell into Joshua's chair with my back toward the woman. Outside the window, the flutter of a sparrow's skittish wings caught my eye. It perched upon the windowsill, pecked at the pane of glass, jerked as if sensing danger inside, and flew away.

IN DUE TIME, THE DOOR SWUNG OPEN and they returned. Joshua entered first and Reverend Wilson and Reverend Cotton followed behind.

Goody Hammer leapt from the rocking chair so quickly that the infant started to cry. She steadied the babe's bobbing head with her hand and stroked her back. "Praise the Lord," she whispered. "You have returned to us, Reverend Wilson. Thank God for your safety."

"Just this morning," Reverend Wilson mumbled, rubbing his eyes. "We have subdued the Indians, as you may have heard. You will see proof of their capitulation outside the meetinghouse where the feet and heads of the slain are being mounted on the spikes of the fence right now. The Lord wills it that we Englishmen prevail."

A moment later, Papa entered, lowering his head to clear the doorway. He came directly from the shipyard in his work apron, high boots and straw hat.

"My God!" I cried out. The others I could contend with by ignoring their words, but I could not contend with my father.

"Leave!" I shouted at him.

Papa opened his mouth to defend himself, but Joshua interrupted. "He stays," he said decisively.

I tried to stand, but Joshua pressed his hands into my shoulders and firmly pushed me into his chair. The four men gathered around me in a tight circle with an efficiency that told me the ministers had done this to other women before. Surrounded by the thick black prunella of the ministers' breeches and the cloaks they wore even in the heat, Joshua's stained breeches and Papa's work apron, I felt as if I had been tossed into a well of a danker kind that smelled of sweat and the sea.

"The child is hungry," Goody Hammer mumbled, walking to the door. "Mercy is unfit so I shall arrange with another to give her suckle," she said loud enough for everyone to hear. She made a display of shutting the door loudly behind her. Joshua bolted the door.

Reverend Wilson spoke first. "We are aware of what

happened, but pray tell us in your own words of the incident."

The incident. I crossed my arms over my chest and pretended not to hear.

Reverend Wilson shook his head and stepped back, allowing Reverend Cotton to come forward.

"I know you study Scripture," he said, stroking the bridge of his round nose. "Was there a story in Scripture that fascinated you? Were you doing what Abraham did when he offered his son to be slain?"

I shook my head and said nothing.

"She cooperates not," Reverend Wilson mumbled in his nasal voice. "Mercy, we've known each other for many years. I've heard your sacred testimony when you were accepted into the Boston Congregation. I've observed you from the pulpit. You've been a pious and useful woman. What has come over you? Has this Hutchinson woman influenced you with her heresy? Has the Satan within her become the Satan within you?"

"'Tis the Hutchinson woman," Joshua confirmed.

I glared at him. How little my husband understood.

Reverend Cotton tilted his head back and stared at the ceiling. He looked annoyed with Reverend Wilson. Beneath his graying beard his throat was blotchy and red. He took stern measure of me. "You tried to harm your child," he said sternly.

I nodded.

"What moved you to such desperation?"

I did not answer.

"Did you not hear the question?" Reverend Wilson shouted. "Admit it, woman, and let us get on with it." He slammed his hand on the table beside him. The vibration jolted me.

"The voices spoke," I choked the words out.

"She hears voices?" Reverend Cotton whispered to Joshua.

Joshua nodded.

Reverend Wilson's eyes flashed. "Whose voices do you hear? Whose are they?"

"The voices of light and dark. The Lord's and Satan's," I answered.

He turned and whispered to Reverend Cotton, "Just like the pronouncement Anne Hutchinson made to Reverend Symmes that the Lord speaks to her."

Reverend Cotton ignored him and addressed me in a calm tone. "What has the Lord told you?"

"That I am forgiven. That I walk in the light. That I am His," I sobbed.

"What about the other voices?" He withdrew a handkerchief from his pocket and I expected him to offer it to me, but instead he wiped his own brow with it. "Did they tell you to kill your baby?"

"They promised me peace if I offered him up." I cupped my hands and dropped my head into them. They promised me peace of mind." I mumbled through my tears, "so . . ."

"So what did you do? Speak clearly now."

"I did as they said."

"When Satan speaks to you, what name does he give?" Reverend Wilson interrupted. "Is it Lucifer? Beelzebub?"

I looked up at him with disbelief. In my mind I could hear his high-pitched voice raising from the pulpit into the meetinghouse air Sabbath next blasting through the rafters, "And Satan spoke to the Jezebel and he called himself Lucifer."

"What does he call himself?" he demanded.

"He gives no name," I whimpered.

"But he promises peace for harming your child? Could ye not find peace in the Lord?"

I shook my head.

"Have you sought peace from the Lord?"

"I prayed. For years I begged for forgiveness. I did good works. I listened to your sermons. I sought grace, but every time I felt a hint of the Lord's compassion, the feeling faded and the Lord showed his wrath toward me once again. He took Michael and Noah and also Ezekiel . . ."

Reverend Cotton knelt down so he was at eye level with me. His voice was gentle. "What sin could a young woman like you have committed that would be so unforgivable in the eyes of the Lord? Our God is a God of mercy, my daughter."

I looked up into my father's ruddy face. His sunburned cheeks had flaked, exposing patches of raw pink skin, and his head was bowed so low that his stubbly chin nearly grazed his neck. He averted his eyes from my gaze. I peered through a crack between the ministers' bodies at the cross bolt on the door. I longed to burst through the blackcoats, yank the bar open and run.

Reverend Wilson stepped forward. His eyes glared from the heat of his own impatience. "Let us get on with it. What sin have you committed?"

I could not say it.

"If I can't reach you with words, Mercy Hoyt, perhaps I can reach you with this," he said. He raised his hand above my head. His mouth was open so wide I could see his yellow teeth and count their number. Then, as slowly as if time itself stopped, his palm, broad as a paddle, descended toward my cheek.

I looked at my father—the man who stood by with downcast eyes watching the blackcoats interrogate me, who had spoken not today, nor yesterday, nor for years in my defense, who walked this earth like Cain, a sad and wounded wanderer shrouded in his own grief. Then he looked up, and in a flicker of a muscle in his cheek I detected a quickening within him. Slowly his lips parted and his mouth stretched into an anguished circle.

"Drop your hand!" he shouted, forcing himself between Reverend Wilson and me. He grabbed Reverend Wilson's arm and released it only when the minister's black-sleeved appendage became limp. "Do not touch my daughter!"

For a moment no one spoke, then I could stand it no longer. The anger of all the years bubbled up like lye in a soap cauldron. I rose from my chair and faced him. "You are a hypocrite," I screamed into his face.

He stepped back. "I will not allow him to lay his hands on you." He slipped his arm around my shoulder and walked me away from Reverend Wilson.

"Papa," I shouted, pulling away from his grasp. "It satisfied you to lay your hands on me that night. Why then should not every other man take his pleasure with me as well?" I broke between the ministers and ran toward the mattress and threw myself upon it. "Here I am, Papa, and the two of you who speak for God. Here I am for all of you. And, my husband, you may watch and then surely you will believe me." I yanked my gown above my knees and spread my legs in invitation.

Joshua ran and covered me with a sheet. "Mercy, hold your tongue." He turned then to the men. "She has been consumed by lies. Now she slanders her father."

Stunned, I sat up.

Reverend Wilson nodded his beet-red face. Joshua seemed unsure of which problem to tend to first, his crazed wife or his defamed father-in-law. He turned to Papa. "Goodman Goodhue, I beg your forgiveness. Mercy speaks foolishness. I have never questioned you, for you are a man of good repute."

"Mercy speaks the truth," Papa whispered.

"She speaks what?" Reverend Cotton asked.

"You art protecting her," Reverend Wilson said disdainfully.

"She speaks the truth," Papa said in a voice at last purged of secrets.

"What?" Reverend Wilson screeched.

Joshua's jaw dropped and his mouth hung open. Six years of secrets had been revealed to him in four words. He glared at Papa with disbelief that in a blink turned into revulsion. He looked at me cowering on the bed, then back at Papa. "My God, Gabriel! What possessed you?" He leapt toward my father, grabbed his shoulders and shook him with the force one might use to shake fruit off a tree.

"YOU . . . ARE . . . HER . . . FATHER!" Joshua released his shoulders. He reared back his arm and hurled the hard knot of his fist into Papa's face.

The ministers backed away and made sputtering sounds.

Papa took the blow as his due; he even moved forward as to invite more. Blood gushed from his nose and he raised his hand to wipe himself. I knew my husband wanted to crack all of Papa's bones like sticks.

Joshua reared his arm again. The ministers did naught to stop him. Then, in a moment of choice, when Joshua could have either struck Papa or walked away, he lowered his trembling arm and walked away. I underestimated my husband. Instead, Joshua lumbered toward me and in a measured movement of self-control lowered himself to the edge of the bed. He bent over and dropped his head into his hands, and he started to rock as if that was all he could do to alleviate his anger. It was up to God to have His way with Papa now, for God alone was witness to the crime he committed. Joshua addressed me. "You told me and I did not believe you. The bed. That's why you burned the bed," he sobbed, staring at me with eyes as sad as death itself.

Joshua leaned into me and shucking all resistance, fell into my lap, burying his face in the sheet that covered my legs. I placed my hand upon his head, feeling him sob.

Across the room, Reverend Wilson draped his arm around Papa's shoulder. "Gabriel, you art a father wishing to protect your daughter, but you must not do so at the expense of truth."

"Do not protect him, Reverend Wilson," Joshua cried out.

"I speak the truth," Papa said. "I pray you hear my confession. I shall confess publicly under oath if necessary."

The benches scraped the floor. The ministers and Papa took places around the table. Joshua and I listened as Papa explained in garbled phrases how he was distracted after Mama's death, of his guilt, and how he drank to forget.

"Mercy should have come to us for help," Reverend Cotton said.

There was a long pause. Joshua shook his head. I knew he was waiting for Reverend Wilson to admit I had come to him, but he did not.

"She did come to you!" Joshua shouted, leaping to his feet. "Reverend Wilson, I was with her the night at Governor Winthrop's when she sought you out. It was before you left for England to fetch your wife. You told her to be—"

"—I recall it not," he said, enunciating every word.

Joshua shook his head in disbelief. "Did you hear that? Like Judas, he denies it."

Papa did not acknowledge the interruption, so intent was he on making his own confession. "Then one evening, I drank such quantity of ale that in my stupor saw only Hannah in the room . . . rocking our baby . . . singing to her . . . preparing the boys for bed. I heard her voice. She was there. I saw her, I did. I believed my Hannah had returned to me, but it was Mercy I took. For a long time I knew not whether it was a dream or a memory," he cried.

"You are uncertain even now?" Reverend Wilson queried.

"I was uncertain. That is what I told myself. I am no longer so. I have been certain since the day Mercy set fire to my bed—after Catherine and I married." He looked directly at me. "There has not been a day since that I did not suffer the memory of it."

"Yet you did not ask my forgiveness?" I said to his face.

"I could not speak of it," Papa said, shaking his head.

"Gabriel, let us now pray for forgiveness," Reverend Cotton said.

And so the ministers turned their attention away from me, to Papa. They gathered around him, opened their Bibles and led him in prayer, reading aloud from Isaiah, Jeremiah, Ezekiel, Jonah and Zechariah, pleading for God's mercy. Finally, upon reading from Romans, they exhausted themselves: "For the wages of sin is death, but the gift of God is eternal life through Jesus Christ our Lord."

Throughout it all, Papa hung his head in contrition.

"I am persuaded you show true remorse, and that the Lord hears you," Reverend Cotton said in his silvery voice. "Now you must make amends with the daughter you have harmed."

I sobbed in Joshua's arms so forcefully that the bed shook. It was then that I began to understand the depths of my madness, that it was the voice of Satan that led me to commit the most despicable act imaginable, and that it was Goody Hammer who saved my child, and that it was with her I had to make amends.

AFTER THE MINISTERS LEFT, Papa approached us.

"My daughter, I beg your forgiveness. It is long overdue. If

I had been less proud, less sure I could do no wrong, and more trusting of you, less afraid, I would have come forward years ago. But I did not."

Joshua held my hand tightly.

"I beg your forgiveness for the damage I have done. Perhaps in the passage of time you shall find it within your heart to forgive me."

"So low the Lord has brought us," was all Joshua could say.

By EARLY CANDLELIGHT, I floated into a fitful sleep. My breasts ached and I moaned. I was aware of Joshua moving about the cottage. A door opened and shut. The voices of passersby heightened and lessened past our window. An owl hooted and a baby whimpered, but when I struggled to give the infant a name, I could not. Then the street grew quiet.

It was nearly dark when I was jolted awake by three quick taps on the windowpane. I looked up to see Goody Hammer's pale face pressed against the glass, peeking inside.

"Shhh," Joshua whispered. "I will tend to it."

The world twisted inside my head. I heard the ominous squeak of the window opening and two voices mumbling in the shadows.

"The child is with Jane. She will give her suck along with Miracle."

"That is good."

"I brought Mercy this. 'Tis a tea useful in calming the mind. It is white dittany grown under the dominion of Venus, valerian grown under Mercury, peppermint and Saint John's wort mashed with syrup of wormseed, and a few ingredients I reveal to no one. The physick must be of the perfect dosage and preparation if it is to operate kindly upon one so unwell. I had often considered this decoction for Mercy, but I did not for fear of conjuring too powerful a physick for such a young woman, but now there is no choice. We will adjust it as we must. 'Tis much like the infusion I prepare for Gabriel."

"Thank you, Goodwife Hammer."

A while later Joshua returned to my bedside carrying a cup of steaming liquid. He sat beside me. "She brought this," he said, gesturing to a jar on the table. "It is a tea for the calming of your mind. You are to brew an infusion of it and drink three cups daily, no more, no less, and when the tea is gone, she shall bring more of it. She claims it should bring you good relief. I have brewed you a cup. Drink now."

I took the cup from his hands and drank. I had fallen to my lowest. This time I willingly followed Goody Hammer's instructions.

Chapter Thirty-Nine

———

I named my daughter Deliverance, a name praising the Lord for the deliverance He granted us. He had rescued our child from harm.

I only had to drink of Goody Hammer's blackish tea for several days to begin to feel its power. Just as I had been blind to the woman's goodness, I had been blind to the powers of the potions she prepared.

It was in a state of calmness that I gave Joshua permission to tell Jane and John everything. As I expected, they responded with a grace that slowly transformed from an understanding that takes place in the mind to one that is felt in the heart.

Again, Jane became my savior. She came to visit when Miracle and Deliverance napped under John's watchful eye. During those first days, she simply sat with me. This time it was she who did not wish to speak. I knew she did not yet own the words to express her disappointment in me.

One afternoon in mid-August, the first day that there was a respite to the heat of summer, I broke the silence.

"You still come. Why?"

"You are my sister."

"After what I've done?"

"I try to comprehend it," she said, reaching across the table and stroking the top of my hand. "I lie awake at night trying to comprehend, and I pray for understanding." Jane had never admitted to praying for help before—except praying to be noticed by John—and there was something different in her demeanor now. It was piety, but not the sanctimonious piety of our ministers, or the zealous piety of Anne Hutchinson, or my way of bargaining with the Lord. Hers was peaceful and vulnerable.

"I have come to my own understanding of what has happened. I don't believe you acted on your own, Mercy." She reached for my hands and held them up before my eyes. "Aye, it was these hands that placed Deliverance in the bucket, but there were stronger hands clutching yours, forcing you to act. Your Papa's hands were there, as were Reverend Wilson's and Mistress Hutchinson's and Satan's. Even my hands were there, because I knew something was amiss, but I did not interrogate you properly."

I looked at my hands and shook my head vehemently. "It was I who tried to drown my child. No other. I must seek forgiveness and accept the punishment."

"Aye. But after the ministers and magistrates deal with you, you shall heal, and you shall feel God's love. And if I have anything to say, you shall have Deliverance home with you soon, for you have it in your heart to be an able mother."

"God's love," I whispered. "From where will that come?"

"It shall come from within." Jane said, tapping her heart. "It will come from those who forgive you, but mostly it will come from forgiving yourself. Your papa begs your forgiveness and he means it. I know he does. But he has been unable to reach you. He has been like an old man tossing a ball to a child but the ball fumbles along the ground between them and the child walks away disinterested before the game can be completed."

"I am interested, and this is not a game."

"Aye. That was a silly comparison, but what I'm trying to say is that you've been too angry to hear."

"I hear it," I said defensively. I stared at a large button at the hollow of Jane's neck.

"You hear, but not enough to forgive. You must forgive him," Jane said, "just as the Lord forgives you."

I nodded slowly. My friend wasn't telling me something I hadn't thought of, but hearing it from her did make a difference.

She leaned into the table. "You must forgive others as well. Perhaps Reverend Wilson was angry with his wife for making him risk blood and breath to retrieve her? Perhaps he was in a rush that evening to pack his bundles? I know only he did nothing. Next time, come to me with your problems and don't go to a man, especially a minister who may be harboring resentment toward his own wife."

"But you weren't here!"

"I'm here now."

I looked at Jane with shamed eyes. I knew she was right. "Pray with me for mercy and forgiveness."

"We will pray, but there is still one more thing I must ask, while I am speaking so freely." She pressed her lips together in thought, reached over and took my hand. "You must also make amends with Goody Hammer. You must drop your accusations of her, for no one would support you in them. I do not believe she is a witch. She is just a healer who mixes potions with prayers and chants. But a witch I don't believe she is. Aye, we have seen a mark, but it may have been a smudge, a rash, a blemish. You do not wish to cause someone pain, even death over a blemish, do you? Think of it this way. Perchance the mark we found on her thigh is no different than the dimple in your chin."

"A dimple in chin, a devil within," I said.

"No, Mercy. That's just an old saying. Think of it another way. A dimple in chin, forgiveness within. Or, a dimple in chin, mercy within. Or, a dimple in chin . . ." she said and stopped. "I'm making a mess of this, but you know my meaning."

I smiled.

"Just ponder it, will you?"

"I am pondering it."

"Goody Hammer saved Deliverance, and now she is healing your mind with her herbs. She must have a gift from the Lord to do that."

I nodded in agreement.

Each swallow of Goody Hammer's tea was bringing me greater calm. It was a bitter tea, but it was as if the bitter herbs held the power to battle the evil spirits that tormented me. A prettier, less powerful potion might not have that effect. After drinking it day after day, the sharp edges of my thoughts became smooth, the depths of my melancholy became but shallow moments of sadness that I could dispel with reason. I thought about Papa. By experiencing these changes in my own mind, I had come to understand the curative effect Goody Hammer's tea had upon his melancholy. I had come to understand the madness, fueled by alcohol, that the tea's absence had created. I was his daughter, cut of his cloth.

"Now to the prayers we were going to say." Jane smiled her impish smile. "I do not carry my Bible with me, nor do I wish to pray from yours. Would it satisfy you if we prayed from our hearts?"

"Aye."

Jane bowed her head and reflected a moment, the way

Anne Hutchinson taught us to do. "Dear Lord. Forgive me for my failure to speak out when I knew a matter of gravity was disturbing my friend. Forgive me for my blindness. Help open my eyes so I might be a more faithful friend."

"You are the most faithful of friends."

"This is my prayer, not yours." She smiled. "Now you pray."

There was no hesitation in my voice now. "Blessed Lord, I am sorry, deeply sorry for my sin against Deliverance. Grant me forgiveness of such depth and meaning and permanence that I find the love within me to forgive Papa and Reverend Wilson and all who have harmed me, as well as those whom I have harmed, especially Goody Hammer."

AFTER JANE LEFT, I sat alone in thought.

Catherine had known nothing of this when she married Papa. Catherine never wished to replace Mama, only to intercede on my behalf as a mother would. Yet I had penalized Catherine because of her guileless association with him. I needed to seek her forgiveness as well.

"Say nothing now," Joshua advised when I broached the subject with him later. "Your father's confession may be enough for her to digest at the moment."

I nodded, but I was not satisfied. Joshua was right about Catherine's troubles at home, but perhaps if I were to ask her forgiveness, she might find it easier to forgive Papa. Joshua was right though in encouraging me not to rush matters, for forgiveness comes as slowly as the formation of wrinkles on our skin, the sprout of a bud from the frozen earth, the graying of hairs on our heads. I knew in time I would venture to her cottage on Sudbury End and unburden my heart to her.

Chapter Forty

———— ❧ ————

Forgiving would take time, as would healing. I knew my husband understood this in the way he understood the transformation of a fallen oak tree into staves that, when bound together within a hazel hoop, blossomed into a bucket; in the way he understood that with an infusion of time and care, and with a craftsman's touch, that which is rough could be smoothed, and that which is broken could be repaired. I knew he was a man of faith. While he believed man's every action is preordained by God to happen in a certain way, he also believed the Lord sets obstacles in our path so we might learn from tribulation. He believes in rebirth.

Several weeks later, I was leaning in the doorway to the cooperage watching him work. Behind him, through the window, the bucket on the wellsweep swayed ever so gently in the breeze, like a head shaking disapproval. Joshua looked up and watched it too.

What was my husband thinking? He had been keeping to himself lately, as had I. Sequestered in our cottage, our conversation was amiable, but like unsure lovers we each held private thoughts we were unready to share.

He set his chisel down on the workbench and turned toward me.

"Slip your apron off, Goodwife. We are leaving this house," he said in a merry voice that belied the circumstances.

"I cannot go outdoors."

"I will be with you," he reassured me.

"Where are we going?"

"Come."

I fussed to make myself presentable, removing my apron, donning my coif, and tucking my braided hair inside it so others would perceive no hint of gaiety in me. He took my hand and we stepped onto the High Street, walking together—me averting the stares of passersby, he steadying me when he felt me tense at the stab of an accusing eye. By now everyone knew of my crime; it had spread throughout Boston as quickly as the news of the quelling of the Pequot Indians. Varying accounts of our public walk would be on the tips of many a wagging tongue by nightfall.

Joshua lifted the parched bough of the Meeting Tree and with a flourish of hand invited me inside. This simple gesture brought back memories of the two of us beneath that tree—when as newcomers to Boston we eagerly and lustfully sought privacy. We were children then, enthralled with our dreams of love. Then, either of us would have bargained our salvation for a kiss or a mere brush of skin.

Joshua smoothed a blanket of dry pine needles for us to sit upon. It was late in the afternoon, nearing the supper hour, and there was not a soul in sight. But even if people did amble by, they would be unable to espy us in our dark clothes that blended with the foliage of the limp and broken tree.

We sat cross-legged facing each other.

"I beg your forgiveness, my husband."

"No need for words. Enough has been said."

"I have harmed you and our child, perhaps beyond repair. Can you ever forgive me?"

He cast his gaze away and he did not answer immediately. His stare had a hardness to it that caused my heart to ache, for I had caused it. He was a man without wrath until I brought it out in him.

He looked down at my hands clasped tightly in my lap. "There was a time when I thought I could not forgive you," he said in a sad whisper. "It was when Goody Hammer carried Deliverance in from the well. At that moment, I wanted to take our child and flee . . . from you . . . from Boston. I wanted never to hear your voice again . . . see your face . . . touch you. Nothing then could make me understand."

As he poured out his anger and fears, I saw in my husband's eyes the darkness that stabbed his soul. He held memories that could never be erased, feelings that until his dying day would weigh down his heart, and fears that would cause him worry whenever he would leave me alone with Deliverance.

He looked into my eyes. "When I learned the truth, in time I began to understand that you alone were not to blame." He wiped his brow slowly with his fingers. "I have done you injustices as well, Goodwife, for I failed to see the signs that were all around me. The bed. The mattress. Your frightened eyes when you awakened after your illness. Your nervousness when I tried to touch you. The fear in your eyes when your father was present. I saw the signs, yet I did nothing. Even a blind man would have seen more. I worried too much about my own reputation and my barrels." Then he spoke as much to himself as to me. "Goodwife, we all get lost along the way."

"Aye," I said sadly, "but most do not fall so low."

We sat in the musty stillness taking cautious measure of each other. Me studying the man I dearly loved but had deceived, he staring at whatever new image he might be capable of rebuilding out of my shatters. I thought of Mama's green bottle lying in shards upon the floor. I could never have repaired it, but had I saved the pieces, perchance I could have smoothed them with a rasp and crafted them into a new object of beauty.

"I was afraid the Lord stopped loving me," I said, wrapping my arms around myself, trying to hold myself together.

Joshua looked deeply into my eyes. "He never stopped loving you. He loved you enough to keep you from harming our child, did He not? He loved you enough to put Goody Hammer in our midst that morning. I might have slept through the commotion."

Tears welled up in my eyes that I could not hold back. They came rushing down my cheeks. Joshua gave me his handkerchief and I blew and sniffled and made all the noises I had once deemed so unsavory in others, but now I made them without embarrassment. Then, at the sound of myself, I started to laugh a small self-conscious laugh. "Today I'm crying for gratitude, for you . . . for Goody Hammer . . . for Deliverance. I love you, Joshua," I blubbered. "You will never know how deeply I love you."

"I've never stopped loving you either. You are the one I have chosen to live my days with, and no matter what, I shall love you forever."

Joshua's declaration was too overwhelming for me to accept lightly. How could he love me now? How could we bear the weight of the hideous memory we shared?

He pushed himself to his knees and scooted beside me. He wrapped his arms around me as tenderly as he would around a bruised child. This time I felt no resistance. He wiped my tears and comforted me with soothing sounds and calming hugs, and I allowed myself to accept his touch without fear.

"I have news for you," he whispered.

I looked up warily. "What news?"

"Reverend Wilson called upon me yesterday when you were asleep. There will be no civil trial for you because no harm has come to Deliverance."

"Praise the Lord."

"And because you have been mightily distracted."

"Aye."

"I told him you are improving."

"Aye, I am hopeful."

I wanted to be hopeful. There were moments I was hopeful, but I was by no means confident. Would Joshua ever be able to trust me with Deliverance again? Was I to be trusted? Surely he was worried, for what husband would not worry about the sanity of his wife and the safety of his children after this?

There were days that followed when I felt able, and days when I did not. As much as I wanted to believe Joshua, doubts raged through me, especially when I was alone and had time to reflect, and oft in the pitch of night when I awoke and my mind spiraled in thoughts and remembrances. Those nights I was not hopeful at all. But as long as Joshua was beside me and I could call upon him, all would be well. I would need his strength to keep me right, as much as I would need Goody Hammer's decoction to keep the voices at bay.

"You must appear before the congregation for admonishment, Sabbath next," Joshua went on.

"Will you be with me?"

"I will."

"What about Deliverance?"

"We shall learn of it then."

"That is five days away, my husband."

"She shall be returned to us soon."

"I pray to be ready."

"The Lord blessed me with a lovely dream of you last night," he said softly. My husband raised his hand in the air and wove it slowly through the glittery threads of sunlight streaming through the pine boughs. The specks in the air danced around his roughened fingers. "In my dream, you were sitting on a bench outside our door."

"We have no bench."

"Then I shall build us one."

"And the dream will become real."

"It will be real," he assured me. "In my dream our daughter was older and as beautiful as you. She was dressed in an ivory gown, and she sat betwixt you and two more children. Your arms encircled the three of them. In my dream, all was well."

I smiled, but looked up at him cautiously. "I wish not to disappoint you. I have done enough of that already. I am still unsure."

"You shall not disappoint me," he said hopefully.

"With your help I shall not."

"I place no demands upon you. You must mend in your own time, and in the Lord's. For now, let us think the best and prepare for our Deliverance."

THE AFTERNOON AFTER Jane and I prayed together, I began to feel a melting within my heart. I hadn't mentioned it to Joshua because oft before I had found such feelings to be transient—a trick of Satan offered and withdrawn. But as the days passed, my longing for my daughter had not diminished. I began to feel the yearning and impatience, the planning and the need for preparation most women feel during the forty weeks their child grows beneath their hearts. At first it was a simple desire to stroke my child's skin as Mama once stroked mine. Then it was a stronger craving to soothe her whimpers, to guard her when she slept and to keep a watchful eye upon her throughout the day. Then it became a desire to prepare for her, to be ready. My mind leapt to Sunday evening. By that time, I will have been sufficiently reduced and shamed before the congregation, and by that time I will know if Deliverance would come home.

Chapter Forty-One

The following Sabbath, shortly after sunrise, Joshua and I set out for the meetinghouse. We left early because, in our nervousness, neither of us felt strong enough to encounter gawkers and taunts along the way.

After passing the Winthrop property, we espied Billy Bowdoin crouched beneath a locust tree with his scrawny knees folded up to his chest. He had just taken a bite of a peach when he recognized us.

"G'day," he cried out in his newsy voice. Then he quickly looked away in embarrassment, knowing where we were heading.

The long thatched roof of the meetinghouse that seemed so far away a moment ago came upon us too quickly, as did the silhouettes of the ghastly heads and hands of the slain Pequot Indians mounted on the spikes of the meetinghouse fence. I was not prepared for the grisly sight. The heads had been drying in the sun for about three weeks and now, shrunken, they were the size of small cabbages. If it were not for the shiny black hair streaming down the heads, and the fingernails on the hands, one would have no inkling they were human.

"Look not at them," Joshua said, quickening his step and holding up his hand to shield me from them.

Reverend Wilson's war mementos, I thought.

A single sheet of parchment had been tacked to the meetinghouse door. Espying it from afar, I knew somewhere on it was written my name. The notice, penned in crude blockish letters, announced the program of the Sabbath service:

Sunday, August 27, 1637
A sermon the Reverend John Cotton
The Lord of Forgiveness

I read the small words below, the words I dreaded to see. "The clergy and magistrates of Boston stand in judgment of Mercy Goodhue Hoyt."

Joshua pulled the door open. The iron hinge groaned in resistance. He gently pressed his hand into my back and guided me inside. The heavy door thudded shut behind us.

Just as my eyes became accustomed to the dimness, Billy Bowdoin pounded the first deep beat on his drum. It would resound up and down every street and hill of Boston, reminding the women to hurry their children, alerting the men to swallow the last bites of their oatmeal, and separating the limbs of the newly married who lingered in bed entwined in their sweet pleasures.

Once I was like them. I recalled the image of my girlish face in the looking glass, my finger coaxing a curl outside my coif for others to admire. I remembered praying for the sermon to be brief, feeling a rush of excitement over whose wedding banns would be read and who would be admonished for what sins. Today I was that sinner who would stand alone to be judged on God's stage by His proxies.

I took my place in the front row nearest the aisle. Joshua sat directly across the aisle from me. We waited motionlessly for the others to arrive. When the room filled, neither of us dared look behind or sideways at each other.

I felt an overwhelming fright. Two long tables covered with white cloths had been set up on the platform in the center, and behind the tables, tall wooden chairs for the magistrates and ministers. I would be called to stand before them.

The ministers took their places first: Reverend Wilson, Reverend Cotton, and Reverend Symmes. Then the magistrates marched in from the back: Governor Winthrop, Thomas Dudley, John Coggeshall, Thomas Oliver, and William Coddington, the only one who made eye contact with me.

Outside, mindless of the spectacle unfolding within, sparrows chirped, horses neighed, young boys teased one another in boasting voices, and a breeze tired of summer rustled through the leaf-laden branches of the hickory trees that flapped gently against the high windows.

I did not hear much of the service. I did hear when Reverend Wilson called my name.

"Mercy Goodhue Hoyt." He skewered me with his eyes. Jane, who had taken a seat beside me, gave my fingers a gentle pull that forced me to stand. As a spider threads its web, I followed the beam emitted by Reverend Wilson's eyes and stepped up on the platform where sinners stand. My feet pressed into the same wood that had supported fornicators, thieves, and murderers. "Face the congregation, will you."

I turned as he instructed.

"May God have mercy on you Goodwife Hoyt," Reverend Wilson said.

I hung my head and stared at the floor.

"I shall not repeat this woman's crime in detail, for you

have heard of it, I am sure. All that must be known is known."

There were whispers and squirms among the people. Men and women adjusted themselves on creaky benches, chests breathed shallowly in anticipation.

"You have offended the Lord, and in doing so you have disgraced your family and this family of saints. We are living in a time of tribulations, and for our sins the Lord is punishing us in many ways."

I raised my head and found Joshua. Again, I looked into his eyes and silently told him of my contrition, as I knew I would every day of our lives.

"Our homeland is threatened with war. In this new land where we dreamed of safety, the barbarians have assaulted us with a vengeance." I thought of the hideous rotted heads and hands out front.

Reverend Wilson, still exhilarated by his brief encounter with war, seemed intent on reminding the congregation of it. He spoke in his nasal voice, slowly enunciating every word. "I have met the savages, but mercifully the Lord has halted them before they threatened Boston, and He willed me to return home unscathed."

"Amen," prayed the congregation.

"But even here in this community of saints, all is not well. We do not abide in harmony. One is jealous of another. One seeks advantage over another. One seeks to pollute the minds of others with heresy. And today we are shamed by the deed of this woman, Mercy Goodhue Hoyt, who stands before us. I am inclined to believe that because we have made ourselves ripe to Satan's overtures, he now dwells in our midst, as he also dwells in England."

I looked at Goody Hammer, but this time I did not accuse her.

"When shall this torment end?" he shouted.

Except for the clearing of a throat or two, the room was silent.

"Goodwife Hoyt. Look up and face the men and women whose trust you have violated. You have violated the trust of your own husband."

Joshua's eyes met mine and in them I saw sadness, but also compassion.

"You have violated the trust of your own father and your family!"

In the center of the men's section, I located my father who was leaning forward on the bench as if he was preparing to leap up and rescue me if I cried out for help. Stay in your seat, Papa. You may wish to defend me publicly, to take blame for my madness, to publicly purge your heart of your own sins, but today I stand alone for mine, and no matter what Jane says to the contrary, I alone am responsible.

"You have violated the trust of every mother in the Boston Congregation who has birthed a child and lost a child through no ill-doing of her own."

I lifted my head and felt the piercing sting of judgment from women who sat facing me, each of them purer than me. They observed me with stony faces. Goody Coddington's narrow countenance was sunken and drawn. Goody Aspinwall, whose smile always deepened at the mention of the Lord, was grimacing as if she had seen Satan. Catherine, who had birthed four children, averted her eyes from my gaze. But Goody Hammer saw me clearly, for she alone understood my troubled mind.

"Mercy, are you of a contrite heart?"

"I am."

"Speak loudly so we might hear you."

"I am of a contrite heart."

I looked over my shoulder and caught Governor Winthrop's eye. He looked away. Thomas Dudley's countenance seemed chiseled in stone; not a muscle on his face moved, nary a breath seemed to emanate from between his liverish lips.

"What is the just punishment for your sin? Is it time in the gaol or is time lived the prison of your heart sufficient? I am persuaded that no mother or father in this room would think any punishment seems adequate for the crime you had attempted," he said slowly, lingering upon every word. "I have heard other testimony, though, that you have been under extreme duress. Is this true?"

"It is, sir."

"What has been the nature of your distraction?"

"I was fearful for my spiritual estate." Please Lord, do not have me explain before everyone what I explained before to the ministers. Do not ask me about the voices that spoke to me. Spare me that.

"'Tis only right to fear the Lord's judgment. We must fear the Lord each day. But your fear has manifested in the most extreme way, has it not?"

"It has."

For a moment Reverend Wilson was silent. Then he resumed speaking. "This is your first offense, Goodwife Hoyt. Until these days of madness, when Satan took possession of your mind and spoke to you, you have pleased the Lord. You have been a useful woman in our community. Because of your past good works I am persuaded that the Lord will show you mercy, and for this reason we too will be merciful. We will spare you the dankness of the gaol where you would be in the company of the beastly Indians we have captured. This would do you no good. Nor would it benefit you to be cast out of the congregation at a time when you are most in need of the saints of Boston. Instead, you shall be taken to the pillory immediately following our service and shackled there until nightfall. You shall have neither food nor drink. Following your release, you shall be shunned by the Boston Congregation for one year."

Then he lifted a red cloth from the table and held it up for everyone to see. The cloth was embroidered with a thick black D. The stitches were tight and angry, sewn by a heavy hand. "The D is for distraction, Mercy Goodhue Hoyt . . . for the anxiety that took over your mind and set you on the precipice of destruction. Joist Brown shall affix it to your bodice now and you must wear it during your shunning, whenever you step out of your home. You must wear it in the marketplace, the meetinghouse, your garth, and always when you fetch water in your well. Let it serve as a reminder of your shame."

Joist Brown had risen from his purple cushion and was moving toward me. He was careless with his pins and he deliberately rubbed his hand against my breast. I closed my eyes as he worked. He whispered ever so quietly: "D for Distraction . . . Deranged . . . Devils . . . Deliverance."

"What about my daughter, Reverend Wilson?" I blurted over Joist Brown's taunts.

"Your daughter shall be returned to you at nightfall," Reverend Wilson said.

I closed my eyes and exhaled.

"Goodwife Hammer alone shall call upon you daily. She will see to it that the rest of us shun you in isolation and shame. Do you understand?"

For the next year I would be considered dead to the community. Not a "G'day" would be uttered to me, nor a cut of mutton or loaf of bread sold to me. Not so much as a handkerchief dropped from my hand would be retrieved. It would be up to Joshua to bring food into our home. Then I remembered my milk had gone dry.

"Aye, but Reverend Wilson, sir, may Goodwife Loring continue to give suckle to my daughter?" I was embarrassed to ask such a personal question of a man, and to do so publicly, but I had to know. There was an uncomfortable shuffle of bodies in the men's section.

"Aye," he mumbled.

"Thank you, sir."

"Your husband, Joshua Hoyt, is a man of eminent parts. We are persuaded he shall guide you on an orderly path. May he see to it that you improve your time on this earth."

Joshua nodded dutifully.

"Do you have any final words to say, Goodwife Hoyt?

My eye traveled to Goody Hammer. Aye, I had something to say about this woman who saved my child's life. How would I say it? But just as I opened my mouth to speak, the meetinghouse door creaked open and a brilliant flash of sunlight blasted in. Then, as if a forceful hand cleaved the light, Anne Hutchinson stepped into it and strode down the aisle.

"Mistress Hutchinson," I exclaimed.

Heads turned and whispering began. I glanced over my shoulder at Governor Winthrop who was stiffening himself against the back of his chair, and at Reverend Cotton whose face reddened at the sight of her.

She stopped in front of me.

"What disturbance is this?" Reverend Wilson asked her angrily.

"I told Mercy I would come, but I had been detained for weeks in Wollaston. I heard what happened just this morning from Mary Dyer."

Reverend Wilson stepped down the riser. "Woman, you boldly disturb our service . . . you enter at the end . . . you are irresponsible," he stammered.

Anne paid him no heed. Her eyes were fixed on me, and she whispered, "The Lord be with you, my daughter. Ours is a forgiving God. Ask and you shall be forgiven, just as you have forgiven those who have harmed you."

Mistress Hutchinson had not forgotten me. As Joshua said, I was not her family and her family had to be tended to first. Yet she did come.

"Goodwife Hoyt!"

Reverend Wilson's voice brought me back to the business we had been addressing before Mistress Hutchinson's arrival. "Repeat to the congregation what you said before this overbold woman interrupted us, will you?"

Anne Hutchinson took a seat beside Jane and they both nodded support.

I looked at the old woman behind them. "Goodwife Hammer, you are a prime woman among us. Thank you for saving my child. Thank you for saving me." Goody Hammer nodded slowly and tipped the brim of her hat. If I was not mistaken, a trace of a smile crossed her lips, but then in the shadows it faded. "I ask God's forgiveness for my misjudgment of you, and all others I have harmed."

"We have heard enough. Take her away," said Reverend Wilson. Joist Brown had already risen from his cushion before the minister uttered his final words: "Goodwife Hoyt repents."

JOIST BROWN GRIPPED MY ELBOW and shoved me down the aisle, a stained bride accompanied by the grimmest of bridegrooms. I stared ahead at the door and stumbled toward it. He lifted the latch, kicked the door open with his boot, and forced me into the sunlight.

"Does God's sun offend you, Goodwife Hoyt . . . though there is nothing good about you I can see?" he hissed into my ear. "I would lock you up forever if the judgment was mine to make. But lucky for you, it was not. I am the father of eight, and I know the pain of what you have done to your child and husband. You have shamed 'em, Goodwife Hoyt," he said, spitting out my name as if it were rotten meat. "They were soft on you. They should have cast you out of the congregation."

"I am a sinner, sir, but I have been forgiven."

"Let the Lord be the judge of it." With a menacing grip on my shoulder, he led me around the corner to the back of the meetinghouse. The edge of the pillory pit was seventy-five steps away. I had counted them. We would then step down a steep incline into the pit. The sun had been beating on the parched earth all morning, causing a thin veil of air to shimmer over it. The only shade came from the crosshatched shadows of the cage, the low-banded shadow of the stocks and the cross of the pillory upon the ground. I squinted up into the cloudless sky that like the fist of the constable showed no mercy.

Joist Brown shoved me down the incline. "No time to play the damsel now."

I looked sideways at him. He smirked when I lost my footing. His belly hung over his breeches and he was breathing hard from the short walk. When he opened his mouth, I could see his few teeth were black as rotten kernels of corn. I straightened my back to show him my strength and also to feel a final stretch of my spine in anticipation of the bent position I would be locked into for hours.

Voices emanated from the direction of the meetinghouse; the congregation was on our heels. I knew some people brought canvasses to sit on, some carried food in their pockets, and some brought their children to warn them of the consequences of sin. Today I would be the gazing stock, the afternoon's entertainment, the week's lesson.

The constable pointed to a block of wood at the base of the pillory.

"Step you up, Goodwife," he said gruffly.

I stepped up and leaned into its centerpost.

Joist Brown unlocked the clamp with an iron key, one of many he carried on a thick chain around his waist. Then with sadistic pleasure, he opened its heavy arm as if he were separating a giant pair of scissors and stared at me with his ditchwater eyes, waiting for a reaction. I swallowed hard. The three half-circle grooves where I was to lay my head and wrists had already been sanded smooth by the skin of many sinners who had been clamped there before me. That day my sweat would blend with whatever traces of theirs remained in the parched wood, evidence of all our sins.

"Spread out your arms. Set 'em in place and make yourself comfortable," he scoffed, "and lower your fair head."

The wood was smooth but hot, and I flinched.

"Keep your head steady. That be my advice to you." He clamped the pillory arms shut and locked them with the iron key. He stomped away, then paused and looked over his shoulder. "Give me a smile now, pretty one, or I should throw this key away," he threatened, rattling the keys on his chain.

For as long as I could stand it, I kept my eyes pinned on the ground. There was chatter coming from the crowd, and for a while that was all there was. Just chatter. Then the mood of forgiveness Reverend Wilson had proposed inside the meetinghouse faded and the taunts began.

"Look up, sinner!"

"Give us a smile, will you!"

"Crazy one!"

"Madwoman!"

"Baby killer!"

It was "baby killer" that stabbed like a lance in my heart. "Look up and face your accusers," the same voice cried out. Still I did not look up. The sun stung at my back and neck. I grimaced in pain.

Someone flung a tomato at me, which struck my ankle. Then an egg splattered against the pillory's centerpost and its slimy yoke, sliced by thin shards of shell, slid to the ground. Flies found it and buzzed around in frenzied delight. Pebbles and rocks came hurling at me. I jerked my head to avoid their onslaught, and groaned from the scruff of wood against my neck. This quick movement forced me to look up. Just then, a pinch-mouthed woman, who in the best of times had been unable to grant me more than a scowl, stepped to the edge of the pit and hurled a peach toward me. "Sinner!" she shrieked. The rotten fruit struck my left hand squarely and splattered. Clumps of it dribbled to the ground. Flies that seemed to multiply in the steamy air swarmed around the peach pit, and a cone of them rose and buzzed around my sticky hand. The stench of the rotten fruit and the egg nearly made me retch. With my arms pinned, I could not wipe my tears. And best I could not, for these were the humiliations I deserved.

I searched the crowd for Jane and found her standing directly across from me on the crest of a sun-parched hillock betwixt John and Joshua. Even from a distance I could see that Jane was crying. Ours eyes met and she nodded, as if to say, "Be of good strength. This afternoon shall pass and t'night you shall have your child." She was rocking Deliverance in the crook of her arm. I fixed my eye on my daughter's pink leg dangling from beneath the hem of her gown. Blessedly, she was asleep and oblivious to my plight.

"Baby killer," someone else shouted.

Think of something else. Anything. The past. The future.

With my eyes on Deliverance, I prayed for the time to pass quickly. Quickly enough to heal wounds and dull painful memories. I tried to imagine my daughter grown, but all I could see was her standing where Jane stood now, her soulful eyes peering into the pillory pit at another woman being chastened. I would speak to Joshua of leaving Boston. But where would we go? Deeper into the wilderness to be besieged by Indians? Already we had traveled so far.

My thoughts leapt back to that first morning when our family had rowed to Cape Ann in the ship's boat. We were so excited, all of us jabbering at once.

"Michael, keep your hands out of the water," Mama said. We laughed at how quickly she forgot her words and reached into the water herself, cupping her hand to feel the water's force against her fingers.

"Such wilderness. Where will we live, Gabriel?"

"Worry not about the Indians. They are guileless."

"This is a fine day," Noah beamed.

I remembered the granite boulders that loomed larger the closer we sailed to land. Another ship's boat had already pushed up upon the beach and people were disembarking, the women hoisting their skirts up to keep them dry, the children splashing barefooted into the surf, the men attempting to enforce some decorum. The sun was dazzling that first morning, and I remembered seeing blindingly beautiful colors—reds, yellows, blues and browns, each of them more vibrant in the sunlight then they actually were. I remembered thinking that each of us was an individual pot of paint, arriving to make an impression on the canvas of America. "We bring to this land only what we are," I murmured to Michael, who was sitting beside me on the edge of the seat. He looked at me as if I were sunstruck. But I knew what I meant. We would either create a fine work of art in this new land, or our colors would run together and become mud.

This land. This America. A refuge? A city on a hill? A step closer to heaven? America was none of these things. It was just land—sprawling, vacant land we were free to mark as our own with our prayers, prowess, preachers, and progeny.

Deliverance's bare leg wiggled. Jane adjusted her in her arms. Was she whimpering? Had she opened her eyes enough to be blinded by the sunlight? From afar, I could not tell. My child was like the land—this I knew—innocent and fresh, awaiting my influence. But in the end I could give her only what I had.

John leaned into Jane and whispered something that made her smile, a small smile that perchance lifted her spirits. John, that peacock of a man who arrived in America donning celadon and feathers, who danced in celebration of his new life and new wife and the miracle he had planted within her. Even though John had taken to wearing black like the other men, he had shown the colors of his faithfulness to our family, and his love of Jane, who in every respect was his perfect helpmeet.

Standing beside the two of them, Joshua seemed sad and alone. I could not imagine the thoughts that ran through his head at the sight of me, bedraggled and tearful, besieged by flies. I prayed for the grace to become the goodwife he deserved. Now, without the haunting presence of my father in our bed, I was free to renew my covenant with this man of trust and restraint.

And Papa? Where was Papa? I craned my neck to the left and espied him leaning against the trunk of a broad white oak tree, much like the one our family had gathered beneath to study the Scripture on our first day in Boston. Only now, it was Catherine and not Mama who stood beside him, a pace away, tall and formidable.

I recalled the verse we recited that first day. It was Isaiah 44: 22. "I have swept away your offenses like a cloud, your sins like the morning mist. Return to me, for I have redeemed you." I repeated it in my mind, and then aloud for I needed to hear the words. I tapped out the number of the repetitions on the wood of the pillory with my fingers.

Throughout the repetitions, I never took my eyes off Papa. When I completed the final verse, he nodded knowingly and I nodded back as best I could. Catherine stepped closer to him. Her skirt pressed against the coarse cloth of his breeches. I prayed for the mending of their differences.

Just then, a gaggle of young girls, about ten of them, broke through the crowd and stood on the precipice of the pit, and like the grown women who preceded them in years and passion, they taunted me. They linked arms and began to sway from side to side, and sang. But by then, in the heat of the sun, amidst the other taunts and cries, their insults were soundless, dizzying words emanating from open mouths, and their faces were pink orbs wobbling atop a whirling stream of colors. Then suddenly, the tallest girl on the end tottered forward and slid down the incline, dragging the other girls behind her. They giggled as their bodies toppled one upon another into the pit, the mass of them consumed in the billowing cloud of dust their shoes kicked up. They were mere steps from me. The tall girl, the leader, who was about fifteen, pulled the others around me, endeavoring to form a circle. Laughingly, they stretched their arms until the first and the last girl linked hands. They danced around me. Streams of browns, blues, russets and greens spun past me like ribbands, and they sang.

"Mercy, whose baby have you drowned t'day?"

"Not mine," answered the chorus.

"Whose baby . . ." they repeated in taunting, shrill tones.

Goody Hammer leaned over the pit. She had risen out of nowhere. Her hands were on her hips and her lips were tightly pursed. Then in a blink, she disappeared.

Amidst the swirling skirts and the streaming frenzy of their rounds, Goody Hammer inserted herself into the middle of the group, and with a slice of her hand and flash of her bad eye, she stopped the circle from spinning. She admonished the girls one by one. She called them each by name, for she knew them all.

"Sobriety Cowlishaw, the Lord is watching you this very minute.

"And Mary, have you nothin' better to do with your time than torment this poor creature who has suffered enough, and needs now to heal?" That girl was Mary Harding, the youngest daughter of Goody Harding, the mother of twelve. The girl's face turned wooden at the scolding.

"And Temperance, what has become of you? I slapped the first cry out of you the day you were born, and is this how you use the voice the Lord has given you? Make your way home now."

"But Goodwife Hammer," she argued, "we did not mean—"

"There are no buts but contrition, Temperance. Now run to your mama who is there on the hill and tell her to take you home, and beg her forgiveness, will you?"

Goody Hammer knew each of the girls' names, but she also knew each of their natures, just as she knew Jane's and mine.

"Be off with you then!" she called after them.

I watched the girls scurry up the embankment, slipping

and sliding in the dust, eager to flee Goody Hammer as fast as their young legs would carry them. On level ground they scattered like field mice. Their rapid departure caused most of the other spectators to leave, with the exception of Joshua and Jane and John and Papa and Catherine, who had joined together beneath the shade of the white oak at the top of the knoll.

Mama had once told me that sometimes it took a lifetime to understand what it was that made a person cold or warm, attentive or distant, critical or loving, and that it sometimes takes an equal amount of time to understand one's resistance toward them, which is oft a thin disguise for one's need of them. That's how it was with Goodwife Hammer. There, bound in the pillory where I had endless time to ponder the circumstances of what brought me so low, I realized that in her crude manner Goody Hammer had always wished me well.

I recalled the morning in the grove when Goody Hammer gave her testament to become a member of the Boston Congregation. Reverend Wilson had called her up front by her given name, Esther Hammer. Esther. That was the first time I heard it. Today in the prison of the pillory, I realized something I should have known all along—that Goody Hammer was named after Esther of the Old Testament who saved her people from slaughter.

Having dismissed the taunts, Goody Hammer hobbled toward me. She pulled a cloth out of her pocket and gently wiped my face and hands, and then stooped to pick up the eggshells, the peach pits, and the debris decaying around me. She removed it all. Then she returned with a gourd full of water, which she held up to my parched lips. She nodded for me to drink.

I sipped the cool water and looked into Goody Hammer's

eyes. In the watery depth of them I saw the core of goodness that until then I had been blind to, and the godliness that against all of my resistance had made Goodwife Esther Hammer my healer. The old woman remained with me until nightfall, keeping me silent company until Joist Brown returned to release me, his keys jingling on the iron chain that hung low around his waist.

Chapter Forty-Two

⁂

It hadn't taken me long to honor Goody Hammer's invitation, "I leave my Betty lamp burning all the night for those in need of me. Come when you are ready." Nor had I waited for darkness to follow the glow of her lamp. One warm afternoon shortly after Deliverance had been returned to us, I pinned the D on my chest, wrapped Deliverance in a blanket to protect her from an autumn wind, and trekked up the hill toward the graveyard.

At the crest of the hill, the stone chimney of her cottage arose into the autumn sky, and from it ascended soft puffs of smoke. Goody Hammer's dwelling was a squat earthen structure with a rounded door and a flat thatched roof built into the side of a hill—so much a part of the hill it was that cattle grazed upon her roof. To the right was a clump of birch trees, their white bark alive with the breath of the wind. To the left was a copse of maple trees brilliant in autumn's red and golden hues. Surrounding her property was a twisted fence composed of branches and twigs built high enough to keep out the deer and the wolves. I found my way to a gate to which Goody Hammer had attached a ring of wee trumpet-shaped silver bells. I jiggled the bells to announce my arrival and pushed the gate open.

Her garden was unlike any I had ever seen. Beyond a hedgerow of mandrake were mounds of herbs and shrubs in a multitude of shades of green, splashed by sunlight, stretching before me in neatly tended rows. I followed the stone footpath that led to her door, identifying the plants I was familiar with along the way: rosemary, sage, chives, parsley, mustard, and tansy. Many of the others were mysteries to me. Later I was to learn their names: chamomile, feverfew, pennyroyal, wormwood, sumac, shepherd's-purse, yarrow, rue, mullein, St. John's wort, burdock, cold water root, flowering hemp— enough names and varieties to make my head spin.

I crouched down to inhale the spiky needles of rosemary. As I continued down the footpath, the fragrance of her plantings nearly made me swoon.

Elijah tottered out from behind the cottage and brushed against my skirt.

"He welcomes you as do I," Goody Hammer laughed, rising up from behind a tall stalk of flowering lavender. The wide pocket of her apron was overflowing with the purple-blue flowers and she held even more in her hand. "For an infusion for a babe with colic," she explained. "What is left will make a handsome bouquet for the table." She took my arm and led me to her door. On the doorpost was a spirit stone bearing a crude figure of a man surrounded by amulets and charms. "It keeps evil forces away," she explained when I stopped to study it.

It was warm and dim inside her cottage and the air there carried the scents of lavender, rosemary, and must. It was not unpleasant at all. Goody Hammer scurried about. She set a wide herb basket near the hearth and lined it with a pillowbear. Carefully, I set Deliverance upon the soft cushion inside the basket so as not to awaken her. My infant still suffered from the colic that vexed her at night. Now in the daytime she was making up for the sleep she deprived us both of. I tucked the quilt around her. Elijah followed my every move. Then, exhausted as well, he curled his ancient body around her basket, made low sleep sounds and napped.

It took a moment to become accustomed to Goody Hammer's surroundings so different were they from the sparseness in most of our homes. She had no more furniture than the rest of us—a table, a chair, and a cot in the corner heaped with quilts. But her dwelling was neatly cluttered with an abundance of drying plants and herbs—squat bouquets tied to the rafters with string, massive flowering bunches of dried herbs that dangled into the room at various levels, more herbs set on cloths on a table by the window to dry. Her cottage was an extension to the sylvan bounty of her garden.

The walls were lined with shelves and on the shelves were tens of glass jars of varying sizes abutting each other like an infantry in dark uniforms. The jars contained leaves as well as pods, seeds, and dried flowers of various sizes and hues. Upon the highest shelf, higher than I could reach, were jars of amulets—thistles, feathers, eagle stones, hound's teeth, iridescent crystals and spiky, furry objects that looked like claws. I shifted my eyes away from them to the hearthstone where she had spread on cloths more herbs for drying. An assortment of iron pots, huge and small, hung from pothooks inside her fireplace. Steam rose in mysterious puffs from the smallest of them.

"Tis water boilin' for the lavender infusion," Goody Hammer said when she noticed me eying the pots. "Then I will prepare another of the powerful feverfew for a soul sufferin' from sadness of spirit. With the grace of God, she shall find good relief in it."

Before I could comment, she asked, "Are you drinkin' the physick I prepared for you?"

"In tea thrice daily," I said.

"How does it operate?" She wrinkled her brow and listened intensely.

"I sleep well. The voices remain silent. And I no longer wish to preach." I answered honestly. "I sleep when Deliverance sleeps. The colic is still with her, ma'am. But that is not why I have come. I have come today to thank you, and to ask your forgiveness for misjudging you."

Goody Hammer stared into my eyes, drew me in with her gaze. "And I you, my daughter."

I reached into my pocket and handed her the pouch of amulets I had dug up from the ground. "These have meaning to you."

She accepted the pouch, felt the contents through the soiled fabric with her fingers, and set it on the table. She refrained from questioning me about how I had the amulets in my possession. We both had an understanding of where they came from.

She looked out the window at the sun still high in the sky and shook her head. "Yesterday is past, t'day there is work to do." She began fussing about busily, setting her mortar and pestle on the table and a knife beside it. "Four hands are more capable than two, so the Lord has surely brought you here to assist me. Satan shall find work for us, if we are not at work for God, don't y'know?" She reached below the table and handed me a ladle and an earthenware pitcher. "Fetch four cups of boiling water and measure it carefully." While I fetched the water she scurried to her wall of shelves and selected several jars that she set on the table beside the lavender. "You will watch now and remember."

"Aye," I replied, easing myself into the chair across from her.

With learning eyes I relaxed and paid attention to her every action. She picked tender lavender leaves off the stalks, chopped the leaves, collected them in a mound, and with a knife divided the mound into four equal parts. She reached for her mortar and with the blade of her knife lifted one of the parts to eye level and took measure of the leaves. She lifted the mortar to below the knife and allowed most of the leaves to fall in. Then likewise she measured in drams of horehound, fennel, asparagus root, and then a speck of cinnamon, each time holding the ingredients high in her hand and sprinkling a precise measure into her mortar. I watched them fall like wee autumn leaves around the base of a tree. She explained what she was doing, but always stopped speaking as she measured, preferring then—as I later learned—to think of her patients and their particular needs, and to pray to the Lord to guide her hand in dropping not a grain too much or too little into her decoction. "When a remedy works cleverly, you must give thanks, and if its properties fail you, then you pray for forgiveness."

That day I recalled many earlier afternoons when, in the midst of my illness, I had watched her prepare decoctions for me. At that time I'd held her suspect, watching her every move with doubting eyes, arguing every word she uttered, silently ridiculing her every mention of Ol' Mim as the reflections of a crone whose fondest memories were only of the past. This time I asked her about Ol' Mim and she did not repeat herself as an old woman might, but told me new stories, and this time I listened.

"Ol' Mim believed that God placed plants on this earth to benefit man, that it is our sacred duty to match plant with disease and to heal. Ol' Mim was not proud. She learned from whomever she could. She could not read, but she asked questions and listened, and the Lord had gifted her with a good memory. She remembered the name of every herb in her garden and the planets that governed 'em . . . Mercury owns flax . . . Venus owns figwort and catmint . . . Mars controls celandine . . . hawthorn is a tree of Mars. 'Twas a Papist monk who taught her the words of healin' that she taught me." In a deep voice, strong and true, Goody Hammer lifted the pitcher of water and began to chant, *"Vidi aquam egredientem de templo . . . et omnes, ad quos pervenit aqua ista salvi facti sunt, et dicent."* A monk taught 'em to Ol' Mim in Loughborough.

I must have grimaced, for she found need to explain. "'Tis Latin. It means, 'I saw water coming forth from the temple on the right side . . . and all those to whom this water came were saved.' Aye, it comes from a Papist," she laughed, "but even some in that group are useful."

I thought of the meaning of water in my own life—the silting North Sea that deprived Papa of his livelihood, the raging ocean that nearly claimed us, the strong waters that had befuddled Papa's senses, the hungry waters that swallowed my brothers, the cool water in our well I had so gravely abused, the tea that heals my mind.

Goody Hammer handed me the pitcher. "Let you pour it into the mixture now drop by drop . . ." "That is right," she said when I did it properly. "You have a steady hand, girl, as I expected."

At that moment an agreement had been made between us, and I became Esther Hammer's apprentice. That was not why I'd come to her that afternoon, nor was it what I expected to happen. But as we worked compatibly side by side, I remembered what my mama said about unexpected changes.

"'Tis the Lord's way of reminding you that He is in charge and not you."

Goody Hammer covered the mortar with a clean cloth, scurried to the fireplace with it in hand, and set it on the warm hearth. "Later we will strain it to cleanse it of harsh elements and pour it into a clean jar for our patient. She flipped her hourglass and we timed it to steep for an hour—"too little is not enough, too much is not good," she cautioned. "I shall deliver it t'night. But before you leave I will dilute a small amount for you to try on Deliverance. You soak a clean cloth in the warm infusion, then let the child suck. We must retrain a child who sleeps all day and cries all night, do you not agree?"

I could not have agreed more.

"Let us now work on the infusion of feverfew."

Chapter Forty-Three

Twice more I saw Mistress Hutchinson. The first of these times was in November of 1637, three months after I had stood before the congregation. It was early in the day, before Boston came alive with activity. Bundled in my cloak with my face hidden in a fur hood to shield me from passersby, I was making my way to Sudbury End to deliver a bowl to a customer of Joshua's. I held the bowl close to my chest to cover the mark of the D on my cloak.

In passing the Hutchinson's home I was stopped by the cry of a baby, and beneath its shrill pitch the sobs of older children. One young voice cried out, "Mama, I need you!" The door to their home was open and William was walking his wife to a carriage that waited outside. Visibly shaken, William carried her Bible and the same overstuffed bag that she brought to births. He held her by the arm, as her walk was unsteady. Her body was bent forward like a tree limb beaten down by the weight of snow. He helped her board the carriage. At first I thought a family of means had sent a carriage to transport her to a birth, but that did not explain the wailing coming from her own children inside the house.

From his window across the street, Governor Winthrop was also watching.

Later, I told Goody Hammer what I saw. It was she who told me (mind you, she took no pleasure in the telling of it) that the General Court had accused Mistress Hutchinson of heresy and that rather than banishing her into the wildernesss in the cold of winter where she would surely die, they removed her from her family to a home in Roxbury where, under the guidance of diverse ministers who would visit her daily, she was to repent. What I had witnessed was her tearful departure.

The final time I saw Mistress Hutchinson was the following March when in the thaw of spring she returned to Boston to stand trial before the ministers. By that time the Coddingtons, the Aspinwalls, and other supporters had removed themselves from Boston in sympathy with her and in protest to her treatment. It was loyal of them to leave, but it left Mistress Hutchinson with fewer advocates to stand up for her.

Throughout the days of her trial, the meetinghouse was more crowded than it ever was on the Sabbath. On the days I could attend, I did not even try to find a seat inside for I knew that as one being shunned no one would sit beside me, and if I did sit on a bench there would be further accusations of me taking more than my share of space. So I stood outside the door and listened. From inside came the shouts of familiar male voices—Reverend Wilson's slow nasal admonishments, Reverend Symmes's overloud diatribes, and Reverend Cotton's pleading efforts to convert Mistress Hutchinson to his way of thinking. But now his voice held more vinegar than honey. They were arguing Scripture. While the blackcoats made a show of their knowledge of the Bible, it was Anne, though, who confidently refuted them verse-by-verse from Isaiah to Galatians, from Samuel to the Acts of the Apostles, often besting their arguments, which enraged them even more. While I admired Anne's courage, I also feared for her safety.

On the last day of her trial, Reverend Wilson rendered the ministers' final judgment. Although I could not see him from my place in the crowd, those who were inside said he stood on his platform and shook his finger down at her face. Catherine, who was there, said his whole body trembled as he denounced her. He was so forceful that Catherine could feel the shake of his venom in the floorboards beneath her feet. She recorded his words in her journal and read them to us later. "In the name of our Lord Jesus Christ and in the name of the church . . . I cast you out! I deliver you up to Satan, that you may learn no more to blaspheme, to seduce, and to lie. I command you as a leper to withdraw yourself out of the congregation."

Over the shoulders of other gawkers, I caught a glimpse of Anne passing through the heavy doors. Mary Dyer offered her an arm and she took it. Her face was white against her dark hood, and beneath her cape I saw her stomach swollen with still another child. Weary of mind and body, she was not broken of spirit. She held her gaze straight ahead and her head high—a demeanor the gossips called haughty. At one point she turned back to face the ministers inside the meetinghouse. In a voice that surprised me for its strength, she called back to them, "The Lord judges not as man judges. Better to be cast out of the church than to deny Christ!"

IT WAS NOT THE LAST WE HEARD of Anne Hutchinson. Eventually, word came from Rhode Island, where she settled, that she had given birth to her sixteenth child. This birth, sadly, was a monster birth, the kind that thrusts every mother into the purgatory of pain and self-examination. Governor Winthrop took pleasure in passing that news around Boston.

The child was not a child at all, he told many, but a mass of twenty-seven clumps, none of them of human shape.

Reverend John Cotton also made use of Mistress Hutchinson's tragedy at the Thursday lecture. Addressing the women of the congregation, he reminded us that just as God punished Anne Hutchinson with a monster birth for her heresy, He would punish any of us who continued to be infected with the leprosy of her opinions.

It was at that lecture—when I watched John Cotton's threatening gaze pass over our faces, one by one—that I decided that while my body would continue to occupy space in the meetinghouse, my mind would no longer be present within its walls. I could not renounce Anne Hutchinson's teachings for the good they had given me, and when our ministers spoke of God's wrath, I could send my mind cleverly to other places— to my God as I knew Him to be, to the lavender and sage in Goody Hammer's garden, to the bands of colorful lace that Jane continued to sew on the inside of goodwives' hems and on petticoats. Anywhere but to the blackcoats and the seeds of fear they planted.

Chapter Forty-Four

1685

As the years passed, I came to rely upon Goody Hammer not only for decoctions to ease my mind, but also for remedies to relieve my own children's coughs and fevers. In short time I found I could be of use to her by writing down her recipes, which she had never done because although she could read, she was able to write only her mark. I became such a constant presence in her home that Deliverance and our sons grew up believing that mortars and pestles were their playthings, that every illness affecting our brethren could be cured by a draught, an infusion, or a posset, and that Goodwife Hammer's garden was their private forest filled with magic. As well as knowing their letters and numbers, they readily became acquainted with the names of every herb and flower in her garden, and humbly accepted the consequences of a snap of a willow branch on their legs if, in the exuberance of play, they trampled her precious plantings.

It was Goody Hammer's influence that sent our first son, a studious boy named Joshua, to study medicine in Edinburgh, and it was Joshua's influence that sent our second son, a gifted but less bookish boy named William, to become a cooper. Goody Hammer's influence was the strongest upon Deliverance, however. Working alongside us she too learned the medicine and the magic, the chants and the prayers passed on by Ol' Mim.

In one's life many days are filled with repetition. Our days are like dried herbs in a jar—the flakes are limited in number and most of them look alike. But there are special days that stand out amongst the many. They twinkle like gold, sparkle like jewels, and these are the ones that live at the forefront of memory.

There is an image of Deliverance and Goody Hammer I shall always hold in my mind. Late one evening, when Deliverance was about fifteen, I had just returned to Goodwife Hammer's after delivering a salve to a goodwife with an irksome rash. The moon was full and on the glistening hillock beside her cottage, Goody Hammer and my Deliverance stood washed in hazy gray light, their coifs dangling from their fingertips; their long hair, silver and chestnut, blowing in the wind. From afar, I listened to them praying in voices strong and true. I watched them lift their skirts, and in the graceful manner of nature's handmaidens performing a dance, they both set one foot behind the other and curtsied to the moon. I could almost hear Goodwife Hammer say to Deliverance, "You'll be a healer like me one day, won't you?" I could have joined them, but I did not, choosing that to be their time. I had many such moments with Goody Hammer in the past, and I wished this one to belong to Deliverance.

As time passed, Goody Hammer became less able to help all of those who called upon her. Gradually she weakened in body and mind. The skin on her face became as sheer as a veil. It was as if the life that was draining from her was rising up in me and in Deliverance, like water diverting from a weak stream into more robust ones.

Her death came quickly. One afternoon in the spring of 1660, after the snow had melted, she insisted upon delivering a poultice to a woman who just given birth. She was an ancient of eighty years then. She would not listen to reason and stay indoors. She said she needed to breathe fresh air and to check on the babe whose life she helped begin. That day, as she made her way across the High Street, she lost her footing and collapsed. It was a sad evening when at sundown we carried her coffin to the graveyard, Deliverance and I at the head of her coffin and four of the women she had nursed with tonics similar to mine, at the heart and feet. The drummer boy followed behind.

To my surprise, a fortnight after her death, my beloved Joshua purchased her cottage from the Commonwealth of Massachusetts. It is there we now live, and it is there that Deliverance, now a widowed woman, and I continue Goody Hammer's work—planting, watering, and weeding the garden; blending salves, teas, ointments, syrups, and poultices; recording our remedies carefully in a notebook, along with each one's operation and the payment we receive in goods, coin, or kindness. Although Deliverance has begun, with our ministers' permission, to tend to pregnant women and assist them through their travails, I prefer to remain with my herbs and recipes working within the private walls of our cottage.

I owe a debt of gratitude to Goody Hammer, for she saved my life—not only on that infamous day in August, but on every day following when she taught me, trusted me, and was there to lift me from the melancholy I still occasionally slip into. She helped me improve my time on this earth. She gave me work and purpose and guidance until I was able to live without her. And Joshua, my faithful husband, was her willing accomplice in my healing. He, too, never lost belief in me and was true to his promise to love me forever.

It is our nature to wish to save those we love, but the Lord did not allow me to save Joshua. Like Ezekiel, he had disease of the heart, and for a long time Deliverance and I treated him with the stalks and leaves of burnet infused into claret wine, and later with motherwort that powerfully aids the trembling of the heart, and finally with a tincture of hawthorn berries. But the Lord did not will him to become an ancient. Nearing the mark of forty-eight years, he died peacefully in his sleep. Again, it was with overwhelming sadness that we trekked to the graveyard, this time the men carrying the pine box, and me, Deliverance, and our sons following behind, our heavy hearts beating to the doleful beat of the drum.

I had been blessed beyond belief with Jane's friendship that continued until her passing last May, a year after her John had gone to God. A fortnight after her mother's death, Miracle gifted me with a packet of letters, tied with a red ribband, that I had written to Jane before she had come to America. "My mother wanted you to have these letters to keep with those she wrote so you might have a fuller picture of your days together."

As I sat at the table combining our letters, Jane's and mine, I thought of how our lives together had been like a braid— Jane's golden plaits entwined with my chestnut ones, and our plaits woven with the lights and darks of many other lives— Mama's, Papa's, Goody Hammer's, Joshua's, John's, and the lives of our children and grandchildren. As I was working, a soft breeze passed through the window and brushed against my cheek. I took it as a sign of Jane's approval, and feeling her spirit inside me, I pressed one of her letters to my chest.

As for the Bible, I now read only the verses that sustain me. I do not allow myself to be surrounded by fear, the way many of those of our persuasion are. I think now of that old meetinghouse, ravished by fire many years ago, and how it has been replaced by a larger structure. Our new meetinghouse is as unadorned as the old one—except for one addition: a painting of an enormous eye on the front of the pulpit. The eye serves as a reminder, especially to the children who now sit upon the pulpit steps during sermons, that God is always watching and nothing we say or do, even in the black of night, goes unnoticed.

It is my belief that this eye, large and unblinking, is the maker of nightmares. It is a disturbing sight that my children have seen only because I was forced to frequent the meetinghouse as a young mother with them in tow. It is the bearer of bad dreams, and today I will have nothing to do with it. This drawing is the creation of man. The Lord I believe in does not want us to be always afraid.

Our cottage is on a sheltered lane, so I no longer have to watch the pious churchgoers walk to the meetinghouse and observe the sanctimonious looks of piety on their faces. But sometimes in summer, when the air is still and the windows are open and the lanes are emptied of people who have gone to services, I hear the preaching of ministers like Increase Mather who breathes hotter fire than Zachariah Symmes, his face flushed with holiness, his voices rising to the firmament then dropping to the depths, railing with threats of hell and damnation. Their discourses I have no interest in hearing, for I believe I have heard enough of them in my lifetime. Many old women allow themselves to be carried to the meetinghouse on chairs, or arrange to be pushed there in carts by their dutiful sons. But I decline such offers. I do not wish to be carried on a chair like a queen throughout the streets of Boston. That is one reason, but if I am to be as honest as a saint, the main reason I no longer go to the meetinghouse is because I do not wish to be in the presence of the blackcloths, who in my lifetime have done me few favors. I recall my many encounters with them: my desperate pleas to Reverend Wilson, their admonishments of hundreds of sinners in the grove, my own trek to the pillory pit, the humiliating D pinned to my chest for all to see—and now I wish to see no such harshness dealt out to others. As an old woman of seventy years, I choose now to worship a forgiving God in the stillness of my cottage, surrounded by bouquets of herbs—tender, fragrant, and hopeful—that lift my spirits to heaven.

The End

From the Author

$\rm M$ERCY GOODHUE is a work of fiction inspired by a seventy-eight word entry that John Winthrop made in his journal on August 5, 1637:

A woman of the Boston Congregation, having been in much trouble of mind about her spiritual estate, at length grew into utter desperation, and could not endure or hear of any comfort, etc., so as one day she took her little infant and threw it into a well, and then came into the house and said, now she was sure she would be damned, for she had drowned her child; but some, stepping presently forth, saved the child.

In the margin, Winthrop had written, "Hett woman distracted."

I first came across this journal entry when I was researching the Puritans for a Master's thesis at Stanford University. Winthrop's story was so sad and tragic that it lingered in my mind long after my thesis was completed. How could religion, whose purpose is to provide hope, create such hopelessness in a woman? What combination of life experiences, religious pressure, and psychological makeup could have predisposed this woman to such desperation? Then when I began to write fiction, I realized it was the "Hett woman's" story I wanted to tell. So I dug deeper into Puritan history.

I walked the streets of Boston trying to erase from my mind the visual cityscape, landfill, freeways—all evidence of the growth that had occurred since the 1630s. I imagined what it would have been like walking those dusty lanes in a time when government was a theocracy, God was a harsh judge, witches were believed to be real, medicine was mixed with superstition and magic, women were expected to "be fruitful and multiply" from marriage to menopause, and when women suffering from psychosis were considered to be possessed by Satan.

During her lifetime, the typical Puritan woman experienced six to eight pregnancies, and whenever she prepared for birth, she also prepared for death because one mother in every thirty died in childbirth. Puritan women (and men) also carried with them, as scholar David E. Stannard points out, a "never-ending, excruciating uncertainty" whether they were among the saved. For the mentally healthy woman, life must have been stressful. For the woman prone to depression or other mental illnesses, it must have been unbearable.

Although we've come a long way since the times of the Puritans, it's important to remember the issues women dealt with then are the same issues modern women face today: rape, gender inequality, incest, postpartum depression. And for women living in less modernized countries, their problems are frighteningly comparable to those of women in 17th century America.

THE PROTAGONIST, MERCY GOODHUE HOYT, is loosely based upon the historic Anne Needham Hett who was the woman John Winthrop wrote about. She was born in England in 1613 and sailed to America on the Winthrop Fleet in 1630. According to the passenger manifest provided by the Winthrop Society, there were no other Needhams in the Winthrop Party, so Anne possibly traveled as an indentured servant. Her husband, Thomas Hett, was a cooper from Folkingham, Lincolnshire who arrived in New England in 1635. Anne and Thomas married sometime before 1637, the year their daughter Hannah was born. The Hetts relocated to Hingham, Massachusetts in 1637, perhaps seeking a fresh start after Anne attempted to drown Hannah. Records show that Hannah was the first of their six children: Eliphalet, Thomas, Mehitable, Mary, and Israel.

Unlike the fictional story of Mercy Goodhue Hoyt, Anne Needham Hett's story did not end with one attempt at infanticide. John Winthrop made two additional entries in his journal that provide further insight into this tragic woman's mental state, which continued to deteriorate before it improved. The first is dated five years later, April 18, 1642.

A cooper's wife in Hingham, having been long in a sad melancholic distemper near to phrensy, and having formerly attempted to drown her child, but prevented by God's gracious Providence, did again take an opportunity, being alone, to carry her child, aged three years, to a creek near her house, and stripping it of the clothes, threw it into the water and mud. But, the tide being low, the little child scrambled out, and taking up its clothes, came to its mother who was set down not far off. She carried the child again, and threw it in so far as it could not get out; but then it pleased God, that a young man, coming that way saved it. She would give no reason for it, but that she did it to save it from misery, and withal that she was assured, she had sinned against the Holy Ghost, and that she could not repent of any sin. Thus doth Satan work by the advantage of our infirmities, which should stir us up to cleave the more fast to Christ Jesus, and to walk more humbly and watchfully in all our conversation.

The child was Eliphalet, a son. For this offense, for her unwillingness to repent, and possibly for some additional misbehavior that went unrecorded, Anne was cast out of the Boston Congregation. We do not know whether she was excommunicated a short time after her attempted murder of Eliphalet, or whether her sentencing was delayed. The following diary entry made more than a year later reports that Anne recovered sufficiently enough for the congregation to accept her back into the fold.

On July 22, 1643, John Winthrop wrote of her again:

The wife of one Hett, of whom mention was made before, being cast out of the church of Boston, the Lord was pleased so to honour his own ordinance, that whereas before no means could prevail with her either to reclaim her from her wicked and blasphemous courses and speeches, etc. or to bring her to frequent the means, within a few weeks after her casting out, she came to see her sin and lay it to heart, and to frequent the means, and so was brought to such manifestation of repentance and a sound mind, as the church received her in again.

After the second attempted drowning incident, we know that the Hetts relocated several times: From Hingham to Rehoboth, Massachusetts in 1645; to Hull in 1647; Malden in 1653; and finally they settled in Charlestown in 1658, where Thomas died at the age of fifty-six and Anne at seventy-five.

Although Mercy and Joshua are fictional characters, I have attempted to tell their story within the context of historical events, personalities, and attitudes. We see the Puritans' obsession with religion and their preoccupation with their own salvation. Constantly, they watched for the signs of salvation or damnation in themselves and each other. We see their belief in witchcraft; the authoritarian leadership of the stern but well-meaning John Winthrop; the zealotry of ministers like John Wilson, George Phillips, John Cotton and Zachariah Symmes; the fracture that the charismatic Anne Hutchinson caused within the Boston Congregation; and finally the brutal war with the Pequot Indians. In addition to the historical characters mentioned above, the Coddingtons, Aspinwalls, Coles, Henry Vane, Mary Dyer, and of course, Anne Hutchinson and her family were contemporaries of the Hetts.

The others characters are fictitious: Goodwife Esther Hammer is loosely patterned after the midwife Jane Hawkins, who was denounced by John Winthrop as being "notorious for familiarity with the Devil." In 1638, the General Court of Massachusetts forbade Jane Hawkins from questioning "matters of religion," to "meddle in surgery, or phisick, drinks, plaisters or oyles." She was eventually banished to Rhode Island, a haven for dissidents.

As for the other historical characters:

John Winthrop continued his distinguished career in public service as governor, deputy governor, or member of the General Council until his death in 1649 at the age of sixty-one. Throughout his life, he remained true to his "city on the hill" principles that leadership and authority should reside with the educated and the saintly, and that government should be a theocracy. Only reluctantly did he, during his later years, begin to relinquish authority to freemen outside the tight circle of the Massachusetts Bay's leadership. In counterbalance to his often heavy-handed public dealings, Winthrop was reputed to be a loving husband and father. Following Margaret's death in 1647, he married a widow, Martha Cotymore of Boston. He fathered sixteen children, eight of whom reached adulthood.

Anne Bradstreet, who is a minor character in this novel, has gone down in history as the first female poet in America. She took her work seriously, but kept her poems private, as women of her time were not encouraged to pursue such endeavors. She died in Andover, Massachusetts in 1672 at the age of sixty.

Anne's husband, Simon Bradstreet, became a judge, legislator, and twice governor of the Massachusetts Bay colony.

Anne's father, the crusty Thomas Dudley, was reelected governor in 1640, 1645 and 1650, and was one of Harvard College's first overseers.

Four months after Anne Needham Hett attempted to drown her infant, Anne Hutchinson was accused of heresy and banished from Boston. Governor Winthrop and the magistrates presided over her trial, where they acted as both judge and prosecutor. It was winter when she was banished, and the Hutchinson family's departure in the bitter cold would have surely resulted in their deaths. So with some mercy, Anne was held under house arrest in the Roxbury home of a minister, where she suffered depression. The following March, she was subjected to one final clerical inquisition where, over several exhausting days, she was browbeaten by Reverends Wilson, Phillips, Symmes, Cotton and others, then forced to recant her theological views. In the end, her beloved mentor, John Cotton, turned his back on her when the pressures from the other ministers became too strong for him to bear. In historical accounts, Cotton rationalized that it was Anne who abandoned him by taking his teachings and twisting them to suit herself.

Several months after the Hutchinsons moved south to Rhode Island, Anne, shaken and probably experiencing menopause, delivered a "hydalidiform mole." A local doctor analyzed the tissue she delivered and shared his findings with the Puritan magistrates who concluded that the Lord allowed this "monstrous" birth to occur as evidence that they made a wise decision in banishing her.

When William Hutchinson died in 1642, Anne and her six youngest children moved to an isolated area on Long Island Sound where she continued to preach and minister to the Indians. She would have nothing more to do with the Boston Congregation. It is believed that she became a Quaker. A year later, she and five of her children were savagely tomahawked to death by a band of Indians desiring to clear their land of the white intruders.

Anne Hutchinson's best friend and loyal sympathizer, Mary Dyer, also came to a tragic end. When Reverend Wilson pronounced the sentence of excommunication on Anne, Mary Dyer rose and left the church in sympathy with her. Subsequently, she too was excommunicated. Shortly before Anne's excommunication (unbeknownst to most others at that time) Mary gave birth to a stillborn and deformed fetus "so monstrous and misshapen as the like hath scare been heard of." Anne Hutchinson was her midwife. Although Anne and Reverend Cotton were estranged by then, it was Reverend Cotton to whom Anne ran for advice on what to do with Mary's malformed baby. Benevolently, Cotton advised Anne to bury the baby without baptism so that there would be no public record of it. Anne followed his instructions, but another woman in attendance at the birth reported it to the authorities. Again, the ministers made much use of the symbolism of both Anne's and Mary's "monstrous births."

Mary Dyer and her husband also moved to Rhode Island. In the 1650s she joined the Society of Friends and became a Quaker. In 1659 she returned to Boston to visit some Quaker friends. Having been banished from Boston, she was arrested and sentenced to death and was literally on the scaffold when she was granted a reprieve and escorted out of the colony. The following spring, when she boldly returned to town, her death sentence was carried out. After her death, a member of the General Council scoffed, "She did hang as a flag for others to take example by."

William and Mary Coddington, who had been sympathetic to Anne Hutchinson, left Boston in 1638, along with the Aspinwalls who also had enough of the oppressive religious climate. They too settled in Rhode Island. Later in life the Coddingtons and perhaps the Aspinwalls became Quakers.

John Cotton continued his ministry in the Massachusetts Bay colony until he died in 1652 of a throat condition that in his final days silenced his golden voice. But his ministerial influence continued through the work of his descendants, the harsh Puritan preachers Increase Mather and Cotton Mather. (John Cotton's widow, Sarah, married Reverend Richard Mather, a friend of her husband's. John and Sarah's youngest daughter, Mary, married Richard Mather's son, Increase.)

Throughout most of their lives both Increase and his son, Cotton, were staunch believers in witchcraft. In the 1680s, Increase Mather published *Essay for the Recording of Illustrious Providences,* a defense of witchcraft in which he cited the "monstrous" births of Anne Hutchinson and Mary Dyer as examples of God's retribution. (In his diary, John Winthrop speculated that each of the twenty-six or twenty-seven lumps of tissue that Anne Hutchinson delivered when she miscarried in 1638 represented a point of heresy she was accused of.)

In October 1692, Cotton Mather published *Wonders of the Invisible World,* in which he reiterated his belief in spectral phenomena and his approval of the Salem witch trials. Both father and son initially supported the Salem Witchcraft Trials of 1692-93, where at the instigation of a band of crazed girls, two hundred were accused and twenty men and women executed. Between 1647 and 1693, the most intense period of witch fear in New England, twenty-two midwives were accused of witchcraft. The first midwife to be hanged was Margaret Jones of Charlestown, in 1648.

Bibliography

Asburn, Frank D., Editor. *The Ranks of Death, A Medical History of the Conquest of America.* New York: Coward-McCann, Inc., 1947.

Adair, John. *Founding Fathers, The Puritans in England and America.* Grand Rapids, Michigan: Baker Book House, 1982.

Bailyn, Bernard, Editor. *The Works of Anne Bradstreet.* Cambridge: Harvard University Press, 1967.

Battis, Emery. *Saints and Sectaries, Anne Hutchinson and the Antinomian Controversy in the Massachusetts Bay Colony.* Chapel Hill: The University of North Caroline Press, 1962.

Braithwaite, William C. *The Beginning of Quakerism.* London: Macmillan and Company, 1912.

Bremer, Francis J. *John Winthrop, American's Forgotten Founding Father.* New York: Oxford University Press, 2003.

Bremer, Francis J. *First Founders, American Puritans and Puritanism in an Atlantic World.* Durham, New Hampshire: University of New Hampshire Press, 2012.

Bush, Sargent, Jr., Editor. *The Correspondence of John Cotton.* Chapel Hill: University of North Carolina Press, 2001.

Caffrey, Kate. *The Mayflower.* New York: Stein and Day, 1974.

Childs, Francis J., Editor. *The English and Scottish Popular Ballads*, New York: Dover Publications, 1965.

Collins, Gail. *American's Women, 400 Years of Dolls, Drudges, Helpmates, and Heroines.* New York: William Morrow, 2003.

Crowley, Vivianne. *Wicca, The Old Religion in the New Millennium.* Element Books, Ltd., 1996.

Daniels, Bruce C. *Puritans at Play, Leisure and Recreation in Colonial New England.* New York: St. Martin's Press, 1995.

Dow, George Francis. *Every Day Life in the Massachusetts Bay Colony.* New York: Benjamin Blom, 1967.

Earle, Alice Morris. *Home Life in Colonial Days.* New York: Grosset & Dunlap, 1898.

Earle, Alice Morris. *The Sabbath in Puritan New England.* Fifth Edition, New York: Charles Scribner's Sons, 1892.

Elliott, Emory. *Power and the Pulpit in Puritan New England.* Princeton: Princeton University Press, 1975.

Fischer, David Hackett. *Albion's Seed: Four British Folkways in America.* New York, Oxford: Oxford University Press, 1989.

Fraser, Rebecca. *The Story of Britain.* New York: W.W. Norton & Company, 2003.

Gowing, Laura. *Common Bodies, Women, Touch and Power in Seventeenth-Century England.* New Haven and London: Yale University Press, 2003.

Greven, Phillip. *The Protestant Temperament, Patterns of Child-Rearing, Religious Experience and the Self in Early America.* New York: Alfred A. Knopf, 1977.

Hall, David D. *Worlds of Wonder, Days of Judgment, Popular Religious Belief in Early New England.* Cambridge: Harvard University Press, 1989.

Hawthorne, Nathaniel. *The Scarlet Letter.* Oxford: Oxford University Press, 1962.

Holy Bible, New International Version. Zondervan Bible Publisher. Grand Rapids, Michigan, 1978.

Holy Bible, Authorized King James Version. Zondervan, Grand Rapids, Michigan, 1994.

Janeway, James. A Token for Children. Adapted from the Second American Edition, 1812.

Kaminsky, Jane. *Governing the Tongue, The Politics of Speech in Early New England.* New York: Oxford University Press, 1997.

Karlsen, Carol F. *The Devil in the Shape of a Woman, Witchcraft in Colonial New England.* New York: Vintage Books, 1989.

Kilby, Kenneth. *The Cooper and His Trade.* Fresno. Linden Publishing Company, Inc., 1971.

Kramer, Heinrich, and Sprenger, James. *The Malleus Maleficarum* (The Witches' Hammer). New York: Dover Publications, Inc., 1971.

LaPlante, Eve. *American Jezebel, The Uncommon Life of Anne Hutchinson, the Woman Who Defied the Puritans.* San Francisco: HarperSanFrancisco, 2004.

Lewis, Peter. *The Genius of Puritanism.* Peter Lewis: 1975.

Markham, Gervase. *The English Housewife.* Montreal: McGill-Queen's University Press, 1986.

Miller, Arthur. *The Crucible.* New York: Penguin Books, 1982.

Morgan, Edmund S. *The Puritan Family: Religion and Domestic Relations in Seventeenth-Century New England.* New York: Harper & Row, 1966.

Morison, Samuel Eliot. *Builders of the Bay Colony.* New York: Houghton, Mifflin Company, 1930.

Moseley, James G. *John Winthrop's World.* University of Wisconsin Press, 1992.

Philbrick, Nathaniel. *Mayflower.* New York: Viking, Penguin Group, 2006.

Potterson, David, Editor. *Culpeper's Color Herbal.* New York: Sterling Publishing Co., Inc., 1983.

Powell, Sumner Chilton. *Puritan Village, The Formation of a New England Town.* New York: Doubleday & Company, Inc., 1965.

Reis, Elizabeth. *"The Devil, the Body, and the Feminine Soul in Puritan New England," The Journal of American History, June 1995.*

Rosebaum, Ron. *"First Blood," Smithsonian Magazine, March 2013.*

Savage, James, Editor. *The History of New England, 1630 to 1649 by John Winthrop*, Esq., Volumes I and II. Salem, New Hampshire: Ayer Company Publishers, Inc., 1992.

Scholten, Catherine M. *Childbearing in American Society: 1650-1850.* New York: New York University Press, 1985.

Schweninger, Lee. *John Winthrop.* Wilmington: University of North Carolina, Twayne Publishers, A Division of G.K. Hall & Company, Boston, 1990.

Sharpe, James. *The Bewitching of Anne Gunter.* New York: Routledge, 2000.

Stannard, David E. *The Puritan Way of Death, A Study in Religion, Culture, and Social Change.* Oxford University Press, 1977.

Thwing, Annie H. *The Crooked and Narrow Streets of Boston, 1630-1822.* Detroit: Singing Tree Press, 1970.

Ulrich, Laurel Thatcher. *Good Wives: Image and Reality in the Lives of Women in Northern New England, 1650-1720.* New York: Vintage Books, 1991.

Ulrich, Laurel Thatcher. *A Midwife's Tale, The Life of Martha Ballard, Based on Her Diary, 1785-1812.* New York: Vintage Books, 1991.

Ulrich, Laurel Thatcher. *The Age of Homespun.* New York: Alfred A. Knopf, 2001.

Warner, Michael, Editor. *American Sermons, The Pilgrims to Martin Luther King, Jr.* The Library of America, New York: Penguin Putnam, Inc., 1999.

Wertenbaker, Thomas Jefferson. *The Puritan Oligarchy, The Founding of American Civilization.* New York: Grosset & Dunlap, 1947.

Wertz, Richard W., and Wertz, Dorothy C. *Lying-In, A History of Childbirth in America.* New Haven: Yale University Press, 1977.

Williams, Selma R. *Divine Rebel: The Life of Anne Marbury Hutchinson.* New York: Holt, Rinehart and Winston, 1981.

Gratitude

There are many I must thank for making this book possible. First, my sincerest appreciation goes to Professor Edith Gelles, senior scholar at the Clayman Institute for Gender Research at Stanford University, who, in a course on Women in Colonial and Revolutionary America, taught me the discipline and joy of historical research, and unknowingly introduced me to the excerpt from John Winthrop's diary that led to this book.

Secondly, my gratitude goes to Sandra Sanoski, friend and graphic designer for her attention to detail, obedience to history, and commitment to capture the essence of Mercy Goodhue on the cover.

Many readers have contributed to refining my many drafts, and have provided insight and encouragement along the way: Barbara Arendt, Susan Bono, Kate Campbell, Marlene Cullen, Christine Falcon-Daigle, Joan Jareo, Chuck Kensler, Lee Kern, Margit Liesche, Julia Lord, Halina Marcinkowski, Drew Meadors, Ed Rau, Pat Tyler, Maria Teresita Stark, Dr. Mark Sloan, Tom Thomas, Amy Meadors Warda, and Jeri Winkels.

Finally, thanks to the many librarians and scholars at the Massachusetts Historical Society, the Winthrop Society, the Green Library at Stanford University, and the Sonoma State University Library who have generously offered me access to their collections and provided me research space in their comfy reading rooms that smell like old books.

And lastly, more love and gratitude goes to my husband, Lee Kern, who has patiently lived with my obsession with the Puritans for the greater part of our twenty-year marriage. Little did he know then what he was getting into.

Discussion Group Questions

1. Discuss the personal, environmental, and religious factors that lead to Mercy's descent into madness. What other factors affected her breakdown?

2. What has changed for American women since the 17th century? What hasn't?

3. Do you believe if Mercy lived today, she would be afforded better medical and psychological help?

4. What types of madness are manifest in this story? In Mercy? In Gabriel? In the Puritan community at large?

5. What and who is important in Mercy's journey toward forgiveness and creating a new life for herself?

6. What role does Goody Hammer play in Mercy's plight? Was she part of the problem as well as the solution?

7. Who were the heroes of this story? The villains? Do you feel sympathy toward Gabriel?

8. Discuss the perils of childbearing in 17th century America, also the bonding that took place among women in the ritual of childbirth.

9. Do you take Gabriel's confession at face value, or do you believe he knew what he was doing when he raped Mercy?

10. What was Jane's role in this story?

11. How would you compare the minister and magistrates of Puritan America with the lawmakers and religious leaders of today?

12. Discuss the irony of a godly community beset with brutality?

13. To what extent did John Winthrop's "A Model of Christian Charity" speech provide a workable founding vision for America? Was Winthrop's plea for American exceptionalism fulfilled or unfulfilled?

14. Goody Hammer "meddled in phisicks and oyles" decades before the Salem Witch trials in 1692. Discuss the dangers of being a healer and midwife in the 17th century.

15. Discuss the all-encompassing impact that religion had on our earliest forefathers, and also the dangers of a theocracy? Was Anne Hutchinson brave or foolhardy to step outside her boundaries as a woman?

For more information on Elizabeth Kern and her novels, please visit www.elizabethkern.com

About the Author

A native of Chicago, Elizabeth Kern received a B.S. degree in Communications from the University of Illinois. After a thirty-year career in Corporate Communications, most recently at Apple in Silicon Valley, she received a Masters of Liberal Arts degree from Stanford University. It was at Stanford that she developed her interest in Colonial American history and the endlessly fascinating Puritans.

MERCY GOODHUE is Kern's second novel. Her debut novel, *WANTING TO BE JACKIE KENNEDY*, was a semi-finalist in the 2010 Amazon Breakthrough Novel Award Competition.

She is the mother of two grown children, Amy Meadors Warda and Drew Meadors. Kern and her husband, Lee, live in the gentle hills of Sonoma County, California.

Author's website: www.elizabethkern.com